Shattered Vows

Sister Veronica rummaged through her desk drawer and found the new box of chalk. Opening it, she walked over to the blackboard along the right side of her classroom and placed several pieces in the tray. It was gloomy in the room. A mild April rain was falling outside, streaking the windows, which hadn't yet had their spring cleaning. Despite the dismal day, Sister's mood was buoyant.

It was Saturday morning and the week's Easter break was nearly over. The children would be filing back into class on Monday, chattering excitedly as usual. As a teacher, it was up to her to see that she slipped enough fun into their lessons so she could hold their interest. She was pleased that her students liked her.

Sister Ronnie, as everyone called her, was twenty-eight. All she'd ever wanted to be was a teacher, almost as fiercely as she'd wanted to be a holy sister. Satisfied with her life, she was seldom without a smile.

Happily busy with her tasks, she didn't hear her door silently open, nor the soft footsteps of the man walking toward her. By the time she sensed someone else in the room and had straightened to turn, the wire was already twining around her neck.

Sister Veronica slumped to the floor soundlessly. The man reached into his pocket and placed a mass card alongside her outstretched hand. The card read simply,

FORGIVE ME

NOWHERE TO RUN ... NOWHERE TO HIDE ...
ZEBRA'S SUSPENSE WILL *GET* YOU —
AND WILL MAKE YOU BEG FOR MORE!

NOWHERE TO HIDE (4035, $4.50)
by Joan Hall Hovey

After Ellen Morgan's younger sister has been brutally murdered, the highly respected psychologist appears on the evening news and dares the killer to come after her. After a flood of leads that go nowhere, it happens. A note slipped under her windshield states, "YOU'RE IT." Ellen has woken the hunter from its lair ... and she is his prey!

SHADOW VENGEANCE (4097, $4.50)
by Wendy Haley

Recently widowed Maris learns that she was adopted. Desperate to find her birth parents, she places "personals" in all the Texas newspapers. She receives a horrible response: "You weren't wanted then, and you aren't wanted now." Not to be daunted, her search for her birth mother—and her only chance to save her dangerously ill child—brings her closer and closer to the truth ... and to death!

RUN FOR YOUR LIFE (4193, $4.50)
by Ann Brahms

Annik Miller is being stalked by Gibson Spencer, a man she once loved. When Annik inherits a wilderness cabin in Maine, she finally feels free from his constant threats. But then, a note under her windshield wiper, and shadowy form, and a horrific nighttime attack tell Annik that she is still the object of this lovesick madman's obsession ...

EDGE OF TERROR (4224, $4.50)
by Michael Hammonds

Jessie thought that moving to the peaceful Blue Ridge Mountains would help her recover from her bitter divorce. But instead of providing the tranquility she desires, they cast a shadow of terror. There is a madman out there—and he knows where Jessie lives—and what she has seen ...

NOWHERE TO RUN (4132, $4.50)
by Pat Warren

Socialite Carly Weston leads a charmed life. Then her father, a celebrated prosecutor, is murdered at the hands of a vengeance-seeking killer. Now he is after Carly ... watching and waiting and planning. And Carly is running for her life from a crazed murderer who's become judge, jury—and executioner!

Available wherever paperbacks are sold, or order direct from the Publisher. Send cover price plus 50¢ per copy for mailing and handling to Penguin USA, P.O. Box 999, c/o Dept. 17109, Bergenfield, NJ 07621. Residents of New York and Tennessee must include sales tax. DO NOT SEND CASH.

PAT WARREN
SHATTERED VOWS

ZEBRA BOOKS
KENSINGTON PUBLISHING CORP.

ZEBRA BOOKS are published by

Kensington Publishing Corp.
850 Third Avenue
New York, NY 10022

Copyright © 1995 by Pat Warren

All rights reserved. No part of this book may be reproduced in any form or by any means without the prior written consent of the Publisher, excepting brief quotes used in reviews.

If you purchased this book without a cover you should be aware that this book is stolen property. It was reported as "unsold and destroyed" to the Publisher and neither the Author nor the Publisher has received any payment for this "stripped book."

Zebra and the Z logo Reg. U. S. Pat. & TM Off.

First Printing: May, 1995

Printed in the United States of America

ONE

As she hurried up the stone steps leading to St. Matthews Catholic Church on Detroit's east side, the young woman pulled up the collar of her coat against a cold March wind. The smile of her fiancé, who was waiting for her just inside the vestibule, warmed her immediately. "Sorry I'm late," Debbie Morgan said, moving into his welcoming arms.

Tom Vanderlind kissed the young woman's forehead. He was twenty years old and on top of the world. He didn't mind that Debbie was a little late, didn't mind anything these days. In three months they'd be married, and he'd be the happiest man in the state of Michigan. Maybe the world. They'd made a seven o'clock appointment to meet with Father Fred Hilliard to plan their June wedding. It couldn't come too soon for Tom, who'd been in love with Debbie since their high school days.

"I've already seen Father Fred," Tom said as he walked with her into the quiet old church. "I told him we wanted to light a candle first. He said he'd wait for us in his office."

Debbie adjusted her collar and slowly moved down the center aisle, holding Tom's hand. St. Matthews was the oldest house of worship in the city, its hard pews uncomfortable, its stone walls keeping the interior cool in winter and summer. Though she was only nineteen, Debbie was old-fashioned and she preferred this church in her former neighborhood over the more modern ones. In just a few short weeks, she thought to herself, she and Tom would be walking down this aisle as man and wife. She shivered in anticipation.

Tom squeezed her hand. "You okay?"

"Yes, just excited."

The interior of the church was dim; only one recessed light illuminated the altar. Soft candles glowed in wall sconces along the gray walls. The air was heavy with incense as they moved forward in the hushed silence.

Suddenly, they heard the squeak of a door opening on rusty hinges, then quickly closing, and they both turned around. But there was no one in sight; they were the only two in the cavernous church. Debbie giggled nervously and they walked on.

Several vigil candles were flickering in their red glass globes as they approached. Tom slipped a folded bill into the lock box, then struck a long match into flame. Taking Debbie's hand, he held the fire to the wick.

"Let's go say a prayer," Tom suggested. Taking Debbie's hand, he led her to the center aisle. As he was about to turn into the first pew, he noticed a woman in a black coat awkwardly slumped onto the kneeler in the row behind. "Do you think she fainted?" he asked Debbie softly, motioning with his head.

"It's one of the sisters," Debbie said, looking over Tom's shoulder and seeing the short veil over the woman's blond hair.

Tom tapped gently on the woman's shoulder.

"Sister, are you all right?" When she didn't move, he gripped her under the arms and pulled her onto the seat. It was then that he saw the thin wire twisted around her neck and her bulging eyes staring up at them unseeingly. "Oh my God," he whispered.

His fiancée's scream of horror echoed through the high-ceilinged building.

The homicide division of Detroit Police Headquarters was located on the first floor of the Beaubien Street station. It was tucked away in the back, reachable only through a winding corridor that seemed to discourage visits from anyone except those with a genuine need to be there. No one who walked through its doors would ever describe the area as cheery.

The squad room was large, noisy, and rarely neat. Cream-colored utilitarian desks with Formica tops were nose to nose, two by two, some partitioned off into semiprivate cubicles. The tiled floor was a brown-and-tan design that had long ago been worn off. The walls were industrial beige and the smell was something you never quite got used to: smoke, sweat, and disinfectant. Captain Renwick's glass-enclosed office was at the far end.

Even though the hour was late, phones were ringing, voices shouted in from the hallway, keyboards clattered. In one small cubicle, Senior Detective Ray Vargas shoved back his chair, deciding it was time to call it a day. It was seven-fifteen and he'd been at it for just over twelve hours. Visions of a thick corned beef on rye with a deli pickle and a cold beer danced in his head as his empty stomach rumbled. Then his phone rang. For a split second he considered walking away, but he relented. They'd find him, he knew. In this job, you could run but you couldn't hide. "Vargas here," he answered.

He bent to grab a pen and pad, writing as the raspy voice on the other end of the line, which he'd immediately recognized as belonging to the desk sergeant, Dick Mulrooney, dispassionately outlined the details of the crime. "Yes, I know where St. Matthews is." The church was a couple of miles from the small colonial on Chandler Drive he'd bought four years ago. "Make sure the officers tape off the scene. I'm on my way."

Hanging up the phone, Ray glanced over at his partner as she pulled on her gloves. Detective Sergeant Mary Margaret O'Malley was the only female detective in Homicide, a woman even hard-nosed seasoned cops liked and admired. Meg had just been telling him that she was looking forward to cooking dinner for her husband that night, then building a fire and curling up with a good book. Dennis O'Malley was desk sergeant at a west-side precinct and, between their two careers, they seldom had time off together.

Ray didn't have the heart to ruin her evening.

Shoving his notepad in his pocket, he reached for his overcoat as she waited, watching him with patient eyes. "Go on home. I'll get this one," he told her. Married cops, male or female, had it rough, Ray thought. Which was only one reason Ray believed that his profession didn't mix with long-term commitments.

"What is it, Ray?" Meg asked quietly. "I heard you say St. Matthews."

"Yeah." He shrugged into his coat, wishing she'd left before the call. There was no way to pretty this one up. "A young couple found a nun strangled in one of the pews." He watched her full lips tighten. As a Detroit cop, she'd seen more than her share of victims. As a Catholic, this one would be twice as hard on her. "Let me take it, Meg."

"No." She grabbed her purse and slung the strap over her shoulder. "We're partners, remember? Don't go soft on me, Vargas."

He dug out his car keys. "All right, but don't say I didn't warn you." Strangulation victims were never a pretty sight.

Ray folded his six-three frame behind the wheel of his Ford wagon, rolled out of the Beaubien lot and headed for Jefferson, driving carefully as was his custom. The air was cold but dry, though he doubted that winter was through with them yet. What little snow remained was in occasional grimy patches.

He'd never seen the point in racing to the scene of a murder. As he'd often told his former partner Sam English, the dead weren't going anywhere. The boys in blue would handle things till he and Meg arrived.

"Eight years on the force and I've never run across the murder of a nun," Meg said, wishing that record had remained unbroken. "Why would anyone want to kill a sister?"

Ray didn't consider himself a cynic, yet he'd given up trying to figure out why people killed. Their reasons seldom made sense to him. A ten-year veteran, he'd leaned over more bodies than he cared to count. In college, he'd been a psych major, which was supposed to give him insight into the human mind, the psyche, feelings and motivations. When applied to the almost daily slaughter he witnessed, it wasn't very useful. He tried to come up with a plausible explanation for Meg.

"Could be she interrupted a robbery in progress." Though that was highly unlikely. A robber might carry a gun or a knife, but strangulation had all the earmarks of a killer filled with anger.

Last fall, he and Sam had spent weeks tracking a strangler hell-bent on revenge. Sam had almost gotten killed before they'd captured the man. One of the killer's near victims had been the prosecuting attorney's daughter, Carly Weston, the woman Sam had wound up marrying. Recently, when Sam had learned he was going to be a father, he'd asked for a transfer to a desk job. Ray didn't blame him, though he knew that personally he'd go crazy working a nine-to-five, stuck inside all day, every day.

Meg turned to look at Ray, one auburn eyebrow upraised. A true redhead with the temper to prove it, she took a lot of kidding. But everyone knew she couldn't stay angry for long. "A robbery? Have you ever been in St. Matthews?" She didn't wait for a reply. "It's an old parish in a working-class neighborhood. The poor box probably doesn't take in enough in a week for one good lunch. Even the collection basket total is barely enough to pay the heating bill. If it weren't for the tuition from the parochial school, they'd probably have to close the doors. A thief who'd try St. Matthews would have to be either new to the city or really stupid."

"All thieves are stupid, if you ask me," Ray said, heading down the freeway ramp.

"Did you ask Sarge to call the M.E.'s office?"

"Yeah. I asked for Doc Freemont." He'd worked with the chief medical examiner on several cases and thought they might need his expertise on this one. The man everyone called Doc was nearing sixty, yet was still the best in the business. Once the press got hold of the news and splashed the nun's death all over the front pages, they'd need hard answers to calm down an outraged public. The clergy were sacrosant. The department couldn't afford to screw up.

Ray's stomach grumbled again, reminding him that he hadn't eaten in nearly eight hours. God only knew when he'd get that deli sandwich tonight. Though it went against the grain, he stepped down on the gas pedal.

"I doubt she even saw her assailant," Dr. Lester Freemont said. He stood with the two detectives, looking down at the nun's body as she lay on the scarred wooden bench. "I'd guess she was kneeling right about here"—he pointed to a place on the kneeler—"and the killer put the wire around her throat from behind and pulled it taut."

Despite her years of experience, Meg struggled with an involuntary shiver. Sister Angelica was wearing a black coat over a white blouse and dark suit. They'd been told she'd taught first grade at St. Matthews Elementary School and was only twenty-six years old. The rosary beads she would never finish reciting were still clutched in one of her hands. Dear God, what monster had done this to her?

She'd been pretty, Ray thought, taking in her fair, wholesome face and innocent blue eyes. "No other marks on the body, Doc?"

"Not that I can see. I'll know more when I get her on the table." Dr. Freemont used the eraser end of his pencil and moved the collar of the woman's blouse to reveal the thin green wire deeply embedded in the bruised flesh of her neck. "Looks to be a common variety, just barely thicker than dental floss."

Ray had seen the type before, in florist shops, hardware, and craft stores. That narrowed it down to several thousand locations. "Got a fix on the time of death?"

The doctor glanced at his watch and saw it wasn't quite eight. "I think I'd be safe in saying less than an hour ago."

Ray made a note in his pad. "I talked with Father Hilliard outside. He said that it was the sister's habit to step in for private prayer each evening after dinner. She left the convent across the street about a quarter to seven."

At the back of the church, the heavy door squeaked open and one of the officers walked in. "Her mother is out here. She's pretty upset." He looked imploringly at Meg.

"I'll talk with her," Meg said as she walked toward him, intent on preventing the mother from entering and witnessing the gruesome scene.

"Forensics coming?" Dr. Freemont asked.

Carefully placing his pen in his pocket, Ray nodded. "They're on their way." He leaned down and peered at the stone floor directly behind the pew where the woman's body had been found. "I want everything they find sent to the Trace Analysis Unit. I doubt they'll pick up anything, but we need to try. Too bad there's no snow. Maybe we could have gotten a footprint or two on the steps or the parking lot."

"I'll have my report on your desk by midafternoon tomorrow, and the wire as well," the doctor said, sitting down on the front pew across the aisle. Forensics would take about an hour. He'd have to wait them out. He'd been called away from his dinner table and wished they'd hurry.

Ray nodded and headed for the door behind the

altar, which led to Father Hilliard's office. The badly shaken priest had said that the young couple who'd found the body were waiting for him there.

He knocked once, then opened the door. The two young people sat huddled on a short couch across from the priest's desk. The girl seemed young and frightened, her face puffy from crying. Her fiancé looked a little green around the edges as well. Real-life death wasn't at all like the TV shows. Ray introduced himself as he pulled a chair over to the couch.

"Tell me what you saw, everything, from the moment you walked into St. Matthews," he said, hoping to put them at ease with a brotherly half-smile.

Tom Vanderlind swallowed around a huge Adam's apple. He'd never been questioned by a cop before. This one was big and intimidating with his beard and badge, his smooth manner. His gray eyes were impatient and his manner no-nonsense. He'd hate to go up against the detective as a suspect, Tom thought.

Ray listened as the couple told their story in fits and starts, all the while twisting their tightly gripped hands and squirming on the seat. "You say you heard the main door open after you were inside, then close again, yet you didn't see anyone?"

"That's right, sir," Tom said, his pale face serious. He hated appearing so shaken in front of Debbie, but the fact was that he couldn't stop seeing the nun's body in his mind's eye. "Someone could have been in the shadows of the vestibule. Maybe he slipped out after we started walking down the aisle."

"Oh God," Debbie moaned, the tears beginning again, "do you suppose it was the ... the killer?"

"Shh, honey. Don't cry anymore." Tom slid a thin arm around her and pulled her close.

"Did you hear anything that may have been footsteps?" Ray wanted to know. "Sounds really carry in this old church."

"No," the both chorused.

Ray took out his notebook and wrote down their names and addresses, then handed him his card. "If you remember anything else, please call me."

They left hurriedly, anxious to be away from him, from the aura of death all around them. Leaving the priest's office, Ray couldn't blame them.

"Got something for you, Ray," Doc called out as Ray walked back into the main church. He held out a sealed plastic envelope containing a white card.

Ray took it, angling it in the dim light to read the short message. Three words were printed in block letters: PLEASE FORGIVE ME.

"Found it under her body, sticking out of a pocket," Dr. Freemont told him. "Five'll get you ten the guy wore gloves, but I put it in an evidence envelope anyway."

A pen-and-ink sketch of the risen Christ was in one corner and a lighted candle in the other. "Looks like a mass card. Thanks, Doc. I'll check it out." Walking toward the back, he saw the two guys from Forensics enter.

His hunger had turned into a headache, but he wasn't done yet. He still had to go across to the convent where Sister Angelica had lived, and talk to the nuns who'd known her.

On days like this, Ray wondered if there were an easier way to make a living.

* * *

The Reverend Mother Magdalen was in her late fifties and wore the abbreviated nun's habit of dark skirt and jacket with a white blouse and short veil over her graying hair. She sat in a stiff-backed chair in the overheated convent sitting room and struggled with her emotions as she told Ray and Meg that everyone had loved the sweet-faced young nun who was in her first year at St. Matthews.

"I've been here less than two years myself," she said in a quivery voice. "Before my promotion and subsequent transfer to St. Matthews, I'd been at another Sisters of St. Joseph convent in the upper peninsula. Nothing like this has ever happened in any of our parishes." She sniffled into a lace-trimmed handkerchief. "The person who ... who killed Angelica must be very ill. We'll pray for him tonight, all of us."

Ray wished he could be so forgiving. "We're going to need a list of all of Sister Angelica's friends on the outside, her family members, anyone she visited occasionally or who came here to see her. A list of her students and their parents. The faculty. And, of course, we'll need to talk to all the nuns here as well."

The reverend mother sat up straighter, her expression changing from mournful to indignant. "I hope, Detective, that you aren't suggesting that any of our sisters could be involved in so heinous an act."

Ray could clearly see the former teacher within the otherwise amiable nun. "Of course not. I'm hoping they can help us by shedding some light on Sister Angelica's acquaintances and her outside activities."

The woman relaxed fractionally. "Well, I suppose that would be all right. However, everyone's quite upset. I would hope you would take that into consideration."

"Certainly we will," Meg interjected. "I know we'll all rest easier once the person who did this is found." She smiled at Mother Magdalen. "Would you be so kind as to bring the others in?" The sitting area wasn't very large, but it was the only room they'd been told that outsiders could enter.

Somewhat unsteadily, the reverend mother rose. "Yes. If you'll wait right here." She silently slid closed the double doors as she left.

Ray sat back, releasing a frustrated sigh. "Maybe you'd better do the questioning. I seem to ruffle the lady's feathers."

"She's just upset." And probably not used to being around men, Meg thought. Especially not a tall, attractive one like Ray Vargas, with his college-professor looks, his neat, full beard, his tweed jacket and button-down oxford shirts. He even wore a tie much of the time, something most of the guys in the squad room kept in a bottom drawer for court appearances only. She'd partnered with several other detectives through the years, each of whom would have shocked the pants off Mother Magdalen, not only with their chosen wardrobe but their colorful language. The reverend mother might have been surprised to learn that Ray was the most compassionate cop on the force.

Ray stood and removed his overcoat, then sat back down. "Is it hot in here or is it me?"

Meg unbuttoned her own coat. "I think it's warm, too. What did Father Hilliard say about the mass card?"

"He said it's not from St. Matthews."

"I've never seen one quite like it. Usually there's a parish name imprinted on them."

Ray fingered the pipe in his jacket pocket longingly. If he couldn't eat, he wished he could at least smoke. "Terrific. There're probably a hundred Catholic churches on the east side and suburbs. Shouldn't take more than a couple of weeks to hit 'em all."

Meg thought of their already overburdened case load and sighed. "Plus hit a hundred-plus stores trying to trace that wire. Piece of cake."

Ray's thoughts shifted to the media, knowing this murder wouldn't stay under wraps for long. "I already told the priest that I don't want him to mention the mass card to anyone. The reporters will undoubtedly find out about the wire, but I want to keep the card between us."

"Fine. It'll also be a way of ferreting out the compulsive confessors." Each time there was a sensational murder, any number of disturbed people would show up, dying take credit for it. It was something every police precinct had to deal with.

Ray heard the double doors slide open and got to his feet, bracing himself to face a dozen or so weepy nuns.

He'd rather have faced a root canal.

Hamtramck was a small Michigan city entirely surrounded by Detroit. Settled mostly by Polish immigrants, the neighborhoods boasted several beautiful churches and schools. The houses were older, mostly two story, and often divided into several apartments. The working-class people who inhabited the area were proud that their neighborhood was relatively crime free, its residents almost exclusively Roman Catholic, hard working, and spotlessly clean. Many were born, lived, and died there.

On Norwalk Avenue between Joseph Campau and Conant, Rosie Pulaski swept her back porch and noticed that the gray paint was peeling badly. If only her Joe had lived, he'd paint it come spring. He'd been such a good man, but he was gone five years now. They'd gone to school together in Warsaw, married and traveled to the States forty years ago.

Rosie sighed, her heavy breasts heaving beneath her thin coat. It wasn't easy for a widow to make ends meet. One of her sons was a Jesuit priest living in Novi and the other had married a woman with fancy taste and moved upstate. Neither could help his mother. Still, life wasn't so bad. She had her health and her church just a few miles away.

Every day Rosie knelt in front of the baby Jesus on her bedroom dresser and thanked Him that Joe's insurance had paid off the house. Of course, she'd had to rent out the upstairs, the small apartment where her mother had lived until she'd died only months before Joe. Between the rent money, Joe's small pension, and social security, Rosie managed just fine.

She moved to brush off the porch steps, automatically glancing up the back stairs. The lights were on in the upper kitchen; her tenant must be home. Rosie smiled as she thought of the young man who'd rented from her for two years. Such a polite fellow, in his middle twenties and quite handsome. He always greeted her warmly, asked about her health, and even brought her flowers now and then. Small bunches of violets.

She was lucky to have him. Some of her friends who rented out their upper flats complained about families with kids making messes and others moving out at night with money owing. She knew his last name, but she had trouble remembering it. She called him Wladek, the Polish translation of Walter, his first name. He was so quiet, sometimes she didn't know he was there. He never played the TV or the radio loud, and never had he had a visitor. Rosie often told him he was too young not to have friends, maybe a special girl somewhere. He would laugh and say she was his best girl.

She wasn't sure where he worked, but he came and went at odd hours. Why should she care? Rosie asked herself. He paid his rent on time every month. In cash.

Stepping down onto the back walk, she swiped her broom at the fallen twigs and several scraps of paper that had blown into her yard. Her mother had always said that just because you didn't have a lot of money didn't mean you couldn't be clean. Rosie agreed. She wondered how Wladek was keeping things upstairs. A man alone, did he even know how to vacuum and dust? She hoped so. He seemed very tidy about himself, his clothes always clean, his soft-soled shoes never muddy.

Rosie bent over to pick up a candy wrapper, then straightened and brushed back a lock of gray hair that had come loose from her combs. What Wladek didn't know was that she had a key to his apartment. She'd never been the sort who'd step in uninvited. Still, maybe one day when he was gone, she'd surprise him and go upstairs to give the place a good cleaning. It'd be like thanking him for the little flower bouquets.

Finished with her sweeping, she gripped the handrail and climbed the stairs. Helen Koberski would be coming soon to pick her up in her Chevy sedan for the bingo at the church hall. She'd just have time to take off her apron and change her shoes. Rosie entered her house and locked the back door.

Sister Veronica rummaged through her desk drawer and found the new box of chalk. Opening it, she walked over to the blackboard and placed several pieces in the tray. It was gloomy in the classroom, a mild April rain streaking the windows, which hadn't yet had their spring cleaning. Despite the dismal day, the woman's mood was buoyant.

Chalk in hand, she began to write out a list of goals for her third-graders for the coming week. It was Saturday morning and the Easter break was nearly over. The children would be filing back into class on Monday, chattering excitedly as usual. They loved their vacations, of course, but Sister Veronica knew that they enjoyed being with their friends and the challenges of learning. As a teacher, it was up to her to see that she slipped enough fun into their lessons to hold their interest. She usually managed just fine and was quietly pleased that her students liked her.

At twenty-eight, Sister Ronnie, as everyone called her, had been teaching for four years. A teacher was all she'd ever wanted to be, almost as fiercely as she'd wanted to be a holy sister. She loved living at the convent, the friendship of the Sisters of St. Joseph, and the children who attended St. Matthews. Satisfied with her life, she was seldom without a smile.

Finishing, Ronnie decided it was uncomfortably muggy in the classroom today. She couldn't open the windows, but she could slip off her veil. Setting it on her desk, she ran a hand through her short blond hair before moving to the stock cupboard.

One last chore, to check her supplies, and then she could leave for the day, knowing her classroom was ready for school to resume.

Bending into the cupboard and concentrating on her inventory, she didn't notice the door silently open, nor did she hear the soft footsteps of the man walking toward her. By the time she sensed someone else in the room and straightened to turn, the wire was already twining around her neck. She raised her hand to her throat, but it was too late.

Sister Veronica slumped to the floor soundlessly. The man reached into his pocket and placed a mass card alongside her outstretched hand.

"Forgive me," he whispered, then turned and let himself out as silently as he'd entered.

"Hamlet, will you hold still?" Ray wrestled with his rambunctious Great Dane on the backdoor landing, trying to wipe the mud and rain from the dog's paws before letting him into the house. Unfortunately, Hamlet thought his master wanted to play.

"I'm not going to take you running with me from now on if you won't cooperate," Ray told him. Unrepentant, Hamlet turned his big tan head and swiped his long wet tongue across Ray's cheek. "Oh, thanks. I needed that." He dragged the towel across the animal's powerful shoulders and along his back, then gave up. "I guess that's as good as it gets, pal."

As he opened the door to the kitchen, Hamlet bounded inside. The pet shop owner's warning drifted back to Ray, telling him that Great Danes weren't indoor dogs, that they were clumsy and tended to lope instead of walk, often knocking over unsuspecting people and small furniture that got in their way. Sighing, Ray closed the door, thinking the advice had been on target. However, after three years, he wasn't about to get rid of man's best friend over a few broken vases and bruised thighs.

As Ray slipped out of his wet shoes, Hamlet bounded over to him, his water dish hanging from his large jaws. His habit of carrying around his empty dishes whenever he was hungry or thirsty always earned him a scratch behind the ears. "Okay, I get the message." Ray filled the water bowl, tossed some dry food into the other dish, and set them both in the corner of the kitchen. Hamlet rushed over and dug in.

In the bathroom, Ray grabbed a towel and had begun drying his hair when he heard the phone ring. Who could it be? he wondered, walking into the bedroom. It was his first day off in weeks. Frowning, he grabbed the phone on the third ring. "Vargas here."

As he listened to the desk sergeant, his scowl deepened. "Judas Priest," Ray muttered. There'd been another strangling at St. Matthews.

TWO

Toni Garette sat back in the cushioned lounge chair on the glassed-in rear porch of her parents' Grosse Pointe Shores home and smiled at her cousin. "I'm so proud of you for this latest promotion, Mo. And we're all so glad you're going to be living closer to us."

Sister Maureen Garette stirred sugar into her iced tea. "Me, too. It seems as if I've lived in every parish in Detroit. I'm anxious to settle down somewhere, to hang my nun duds in the same closet for a while."

Toni laughed. Mo's sense of humor was laced with an irreverence that showed she didn't take herself too seriously. Only a few people knew how long it had taken her cousin to get to this point. After a long uphill struggle, at last Mo seemed truly happy.

Though they were quite different, the two women were very close. Which was why Toni was so glad that Mo had been appointed vocational guidance counselor for the east side and been assigned permanent living quarters at St. Matthews, where she'd moved just the previous week.

"So, how do you like the new convent?" Toni

asked, reaching for her own tea. They'd just finished sharing a curried seafood salad from a new recipe that Toni was testing. As the manager of her parents' upscale restaurant, the Glass Door, she loved inventing original offerings that she'd then pass on to their chef, provided they'd won her approval. "Are the sisters friendly?"

"Yes and no," Mo answered, curling her slim legs up on the two-seater opposite her cousin. "They're awfully subdued and still very disturbed about what happened to Sister Angelica last month. Not that I blame them."

"I read about that. It was horrible. Who'd have reason to kill a nun?" A lifelong Catholic, Toni shuddered at the thought.

Mo shook her head sadly. "I can't imagine. Every night, we pray that the murderer gets caught and gets the help he needs. It's made everyone nervous, I can tell you. Mother Magdalen has warned us not to go anywhere alone."

"That may work for the teachers, but what about you? You drive all over town alone."

"Well, that's my job. I can't very well hire a bodyguard or start carrying a weapon." Mo twisted a curl of her pale yellow hair, a childhood habit, and smiled. "I'm not afraid, really. I mean, I don't go out alone after dark and I'm not careless. I keep my car doors locked and I don't drive down deserted streets. But I can't exactly lock myself in my room until they catch him." Mo took a slow sip of her tea. "Besides, I think it was probably one of those random things. Poor Sister Angelica was just in the wrong place at the wrong time."

"Maybe." Toni gazed out at the gently falling rain. Her mother's flower beds, the ones Jane had planted over the mild Easter weekend, were soaking up the moisture. Geraniums, marigolds, and deep purple pansies nestled among the budding rosebushes. They had a gardener who kept the lawn and shrubs trimmed, but Jane Garette enjoyed working in the earth. Toni hoped a late frost wouldn't kill off the new growth.

She loved their backyard, the tall redwood fencing that afforded them privacy, the maple tree with the two hanging bird feeders, the sour cherry tree in the far corner. And the pool that her father had had put in three summers ago after a mild heart attack so he could get his required exercise.

Toni allowed herself few leisure hours, but what little time she had for relaxation she often spent in the backyard she'd enjoyed since childhood. Friends often asked why at her age she still lived with her parents. Her answer was always the same: because she loved them and her home and, since her father and mother let her live her own life, she saw no reason to move out.

It was as much Mo's home as her own, Toni thought as she swung her attention back to her cousin. "Maybe you should consider moving back here until the case is settled. I know Mom would feel better. Your old room is always waiting."

But Mo was already shaking her head. "I can't, Toni. Please understand. I belong there now."

Toni had never been as deeply religious as Mo, but she respected her cousin's feelings. "I do understand. We just . . . well, we want you *safe.*"

"You worry too much," Mo said, glancing at her watch. "Look at the time. This was super, getting together like old times. We'll have to do it again real soon. But I'd better scoot. I've got some paperwork waiting for me and—"

The phone on the end table rang, interrupting her.

Toni picked it up in the middle of the second ring, listened a moment, then looked up. "It's for you. Mother Magdalen." Handing the receiver to Mo, she bent to gather up the lunch dishes. She carried them into the kitchen, then returned for the glasses. When she saw Mo's stricken expression, she stopped in the doorway. "What is it?"

Mo looked at her, white-faced. "There's been another strangling. Sister Ronnie. Just last night we watched television together." She reached for her veil that she'd set aside on the footstool. "I have to leave."

"I'll go with you," Toni said, not wanting her gentle cousin to face such a thing alone. A ripple of fear raced up her spine as the news sank in. Two nuns strangled within a month of one another. What was happening at St. Matthews?

Huge blue eyes so like her own swung toward Toni. "He ... he killed her right in her classroom. She'd gone over to prepare it for Monday."

Toni drew her close for a long moment. "I hope they get that bastard, lock him up and throw away the key."

Mo pulled back. "No, Toni. He's sick. He needs help."

"Yeah, right. And I'm the Easter Bunny." Toni bent to put on the shoes she'd kicked off earlier. "Come on. Let's go."

Ray pulled his Ford wagon into St. Matthews' parking lot next to the Channel 7 van, his mouth a grim line. Despite the steady rain, the TV cameras were rolling on the stone steps where a reporter was talking with Father Hilliard. Swearing under his breath,

Ray stepped out, zipped up his leather jacket, and walked over.

The reporter, an attractive black woman he'd run into before, saw him approaching and ended the interview quickly, signaling the cameraman to cut it. Smart lady, he thought as he sent her a flinty look before turning to the white-haired priest. The man was obviously shaken. "Could we have a private word, please, Father?" he asked, taking the priest's arm and leading him away. He'd been told that the killer had struck in the school room, so he headed them across the street.

"This is terrible, just awful," Father Hilliard said softly, unmindful of the rain dampening his hair and jacket. "I've called the bishop. I simply don't know what to think."

With a nod, Ray acknowledged the uniformed cop standing alongside his black-and-white as they entered the school. "None of us do, at this point. A word of advice, Father, if I may." Ray stopped short of the classroom door, where another officer and several nuns were huddled. He chose his words carefully. "It might be a good idea not to talk with the media any more. They have a tendency to do a lot of speculating. Sometimes that can alarm people unnecessarily."

Father Hilliard's pale eyes registered confusion and lingering shock. "But I thought if they heard a few words from their pastor, our parishioners might feel comforted."

"Perhaps. What did the reporter ask you?"

"She wanted to know if I agreed that we had a serial killer on the loose here at St. Matthews."

Ray bit back an oath and let the older man continue.

"I didn't know how to answer that. I . . . do you

think these two strangulations could be the work of one madman?"

"I haven't seen the second victim yet." The dispatcher's call had indicated the same M.O., but Ray didn't want to go into that with the priest right now. "I feel it's best not to conjecture, as I said. Not until the facts are known, until the medical examiner's report is in. Your parishioners are probably frightened enough without theorizing about a serial killer, wouldn't you say?"

"Yes, yes, of course."

"Why don't we talk again after I've checked with the doctor? If you could round everyone up, we could meet at the convent." At the priest's vague nod, Ray left him, walking toward the classroom, inwardly cursing the media who often as not added to the problems of most investigations.

He spoke briefly to Mother Magdalen at the door, nodded to the officer and moved inside. Dr. Freemont was sitting in a low chair watching the men from forensics, one dusting for prints, another who'd just finished vacuuming for trace material. Ray was fairly certain, as with the last time, that they wouldn't find anything.

"I wish we could stop meeting like this," Doc said quietly. It was his job to work on dead bodies, to gather his findings and give them to the detectives. Yet some got to him more than others, and these nuns were the worst yet. He had a daughter in her twenties, slim and lovely like this victim, the second young woman to die so horribly in four weeks. And she probably wouldn't be the last. "Same M.O., Ray."

"I was afraid of that." Ray stooped down to stare into the unseeing eyes of the nun, with her discolored face and bloody, swollen neck where the slender wire that had killed her was still twined.

Doc leaned over and handed him the small plastic evidence envelope. "And here's his calling card."

Ray stood and examined the card. The same imprints, the same block-letter printing, the same message. They hadn't picked up a single fingerprint on the last one.

Struggling with his anger, Ray gazed around the classroom. Typically elementary with small desks, neat printing on the blackboard, colorful animals cut out and hung on a large corkboard. A dozen spelling tests displaying happy faces and gold stars tacked on a bulletin board. A picture of Jesus at the front near the teacher's desk, His arms outstretched in welcome. Ray glanced over at Sister Veronica.

He hoped that her faith had delivered her to her savior.

Ray wiped his shoes on the mat at the convent's front door and entered. The vestibule was empty except for a tall blonde who was standing and gazing out the side window, her back to him. She was dressed in a kelly green sweater, designer jeans, and Reeboks. Ray didn't think she was a nun.

When she heard him step inside, she turned. After but a moment, recognition lit up her eyes and she smiled. "Ray. It's been a while."

Toni Garette. He hadn't seen her since the wedding of her best friend and his ex-partner last year. He'd thought her attractive when they'd worked on the Weston case, but hadn't acted on it or mentioned his interest, even to Sam. He had a feeling that Detroit detectives and managers of posh suburban eateries lived in different worlds. "Almost six months now, right?"

"About that, yes." Her eyes slid over his beard. "You've expanded your mustache."

Ray resisted the urge to reach up and stroke his face. "Keeps me warm in these cold Michigan winters."

She was elegance personified, even in casual clothes. Her hair was the color of wheat blowing in a summer Kansas breeze, falling just to her shoulders with airy bangs shifted to one side. Her skin was pale with just a smattering of freckles across the bridge of her nose, the small imperfection oddly adding to her beauty. Her lips were full and moist, the kind of mouth that made a man wonder how she'd taste. But it was her eyes that had always stopped him in his tracks. They were large and as true a blue as the Pacific Ocean about ten miles off shore at high tide. "You've cut your hair," he said inanely.

"Yes. How have you been?"

"About the same. And you?" Undoubtedly, she was dazzled by his wit and charm, his sharp repartee, Ray thought irritably. Some things never changed. Toni Garette still could reduce him to stupid in seconds, a fact that didn't please him.

"Not too bad, until today." She nodded toward the closed doors of the sitting room where the low hum of voices could be heard. "Are you here because of the murders?"

"Yes. Meg and I are investigating. You remember Meg?"

Oddly, for two diverse people, they had several friends in common. That was probably because two of Toni's closest friends had married detectives from the Beaubien precinct. "Sure. The redhead.

How's she doing?" Meg had danced cheek-to-cheek with her big Irish husband through both receptions.

"Good." He frowned at the door, then glanced back to Toni. "What brings you here?"

"Sister Maureen Garette's my cousin. She just moved to St. Matthew's this past week. She was with me when she heard the news." Toni shoved her trembling hands into the pockets of her jeans. "I'm trying to convince Mo to come stay with me until all this is over."

"Can't say I blame you."

"Have you got any leads from the last strangling?"

Ray unzipped his jacket, wondering why it was always so damn hot in this house. "I wish I could say yes, but I can't." They knew some things about the killer from studying the victim and the scene, of course. But they'd gotten nowhere trying to trace the mass card and the florists' wire. She probably wanted to hear about suspects and he was fresh out.

"Same killer?"

"Looks like it. I'll know more after I get the medical examiner's report and the one from forensics." He turned as the two doors slid open. The reverend mother, looking pinched and worried, stood silently waiting. Ray had trouble understanding such patience, such acceptance. If two of his close friends had been viciously strangled, he'd be ready to rip the room apart.

He swung back to Toni and saw her tense impatience. She wasn't the tolerant type either. "Are you coming in?"

Toni hugged her arms close to her body protectively and shook her head, "I think I'd better wait here."

Reluctantly, Ray entered the crowded sitting room.

St. Aloysius Catholic Church in downtown Detroit had few in attendance for the Saturday evening five-thirty mass. Once, in better times, before the gracious apartment buildings of the area had been vacated and then torn down, the grand old church had been packed for every service. But urban decay and a high crime rate had emptied the streets and sent the residents scurrying to the suburbs. All but a hardy few.

Wally knelt in a side pew in the back and watched the handful of worshipers file out after the priest as the mass ended. The candles still burned and the smell of incense was heavy in the damp air.

Outside, the rain hadn't let up for hours. But Wally didn't mind. He liked the rain. It was good for the grass and the flowers. Terry had always liked violets. He'd given them to her often. Even now, he kept a small cluster of violets on his dresser in his flat. To remind him.

He left the pew and walked silently in his rubber-soled shoes down the long aisle to the altar railing. There, he knelt down, clutched his hands together and raised his eyes to Jesus on the cross. He'd sent another sweet virgin to live with Jesus today. She would have no more worries here on earth, no more hard decisions about right and wrong to make. He'd freed her from her earthly cares and sent her to a better place.

Yet the act weighed heavily on his mind, in his heart. Bending his head low, he prayed. *Father, forgive me.*

* * *

It took Ray almost an hour to calm their concerns, to answer their questions, to reassure the sisters at St. Matthews that the police were doing everything possible. He understood their near panic. Generally, nuns were protected, sacrosanct, inviolate. Yet someone was violating them, mutilating, killing. He was the one entrusted to find the responsible individual. He recognized their vulnerability, tasted their fear, and felt their frustration.

"Sisters," he said, winding down and standing up, "the best advice I can give you is to go *nowhere* without a companion. In each case, the killer's victims were alone. There's safety in numbers. Don't go out at night and—"

"Sister Ronnie was strangled in broad daylight, Detective," Sister Maureen reminded him. Though she was as frightened as the others, she also knew she couldn't do her job if she couldn't move about the city freely.

"Yes, you're right. But the school was deserted when she was there. And she was working alone."

"We're teachers," Sister Agnes, an older nun interjected. "We're often in our classrooms alone after the children leave. To straighten up, to do class planning."

"I understand that. You need to coordinate with one another for those times. Leave your doors open. Know who's in the building. Check up on one another." He saw the nervous, irritated glances pass between their worried faces. "I know it's a nuisance. But it just may save your life."

"When, exactly, do you think you'll catch this ... this mad man?" a middle-aged sister in the back wanted to know. She earned a scowl from Mother Magdalen.

"I wish I could give you the hour and date. I can't. As I've said, we're working diligently toward that end." He checked his watch, saw that it was nearly seven. There was little more that he could tell them. "I'm sorry, I have to leave. I've left my card with Mother Magdalen. If any of you remember any small detail you think might be important or if you see anyone suspicious, please call. And thank you for your time."

With something bordering on relief, he left the hot, stuffy room and found Toni Garette seated by the vestibule window. He needed to file his report. Yet he found he wanted to take a detour first and spend a little time with her.

He walked over, carrying his jacket. "Can I offer you a lift?"

Toni stood, looking around him, trying to catch Mo's eye. "I'm not sure yet." She'd ridden over in Mo's car and didn't want to bother her about a ride back after what had happened. She wondered if Mo wanted to return to the house. She'd be safe there. "I need to talk with my cousin a minute."

"Sure." Ray watched her walk away, her back straight, her incredibly long legs carrying her quickly to Sister Maureen's side. She seemed to be trying to convince her cousin of something, but it wasn't working, for Mo was shaking her head. Toni gave in, hugged her fiercely, said goodbye and came back to him. "Where's your coat?"

She shrugged. "I didn't wear one."

Ray slipped his jacket around her shoulders over her protests, and led her quickly to his car. Inside, he turned on the motor, the wipers and the heater before looking at her. "Do you have to hurry home?"

Toni studied his face. It was a nice face, well suited to his neat beard, which was the color of rich chocolate. His eyes were a deep gray and reflected a quiet intelligence. He was wearing a tan V-necked sweater, its sleeves pushed up on his arms, and khaki slacks. She'd liked Ray Vargas the few times she'd met him. He was a big man, yet there was a gentleness about him.

But he was a little too square, too dull, too predictable for her taste.

Still, her parents would be at the restaurant till quite late so she had nothing to rush home for. And she had to admit that being so close to a murder investigation had made the prospect of an evening home alone far less appealing. She rarely went on dates, but this could hardly be construed as a date. "No, not really."

"I haven't eaten all day. Do you like Chinese?"

"Love it."

Shifting into gear, he smiled his first real smile of the day as he drove out of St. Matthews' parking lot.

Wang's was a "joint," a hole in the wall on Cadieux near Warren Avenue. The obligatory dangling red Chinese lanterns and some oddly psychedelic black-and-white wallpaper were the only decoration. But the fake leather booths and Formica tabletops were clean, and the heavenly cooking smells in the moist air just about grabbed passersby by their noses and dragged them inside.

"What do you prefer?" Ray asked, opening the large menu.

"Anything but sweet and sour." Toni made a face. "There's something about all that red-orange sauce." Feeling the warmth of the nearby kitchen, she shrugged out of his jacket and folded it onto the seat next to her. His scent, a hint of tobacco mingled with an outdoorsy aroma, clung to her sweater, oddly appealing.

Ray gave their order to Mr. Wang himself, the only person other than the cook working this gloomy Saturday evening. A young couple with a baby asleep in a carrier in the far corner ate quietly. Otherwise, they had the place to themselves. He poured them each a cup of steaming tea. "I don't even like tea. But somehow, it tastes good in Chinese restaurants."

Toni nodded distractedly, her mind still back in St. Matthews convent with her stubborn cousin. "I wish Mo would have agreed to stay with me for a while." She gazed out the smudged window at the dark drizzle, her spirits not much brighter than the weather. Her mother especially would be upset that she hadn't been able to persuade Mo to return to the house. When she'd talked with Jane Garette earlier, she'd told Toni to insist. Her mother had apparently forgotten that Mo very much had a mind of her own.

"I take it the two of you are close." Ray sipped his tea.

"More like sisters than cousins, really." Toni shoved the sleeves of her green sweater up over her slender arms. "Mo's parents were killed in an auto crash when she was only nine. Her mother was my Mom's sister, so my folks brought Mo to live with us. She'd always been shy, but she really withdrew after the accident."

He was listening, yet assessing her as she spoke,

a bad habit he had no intention of breaking. Working both sides of the brain, he called it. He decided he hadn't been this close to class in a long time. By accident or design, Vargas? his inner voice asked. "You don't have any other sisters or brothers?"

"No. We're both only children, the same age, even born the same month."

"What month would that be?"

"March."

"And how hold were you on this March that just passed?" he dared ask.

Toni raised a careful brow. "Subtle as a ton of bricks, aren't you, Vargas?"

He smiled. "Yeah. Cops are known for their subtlety. You going to tell me?"

"The big 3-0. Over the hill."

His eyes skimmed over the features of her face, taking his time. "A mighty nice hill." He saw the surprise on her face and wondered if it was possible that she didn't think of herself as beautiful. "I've got six years on you. Tell me more about your cousin."

Steaming wonton soup arrived in small bowls with ladle type spoons. Despite the heat, they dug in hungrily. Toni let her memory drag her back as she ate. "After the accident, it was a long while before Mo laughed out loud again. She developed asthma and missed a lot of school. She had it rough. Finally, when she was a junior in high school, she came into her own. She was so pretty and she had this mischievous sense of humor. A lot of guys were nuts about her."

Ray finished his soup and shoved aside the bowl. "But . . ."

"But Mo was marching to a different drummer. Mom and Dad kept trying to interest her in college, but she had her mind made up. She entered the convent at eighteen."

"And now she teaches little children their ABC's."

"No, actually she's a vocational guidance counselor. She advises young girls who think they have a calling to the sisterhood."

Mr. Wang returned and placed brimming oval platters on the table. Cashew chicken, moo gai pork, shrimp tempura, vegetable fried rice. Ray watched as she filled her plate, pleased she wasn't one of those women who nibbled. "But you never had the calling," he said, resuming their conversation.

Toni sent him an incredulous look. "Me? Not hardly. I'm a shade too questioning, far too impatient, and definitely too irreverent for convent life. But I admire those who can handle it. The life is perfect for Mo. She's finally happy."

Ray paused, studying her. "You love her very much."

She looked a little embarrassed. "Well, sure. She's family and we only children don't have many to spare. How about you? Come from a big family?"

He'd learned long ago to mask his feelings when it came to family discussions. "No, just me and a half-brother. What reason did your cousin give for not staying with you until the killer's caught?"

Toni sighed as she stabbed a shrimp onto her fork. "The only one she could, I suppose. That she belongs there." She felt a worried frown form. "Have you learned anything about the man you're after from the last killing?"

"A little. He's able to move about without suspicion, apparently. In both cases, there were no signs of a struggle."

SHATTERED VOWS

They ate quietly for a few minutes as Toni's restless mind considered possibilities. "So he's probably very strong."

"Or very lucky, happening on them when they're really absorbed. One kneeling in prayer, the other cleaning out her classroom cupboard."

Toni chewed her fried rice thoughtfully. "Why nuns? Some religious nut, you think?"

Ray scooped himself a second serving and shrugged. "Maybe a defrocked priest or maybe a nun who was kicked out of her order for some terrible violation." He saw her shaking her head. "You don't agree?"

"Catholics don't often defrock their priests, as a rule. Priests leave the order for reasons of their own. If they have serious problems such as alcoholism, there are recovery facilities to deal with that sort of thing. Some are asked to retire early, but it has to be for a very serious infraction. And I've never heard of a nun being kicked out, although quite a few have left because they wanted to marry. I really can't picture a former nun becoming so violent."

"If you saw what I see on an average week, not much would surprise you. Didn't your cousin ever date? Doesn't she miss not having a chance for a family?"

"She dated some, mostly in groups. She speaks of the other sisters and the people she serves as her family." Toni set down her fork, a smile twitching at her lips. "Is your male ego wounded that a woman would voluntarily not want to marry?"

He smiled. "Not at all. On the other side of the coin, I know a lot of guys who want nothing to do with marriage, especially cops. And then there's you." He leaned forward, his elbows on the table. "You've never married, have you?"

Right back at you, chum, she thought. "No, I haven't." She mimicked his pose and his smile. "And then there's you. Have you ever married?"

The smile slid from his face. "Yeah, once. Long time ago. I learned that the grand institution wasn't for me." His gaze didn't leave her face. "You have the most beautiful eyes. Anyone ever tell you that?"

"In other words, let's change the subject."

"Beautiful *and* smart." He shook his head. "An unbeatable combination."

Toni sat back, comfortably full and surprisingly comfortable with him. "Getting back to our killer, do you think he's got something against nuns or the church? Or is he just a nut who happened to be passing St. Matthews when the urge hit him, twice?"

Ray wiped his mouth and leaned back. "Hard to say. Psychologists can give you profiles on serial killers, if, in fact, that's what we have here. But they vary from case to case. Yeah, I'd guess this guy has something against Catholics. Maybe nuns, maybe not. From what I've seen of the victims, he's angry, filled with rage."

"He's killing to pay back the church for some real or imagined wrong?"

"Possibly."

"Then I imagine you're checking out the loner types who hang around St. Matthews. Parishioners, visitors, workmen. Friends of the sisters. Delivery men, even relatives."

He smiled, rather tolerantly, he thought. Amateurs always had the answers. "We are. But not all killers are loners lurking in corners ready to spring. They often lead a double life, are quite intelligent, and able to function well enough in society to maintain an acceptable public persona. They usually hold down a job. Not all of them are mental misfits easily recognizable at ten paces."

"Are you making fun of me?" she asked as Mr. Wang placed a small tray with the check and two fortune cookies on the table.

"Absolutely not." He admired the way her mind worked, quietly efficient, impatient, zeroing in. He'd learned from conversations with Sam that Toni was a type-A personality who invariably forged ahead and got the job done, which was what she was dying to do with this case.

She wasn't at all the kind of woman he usually spent time with, he couldn't help thinking. The little free time he had, he wanted simple pleasures, uncomplicated conversation, good food, and a mutually satisfactory tumble in the sheets. Perhaps Toni valued her freedom, too.

Ray put several bills on the tray as Toni picked up her cookie.

"Aren't you curious about your fortune?" she asked.

He shook his head. "I don't believe in those things."

Shrugging, Toni followed him out to his car.

Inside, Toni waited for the heater to do its job. The windows fogged up quickly, lending a cozy feel. "My mind keeps going back to these strangulations. Do you think the killings are sexual, that he gets some sort of perverted thrill out of the women dying?"

Ray brushed rain from his hair. "That's always a possibility, but I doubt it in this case." She didn't know about the mass cards and their pleading message. He didn't think he'd go into that with her just yet. "I think he's apologizing for having sinned against someone. Perhaps God. He's asking forgiveness."

Toni gazed at him, puzzled. "Apologizing by killing. That's difficult for me to comprehend."

Ray shifted and the wagon moved forward. "Most of us have trouble understanding a murderer's mind." He drove slowly in the evening drizzle, still reluctant to end their time together, still wondering why that was so. He flipped on the radio and an old Burt Bacharach tune filled the wagon.

Toni was a beautiful woman, and dinner had been an unexpectedly pleasant interlude. But he knew half a dozen attractive women who would gladly share his meals with him. Why was this any different?

The Garette house was dark as he turned into the circular drive. "Do you have a dog?" he asked.

"No, why?"

"Dogs are a good warning system." He got out of the car and went around to help her out, surprised to see she'd already opened her own door.

"We've got a burglar alarm system," Toni said from the porch as she unlocked the door. Inside, she turned on the light and pressed in the code, then held the door for him.

He didn't want to tell her that burglar alarms could be deactivated easily enough by all sorts of people. He looked around at the marble foyer, the winding staircase carpeted in pale blue, the huge chandelier. Impressive, but her parents' taste probably. He wished he could catch a glimpse of a room that she'd decorated as her private sanctuary. "You want me to have a look around before I go?"

The thought had her frowning. "You think that's necessary? I'm about as different from a nun as you're likely to find."

"I'm just an overly cautious cop."

Toni leaned into the archway and hit another button, illuminating the large living room beyond. "I feel pretty safe here, but thanks." She took off his jacket and held it out to him, surprised again how much she'd enjoyed the heavy masculine feel of it. "Thanks for the use of your jacket and for dinner."

"How late do your folks usually work?"

"Midnight, one, sometimes two. It depends. It's Saturday, so they'll probably be late." She walked back toward the door with him. Almost there, her wet Reeboks skidded on the marble. He caught her, drawing her up hard against his body to prevent her from falling.

His large hands held her steady. She had the impression of strength and patience and a barely controlled energy. She saw the pulse in his throat escalate, saw a quick flash of awareness leap into his eyes. And heard her own heart suddenly thudding in her ears.

She'd been wrong. He wasn't nearly as bland, as mild-mannered as she'd thought. The phrase about still water running deep trickled through her mind as she let out a breath and stepped back. "I ... thanks, again."

"Sure." He let go of her, wishing he didn't have to, yet annoyed with himself because he wanted to go on holding her. "If I called one night when you're free, would you want to go out?" The words were spoken before he'd consciously thought to say them.

"Thanks, but I don't date men."

That threw him, but he kept his features even. "I respect people with alternative lifestyles."

"What?" She laughed, a genuine sound. "I do,

too, but that's not the reason. I just find it easier to stay uninvolved."

"I'll bet there's a story there. Want to tell me?"

She glanced at the grandfather clock standing in the curve of the staircase. "Oh, I think it's a little late tonight to exchange life stories."

He smiled. "Then I guess you'll have to go out with me another time and tell me." He couldn't resist reaching up to touch the ends of her hair lightly, briefly. "I'll call you."

She didn't answer, just watched him hurry down the steps and into his station wagon. He'd probably consider her little red Mercedes two-seater convertible a real indulgence. It probably was. But hell, even her father didn't drive a stodgy station wagon.

Toni watched his taillights disappear, closed the door, and engaged the alarm. What was she doing even thinking about Senior Detective Ray Vargas? A nice enough guy, but not for her. But then, she wasn't looking. By the time a woman hit thirty, good, available men were scarcer than hen's teeth, as her friend Carly used to say.

It wasn't that she didn't like men. But more and more they seemed to fall into a couple of very predictable categories. The terminally dull or full-of-themselves arrogant ones, or the your-place-or-mine types. They made an evening spent alone at home with a good book sound heavenly. Lately, she'd spent most of her free time either working or reading, it seemed.

Toni doubted if Ray Vargas was any different. No matter. She'd probably not see him again for another six months.

Walking upstairs, she decided to leave the lights on and call Mo to see how she was doing.

THREE

He needed a Catholic, Ray thought as he loosened his tie. It was unseasonably warm for mid-April, adding to his discomfort. He'd liked to have removed his jacket, but his shoulder holster wouldn't allow it. Scooting behind the wheel, he let out a frustrated sigh. He'd just visited his fourth church office and no one could tell him a thing about the mass card he'd shown them.

The women behind the reception desks had been nice enough, always smiling and soft-spoken. But the moment he showed them his I.D., they stiffened right up, as if his very presence might bring the strangler to their parish. Thanks to the newspapers and TV anchors, the serial strangler, as he'd been dubbed by the press, was the talk of every Catholic community as well as other angry citizens. Speculation ran high as to when he'd strike again. The twelfth of never, Ray hoped.

The office volunteers had glanced at the mass card and quickly shaken their heads. Ray gazed up at Our Lady of Perpetual Help as he started the wagon. Here he'd insisted on talking with the pastor. It hadn't worked. The slight, balding priest had told him he'd never seen the card or anything similar, then excused himself to make an important call. Swell.

If only Meg hadn't come down with the flu, Ray thought as he turned out into noonday traffic on Mack Avenue. It wasn't her fault, of course, and she'd been obviously green around the gills when he'd insisted she go home the previous afternoon. But perhaps as a Catholic, she'd have been able to pry more information from the reluctant ladies who guarded their priests from problems of the outside world like the Secret Service kept watch over the president. Or so it seemed to Ray.

Stopping at a light, he picked up his list. There were six more parishes that comprised the area in and around St. Matthews. He'd have to visit them all in order to rule them out. The media still hadn't learned of the mass cards and Ray wanted to keep it that way for a while yet. If they could only get a fix on where the killer got the cards, perhaps they could pinpoint the neighborhood in which he lived, then trace his activities.

The light changed and he moved ahead. Yesterday, he'd spent hours dropping in on area print shops, hoping one of them might have made up the cards. No luck. Then he and Meg had visited several Catholic supply stores, but that had netted them zero. One had given him a catalog that parishes often used to order stationery and such. After Meg had gone home, Ray had pored through that. And had come up empty-handed.

Someone had to know something about the card. It couldn't have just popped up out of thin air. Checking the address of the next parish he intended to visit, he noticed that it was on Kercheval, just blocks from the Glass Door, the Grosse Pointe restaurant owned by the Garettes. Lunchtime. The place would probably be crowded. She'd likely be too busy to speak with him.

Why did he want to talk with her, anyway?

He'd dropped her off the previous Saturday and said he'd call. Only he hadn't, not yet. He certainly didn't want an involvement and she'd claimed she didn't, either. He'd just gotten untangled from a very nice woman last Christmas. Donna was a court reporter, fun to be with and good in bed. But after months of seeing one another, she'd wanted more. Ray had told her up front not to expect forever from him. She'd decided to move on, no hard feelings. Which was the way he liked things to end.

He didn't think Toni was actively seeking. If a woman made it to thirty without saying her "I do's," she was either very independent or very picky. Or both. He wasn't sure why, but he had the feeling that Toni was like him in that she was too deeply involved in her work to want a relationship commitment. If he read her right, they'd get along just fine.

She couldn't have missed the quick spark of attraction that had flared when he'd held her close for that brief moment. He'd seen her eyes, recognized the signs; he was sure she had, too. He'd thought of her far too often since then. Maybe it was time to find out if there was something more there.

Ray turned into the large parking lot of the Glass Door, already crowded with Mercedes, Lincolns, and BMW's, handed his wagon over to the young attendant, and went inside. The trademark heavy glass door, profusion of large, thriving plants, snow-white tablecloths, pale candles, soft music. Chic matrons taking a break from their shopping, attractive older men in leather sport coats and tassel loafers, young executives wheeling and dealing over lunch as tuxedoed waiters poured their Chardonnay. He'd never visited this restaurant, but he knew it.

Knew it from his years in Boston when his stepmother had needed to ease her conscience for neglecting him and his brother, dressing them up and dragging them out to show them off. Elegant little dinners in the best places teaches the boys to appreciate the finer things in life, she'd commented to their father. And, like the besotted creature he'd become, Dad had agreed. But by then, John Vargas had agreed with everything his wife, Marianne, said and did.

"A party of one, sir?" the tall woman behind the reservation desk asked, interrupting Ray's thoughts.

"Actually, I'm here to see Toni Garette. Is she in?"

"Just a moment and I'll check." Pencil in hand, the hostess drifted away on a cloud of Obsession.

Hands in his pockets, Ray stared out the window until he heard his name spoken, then turned. If she was surprised to see him, she hid it well, he thought. Seeing her dressed in a black linen suit with a white blouse, looking so businesslike, he wished he'd ignored the urge to drop in without phoning. The other night, casually dressed, she'd seemed approachable, vulnerable even, concern for her cousin softening her. Here, in her element, she looked urbane and sophisticated. Off limits.

His expression didn't change, but Toni read him anyhow. "Let's go to my office."

As he followed her through the main dining room and down a long carpeted hallway, he told himself he could easily fit in with this lunchtime crowd. If he had to, if he wanted to. But he'd had too many years of it to want a rematch. He still dressed the part, he supposed, or so the guys at the precinct were always telling him. He'd become used to buying expensive clothes that lasted.

Toni waited until he sat down across from her desk, then closed the door and returned to her chair. Strangely nervous, she picked up a pen so her hands would have something to do. "I hope you've come to tell me you've caught the bastard."

Her language, which seemed too down-and-dirty coming from her, relaxed him. "Afraid not. I've come to see if you had time to give me little help." He nodded toward the area they'd just left. "But I guess you've got your hands full."

"That depends on what you need me to do." She had the feeling it hadn't been easy for him to come to her, and even more difficult for him to ask for her help. Remembering the way he'd held her the previous Saturday night, the brief moment she'd looked up and seen the hungry look in his eyes, she felt her pulse quicken.

Crossing his long legs, Ray explained about the mass card the killer had left with each victim, that Meg was out ill and that he'd spent a frustrating morning trying to get information out of church office personnel. "The minute they find out I'm a cop—a non-Catholic cop, at that—they can hardly wait to get rid of me. I thought maybe, if you had the time, they'd open up to you more." She was watching him, her eyes assessing, her expression closed. On the other side of her door, he heard the clatter of dishes, the murmur of voices, a phone ringing. All right, so he'd made a mistake. "Never mind. It was a bad idea." He stood up, ready to bolt.

She'd decided as soon as he'd begun that she'd turn him down. Detroit had a huge police force. Let him recruit someone from inside. She had two friends who'd gotten involved with cops, and not a day of it had been easy. They were restless men with weary eyes who'd seen too much and had hearts that were firmly attached to their jobs. No sensible woman would want to take on all that.

"No," she heard herself say, despite herself, "it's a fine idea. Let me just tell my maître d' I'm leaving." She picked up the phone, thinking she'd finish going over fabric selections for their new restaurant later. She was used to working long hours.

He stood awkwardly while she talked into the phone, wishing he wasn't glad she'd decided to go with him, wondering why she had. You ponder too much, Vargas, Meg was always telling him. Why can't you accept more at face value? his partner often asked. Because he'd learned at an early age that some of life's worst problems were cloaked in pretty packages, and vice versa.

At the side door, Toni paused as a tall, slender woman with silver-blond hair walked toward them. Toni introduced her mother to Ray and the two shook hands as she explained why the police needed her help.

"Everyone's upset by those terrible murders," Jane Garette said. "I certainly hope you find that monster soon."

"Can't be soon enough for me," Ray told her, noticing the small worry lines around the older woman's eyes. He wondered if Toni had given her parents much to worry about.

"I'll check in later, Mom." With that, Toni walked outside into the sunshine.

Ray settled her in his wagon and headed south. "The next on my list is St. Patrick's. Familiar with it?"

"Not really. But there's a similarity to most of the parishes." She sat back, stealing a look at his profile, wondering why he was a shade nervous today. He'd seemed so confident the other evening. "Is there anything new on the case, that you can discuss with me, that is?"

"Don't I wish." He ran over their meager findings, no prints, same perpetrator, the dead ends. "The frustration's pretty high around the precinct." He glanced over at her long legs, sedately crossed. Nice. "How's your cousin doing?"

"Things are a little tense at St. Matthews, too, as you might expect. But she's going about her job, trying not to worry." Toni had thought of something and hoped he wouldn't mind her mentioning it. "Do you think there's a time pattern to these killings? They occurred almost exactly thirty days apart."

"Like the phases of the moon, you mean? Yeah, we've considered that. Maybe our killer's a strong woman and she starts to fall apart at the end of her cycle."

Toni wasn't buying that. "Men have cycles, too. Just not as obvious. The moon affects all living things."

He saw St. Patrick's ahead on the right and eased over. "Yeah. Right now, my cycle's making me grouchy. If we could get a bead on this guy, I know I'd feel better." In the parking lot, he turned off the engine. "Maybe you could light a candle. Aren't they supposed to be for specific intentions?"

"Yes, but it's not as simple as that. You can't, for instance, bet on a football game, then light a candle so your team will win."

"Too many rules. We atheists have it a whole lot easier."

Toni turned to see if he was joking. His expression was unreadable. "You're an atheist?"

Ray shrugged. "Atheist, agnostic, fallen-away Methodist. All three and maybe more."

How sad, she thought, but decided to keep her opinion to herself. "When did that happen?"

"Probably about the time my mother died, after I begged God to save her." He got out of the car, wondering what on earth had made him tell her something so personal.

Two hours and three churches later, they still hadn't found anyone who recognized the cards. Toni watched Ray take off his jacket, toss it in the back, and climb behind the wheel. He'd removed his tie earlier. The gun nestled against his side looked small and deadly.

"So, how do you like police work? Pretty glamorous, huh?" he asked. It was nice having her along; it definitely broke up the monotony. And he'd been right, the women had opened up to Toni far more than they had to him. She spoke their language.

"It's a lot of leg work, isn't it?"

"Too much." He glanced at the directions he'd written down for the fourth church and pulled out into traffic. "But then, I imagine your job has its dull moments, too, even though you cater to the rich and semi-famous."

"Sure, just like every other job. But I enjoy it most of the time. Especially with the new restaurant we're about to open in Birmingham."

He swung around a slowly moving truck. "Glass Door Number Two?"

"No. We're calling it the Brass Door. I'm designing the interior and working with a new chef we've found to create some really special recipes. Grand opening in June. If you play your cards right, I might invite you."

"I'll keep it in mind. You sound excited. Or just proud, maybe."

"A little of both, I suppose. The whole thing was my idea and it's great fun to see it take shape." Her idea but her father's dream, she thought, the one he'd put on hold after his heart attack. "Mom usually works only weekends now and Dad wants to play more golf. So I'll be going back and forth between the two places for a while."

"That seems like a lot of work.'

"I like to keep busy. Desk work alone makes the days drag."

Ray kept his eyes on the traffic. "I agree. A nine-to-five job works for some people. Personally, I think I'd go stir crazy at a desk job."

"How's Sam adjusting?" According to her friend Carly, Sam's wife, her husband had adapted to desk duty just fine.

"He has his good days and bad. We had a bust going a couple of weeks ago. Drugs. There were maybe six of us on it. Sam was itching to go with us, I could tell."

"A man's priorities change when he has a wife and child on the way. Then again, look at Luke and Stephanie. Two children in three years, but Luke's still out in the field." Stephanie was a friend from her neighborhood who'd married a cop, who'd rescued her from her abusive first husband.

"Yeah, old Luke will never hang it up." But Ray knew the anxiety his friend lived with, worrying about his family. A cop needed a clear mind to focus on his work. Thinking about other things could cost him his life.

"Is that why your marriage broke up, because she couldn't handle your job?"

Ray hesitated for a moment. "Yes and no. We were too young. She thought she knew what marriage to a cop would be like, thought she could handle the stress, the long hours alone. But she was an only child, came from money, and she was awfully spoiled. She needed more excitement than I could provide. So she went looking for it without me."

Toni looked at him speculatively. "So she left you?"

"No, I left her. The day I found her in bed with one of my good buddies. Probably for the best. We didn't belong together." He glanced over at her, saw the quick empathy in her eyes. "How about you? How is it you've never married?"

Toni wanted to know more about his marriage, but knew his question to her was his way of closing the book on that. "Never found anyone who'd put up with me, I guess."

Ray felt certain she was hiding something behind that evasive humor. "Seriously," he said.

Toni sighed, leaning back against the headrest. "Seriously? All right. I came close, twice. The first time we were both just out of college. Nick's Italian and very traditional. He wanted to marry me, have me stay home and raise his children, attend all the socialite charity events like his mother does. He wanted me to be his vision of the perfect wife."

Ray's lips twitched as he stopped for a light. "Did you tell him where to go?"

"Pretty much. The second was more recent." And still stung, she thought to herself. "Devlin's family owns two restaurants on the west side. He's black Irish, dark and very handsome. Looking back now, I think he set out to get me to fall for him."

"And did you?"

"Did I ever." Hard. She'd fallen hard and lived to regret it. "Until I learned that what he really wanted was a merger of our two families. To build a restaurant empire, so to speak. Very flattering, very good on the old ego."

"So that's why you've sworn off men?"

"Not exactly sworn off. But I am very cautious. I'm not fond of being used or of getting hurt. And I've learned that I'd rather be alone than settle for second best."

Picky, like he'd thought. Like he was. He understood perfectly. He'd been there and back, and it hadn't been soul-satisfying. "Second best leaves a bad aftertaste, doesn't it?"

She met his eyes, a little surprised that he understood. "Yes."

They were two blocks from St. Germaine's when the raspy voice of Sergeant Lou Frankell crackled out of Ray's radio. "Two-o-nine, you there, Ray?"

Automatically, Ray reached for his mike and pressed the button. "Yeah, Lou. What's up?"

"We've got a guy on the ledge. Fisher Building, sixth floor. Ramsey and Carter are on it, trying to talk him down, but no go so far. Captain said to call you, said to remind you about the Sawyer kid. This one's even younger and he swears he's going to jump."

Judas, of all days. "I've got a civilian in the car, Sarge."

"Tell them to wait downstairs with the blues. Kid's mother's out of town and his father's dead. Come on, padre. You can do it."

"Right." Disgusted, he rang off. "Got to make a little detour here," he told Toni. "Do you mind?"

But he'd already activated his flashing light and reached up to clamp it onto the car roof.

She didn't think his question required an answer. She'd heard the steely tone beneath the pleading sergeant's voice. Ray had little choice. "Why did he call you padre?"

Executing an illegal U-turn, Ray's lips were a thin line as he aimed the big car toward the expressway, his mind already with the frightened boy who was on a ledge. The last one had been high on drugs, but that hadn't kept the kid from being scared enough to wet his pants. He wondered what this one's problem was.

Toni watched his expression change. He probably hadn't even heard her question, she thought. His profile was hard, grim, focused. His foot on the pedal was firm, his hands on the wheel tense. She could almost see the adrenaline pumping through him. Through the windshield, she saw cars veering out of the way as he drove the needle upward. Sixty, seventy, nearing eighty.

In no time, Ray signaled a right turn, eased up on the gas, and zoomed toward the off ramp and onto Grand Boulevard. Mid-afternoon traffic was light, thank goodness. He saw the Fisher Building, with its spiraled steeple-like roof up ahead on the left. Two black-and-whites had cordoned off the street area. As he'd expected, a crowd had gathered, all heads looking up. A firetruck had just arrived; its ladder was being raised into an upright position. Siren screaming, he careened over the median strip. The sturdy wagon bounced, then came down hard, still rolling. He brought it to a stop a mere foot from the yellow tape line.

Hurriedly, Ray got out, shrugged into his jacket, then remembered his passenger. "I'll be back as soon as I can," he told Toni, then rushed toward the uniformed officer who ushered him inside. In the elevator, the man whose nameplate read Jack Ramsey briefed him.

"The kid's only fifteen. His father's been dead a couple of years and his mother's in Chicago at a meeting. We reached her. She's flying back." The officer was in his mid-forties, with two teenagers of his own. If they ever did anything like this, he'd clobber them a good one. "The little shit stole some money from his mother's purse this morning, skipped school, and spent the day at the movies. Suddenly, he decides he doesn't want to live anymore. Or maybe he just wants attention. I'd give him attention all right, if he was mine. He wouldn't sit down for a solid week."

Ray watched the elevator indicator lights flash the floor numbers impatiently. "Yeah, beatings solve a lot of problems."

Officer Ramsey caught the sarcasm in his tone. "Parents are too damn soft these days, I say. My dad used to warm my pants a lot. Didn't hurt me none."

"It turned you into the same kind of father, didn't it?" Ray struggled with his anger, knowing he needed to keep his cool at a time like this. "You ever hurt real bad, Ramsey? Or were you ever lonely, scared, mixed up? Ever think it might be that kind of thing that sent that kid out on a ledge six stories above the ground? Fifteen-year-olds don't threaten suicide just to get attention. By the time they crawl out there, they need a whole lot more than mere attention."

The doors finally slid open on the sixth floor and Ray hurried out.

Ramsey walked fast to keep up with Ray's long

strides. "Hey, I didn't mean nothing, you know. You're right. The kid's probably got good reasons." His voice lacked conviction.

Reaching the office doorway, Ray saw that the officers had cleared everyone out. The name on the door read ABIGAIL MCCARTHY, M.D. "Do we know who she is?" he asked.

"Yeah," Ramsey answered. "It's the kid's mother's office. He'd come to talk with her. Didn't know she'd left town."

A close, loving relationship, Ray thought. Two sets of double windows faced him, separated by a wide stretch of wall. The other uniformed officer was sitting on the edge of the open one. Ray walked over to him and introduced himself. "How's he sound to you, Carter?" he asked the young cop.

"Scared shitless, sir. But pretty determined. I slid a can of Coke out onto the ledge, but he wouldn't grab it until I ducked back inside. He's been crying, hands shaking. Says no one will miss him if he jumps."

Ray felt the weight of it, the fear like a cold ball in his stomach. These things could always go either way. "Let me see what I can do." He slipped off his jacket, then his gun holster, before moving to the window and peering out carefully.

Seated cross-legged, it was apparent that the boy was thin and tall with coltish legs, acne marking his face. Ray swallowed, feeling as if he were gazing into a flashback mirror. He forced himself to recall his training, the part that said an effective officer had to remove himself emotionally from his subject. Get him to like you, then to trust you. Carefully, he sat down on the window ledge and leaned his upper body out. "Hi," he said cautiously.

The boy's head swiveled toward him, his sandy

SHATTERED VOWS 59

hair shifting in the breeze. "Don't come out. I mean it."

"I'm not," Ray assured him. "But I wish you'd come in so we could talk."

"I don't want to talk."

"You came here to see your mother. I'll get her for you if you'll come back inside."

"Too late." He leaned slightly toward the edge of the precipice. "She don't care. She won't miss me."

"What makes you think so?" Keep them talking, so the manual said.

"She's got Donald. They're getting married. I'm just . . . in the way." He swiped at a tear that escaped his eye.

"What's your name?" Ray asked gently.

"What do you care?"

Ray shrugged, trying for nonchalance as the kid's dark eyes stayed on him. "I care because I know how you feel. I—"

"No one knows how I feel. Mom's too busy. They're going to the Bahamas on their honeymoon. I have to stay home with old Gertrude Goatface."

Ray smiled at that. "Your housekeeper, I'll bet. We had one named Hilda. Only my brother and I called her Hilda the Hun. Man, she was the worst cook that ever lived."

The boy nodded. "Yeah, Gertie, too. Pot roast and stew and garbage like that. She told me hamburgers were invented by the devil." The boy's curiosity about Ray won out. "You a cop?"

"Yeah, but I wasn't always a cop. My mother died when I was seven. My Dad married again and they traveled a lot. I had to stay home with Hilda."

"Did you hate it? Were they always telling you to do your homework or go to your room? Did they ever want you around?"

Not so's you'd notice, kid. He wouldn't lie, but he wasn't about to tell this boy how it had really been for him, either. The unvarnished truth might send him over the edge and quick. "Yeah, I hated it, and yeah, they sent me to my room a lot." *Take your brother out to play, Ray. Here's some money. You boys go to a movie, will you? Take good care of Pete, Ray.*

"Did you ever run away?"

Ray slowly shook his head. "You know why? Because some problems you can't run away from. You know what I did instead? I found someone to talk to, someone who understood."

"Yeah, well, good for you. I got no one like that." He finished the Coke and crunched up the can with long, lean fingers.

"I'll bet you do, if you think about it. someone at school, maybe a teacher. A relative. An old friend of the family." Even as he suggested it, he wondered if it would be enough, if this boy needed far more than that. "Or me," he said, before he could stop himself. "You could talk to me. I'd listen." The boy wasn't a druggie, just a lost kid, like so many others.

The teenager stared at his sneakers, then looked back at Ray, measuring him, wanting to believe. "Mark. My name's Mark."

"Okay, Mark. Can you think of anyone?"

"Who did you find to talk to?"

"A teacher. Mr. Bradley. He was the basketball coach and I was the tallest kid in class. He taught me how to play ball and he listened to me. For about three years, he was the reason *I* never climbed out on a ledge. I see you're pretty tall, and still growing. Maybe you want to give basketball a shot."

SHATTERED VOWS 61

"I don't know." The boy's eyes were thoughtful. The most popular guys were on the basketball team. He felt like a nerd alongside them. "Mr. Grafton's my science teacher. He ... he says I have great potential." He shot Ray a look, as if to see if he was being believed. "But Mom says she wants me to be a doctor."

"What do *you* want to be?"

"I'm not sure. I like science a lot."

"I don't see why you have to decide that right now. Maybe you could talk some more to Mr. Grafton." He scooted fractionally closer, edging farther outside. "But my offer stands. I'm not going to back out on you, Mark. I went through what you're feeling now. And I survived. You can, too. But you've got to want to."

With huge, solemn eyes, the boy studied Ray.

In the cordoned-off parking lot, Toni shifted her weight from foot to foot, unable to take her eyes from the urgent little drama playing itself out six floors up. While she watched and waited, she learned quite a bit about Detective Ray Vargas from listening to his fellow officers in the parking lot.

"Who's the guy who went up?" a short black officer asked.

"They call him padre down at the precinct," the taller cop just inside the yellow barricade answered. "He's talked quite a few would-be jumpers down, one just a few months ago."

"Oh, yeah, I know him. Vargas, right, from downtown? He's a straight shooter, all right. Doesn't take any crap, but if he tells you something, you can put your money on it."

"He's good at this sort of thing because of his brother," the taller officer went on.

"I heard that. The brother's a loser, I hear, but

Vargas never gives up on him. He feels responsible, I guess."

Toni took it all in, wondering where this loser of a brother was and why Ray felt responsible for him.

The sun was lowering in the sky, the air turning cool, and she imagined that it was even colder six stories up. Squinting, she saw the man in the white shirt stretch out his hand. She held her breath, waiting. The boy in the blue slowly got to his feet. Then he was inching closer to the window where Ray sat waiting. Finally, he was close enough for Ray to grab his hand.

Toni let out a nervous huff of air as she saw Ray draw the boy inside, then envelop him in his arms. Unbidden, tears burned the backs of her eyes. Certainly a side of the man she hadn't suspected. Of course, she'd sensed a gentleness to him. But she'd also seen the utterly focused detective doing his job. Talking a kid out of jumping off a ledge was something that not every police officer could do with success, no matter how good they were in other areas.

Detective Vargas continued to surprise her. She wasn't sure if that was part of his charm or something to be feared. She didn't particularly like surprises.

He was an atheist, he'd told her. Sure he was. No atheists in foxholes, the saying went. And probably none on window ledges six stories up, either.

Walking back to the car, Toni waited for him to return.

The headaches were coming more frequently. Wally fixed the ice bag, then went to lie down in his dim bedroom. He was sweating again, profusely. He needed quiet, he needed darkness, he needed peace. He didn't turn on the lamp, but instead had lit several candles.

The dreams wouldn't let him be. He'd pushed them back for nearly two years. After that first time at the lake, the incident that had caused him to lose control, he'd had peace for all those months. He'd even dared hope it was over. The sinner who'd dragged him down was gone from his life finally.

May she rot in hell for the hell she'd made of his life.

He adjusted the icebag more comfortably on his forehead. The pain made his vision blur, his stomach roll. He'd been sick a while ago, so sick that he'd feared his landlady might have heard. These old houses had high ceilings and creaking boards that let every sound filter through. He was always so careful, so quiet, not wanting to arouse suspicions.

And it had worked for two years. Then the dreams had begun again and he'd been forced to act. He hadn't wanted to, but some things were beyond a mere mortal's control. God knew that. God understood him. He always made a good act of contrition, kneeling before Him, begging forgiveness. His early training had taught him that no sin was too big for God not to forgive.

The first one hadn't really been a sin. He'd rid the world of a sinner, a liar, a thief who'd stolen his future. It was because of that sinner that she had left him, that she'd turned from him, that she was forever lost to him.

So sweet, so pure. She'd been like an angel, one that had almost been his. But he'd faltered and sinned. And, just as he'd made the sinner pay, he, too, would have to pay one day. He knew that, was willing to accept his punishment.

But not yet. He still had work to do, still had a mission to complete. It was all clear to him now. The dreams told him exactly what needed to be done. He was merely an instrument carrying out orders given him in dreams.

If only the dreams would stop for a while, would let him rest, if only the pain would go away. Sometimes he felt as if the top of his head would explode.

The worst thing was that no one understood. There was no one he could talk with, to get absolution from. He'd tried to tell a priest once, but he'd wound up running out of the confessional, his heart pounding, his head hurting, his face running with sweat. There was no on left for him. No one he wanted to be with who would understand.

He was lost, alone, waiting. Soon, he'd have to seek out another sweet-faced virgin. He would send her to be with Jesus.

It was the only thing that stopped the pain.

FOUR

Ray held up the piece of wire, studying it yet again. "It looks so damn *ordinary*," he told Meg.

"It *is* ordinary. I've checked with half a dozen hardware stores, building supply outlets, gardening shops, florists. They all sell something similar. And Father Hilliard says he'd found spools of them from time to time in the prep room in back of the church where the flowers for the altar and for weddings and funerals are delivered and arranged. Anyone could have picked one up there."

"Yeah, anyone. So we're looking for a hardware salesman or a builder or a gardener or a florist or a deliveryman with a grudge against Catholics. Terrific." In disgust, he tossed down the green wire.

"What we're looking for is a madman." Meg brushed a hand through her short red hair, feeling her partner's frustration. They hadn't been able to track down the source of the mass card nor come up with any leads whatsoever. Damn! The killer had to have made some mistake. He had to be traceable somehow.

Leaning back in his desk chair, Ray let his eyes wander around the squad room. A burly man wearing handcuffs, a skull-and-crossbones tattoo on his upper arm, sat sullenly alongside a desk where an officer talked on the phone. Across the room, a hooker let out of night lockup was reaming some guy up one side and down the other for being late with her bail money. And someone's mother was crying loudly as an officer marched her son away.

Business as usual.

He felt oddly restless, the way he always did when a case was going badly. The papers were having a field day, not letting the stranglings fall off the front page for a day. The captain had chewed his ass good yesterday, saying that Monsignor Clancy had called the mayor demanding action. As if he and Meg had decided the murders could wait and had gone off on a holiday.

"What makes me nervous is that we don't know when he'll strike again," he told Meg.

Meg nodded in agreement. "We've done about as much as we can. It seems like all we can do now is wait." They had had seven calls from the rectory and convent so far, reports of suspicious persons. Only they'd all turned out to be ordinary citizens going about their business. "I'm not sure I buy this thing about cycles. He may not wait thirty days. Maybe he's getting off on the publicity."

"What triggered him to begin with, is what I want to know." Ray stroked his beard thoughtfully as he reread the medical examiner's reports on the two victims. He'd spent a good part of the past week personally going over the list of parishioners with Father Hilliard, all twenty-two hundred of them. He'd asked the pastor to point out anyone who might be the least bit suspect. The priest had come up with only four possibilities. When Ray checked them out, he found that one had died, another had moved away. The third was a closet homosexual who showed up for mass infrequently and the fourth a single man who'd had a record of child molestation dating back ten years.

They'd questioned the last man at length, but he appeared to be in the clear on this one. Though Ray didn't think he was their man, he'd put a watch on the guy anyhow. He was also methodically checking out about two dozen others who were new to the parish or the area, or whose record cards had seemed out of sync. So far, he'd found two deadbeat dads way behind on their child support and a woman who'd violated a shoplifting probation.

"Hey, Vargas," the desk sergeant called out, "someone asking to see you."

Ray swiveled about and nearly groaned out loud.

Meg peered through the doorway and shook her head. "Mort Ziltzer. Why don't you tell that weirdo to go take a flying leap?"

"He's just a harmless old man," Ray said, rising.

"Yeah, one who swears the microwave in the apartment above his is interfering with his hearing aid, his TV reception, even his thoughts. Honestly, Ray. Why do you bother?"

"Damned if I know." Maybe because talking with Mort was better than sitting around beating his head against a brick wall over the St. Matthews stranglings. Maybe because poor old Mort seemed to have no one to turn to and Ray knew how that felt.

Captain Renwick's office door swung open. "Vargas, O'Malley. We've got a suspected arson call. I need you on this one right away. There's a guy inside the building with a bullet hole in his chest."

Meg walked over to get the details while Ray approached Mort. "Sorry, pal. I'll have to catch you later."

"But Detective Vargas, the woman upstairs is driving me crazy. There's this here buzzin' in my ears all the time. Ain't there somethin' you can do?" The old man scratched at his scruffy beard as he shuffled after Ray.

"Not a whole lot. At least, not right this minute." As Meg caught up with him, Ray put his hand on the old man's arm. "Hang tight, Mort. I'll see you tomorrow." He walked away, the troubled man's expression lingering in his mind. He wished he didn't care, didn't feel responsible for all the lost, the lonely, the crazies.

On the run, he reached his wagon and jumped in.

It had been a hellish two weeks. Ray was tired, frustrated, restless. And hungry.

He worked at clearing off his desk so he could get the hell out of there. They'd wrapped up the drug sting at least, and nailed the creep who'd gotten impatient and carved up one of his own delivery boys. He'd spent two days in court waiting to testify on an earlier case. He'd spent three evenings on a city basketball court teaching young Mark McCarthy the basics of the game, then just sitting around shooting the breeze and playing chess together. Ray wasn't sure which one of them got more out of their time together.

He and Meg and the fire marshal had spent a lot of time tramping through the fire-ravaged ruins of an old factory off Milwaukee just south of the freeway, looking for clues. So far, they didn't know if the fire had been started to cover up the murder or if the victim had happened along as someone was torching the place. The dead man turned out to be one of the developers who'd negotiated with the city to tear down three blocks of old buildings for urban renewal. Ray had a hunch; the whole thing smacked of insurance fraud, but so far, he hadn't been able to prove anything.

He shut the last file drawer, then stood to stretch his weary muscles. Meg had gone home half an hour ago. It was only six, yet he felt as if it were nearer midnight. What he really should do is drive home, fall into bed, and sleep for twelve hours. What he did instead was pick up the phone.

In moments, Toni was on the line, sounding efficient and slightly impatient. He smiled, picturing her in another one of her neat business suits, her hair shiny and fragrant enough to make a man ache. He had no reason to call her except the most foolish one: he wanted to.

"I've got someone I want you to meet," he began.

In her office, Toni sat back, recognizing his voice immediately, aware of a rush of warmth. "Is that right, Detective? And who might that be?"

"I want you to come to my house and meet my puppy." It had been some time since Hamlet could be called a puppy, but he'd decided to appeal to her female heart, the one that probably reached out to all things small and furry.

Her smile widened. "Your puppy? Now that's an original approach."

"There's more. I have this Italian friend. Owns a pizza joint. I'm thinking about getting a large to go, loaded with the works, including extra cheese and Sal's homemade sauce. Have you eaten?"

"As a matter of fact, I haven't. Tell me, do you ever eat anything but junk food?"

"I try not to. Messes up the metabolism."

The laugh came easily to Toni. She was happy to hear his voice. He couldn't possibly imagine how often she'd thought of him over the past weeks, remembering him up on that ledge, pulling that troubled boy inside. He'd driven her back to her car that evening as if nothing out of the ordinary had happened. Maybe for him it hadn't. For her, something special had begun, something that set her to wondering what was between them. Something she wasn't sure she wanted to pursue.

"Should I bring some wine? Red, I suppose. I don't make my own, but I could pick up a bottle."

Ray smiled at the humor in her voice. That's exactly what he needed, a light-hearted evening with a beautiful woman. "I've got some Dago Red that Sal made. Guaranteed to put hair on your chest."

"Just what I need. What time?"

"I'm leaving now. I'll swing by and get you."

"I've got my car here. Why don't I just meet you at your place?" She liked having her own transportation. That way she could leave when she felt like it. "Say, an hour?"

That independent streak, he thought. "Okay." He gave her his address, then hung up.

He felt like whistling, but curbed the urge. Instead, he grabbed his jacket and made for the door. But not fast enough.

"Detective Vargas, I been waitin' for you." Mort Ziltzer, his eyes red-rimmed and his nose running, got up from the row of chairs outside the squad room.

"I'm in kind of a hurry, Mort," Ray said. The guy's timing was lousy.

"I won't take long, honest." Mort swiped a wrinkled sleeve under his nose. "Now she's got a toaster oven, you know. I can't think, I can't sleep it's so loud."

Cursing silently, Ray nodded. "All right, come

with me and we'll talk. But I've got only ten minutes."

"Sure, sure. You're a busy man. I know." Mort followed the detective into a glassed office, his old sneakers shuffling.

Ray chewed around a gooey mouthful, the cheese thick and stringy. "This isn't pizza. It's a slice of heaven."

Toni swallowed a much smaller morsel. "Don't you ever worry about cholesterol? Fat content? Your heart, your arteries?"

"Yeah. And I worry about who's got the bomb, about the ozone layer, and how the Tigers will do this year. But not tonight." He smiled at the face she made as he wrapped his mouth around another huge bite.

Seated at his butcher block kitchen table, he studied her from under lowered lashes as he ate. She'd taken the time to run home and change into an oversize blue sweater the color of her eyes and jeans with penny loafers over bare feet. The fingers that held his pizza itched to dive into all that hair.

"Did you lock up any bad guys this week, Detective?"

"Mmm." He wiped his mouth and hands on a paper napkin. "A few. Cater any ritzy bashes?"

"A few." She smiled at him over the rim of her glass. He'd been right. The homemade wine was tart and packed a punch. "Anything new on our strangler?"

Regretfully, Ray shook his head. "No, and it's making me nervous. Each day that goes by, I wonder if he's going to strike again. And when."

"Mo drove to Lansing yesterday to take some

special class in vocational counseling. It's selfish of me, I know, but I was glad to see her leave, to get her out of harm's way." She debated on having another piece of pizza, then gave in. "Do you have any idea why he picked St. Matthews?"

Finishing his third piece, Ray sat back. "Not any more than we've been able to determine why he picked those particular nuns. My personal opinion is that it was random. He killed the ones he found alone. I sure hope those nuns are listening to our warnings and not venturing anywhere by themselves."

Toni chewed thoughtfully. "Random. You make it sound as if the urge to kill comes over him and he goes looking for a victim who's unprotected."

He nodded. "Basically, that's about it. Just like with most rapists. Pressure builds up, they need the release, and they hunt for a victim. They find one alone and *bam!* Doesn't matter if she's young or old, short or tall."

She set down the pizza, suddenly losing her appetite. "But we talked about this before and you said, in this case, his motive didn't appear to be sexual. What kind of release does he get from killing?"

"That's a good question and I don't have a good answer. Psychiatrists will tell you that a serial killer is driven to kill to satisfy some internal need. Revenge, forgiveness, rage at impotence, to avenge memories of an abused childhood. And a few who just plain have a taste for it. Any number of reasons. They kill a victim and the need is gratified. For a while. But it rears its ugly head again. And, in most cases, the need escalates as the killer's grip on reality deteriorates."

"I guess you've studied this quite a bit."

"I read up on it extensively last year when Sam

and I were hunting the guy stalking Carly. But he was a little different. A precise number of people had wronged him, in his opinion. And he set out to kill them one after another. Made up a list and crossed off each one methodically. Revenge serial killers are the exception. Most are random."

"Random, but of a type. Like Ted Bundy, who killed only young college girls that fit a particular description."

"Right." He poured more wine for both of them. "And the woman in Florida who killed middle-aged men who reminded her of her abusive father. These are the really dangerous ones, because they never run out of victims. There are literally thousands of men in this country alone who'd remind that woman of her father, for instance. Once the police can tap into the key, the common factor, they at least have something to go on."

"And that hasn't happened in this case yet?"

"Unfortunately, no. It's not easy, with just two victims, not that I want there to be more. But you can see what I mean. The women were both nuns, in their twenties, pretty and blond. Both were sisters of St. Joseph and teachers at St. Matthews. That's it. We can't come up with any other common thread. They didn't even know one another until recently, their childhood histories don't include a mutual acquaintance who's since flipped out. That's why I believe, at this time, that they were random victims."

Toni shuddered as a chill crept up her spine. "It's just so awful."

"Many aspects of my job are pretty awful."

"But some are rewarding. Have you had any contact with Mark?" He'd told her a little about the boy on the ledge that evening, but not a great deal. He'd appeared quite moved by the whole thing, yet reluctant to discuss the teenager.

"We're in touch. I'm teaching him basketball at the park a couple of blocks from here and some evenings we play chess." Abruptly, Ray got up to clear the dishes. "He's a good kid. It was a drastic move he made, but it may have been a wake-up call for his mother. Mark tells me she's postponed her second marriage, probably hoping that her fiancé will take more interest in the kid. I give her credit for trying."

Toni rose and carried the pizza box to the counter. "I suppose. But why is it she hadn't noticed how unhappy her son was up to now? Surely there were signs. A kid doesn't just wake up one morning and decide to kill himself."

He handed her a plastic zipper bag for the leftovers. "Plenty of signs, I'm sure. But some parents just tune out. They have problems of their own and they don't need more. They figure the kid will outgrow whatever's bothering him."

She placed the pizza in the bag and then in the refrigerator. "Is that what happened to you and your brother?"

Her question took him by surprise. She listened when people talked, really listened. He'd mentioned having a brother only once. He'd have to remember to watch what he said around her. "Something like that." He picked up his wine glass. "Let's go into the living room."

Changing the subject again, Toni thought. She followed him in, wondering why she cared enough to probe.

Sister Bernie checked her watch, then glanced out the front window. Nearly eight and dark out, of course. She hadn't meant to stay so long at her parents' home. But her mother was recovering from heart surgery and she'd wanted to make sure she was eating well. It seemed to take forever to get her father to understand what she was saying because he was hard of hearing and too stubborn to get a hearing aid.

Frederick Street wasn't in the best of neighborhoods anymore. The Warren and Mt. Eliot area had once been lovely, with houses, large families, and the noisy laughter of children. But the factories had closed, the children had grown up and moved away, and urban decay had taken over. So sad, Bernie thought as she straightened her mother's starched curtains.

"Now Mama, I've put the rest of the roast in the fridge," Bernie said, hunkering down alongside her mother's chair. "There's a bowl of vegetables, too. Enough to heat up for tomorrow's supper. And there's that pot of soup I made. You should have plenty for several days."

Her mother reached out a frail hand. "Thank you, dear. I'm so glad you could come."

"I'd stay longer, but it's getting late." She kissed the thin cheek, wishing she could move her parents to a bright, sunny condo in the suburbs. Sighing, she straightened, and moved to the rocker where her father was reading the paper. "Papa, I'm going," she said, raising her voice.

"How's that?" the old man asked.

Leaning closer, Bernie repeated her words, then kissed him, too. He clung to her a long minute, bringing tears to her eyes. Why was growing old so hard? she wondered as she picked up her satchel and walked out the door.

The car she'd borrowed from St. Matthews was

parked at the curb. Mother Magdalen wasn't going to be happy with her getting home so late. She'd given Bernie permission to visit her parents with the promise that she'd be back before dark. Well, she'd just have to understand.

On the bottom porch step, Bernie looked both ways and saw no one. Quickly, she moved to the car, unlocked the door, and got behind the wheel. She locked herself in, then relaxed. Inserting the key, she turned it. There was a funny, straining sound, but the motor didn't turn over.

Nervously, she tried again. It was a six-year-old Plymouth and a little stubborn at times. The same sound came with no results. Now she'd be even later getting back. Frustrated, Bernie bent her head and sent up a small prayer, then got out of the car.

Her father wouldn't have heard her efforts, and even if she fetched him, he knew little more than she did about cars. Tow trucks didn't like to come down into this area, she knew. Maybe it was something simple, like a disconnected wire. The street lamp was at the corner four doors away and offered very little light. But she raised the hood anyway, propped it up and peered underneath.

It looked like a foreign maze. Gingerly, she touched a couple of wires, but everything seemed intact. Turning around, she saw a man strolling toward her, seemingly in no hurry. He was about her age, average looking, with neatly combed hair and clean clothes. He appeared safe enough. And most people were willing to assist a nun.

Bernie smiled at the man as he neared. "I have a little problem here. I wonder if you'd mind taking a look." Ducking her head back under the hood of the car, she squinted at the confusing array of parts. "It just makes a funny sound and won't start."

The man stopped alongside her and stood for some moments, making no move to assist her. Wondering at his silence, Bernie turned toward him.

It was then that she saw the slender green wire stretched between both of his large hands.

"Does Mark like basketball?" Toni asked, returning to a safe topic.

"Yeah, and he's not a bad shot. He's got the height for it, but he also has this notion that he's a nerd because he gets good grades. Excelling at a sport might give him some confidence with his peers." If he'd stick with it, if the adults in his life encouraged him. If the stepfather-to-be had some parenting skills, Ray thought. "And he's also in counseling. We can't discount the fact that he crawled out on that ledge."

She watched him sit down on the couch, an invitation in his eyes, but she wandered over instead to check out his crowded bookcase. At a corner table, she saw a chess game set up. "He's very fortunate that you showed up and talked him back in."

Ray merely shrugged. "If not me, then someone else would have."

"I don't agree. He wouldn't have changed his mind for just anyone. You obviously were able to relate to him in some important way." Maybe because of his background, the one he didn't want to discuss, Toni thought. She turned to study the shelves.

Books, he had a ton of them. Hemingway and Joyce, Keats and Crichton, rows of detective novels, several *New York Times* crossword puzzle volumes. Two shelves of CD's. Garth Brooks, the Boston

Pops, Barbra Streisand. "Your taste runs the gamut, I see."

"I like to try everything once." What he wanted to try right now had nothing to do with books or recordings. He wanted to kiss her, to hold her, to see how she'd fit in his arms.

Wandering back, Toni moved to the fireplace mantel and admired his collection of carved horses. "This one's made of olive wood, isn't it? Were you in Israel?"

"A long time ago."

She swung around facing him, crossing her arms over her chest. "You've traveled a lot?"

She wasn't going to give up, he thought. He decided to tell her a little. The innocuous parts. "When I was a teenager. My father owned a television station and a couple of small newspapers in Massachusetts. We were always going somewhere. Europe, South America, Japan."

"I envy people who've been all over. I always wished we'd have traveled more, but my folks were so tied to their restaurant. Still are." And now, so was she. More than ever.

"But you aren't. You could go now, if you wanted to."

Toni tossed back her hair, knowing he was right. "Maybe I will one day." She decided to shift gears. "Where did you go to college?"

"Harvard." He watched her carefully. To her credit, she didn't look shocked. Quite a few in his past had. No one expected a Harvard grad to become a cop.

He seemed to be waiting for a reaction. Actually, she'd suspected he was well educated, more erudite than she'd originally guessed. "I thought I detected a bit of an East Coast accent. How did you wind up in Michigan?"

The trouble with sharing life stories was that some people always wanted more. "It's a long story, but I'll boil it down for you. One day I decided to walk away, from everyone, from everything. I didn't have much money, so I went to the bus station. I asked where the very next bus leaving was headed. The man told me Detroit. So I bought a one-way ticket. End of story."

Toni was sure there was a whole lot more. She was also sure she was not going to get the whole story, not tonight anyway. A deep-throated bark coming from the vicinity of the back door gave her a natural segue into another subject. "So, am I ever going to meet your puppy?"

Ray had insisted that Hamlet stay out back until they'd finished eating, knowing what a beggar the Great Dane was. "All right, but brace yourself. We don't have a lot of visitors." Ray rose to open the back door.

Hamlet came bounding in and nearly knocked Toni backward onto the couch. Sitting down heavily, she let him put his big head into her lap. "He's beautiful," she told Ray as he joined her. His coat was a sleek tan with several distinctive black markings, as if dropped by an errant paintbrush. His wet tongue darted out to lick her hand while his big brown eyes adored her.

"He's a big baby," Ray said, his tone affectionate. "I've sent him to obedience school twice. Can't teach him to heel, to roll over, to walk on a leash, can't even keep him off the furniture. He eats more than a lumberjack and although his bark is deep, he'd probably lick an intruder's face, he's so damn friendly. He's a pain in the butt."

She smiled into his eyes. "And you love him."

Ray reached over to stroke Hamlet's head. "Yeah, I guess I do." The dog continued to lick her. "Go lie down, Hamlet." Big brown eyes shifted to Ray, looking comical in his disbelief, begging for a few minutes more. "Now!"

Grudgingly, Hamlet backed up, turned, and went to his rug by the hearth, curling up and sending Ray a wounded look.

Toni smiled. "And you said he's not obedient."

"Only as a last resort." Stretching one arm along the couchback, Ray felt the warmth of the wine relaxing him. As Toni angled her body to face him, he reached out to brush back a strand of her hair. "I'm glad you agreed to come over tonight. I wanted to ask you out back when Sam and I were working on the Weston case last year." Except he'd been seeing Donna then, a relationship that had already gotten rocky.

"That surprises me. You didn't ever call. You hardly spoke to me at their wedding."

"I thought we were like oil and water. They don't mix, you know." One touch wasn't enough. His hand went back for more, reaching out, running his fingers through the silky thickness of her hair. "I've been wanting to do this all evening."

She felt the heat of his touch, saw it in his eyes, and her heart began a double-time beat. Careful here, she told herself. "Have you changed your mind?"

"No. I still think we don't mix. But I want you anyway."

Toni felt a sudden need to throw caution to the winds, to see where this might go. "I've never kissed a man with a beard."

He bent his head and touched his mouth to hers.

He came on slowly, patiently, gently. Then pulled back and waited until her eyes drifted open. "Well?"

"Well, is that the best you can do?"

She'd pegged him right. He couldn't resist the challenge. The second kiss was powerful, had her blood racing and her mind emptying. His arms slid around her, bringing her close up against his broad chest. The masculine feel of his beard grazing her face was surprisingly erotic. His tongue slipped inside and mated with hers. Eyes closed, Toni let him take her deeper.

She was sophisticated, the epitome of the cool, controlled blonde. But she didn't kiss like one. He felt her heated response, the shock of it. Her mouth moved under his, her awakening need flowing to him. He could taste her desire, feel her excitement. He wanted her so badly that his fingers shook as they crept under the hem of her sweater and found her warm, naked skin.

At the touch of his hands on her back, Toni broke the kiss. His eyes were pewter gray and dark with arousal. She wanted him, too; so quickly, so fiercely that she ached with it. Was this the same man she'd thought dull, square, and predictable? A time or two, she'd reached out for what she'd wanted, and taken it then and there. This wasn't one of those times. He wasn't one of those men.

He was a man who'd managed to touch her heart before she'd tasted his kiss. In the past, she'd given her body on occasions of her own choosing. But she'd never given her heart, not completely. Suddenly, inexplicably, she felt the need to throw up her guard.

She eased back, averting her gaze. "I . . . I wasn't quite prepared for that."

He felt as shaken as she. Letting out a breath, he

let go of her and ran a hand through his hair. No use pretending he didn't know what she meant. "Neither was I."

She needed some time to think, some distance. While she might have opted for an affair, one she could easily walk away from when the time came, this was a horse of another color, she feared. She wasn't altogether sure, once she gave in, if she could stroll casually away.

She needed to leave because she wanted so badly to stay. Straightening her sweater, she stood. "You were right. Oil and water. Let's just forget this happened, okay?" She walked over to where she'd left her shoulder bag and picked it up.

"Okay, it's forgotten." In a pig's eye, he thought. Rising, he followed her to the door. Hamlet let out a low moan and got up. Ray waved him back.

Hoping her face didn't reveal her feelings, Toni turned to face him. "It's best this way. We both have busy lives. As I mentioned, I don't want an involvement and—"

"And neither do I. Right."

"Thanks for dinner."

But he couldn't let her go like that. Could not. He whirled her around, lifted her to him and crushed her mouth with his. Incredibly, she opened to him, too surprised not to respond. He ground himself against her, wanting to ignite her, to give her something to remember after she'd left. He felt her hands bunch in his shirt. He inhaled her heated female scent and pressed his growing erection into the soft juncture of her thighs. He heard her soft moan of pleasure and drank it in.

Then he released her just as suddenly, and gazed into eyes stunned and confused. Sweeping a hand over his hair, Ray struggled to slow his breathing.

Toni clenched her hands to still the trembling. "What . . . what was that all about? I thought . . ."

"That was one for the road. Lock your doors and drive carefully. Good night, Toni."

Drawing in a deep breath, she turned and left quickly. Oil and water, she kept telling herself as she finally managed to unlock her car on the third try. Oil and water don't mix.

"There you are, Wladek." Rosie Pulaski closed the back fence gate behind her and hurried toward her porch. "You're late getting home tonight."

The young man paused at the bottom of the stairs. "Hello, Rosie. How's my favorite girl?" He was feeling good, really good. He'd done a fine job tonight and he was at peace. He could afford to brighten his landlady's day.

"Oh, go on with you." She giggled girlishly. "You had to work late?"

"Yeah, I guess you could say that." From behind his back, he brought out a small bouquet of violets. He'd intended to put them by the picture on his dresser, but Rosie looked so lonely. "This is for you."

"Oh, you sweet boy." She reached to take the flowers, wondering why her own sons weren't so thoughtful. "I made extra soup, and I got fresh rye bread. Why don't you come in and have a late supper with me?"

His headache was gone, all gone. He did feel hungry, now that he thought about it. "That sounds good." He offered her his arm. "Let me give you a hand. These steps are steep."

She was so lucky, Rosie thought as she let her boarder help her up the stairs. He was so thoughtful.

Not even her Joe brought her flowers so often. Only on her birthday. The least she could do was feed the boy now and then.

Humming softly, she unlocked her back door.

FIVE

Ray hated having to visit the morgue. He'd bent over dozens of bodies in hotel rooms, parks, alleys. But that didn't bother him half as much as the medical examiner's domain, with its glaring bright lights, the wall of sliding refrigerated shelves containing cadavers, the harsh chemical smells no deodorizer could ever mask.

He'd gotten the call late the previous night, but Sister Bernie's body had already been placed in the ambulance and was on its way to the morgue. He'd decided there was no point in rushing, that he'd talk with the M.E. after he'd done his thing.

Dr. Freemont was waiting for him.

"We've got a little something new on this one, Ray," Doc said, pulling back the sheet and revealing the woman's face and neck.

Ray unwrapped a breath mint, hoping the peppermint flavor would overpower the sudden bitterness in his mouth. Times like these he missed smoking, missed the way the nicotine had dulled his taste buds and sense of smell. He'd quit five years ago, yet he longed for a cigarette now. He'd tried a pipe for a while and had given that up recently as a poor substitute. "What's that?" he asked.

The M.E. held up a small plastic pouch. "This is part of a gold chain the victim had around her neck. At first I thought it might have broken and fallen into her clothes or that it was left at the scene. Even had one of the boys go back and recheck the area. Nothing."

Ray examined the approximately three-inch-long links of gold. "Go on."

"I believe the perp yanked the necklace from her and that that small section got caught in the wire and stayed in the grooves of her neck. I got to thinking and went back to check the other two nuns. One had no such markings, but the second victim had tiny indentations in the flesh at the back of her neck, that could have been made by a chain like that one being jerked off her. I'd missed it the first time because of the swelling from the wire."

"So you're thinking that at least two of the three were wearing chains, and that the killer ripped them off and took them with him?"

"That's right."

"A souvenir." He knew that some murderers, especially serial killers, liked to take some remembrance, to keep and look at later, to help them relive the event. "Pretty sick, isn't it?"

"Yeah, well, murderers are pretty sick puppies, wouldn't you say?"

Ray pocketed the plastic envelope. "You're right about that. Anything else?"

"Here's the mass card." He handed over a second envelope. "Same message. It was in her jacket pocket."

He felt the rush of anger, of impotent rage. "How in hell does he manage to loop a wire around a woman's neck, strangle her to death, yank off her necklace, and slip a card in her pocket—all on a residential street where *anyone* could be looking out a window, or walking their dog, or driving by? How does he have the balls to risk it? How does he get away with it?" Ray shoved a restless hand through his hair, wanting to hit something hard. "The other two cases, he was safe from detection, at least, but—"

"Not really," Dr. Freemont interrupted. "Someone could have walked into that church; the priest was there. Another teacher could easily have been in that school. I agree, the guy seems to get off on risk-taking. So far, he's been damn lucky and no one's spotted him. I'd guess probably because he's everyman, you know." Doc shoved his glasses higher on his nose as he looked up at Ray. "Average. Doesn't stick out in a crowd. The kind of guy you see daily, but you never really *see*. Know what I mean?"

Ray let out an exasperated sigh. He'd already had a call from Renwick that morning. The captain's ass was on the line and he didn't like the feeling. Unfortunately, they were no closer to cracking the case than they were the night they'd found the first victim. "I know exactly what you mean. Some workman who comes and goes and becomes almost a fixture, so when he's in your line of vision, your eyes just roll over him. Like he was a living room chair you know is always there. That's why we interviewed everyone who works at and around the school and church. Came up with nothing."

Doc pulled the sheet back over the victim.

"This one's got me worried," Ray said quietly. "Okay, so she was also a teacher at St. Matthews. But she was miles from the convent. What did our guy do, follow her and wait in the shrubs of her parents' home? How did he know she'd be there that night?" He was thinking aloud, not really expecting an answer from Freemont.

"I wish I could tell you more," Doc said. "Time of death was right around eight. But she wasn't found until after ten. Some guy walking his Doberman found her. Not a lot of strollers in that neighborhood."

The futility of it raged through him. The victim lay there, dead in the street alongside her car, right in front of her parents' house, for two solid hours before anyone noticed. Judas, but it was getting to be a rotten world.

"Thanks, Doc."

Freemont nodded. "I'll have your report by morning. I've got a couple of autopsies yet today."

"No problem." Ray hurried out, refusing to take a deep breath until he was well into the parking lot. It was raining again even through April was over and it was early May. He didn't mind as he gulped in a lungful of muggy air. Anything was better than the antiseptic aroma that had surrounded him in there.

Meg was over at the convent questioning Mother Magdalen and the nuns once again, trying to retrace Sister Bernie's activities of the previous day. Maybe she told someone where she was going and the wrong person overheard.

He hoped Meg was faring better than he was.

"You're working too hard," Jane Garette said as she stood in the doorway of her daughter's office. She'd been there several minutes and Toni had been so absorbed in what she was writing that she hadn't even noticed.

"Hi, Mom." Toni put down her pen and leaned

back, smiling at her mother. She looked so nice today, dressed in a light green linen dress, very springlike, her silver-blond hair coiled in the French twist she usually wore. It was like looking into a mirror twenty-five years down the road, Toni thought. If she moved into middle age looking as attractive as her mother, she'd have no complaints.

Jane walked in, seated herself, and crossed her slender legs. "Did you hear what I said? You're here too many hours or you're over in Birmingham overseeing the new place. Yesterday, you even subbed for Maria." Their hostess had taken ill and had had to leave early.

"I didn't mind. It was a nice change of pace." She knew what her mother was getting at. She *was* working longer hours. Deliberately. It was easier to sleep if she tired herself out each day. "Are you complaining because I'm concerned about the business?"

"I can hardly fault you for that." But Jane Garette saw the shadows under Toni's eyes. And in them. That usually meant sleepless nights and hidden worries. "Are you all right? Is there anything you want to talk over?"

Toni averted her gaze. One of the minuses of working and living around her parents was that they saw things she didn't want them to see. "No, not really. I'm fine." She glanced toward the open door. "Lunch crowd thinning out?"

Her daughter had always been good at changing the subject. There was little Jane could do to get her to confide in her if Toni didn't want to talk. "Yes." She stood. "I've decided to take a couple of hours off this afternoon. Would you like to go shopping with me in the Village? All the new spring things are out."

Ordinarily, Toni probably would have gone. But the prospect didn't enthuse her today. "Thanks, Mom. But I've got some work here I really want to finish. Rain check?"

Jane sent her a smile. "Of course. See you later."

Alone again, Toni swiveled her chair around so she could look out the window. The Glass Door was situated on an incline, giving her a good view of a small garden bordering the parking lot. Budding trees, yellow crocus plants, rows of red tulips. Lovely. A vision that should be soothing, calming.

Why this restlessness, then?

It had been two weeks since she'd shared a pizza with a tall detective named Vargas. And some red wine. And a couple of dizzying kisses. Now we've come to it, she thought.

She was woman enough to know that he wanted her in his bed, and smart enough to realize that that didn't necessarily mean he wanted her in his life. Which would be fine with her, and had been before. A strong mutual attraction, some time spent together satisfying that need, and parting friends.

That scenario didn't fit this man. She was having trouble getting a fix on him. Ray wasn't a TV cop, all flash and dash. He was real, sincere, compassionate, the genuine article, not some writer's idea of a romantic lawman.

But he was also hard, focused, unrelenting. And he appeared to have a past that seemed to haunt him, one he was reluctant to reveal. She wondered what his secrets were even though she knew they were none of her business. She had a few herself. He didn't pry, yet she could scarcely stop asking him questions.

Not good. The whole situation was not good. Physically, in his arms, Ray had made her feel a great deal more than she'd guessed a simple kiss would provoke. If she were ever to get serious again, she wanted more than physical compatibility, more than good sex. She wanted a man who could give himself wholly to a woman and love her unconditionally. There were days, and nights, when she doubted such a man existed.

She certainly doubted that Ray Vargas was that man.

So that should be the end of it, Toni thought as she turned back to her desk. Foolish to long for or worry over a man who couldn't give her what she wanted, offer her what she needed. Best to stay away from personal entanglements, as she'd once vowed she would. She wasn't a teenager anymore struggling with a crush. She'd been down this road before and been smart enough to bail out before she'd gotten badly hurt. Ray could hurt her, she knew.

Picking up her pen, Toni bent to her work. It was better this way. Clean break. Far better.

She almost believed it.

"How's our daddy-to-be?" Ray asked, taking the chair alongside Sam English's desk. "Still having morning sickness?"

Sam set aside the report he'd been studying and smiled at his former partner. "I guess I'll survive. How goes it with you?"

Ray crossed a leg over his knee and grasped his ankle. "I hate to admit it, but we're up against a blank wall. Three strangulations and we haven't got a clue. Not one."

Sam heard his frustration, and remembered how he'd felt the previous fall when they'd been in pursuit of another serial strangler. That guy had killed with his bare hands. And he'd been after Carly. Sam clenched his fists reflexively. "I've been following your case. No common thread?"

"Only nebulous ones. All nuns from St. Matthews, all belong to the same order, all teachers. All blondes with blue eyes. There it ends." Ray stared out the window at the bright May day and wished the sunshine could lift his spirits. "I'm getting so I want to post a bodyguard on every blue-eyed blond nun on the east side."

Sam rubbed the back of his neck thoughtfully. "That's three in one parish. How many more can there be that fit that description?"

"I'm not sure." Something to look into. There was one in particular he was concerned about. "Toni Garette's cousin lives in that convent, but she's not a teacher. Trouble is, she drives all over town counseling. It'd be a full-time job keeping track of her. That sort of freedom worries me, and she fits the description."

"Could you get her to allow you to track her?"

"Exactly what I asked her." Ray grunted his disapproval. "Damn, she's stubborn. Said she can't do her work effectively if someone's following her. And she told me that the Lord will take care of her so I shouldn't worry."

Sam shook his head. "You've got your work cut out for you." Carly had told him a week or so ago that Ray had taken up with Toni Garette. The news had surprised him. "How are things with you and Toni?"

Ray's forehead creased. "What do you mean?"

"I thought you were seeing her?"

"I ran into her at St. Matthews with her cousin. Nothing more to it than that." *Liar.* Ray uncrossed his legs and stood. "I've got to get going. Say hello to Carly for me."

"Right." Sam watched his ex-partner go. His response to his question about Toni had been swift and agitated. Something there. Ah well, none of his business. Besides, he knew how adamant Ray was about staying footloose and fancy free. Sam went back to his report.

Across the squad room, Ray grabbed his jacket. He had an appointment with the fire chief on the arson case. It seems they'd found a gun in one of the rubbish tins outside the burned factory.

"Check me out, Sarge," he said to the man at the desk as he made his way to the parking lot.

It was Toni's favorite time of year and her favorite time of day. Spring, early morning. The late May sunshine was already warm and the dew was heavy on the grass as she strolled the backyard with her coffee cup in hand, checking out her mother's flower beds. Everything was in bloom and the air was fragrant with the smell of newly mown grass.

She waved to the gardener her father had hired recently as he finished cutting the front lawn. The pool man was due this morning to remove the winter cover and open the pool in preparation for summer. A mother robin flew to her nest in the cherry tree, carrying a morning snack to her babies as they chirped a hungry welcome. She felt a light breeze ruffle her hair and smiled at the sun as it crept upward.

It felt good to be alive today.

She'd been working awfully hard lately, Toni thought. The opening of the Brass Door was only a month away and she'd been there almost daily, in addition to putting in time at the original restaurant. Which was why she'd decided to take the morning off and just relax. Read a book, sit in the sun, sip her coffee. A little mental R & R.

Jane Garette was having her morning at the beauty shop—hair, nails, pedicure. And her father was golfing at Lochmoor. Walking back inside to refill her cup, Toni decided that stealing a few hours of peace and quiet was good for the soul.

By ten o'clock, she'd shifted from her front to her back on the lounge chair and switched from coffee to iced tea. Flipping over, Toni adjusted her white shorts and tugged down her blue terrycloth top. Maybe this year she could acquire a tan. You could never count on too many days in Michigan's unpredictable weather to allow for tanning, but she could try.

When she heard her name called from the gate leading to the backyard, she got up with a frown of annoyance at the interruption. But she smiled a greeting when she saw Bill Emery from the pool service and opened the gate for him.

"Beautiful day, isn't it, Miz Garette?" the rotund little man asked, dragging in his equipment.

"It sure is. I'll be on the patio if you need me, Bill." She strolled back to lie down again and resume reading. The book was a Sara Paretsky mystery, the sort Toni loved. Yet it wasn't holding her interest today. Her mind kept wandering.

She'd been given a message two days ago when she'd returned to the Glass Door that Ray had called. She'd phoned him back, thinking his call might be about the stranglings, only to be told he was out. She'd left her name and number, but he hadn't called again. Perhaps it was for the best.

Toni set her book aside, raised her arms, and

rested her head on her crossed hands. Being with Ray was like window shopping without a nickel in your jeans. You saw things you couldn't have and you wound up frustrated. He made her want him, yet she knew that giving in to that need would probably be a mistake. Their separate lives would never mesh. He knew it, too, which was probably why he was staying away. Sometimes it was smarter to ignore an itch rather than scratch it. Harder, but smarter.

She was better off with no man to worry over, to wonder about, to make plans around. She had a busy life and she liked it exactly the way it was.

Didn't she?

Toni closed her eyes, thinking that if she dozed off she might rid herself of the small headache that had begun a short time ago. She was almost asleep when she heard a man's agitated yell. Jumping up, she blinked in the bright sunlight and saw that Bill was at the deep end of the pool, peering down into the water.

"Miz Garette, come quick. I found something."

Grabbing her sunglasses, Toni hurried over. "What is it?"

"More like someone than something. Look." He pointed to a figure bobbing in the murky winter water.

"My God!" Toni stepped back, horrified. "It's a body." The dark form was floating facedown in the water, unrecognizable.

"Yes, ma'am. Sure is." Bill had been servicing pools for nearly twenty years and had never run across anything like this. A rat or two, mice certainly, and one time a stray cat that had drowned. But never a human. "I'd just about gotten started when I saw it." He removed his Detroit Tigers cap and brushed back his damp hair before slapping the cap down onto his head again. "Sure never seen nothing like this before."

"There's no question the person's dead?" Toni's voice sounded strange to her ears.

"No, ma'am. I pushed at it with my skimming pole. It's dead all right."

Questions flooded Toni's mind. Who could it possibly be? A homeless person who'd picked their yard to camp in and somehow stumbled into the pool? How long had the body been in the water? She felt an involuntary shudder as she turned to Bill. "I'm going to call the police. We'd best not touch anything until they get here."

Hitching up his pants, Bill nodded. "Don't worry. I won't."

The poor man looked as shaken as she felt. "There's iced tea in the pitcher on the patio," she called over her shoulder as she rushed inside. "Help yourself."

In the kitchen, Toni found that her hands were trembling. It took two tries to dial the number and get it right. Perhaps it wasn't Ray that she should call, but he was who she thought of first. If he couldn't help her, he'd direct her to someone who could.

"Sergeant O'Malley," Meg said into the phone.

"Oh, Sergeant, this is Toni Garette. I was calling Detective Vargas." Toni was confused at hearing the woman's voice on Ray's line.

"He's out, Toni. Can I help you with something or shall I take a message?" Meg had heard that Toni had been with Ray during the near suicide at the Fisher Building a while back, and wondered if the two were seeing one another.

"We need some help. Our maintenance man is here, and he just found a body in the pool."

Meg grabbed her notepad. "Male or female?"

"I don't know. The water's murky. We haven't touched it."

"I think Grosse Pointe will want to handle this and—" Meg stopped herself and suddenly sat up straighter. "Uh, wait Toni. Do you think it might be a nun?" The last killing hadn't occurred at St. Matthews, and Toni had been on the scene the night Sister Ronnie had been found in the school. A vague connection, but a possibility, Meg thought.

"A nun?" Toni glanced out the kitchen window in the direction of the pool, where Bill was standing staring down as if the body might disappear if he looked away. Fear shot through her. "I don't know. Please send someone."

Jurisdiction was important, Meg knew. Detroit versus Grosse Pointe or any of the other suburbs. The men in charge could get their noses out of joint easily. Nevertheless, Meg decided to take a chance. If it turned out to be an unconnected homicide, she'd call the guys on the Hill herself. "We'll be right there, Toni. Don't touch anything. And don't let the pool man leave."

"All right." Toni hung up, feeling dazed, wishing Ray had been in. Suddenly, she longed for his big, comforting presence.

She'd slipped on slacks and a gauzy blouse, informed her father via his cellular phone and notified her mother at the beauty shop, then she'd gone out back again to wait with Bill. A nervous man, he'd downed three glasses of iced tea and, pacing, had told her about several rescues he'd made since working pools. A four-year-old child, a miniature poodle, a baby bird. But he'd never run across a dead body, no sir, never. His pants at half mast, the man was visibly distressed. It was with a sense of relief that Toni heard the police arrive.

Letting the two uniformed officers in through the gate, Toni turned to Meg and greeted her. "I can't imagine how this happened," Toni said, walking back with the attractive red-headed sergeant. "We keep that pool cover on from September through May." She pointed to the plastic casing Bill had rolled up and left on the lawn.

"We'll try to get some answers for you," Meg said as she stood alongside the diving board with Toni, watching the officers and Bill scooping the body out with a large net. She'd beeped Ray to tell him where she was headed. He'd said he'd check back with her as soon as he finished up in court, but he estimated he'd be tied up for another couple of hours.

Toni thrust her hands into the pockets of her slacks to still their trembling. It was one thing to read about this sort of thing in a novel and quite another to have it happen in your own backyard. Both her parents would be unnerved. Toni wondered how V. I. Warshawski would handle this one.

"Do you really think it might be one of the sisters?" she asked Meg. "All the way over here?" They were easily ten miles north of St. Matthews. She had a sudden urge to call Mo, but decided it would be silly to alarm her unnecessarily.

"Anything's possible, Toni." Meg noted the concern in the woman's eyes and tried to keep her voice calm. "Our strangler's branched out, as I'm sure you've read. But this person could be entirely unrelated to the case, a trespasser who stumbled into your pool and drowned. A vagrant. There are any number of possibilities."

Toni prayed Meg was right.

She shivered as the men placed the bloated body on the patio.

"Why don't you stay here?" Meg told Toni as she started toward the men. "Drowning victims are never a pretty sight."

But Toni was determined. "I'll be all right." Following behind Meg, she slowly circled the pool.

Meg took in all the details immediately. A Caucasian female wearing black pants, a loose black jacket, sensible shoes. Fearing the worst, she signaled the officers. "Turn her over, please." Despite the disfigurement, it was clear the woman was both young and blond, her blue eyes staring up at a sunny sky. And around her neck was the telltale wire.

Swallowing hard, Meg swiveled around to intercept Toni. She'd interviewed all the nuns at St. Matthews and had immediately identified this one. "Toni," she said, touching her arm. "Don't go any farther."

Toni looked into the sergeant's eyes a long minute, then shook her head. "No. Please, no."

Taking her by the shoulders, Meg urged her back toward the house. "Where are your parents, Toni?"

Toni pulled from her grasp. "I want to see. I've *got* to see."

"I don't think that's a good idea—"

But Toni was adamant. "Let me go." She whirled away and moved closer to the still form on the cement. Her hand flew to her mouth and she let out a deep wail as recognition slammed into her. She'd feared, even suspected, and now there was no escaping the fact. "Mo! Oh God, not Mo!"

With an anguished cry, she sank to her knees.

* * *

It was late afternoon before Ray learned what had happened. The court case requiring his testimony had lingered on and his time on the stand kept being postponed. It was nearly five as he drove up into the Garettes' circular drive and parked his wagon behind Meg's black Mustang. The officers, the ambulance, and the forensic people had all finished and left. A small cluster of neighbors were huddled in the driveway next door, talking in hushed tones. A woman across the street was leading a toddler indoors. Murder made people uneasy.

John Garette, a tall man with glasses and a receding hairline, answered the door. "We've been expecting you, Detective Vargas. Please come in."

"Thank you, sir." Ray entered, recalling momentarily the only other time he'd been in that foyer, the first evening he'd held Toni and felt that quick jolt of sensual connection. "I'm so sorry about your niece," he said sincerely.

"Yes, thank you," John said, leading him into the living room, with its white carpeting and marble fireplace. "Please, sit down."

Toni's mother was on the pale blue couch by the window, looking red-eyed but composed. She started to rise but Ray stopped her. "Please, don't get up." Again, he offered his sympathies, something he had to do too damn often, it seemed.

"Have you *any* leads on this monster, Detective?" Jane asked, reaching for a tissue in the pocket of her linen slacks.

Ray glanced at Meg, who was seated in the wingback chair; she shook her head. "Not yet. I wish I could tell you differently." He glanced quickly around the room. "Is Toni at home?" She had to be hurting. He knew how close she and her cousin were.

"She's upstairs," Jane said. "She's taking this very badly. Toni and Mo were raised like sisters, Detective." Her eyes drifted to the stairway. "I know she's in a great deal of pain."

Pain. The sick bastard with his deadly little wires had caused a hell of a lot of that. And they still hadn't a clue as to his identity. He shifted his gaze to Meg. "You get everything you need?"

"Yes. I was just waiting until you arrived." She looked at Jane. "Is there anything else we can do?"

"Just find him," John interjected. "Find him before he kills another innocent woman."

Meg rose. "I promise you we will." The question was not *if* but *when*. "Coming?" she asked Ray.

It took him but a few seconds to decide as he turned to Jane. "Do you think it would be all right if I went upstairs to see Toni?" He didn't explain. Just waited.

Jane glanced at her husband, then back to Ray. "I suppose it would be all right." She'd met the detective at the restaurant and had had several conversations with Toni about him. Several rather unsatisfactory conversations. Was something going on between the two of them? she wondered. If so, perhaps he could get through to Toni. Neither she nor John had been able to.

"Thank you. I appreciate it." He turned to Meg. "I'll see you in the morning."

While John saw Meg to the door, Jane walked with Ray to the blue carpeted stairway. At the first step, she touched his arm. "Toni looks and acts very strong, but she's quite fragile really."

"Yes, I know."

She saw compassion in his eyes and felt reassured. "She's probably in the attic. She only goes there when she's truly upset. The door at the end of the hall."

With a nod, Ray started up. At the attic landing, he shed his coat and tie, draping them over the banister. Continuing on, he saw that a dim light was burning. The high windows of the attic were grimy with winter dirt. There was a musty smell to the room. Walking slowly, he saw her at the far end of the room, sitting on the top of a short stairway that led down to another storage area containing a large armoire and highboy dresser.

She was wearing black slacks and a loose fitting yellow shirt, and she was barefooted. Scattered on the floor were an assortment of old clothes, delicate silks, gauzy prints and faded satins, long dresses from another era. In her hand, she held a wide-brimmed straw hat with a limp cluster of artificial roses.

He was sure she'd heard him approach, but she didn't look up.

Toni fingered the frayed pink ribbons of the old hat. "We used to come up here and play dress-up when we were kids," she said, her voice barely audible. She glanced toward a cheval glass in the corner, its mirrored surface covered with a layer of fine dust. "We'd put on our grandmother's long dresses and borrow some of Mom's shoes." She smiled a heartbreaking smile. "We had such fun in those days."

Ray stepped down and sat beside her on the top stair. He couldn't bear to say another *I'm sorry* to her, after she'd likely heard it all day long. He wished he could think of something to ease her pain. "You have a lot of good memories of her. Concentrate on them."

She turned angry eyes on him. "It's not fair. I wasn't ready for her to leave us."

He nodded, knowing her anger wasn't directed at him. Fair? Who the hell ever promised anyone fair? "She was too young to die."

Toni shook her head, her windblown hair swirling around her shoulders. "That's not why. There was so much she had to do. She had so much love to share."

"You have to think about all the good she did in the short time she was here. Yes, she was taken too soon. We can't change that. We have to learn to live with it."

"I don't *want* to live with it." Her voice was strained now, almost breaking. "I want to go to sleep and wake up to find this has all been a bad dream."

He took the hat from her, tossed it onto the pile and pulled her close. "I know. We all feel that way when we lose someone we love." He still remembered crying at his mother's bedside, begging her not to leave him; he'd been only four years old. And when she had, he'd wanted to rewind the clock, too. "She's in a better place now, a place where she's safe." *The Lord will watch over me,* Mo had told him just days ago.

Toni looked up at him. "I thought you didn't believe in God."

"It doesn't matter what I believe. Mo believed."

"Then why did God let this happen to her?" Her face seemed to crumble. "I didn't even get to say goodbye." Then she let go, let the tears come, the sobs break through, giving in to the pain. She clung to him and wept, for Mo, for all of them. Innocents snuffed out by a monster. The church taught its people to love their enemies. But she couldn't, Toni thought. Not this time. She simply couldn't.

The heart-wrenching sounds emanating from her had him aching to ease her distress. But he didn't have the words. So he held her, smoothed her hair, kissed her forehead, rocked her as she cried out her sorrow. He wasn't sure how long they sat like that and he didn't care. It felt good comforting her, holding her. He usually tried to avoid scenes like this, which was why he was surprised to realize he was exactly where he wanted to be.

He was so big, so solid, his comfort so genuine, that Toni clung to him despite herself. Her sobs slowly diminished; she emptied herself of them. Feeling spent, she eased back and searched for a Kleenex. She dabbed at her cheeks, blew her nose, and finally met his eyes. "It's the same bastard, right?"

Meg had updated him on the phone before he'd driven over. The same wire, the mass card tucked into her jacket pocket, waterlogged and barely decipherable. He felt his jaw tighten as he nodded. "Don't think about it any more tonight."

"How can I not?" With a trembling hand, Toni shoved back her hair. "Such a waste."

Because he didn't know what else to do, Ray urged her back into his arms. She needed him and, just maybe, he needed to hold her as well.

Toni nestled there for several minutes, her cheek pressed against his chest, listening to his steady heartbeat. Finally, she inched back and looked up at him. "No one should die before they've really lived," she whispered. "I'm scared, Ray. I don't believe anything has ever scared me like this."

He felt angry and protective at the same time.

"Don't let the fear take over. I'll watch out for you."

Her eyes changed, darkened, took on an awareness. This time it was she who closed the distance between them, reaching for his kiss. As his mouth took hers, she knew she was reaching for comfort more than passion. Everything had shifted inside her. She wanted to feel, to experience, to be loved.

Just this morning, she'd felt glad to be alive as she'd strolled the backyard, unaware that under winter's cover, Mo was already dead. Dear God, how fleeting life was, how capricious fate.

Her arms tightened around him as she deepened the kiss, pressing herself against his broad chest. She wanted the forgetfulness his physical presence offered, to shut out the world, to obliterate everything and everyone. She wanted the oblivion only he could give her.

Ray responded to her, though he knew what she was feeling and doing. He'd seen it before, too often. The living needed to prove that they were still alive in the presence of death. It was frustration and fear driving her. She wanted something to take away the pain, and he was available. He wasn't hurt, just a little surprised at her loss of control. It was so unlike her.

But just as suddenly as she'd reached for him, Toni tensed, easing back from him, embarrassment flushing her face. Had she taken leave of her senses? she thought. She'd all but thrown herself at him, and her parents were just downstairs. In her entire life, she'd never done such a thing. Is this what grief did to her? She placed her hands on her flaming cheeks, wishing she could retract the last few minutes.

Gently, Ray turned her to face him and peeled her

hands away. "It's all right. I understand." When she didn't respond, he squeezed her hands. "Did you hear me?"

Her eyes averted, Toni nodded.

Still holding her hands, he stood and drew her up to him. He kissed her eyes closed, brushed his lips across her damp cheeks, then covered her mouth with his tenderly.

When she opened her eyes, she saw that his expression was filled with concern. "It's okay. I know you understand."

Reassured, he urged her toward the attic steps. "I think you need to rest now. I'll call you in the morning, all right?"

"Yes, fine." She walked down to the second level with him, grateful that her parents were nowhere in sight. At the top of the stairs, she turned to him. "Thank you."

How could she look so beautiful at such a time? he asked himself. How could he want her so much that his insides were churning, he who'd all but shoved her out of his life mere weeks ago? He didn't know how, he only knew it was so.

Reluctant to leave her, he reached for her again, gathering her slender frame to him, kissing the top of her head as her arms encircled him. As he turned to leave, he looked downstairs into the worried frown of Jane Garette.

SIX

Be not afraid, I go before you always...

The music rose to the high ceilings of St. Matthews as the organist played Sister Maureen Garette's favorite song. In the front pew, head bent and eyes burning from the many tears she'd shed, Toni couldn't manage to find her voice. She let the comforting words wash over her and tried desperately to be consoled by them, and by the faith of her childhood.

Next to her, her mother knelt, her back ramrod straight, her eyes dry. Only Toni and John Garette knew what such composure cost Jane, the sleepless nights, the ulcer she'd been struggling with for years. The young woman in the coffin at the head of the center aisle had been like a daughter to her. Jane had no more tears left, only a hollow feeling in the pit of her stomach.

John Garette's pain was just as real. He knew it was irrational, but he felt responsible somehow. For insisting on putting in the pool, for not being home, for not keeping little Mo safe. Intellectually, he knew better, but he was leading with his emotions right now. The old shouldn't have to bury the young, he thought as he wiped away a drop of moisture that trailed down one cheek.

Standing at the back of the church, Detective Ray Vargas kept his eyes moving along the pews, up and down the aisles. St. Matthews was filled to overflowing, though the young victim had been involved in the parish only a few months. The large turnout was probably due to the publicity surrounding the murders; the mourners were there not only for Mo but for those who'd gone before her, Ray thought. The whole community was saddened, incensed, frightened.

He couldn't blame them.

His fists clenched as he thought that the person responsible might very well be there, in attendance. He'd known it to happen frequently, the killer not only returning to the scenes of his crimes, but to attend the wakes of his victims. If only he could pick him out, if only criminals had some scarlet mark that would betray them. He would find him, Ray vowed. And it had better be soon. Four young women in the prime of life had lost their lives already. How many more would die before they stopped him?

He'd assigned several plainclothesmen to attend the service, hoping one of them would spot something or someone suspicious. Uniformed officers also lingered in the vestibule and at each door, more to give the parishioners a feeling of security than for any other reason. Whoever the killer was, he certainly wasn't careless or stupid. At least, he hadn't been so far.

The sisters from the convent were seated directly behind the family, many dabbing at their eyes. Several sisters of St. Joseph had driven in from the mother house in Nazareth, Michigan, to mourn one of their own. Young students whom Sister Maureen had counseled openly wept. Lay teachers and maintenance staff and groundskeepers for St. Matthews, as well as half a dozen priests, lined the hard pews. Ray could see Meg in the back on the other side of the wide center aisle, her eyes skimming the crowd.

Lord, but he hated funerals.

The final hymn ended and the pallbearers moved slowly down the aisle with the casket, followed by the family. Ray gazed out over the assembly, watching for that odd something that might set someone apart. Seeing nothing unusual he moved to unobtrusively insert himself near the family. They would bear watching, especially Toni.

He had a bad feeling about this one. It bothered him greatly that Mo's body had been dumped in the Garettes' pool. Given the nun's busy travel schedule, the strangler could have struck at any number of places. There were no clues on her body to indicate where she'd been murdered; the medical examiner had said she'd been dead only about six hours when found. Yet *where* she'd been found meant that the murderer knew of Mo's connection to the Garettes of Grosse Pointe Shores.

And that might mean that Toni, a blue-eyed blonde, could be in danger. Ray turned to look at her.

Toni's fair skin, offset by a black silk dress, looked paler than ever. Her hair was parted in the middle and pulled back into a twist, perhaps demonstrating her control over that one small aspect of her life, Ray thought. The severe look would have made most women appear hard and unyielding. Toni only looked more beautiful. He moved toward her and touched her arm, sliding his hand down and lacing his fingers with hers. "How are you holding up?"

"I'm all right." She squeezed his hand. "I'm glad you're here." She glanced over at Meg. "All of you." Her parents were moving out to the cars. "Are you coming to the cemetery?"

He saw the need in her eyes. "Yes. You go with your folks. I'll be along." She stood looking at him with such vulnerability in her expression that he found it difficult not to pull her close and reassure her. "If you notice anything out of the ordinary, anything at all, make a note of it, will you?" He saw her nod and felt her tense at the reminder of the killer possibly in their midst. "I'll keep you in sight even though you may not see me."

"Thank you." Lately, it seemed as if she was always thanking someone, Toni thought. Turning, she walked down the stone steps of the church.

Meg joined Ray, a look of concern on her face. "She looks as fragile as glass about now."

"Yeah, I know." Ray turned and saw Luke and Stephanie along with Sam and Carly leaving the church, moving to speak to Toni. Feeling weary, he followed them, Meg close behind.

Meg sat on a folding chair at the back of the church hall where the colleagues, relatives, and friends of Sister Maureen Garette sipped punch and spoke in hushed tones of the sweet woman they'd known. She saw Ray by the refreshment table, talking with Mother Magdalen. The crowd had filtered down to about forty, the faces all familiar to her by now. Although they'd had half a dozen officers at the church and the cemetery, she doubted that the killer had put in an appearance.

Hearing a door open, she turned to see Toni step out into the side yard, probably needing a breath of fresh air. Meg rose and followed her out. She found her standing by one of the pillars, gazing off into a setting sun, her arms crossed over her chest in a defensive posture. "I hope I'm not intruding," Meg said quietly as she stepped closer.

Toni turned and gave her a weak smile. "No, not at all. It's so warm in there." And so cloying, so heavy with the aroma of flowers and sympathy, Toni thought. She'd left before she started screaming.

"I guess summer's nearly here."

Toni shivered involuntarily. "My father wants to cement in the pool. I don't think any of us could ever swim in it again."

Meg fell silent for a moment. "I hate to ask questions at a time like this, but Sister Maureen was sort of vague when I talked with her. Do you know of any men friends she might have had who could have had a crush on her, perhaps, or harbored a grudge?"

"A grudge? Doubtful. Everyone liked Mo. Crushes? Any number of guys had crushes on her, but that was years ago when we were in high school. She joined the convent and after that, men were merely friends. She never had a lover, if that's what you're thinking." More's the pity, Toni thought. Mo wouldn't agree, but Toni felt her cousin had missed out on so much.

Meg let out a frustrated sigh. "It's the same story I hear from the relatives and friends of all the victims. There simply *has* to be someone who has some motive for all this."

"I wish I could help, but you know, sisters rarely go around making enemies. And they don't have close ties to single men, even in their youth. Mo never seriously considered the boys we hung around with as *boyfriends*. They were merely friends, as were the girls. It's a different way of thinking, one that has roots in their calling, I'm sure."

"I think you're right. I'm Catholic, so I understand. I'm just grasping at straws here, trying to find a lead, a link, *something.*"

"Oh, I know. You must be terribly frustrated. I know Ray is."

Meg was glad Toni had given her an opening. "Yes. He seems to have taken a personal interest in this case. As he did in Carly Weston's stalker last year."

It was hard to tell if Meg was fishing or just making conversation, Toni thought. "Well, my family and I appreciate everything that both you and he are doing."

"Ray's a very caring man. I imagine you've noticed. He gets personally involved in quite a few of his cases, though the book tells us not to."

Was that a warning or was Meg hinting at something? Toni wondered. "You mean he gets personally involved with the victim's families, or more specifically with women?" She had trouble believing that. Ray didn't give the impression of being a ladies' man.

"No, not just women. I mean emotionally involved. Like with that young man who almost committed suicide. Ray's teaching him basketball, seeing that he gets professional counseling. And there's this crazy old man who hangs around the precinct. Keeps telling anyone who'll listen that his neighbor's microwave is interfering with his TV reception. No one pays much attention to him. Except Ray. He listens to Mort as if the man's complaints were perfectly legitimate."

Meg sighed. "You see, Ray's never developed the

dispassionate approach to police work that some of us have. That makes him unique, but it takes a toll on him emotionally. It's also part of what makes him so special."

Toni uncrossed her arms and toyed with the top button of her dress, not at all surprised at what Meg was telling her. Yet, she was puzzled. "I've noticed his compassion, certainly. And his empathy with people. I've wondered about what's shaped that in him. Most seasoned police officers have hardened themselves against the pain they see on a regular basis. As you know, I have two friends married to detectives, and both Luke and Sam are pretty good at distancing themselves. But as you say, Ray's different."

Meg leaned against the cool brick of the building. She sensed there was more than passing interest about Ray in Toni. "I think it's because he feels a deep-rooted responsibility, for those under his command, for the victims, sometimes even for the criminals themselves. It doesn't keep him from doing his job and doing it awfully well. But I think he winds up hurting himself more than the rest of us do. That's what happens when you take on the pain of others, when you try to take responsibility for their loss."

Toni was silent a minute. "Why do you suppose he feels such a sense of responsibility?"

Meg shrugged, thinking perhaps she was getting in too deep. "I wouldn't know, though I'd guess it goes back to his upbringing." She flashed a smile, showing a dimple in her left cheek. "Doesn't everything we say and do date back to our childhood?"

"Probably. I understand he has a brother. Is he younger?"

"Yes, considerably. And he's given Ray more than his share of trouble over the years."

"What about their parents?"

"Pete's a half brother. Ray's mother and father are both dead. Pete's mother took off." Meg shook her head. "Not too uncommon these days, I'm afraid."

The stepmother took off and Ray took over. Toni remembered Ray saying that one day he'd gotten fed up, bought a bus ticket, and left everything and everyone behind. She was beginning to piece his past together and ached for the young man he'd been. Life certainly wasn't fair. She drew in a deep breath of lilac-scented air and wished she could go home.

Studying her, Meg couldn't help asking one more question, which was none of her business, really. Except that Ray was not just her partner, but her friend. "You care about him, don't you?"

Toni shifted her eyes to Meg's. She thought about not answering, but then saw no reason not to. "Yes," she said simply.

Meg nodded, hoping that Toni was tougher than she looked. She'd seen Ray get involved with several different women through the years, and remain faithful to each one. For a time. But he never allowed himself to get serious, to truly commit. She doubted if Toni Garette was the type interested in a brief love affair.

"I think I'll go round up my parents," Toni said, pushing off from the pillar she was leaning against. "I'm exhausted."

"I think it's time we all left." Meg walked to the doorway with her. "Toni, if you think of anything that might help solve the case, or if you just want to talk, you know my number."

SHATTERED VOWS 115

Toni's smile was warmer this time. "Thanks."

Meg watched her walk into the hall and flicked her eyes to Ray. She watched him move to Toni's side and slip his arm about her waist, leaning down to talk to her, the gesture intimate. Yes, there was definitely something between them.

Meg couldn't help hoping that neither of them got hurt.

In the back section of St. Matthews parking lot sat a 1980 blue Olds Delta 88 with a burned-out headlight. Inside the car, the man kept his eyes on the side door of the church hall, where the blonde and the redhead had entered. He wished he could have been a fly on the wall and heard their conversation. He imagined the discussion had included the most recent innocent he'd sent to heaven.

Wally drew in a deep breath of cool evening air. The headache was finally gone and he felt renewed. It was like that every time. The pressure would build and build until nothing would help him, not rest or medicine. Not until he found his next angel and sent her on her way did the pain abate.

The redhead was a cop, though she was out of uniform. The blonde in the arc of light was Toni Garette, a relative of the latest chosen one. They'd looked a lot alike, those two. A lot like Terry. The one he'd just sent on her way had been a virgin, pure like all the rest. He wondered if Toni was. He'd been in the church during the funeral mass and seen how that detective with the beard had moved to her side so protectively.

He felt himself grow hard thinking of Toni, and squeezed his eyes shut. She was so beautiful, so soft looking. He knew that bad thoughts about sinful acts would lead him into trouble. Like that time with Angie. She hadn't meant anything to him. But the evil desire had taken him over. And look what it had done—destroyed his life. Nothing had been the same after that. Nothing.

He'd spent weeks on his knees begging forgiveness. But Terry hadn't been able to forgive him. Angie had told on him, but he'd made her pay for that mistake. He shifted uncomfortably on the worn upholstery of the seat as his erection strained against his zipper. He mustn't let his traitorous body take over.

Bending his head, he touched his forehead to the steering wheel and prayed: *Father, forgive me. Please forgive me.*

As the last few mourners trickled out of the hall, Ray took Toni aside. "Why don't you let your folks go in their car and I'll drive you home later. It's only seven. We could get something to eat or just go to my place and talk." Her face was shadowed with fatigue, yet he doubted she'd be able to sleep.

"I don't think so, Ray." She gripped his hand, hoping he'd understand. "Thanks, but I think I need some time alone."

"I understand." He took her arm, walking out with her. "If you change your mind, call me. I'll be home." Too many people around to kiss her, Ray thought. He brushed his fingertips along one silken cheek. "Sleep well."

She lay fully clothed on her bed in the room she'd had since she'd been born, and stared at the ceiling. Memories flooded Toni's mind, years of them superimposed on one another. She and Mo at Mo's parents' funeral, sad and confused children. At their combined birthday party the next year in the family room, when Dad had hired a clown to entertain their friends. The first dance they'd attended, how nervous they'd been getting ready. All the nights they'd chattered away in her bed or down the hall in Mo's, one having crept over after lights-out to be with the other, giggling until Mom came to separate them.

Toni was dry-eyed and found her silent grief just as painful as tears. She couldn't stop thinking, couldn't stop remembering. On the one hand, she didn't want to forget Mo. On the other, she felt as if she were going out of her mind with the kaleidoscope of events whirling through her brain. How long would it go on?

She glanced at the clock and saw that it was only nine. She'd tried to eat the sandwich her mother had fixed when they'd returned home, but she'd had trouble swallowing and given up. She'd liked to have gone outside to sit in the backyard she loved, but that pleasure had been forever altered. She'd taken two Tylenol for the headache that had finally eased. She knew that sleep would elude her for hours yet.

Giving up, she rose, shoved her feet into her shoes, ran a brush through her hair, and grabbed her purse.

Downstairs, she walked to the arched doorway that led into the family room. Her father was reading the paper and her mother was working on her needlepoint, a young Frank Sinatra serenading them from the stereo. "I'm going out for a while," she said quietly.

"At this hour?" John asked, clearly disapproving.

"Is anything the matter?" Jane asked, her brow wrinkling with concern.

Yes, everything's the matter, she thought. "I feel like a drive."

"Going to Carly's or Stephanie's?" Jane asked hopefully. At least with her friends, she'd be safe.

"I'm not sure. Please don't wait up. I'll call if I find it's getting late." The advantages of being thirty, Toni thought. They wanted to ask more, but wouldn't. She wasn't deliberately trying to make them worry, but she also wasn't about to put her need to leave up for discussion.

Toni skipped down the back stairs, avoiding looking at the pool as she hurried to her Mercedes. In moments, she was cruising down Lakeshore Drive, heading south. She'd said she wasn't sure where she was heading. That was a lie. She knew exactly where she wanted to be.

The drive to Ray's in light evening traffic took only ten minutes. As she approached his house, she saw through the living room windows that a lamp was on. A noisy Oldsmobile rumbled slowly by as she pulled into his drive. Ray's wagon was probably in his garage at the back of the lot. She got out, noticing that her hands were less than steady now that she was here.

Maybe this hadn't been such a hot idea after all.

But here she was. The neighborhood was still, most folks settled in for the evening. Next door, she could see a flickering television casting a silvery glow. A dog barked from a nearby backyard. Inside Ray's, she heard Hamlet's throaty answering growl. Or did the dog sense her stepping onto the porch? Heart pounding, she pressed the doorbell.

Inside, Ray frowned at the sound of the bell as he spoke into the phone. "It's more than we've had before, Doc. God knows we needed some good news." The bell rang again. "Listen, can you hold a minute? Someone's at my door." He set down the phone and walked to the front door, where Hamlet was patiently waiting.

She stood there in a shaft of moonlight, her head bent, seemingly examining her shoes. She finally looked up as he swung open the screen. Her eyes were large and vulnerable as they locked on his; she was oblivious to the dog, who rushed out to greet her.

"Did I come at a bad time?"

"No. Come in. I'm just finishing a call." He whistled Hamlet in, closed the door, and went back to the phone. "Sorry, Doc. So when can you do a more thorough workup?" He paused, listening. "Tomorrow afternoon is fine. I'll see you then. Thanks for calling. 'Bye." He hung up and saw that she was crouched by the fireplace, scratching behind Hamlet's ears. Ray moved to her side. He'd wanted her to come, had hoped, but hadn't really believed she would.

Toni placed her shoulder bag on the floor and stood. He looked so damn appealing, so *male,* she thought. His shirt was hanging open and unbuttoned over the suit pants he'd worn earlier, and he was barefoot. She tried to focus on the part of the phone conversation she'd overheard. "Is there some news on the stranglings?"

"The medical examiner just got the report on Mo from forensics. This time, we may have gotten lucky. They found two dark brown hairs under her fingernails. They're going to run some tests and see if they can type them."

"Can they really tell anything from two little hairs?"

"Sometimes. They can tell what part of the body they're from, male or female, young or old, dyed or natural, if there was a struggle. Lots of stuff."

"But not if they came from the killer?"

Her face was still so pale. She seemed nervous yet energetic, restlessly touching a carved horse on the mantel, repositioning an ashtray on the coffee table. "True. But we can probably trace Mo's whereabouts during the day, see who she came in contact with, take hair samples from them to eliminate possibilities. It could boil down to the last person who saw her alive."

Toni shivered, but it wasn't from the temperature, which was quite warm even with a side window open. She glanced out the window at the moon, high in the night sky, and then back to Ray. "I shouldn't have come. I'm rotten company tonight."

He took hold of her hands, stilling them, finding them cool to the touch. "I'm glad you did." He managed to capture her gaze. "Why did you?"

"I'm not sure." Still agitated, she tugged her hands free, walked to the front window, and stood looking out. Two cars she hadn't noticed before were parked across the street, both unoccupied. The only sound was her thumping heart. Why on earth *had* she come?

Patiently, Ray went to her. "Try. Tell me why you're here."

She drew in an annoyed breath, knowing full well why, not wanting to say the words aloud. "Do you remember when we talked, up in my attic?"

"Yes, every word."

"I almost jumped your bones that night." Even the thought embarrassed her.

He took a step closer. "You were hurting."

"I'm still hurting." She swung around to face

him. "Make it go away, please." The fist in her stomach curled tighter as she waited for his response.

Ray saw that she was trembling and wondered if any woman had ever trembled for him before. "Are you sure?" he asked.

Her chin went up a notch and her voice was strong. "Very sure."

He bent his head to kiss her and felt the passion he'd been pushing back flare up instantly. He tugged her closer and swallowed the small sound she made. He tasted her frustration and that breathless hint of panic as she undoubtedly again wondered if she'd made the right decision in coming to him. He would make her glad she had.

Toni concentrated only on him as he continued the assault on her senses, nibbling at her lips, his hands beginning to explore, his tongue beginning to invade. Emotions warred within her—fear and pleasure and impatience and need. Her need for him. Only him.

Steeped in sensation, she felt herself being lifted, then carried up his stairs and into his bedroom. He kicked closed the door. She had a vague impression of a large four-poster bed and moonlight pouring in through slatted blinds before he kissed her eyes closed as he let her slowly slide down his body. The erotic journey had her pulse pounding and her blood rushing like a molten river.

He turned on a low lamp and backed her up till her knees met the hard edge of the bed as his hands skimmed along her bare arms. He saw the quick jolt of hesitancy register in her eyes, then disappear as his hands raised to remove the pins from her hair. "You should always wear your hair down," he said, letting the pins fly, shoving his fingers through the twisted strands, massaging her scalp sensuously as she began to move restlessly under his touch.

He paused to admire the wild cloud of hair settling around her shoulders. "I won't make a move without your consent," he told her. He could be patient now, take the time to reassure her. She'd come to him. "Tell me what you want."

She drew in a deep breath, stepped out of her shoes and kicked them aside, then rose on tiptoe. "This." She stretched to press her mouth to his while her hands pushed his shirt from his shoulders; she let it drop to the floor. "And this." She threaded her fingers along his broad chest, loving the feel of the hair there.

"You're wearing too many clothes," he said, his voice husky.

Slowly, she unbuttoned her dress and let it slide from her. Stepping back, her eyes challenged him to take her to the next plateau. She watched as he made short order of removing her underthings, then heard his swift intake of breath as he gazed at her. Leaning forward, she sank her breasts into him and felt a moan she couldn't control escape from low in her throat. "Oh, God, and this, too."

He swayed against her and with her, letting the sweet friction tease his senses. Then he dipped his head to trail hot kisses along her throat and finally closed his lips over the peak of one breast. He could feel her heart thundering beneath his mouth. He eased back and took both breasts in his hands, finding her small and firm, her skin soft as satin.

Taking her hands, he eased her down onto the mattress, inhaling the lingering scent of expensive bath oil and her own arousal. Her hands fluttered, seeking, anxious. He didn't want to rush this, Ray thought, and consciously slowed his hands, his lips.

The urge to hurry to completion was his to conquer and he did, though it cost him. He wanted to take her up slowly, to make her hot and nearly mad with need, crying out for him, opening to him. But he knew that this first time, he needed to go slowly. She deserved slow loving and an easy touch, especially tonight. He came back to her lips and feasted there, drinking from her.

When her hips arched in invitation, he took his mouth along her throat and traveled slowly south, tasting the heady flavor of her breasts and brushing his bearded face along the tender skin of her flat stomach. He caught her throaty moan as she closed her eyes on a sensual sigh.

Her blond hair was spread on his dark blue pillow in a wild tangle, exactly as he'd imagined it in his restive dreams. Her eyes were hazy with passion and her full mouth was swollen from his kisses. As he stared, she moved fitfully and reached a shaky hand to the waistband of his slacks.

"Are you on the pill?" he asked.

"Yes, but maybe we should use something anyway," Toni answered. She didn't like to consider it, but she had no idea how many others he'd been with.

Pausing, Ray met her gaze. "We need to get something straight. I don't sleep around. Never have. I had someone and that ended last fall, as I told you. No one since. All right?"

He couldn't know how much better she felt. She managed a smile. "Yes, all right. It's been longer for me. Lots longer."

He wrinkled his brow. "Any particular reason?"

"The moment wasn't right, and neither was the man."

"And now?"

She smiled lazily, because this felt right. Very right. To convince him, she slipped her hand beneath his waistband and her fingers closed around him.

He nearly shot off the bed. Easing back, he slipped off the rest of his clothes and came back to run his hands along her strong, slender thighs, needing to take back the control. He knew how much she liked to be in charge. But not tonight. Not this time. He wanted badly to make her lose that famous control of hers, to make her winded and wild for him. Unobtrusively, he replaced his hands with his mouth.

The first climax ripped through her with the power of a tidal wave. Breathless, dazed with pleasure, her hands clutched at his arms as she shook with the power of it. But before she was fully recovered, he drove her up again, watching her climb, watching a sensual flush infuse her face, watching the waves batter her.

This was what she'd been seeking, Toni thought as she lay seeped in stunned pleasure. This mindless loss of self where no disturbing thoughts could intrude and no problems could engage her. There was only here and now, this room, this bed, this man. Her thoughts centered on pleasing and being pleased, on letting go of the world filled with pain for at least a little while.

Coming back to herself, she looked up at him and saw a smile play around that clever mouth of his. "Pleased with yourself, are you?"

"I am. Do you want to quit or do you want more?"

"I want more." She opened her arms. "Come here. I want you inside me."

More than ready, Ray poised himself above her.

"Don't close your eyes." He wanted her to watch as he joined with her. And when he finally did, she arched to meet him, her body straining to get closer, closer. He found the rhythm and saw she was perfectly attuned to him, keeping up, moving with him.

He drove himself into her with a fierceness he'd never experienced before. He watched her eyes try to stay focused on his, until they finally drifted shut as a stunning peak shoved her over the edge. Unable to hold back another moment, he let himself follow.

Toni whispered his name and went limp in his arms, utterly spent, momentarily free.

Across the street, two doors down under the hazy glow of a street lamp, a dark Olds sat at the curb. Scrunched down so no passing motorist could see him, Wally stared at the house that belonged to the bearded detective.

Toni Garette had buried her dead relative, then hurried to be with Vargas, for comfort, he hoped. Surely she wasn't one of the bad ones, the ones so unlike Terry. The ones like Angie. Like himself.

He wiggled in the seat, trying to ignore his restlessness. His body wasn't cooperating as his disobedient mind pictured Toni's long legs, her slender form, so like Terry's. Her blond hair was like Terry's, too, and she had kind eyes that he'd seen light up when she laughed. How many thousands of nights had he imagined Terry with him, undressing for him, reaching for him, loving him?

But no! It would never happen, not to him. He disgusted Terry. She'd told him so. Terry was slow in making up her mind, but once she decided something, that was it.

His eyes drifted back to the lighted windows. Why was it that that cop was enjoying the pleasure of Toni's company, a pleasure that he never could have? Only women like Angie wanted him, Angie, who'd been tainted. He'd had to rid the world of Angie.

The detective would be watching out for Toni since they were such close friends. Wally shoved back his dark hair, thinking he had too much to do yet to risk getting caught watching a cop's house.

He could still watch Toni, but from a distance. It gave him pleasure, too much to give it up. He would daydream, imagine that Toni was Terry and that she wanted only him. Surely God would understand his need to just look if he couldn't touch. But he'd have to be very careful when she was with Vargas.

Was that a shadow that passed in front of one of the windows, or was it Toni? His active imagination removed Vargas from the scene and put himself in the house with her. Oh God, how he ached just thinking about her, picturing her naked and reaching for him.

He was weak. God knew it and so did Terry. He did bad things, sinful things, but sometimes, he couldn't help himself.

One last time, he promised himself, as he scooted down in the seat and slowly unzipped his pants.

Propped up on his side, Ray lay watching Toni sleep. She was exhausted, he knew, and had fallen almost immediately into what he hoped was a dreamless oblivion. Only moonlight covered her as she lay facing him atop the tangled sheets. Her hair fanned out around her oval face, and her chest moved gently with each quiet breath she took. He thought she was the most beautiful woman he'd ever seen.

And the thought scared him half to death.

Ray sucked in a great gulp of air as he stretched his arm up and lay his head on it. He'd had his share of women over the years, though he'd been monogamous with each, as he'd told her. He appreciated the fairer sex to the extent that he enjoyed the way they thought and reasoned. And he mightily enjoyed fencing with them in bed. But there, it had always stopped. Afterward, he'd never been sorry to see them leave, nor had he preferred to wake up with them.

Why then was he already hoping Toni would stay the night?

Because she was different. She'd managed to get to him with her sense of humor, her sense of caring. She'd captivated him with her odd combination of innocence and sensuality. He wanted more and knew he'd want still more again. And he meant to have more. For as long as it would last, they'd be good together.

Gently, he reached out with one finger and brushed her bangs off her forehead.

She opened her eyes and, for a moment, felt disoriented. Then she saw Ray and slowly, she smiled. "Have I been asleep long?"

"Yeah. I missed you." He leaned over and kissed her.

She made a soft, purring sound and stretched lazily.

"I guess you're not one of those women who like to talk after sex, eh?"

She sighed, turning toward him. "Are you one of

those men who want to hear a woman say the earth moved?"

"And if I were?"

Her smile was very female. "Then I'd have to tell you that it damn near whirled off its axis."

He grinned and burrowed his face between her breasts, loving the feel of her, the scent of her. Her hands moved into his hair as he nuzzled his beard against her skin.

Toni felt a reawakening surge of desire ripple through her as his lips and tongue went to work. Impossible, she thought, then gasped as his teeth nipped her gently. Maybe not.

He raised his head up to look at her, his eyes serious. "Did it work? Did I make you forget?"

"Everything. You made me forget my name." She settled her hands at the back of his neck. "Did you really need to ask? You're not insecure, are you?"

Insecure? About lovemaking? he thought. But his laughter died in his throat. Maybe he was, a little. She was so beautiful, and his wife had left him for another man. Correction. Other men, for he'd learned there'd been several. Finally, he shrugged. "Isn't every man?" He rolled over onto his back and propped his hands under his head.

Toni curled onto her side and went to him. "I don't know about every man. I haven't been with very many."

Her statement pleased him.

"And I've certainly never driven to a man's house before and practically begged him to make love to me."

He shifted to look at her. "You didn't beg. You'd never have to beg, not me or any other man." He'd been nearly ready to beg *her*. He reached to stroke her cheek. She turned her face and pressed her lips to his palm. "You're very special, Toni. I hope you believe I mean that."

She raised to meet his eyes, her own bright with a sudden rush of tears. Damn, but she was tired of tears. She smiled. "I believe you. You're special to me, too."

"Will you spend the night?"

Toni let out a whoosh of air as she glanced at the bedside clock. "Midnight! How'd it get to be midnight?"

"Does it matter, Cinderella?"

She sat up, reaching for the sheet. "I don't have any clothes for morning and my folks will worry." She turned to see him patiently watching her, not saying a word. Suddenly, she knew it was exactly the right thing to do. She hated it when people tried to make up her mind for her. "Oh, well, what the hell. Hand me the phone."

SEVEN

Meg rushed into the squad room, red-faced and out of breath as she entered the cubicle she shared with her partner. "Sorry I'm late," she apologized to Ray. Actually, she was a little embarrassed but not a bit sorry. Her husband had a late shift that day and she hadn't been able to resist staying in bed an extra half hour when he'd reached for her. With their disparate schedules, their time alone together was important to them both.

"No problem," Ray said, his manner distracted as he studied the report on his desk.

Shoving her handbag into her bottom drawer, Meg squinted in his direction as she took her chair. "What're you reading?"

"Forensics report on the two brown hairs found under Sister Maureen's fingernail." He handed her the report he'd finished. "Amazing how much they can learn from a tiny hair."

Meg skimmed the report, reading the pertinent facts aloud. "From a white male, middle-aged probably, torn from his head. Original hair color. Trace of a chemical of indeterminate origin." She glanced over at Ray. "Damn shame he had to put her in that pool. Otherwise we'd probably have more."

"I guess we're lucky to have that much, though it doesn't really tell us anything we didn't know." There had been recorded cases of serial killers of other races and also of the female sex, but the majority were Caucasian males between twenty-five and fifty. "Most likely they're picking up a chemical from the pool."

She unbuttoned her suit coat. "Are they going to try to pinpoint it?"

"That's what they told me." Though he doubted they'd learn what it was, diluted as it had been. The mass card in her pocket had been too soggy to read, but the remnants looked to be the same type. And Mo also had had a small gold chain ripped from her, the small clasp left behind, caught under the green wire.

"So I guess all we have to do is round up all the middle-aged white men with brown hair and easy access to green wire within a five-mile radius of St. Matthews, and we've got our man." Meg blew out a disgusted breath.

"That's about it. I've got another couple of men checking area florists and nurseries for possibles. But we're liable to come up with fifty or more suspects. That's a fairly common description." It even applied to him.

Meg studied Ray carefully. She couldn't remember seeing him quite so dejected. He was truly upset over this case, almost taking it personally. And she thought she knew why. "How's Toni handling things?"

He shrugged. "Not well. And her folks are shattered." He looked across the span of both desks at his partner, his gray eyes shadowed. "For that alone, I'd like to get this bastard."

"I hear you." Had he really fallen this time, or

was Toni just the next diversion for him? Meg had watched several fellow detectives, all having sworn off permanence with any woman, fall like giant oaks over the past few years. Luke Varner, who'd risked his life for Stephanie. Sam English, who'd been taken captive by the madman who'd stalked Carly. The more adamant about going it alone they were, the harder they fell when the right woman came along, Meg believed. She had no idea if Toni was the right woman for Ray. However, she did know that she hadn't seen this level of concern on his face before. "Toni carries off the image of a tough businesswoman quite well," Meg went on. "But underneath, I think she's very vulnerable."

Ray busied himself making an airplane out of a piece of graph paper. "Yeah, she is." He thought of the way she'd sobbed in his arms in the attic, and of the way she'd come to him and asked him to make her forget. Though they'd shared a long, loving night, he wondered if she'd come to him again when she didn't need comforting. "She'd hate it if she thought we saw through her facade."

"Her secret's safe with me." Meg flipped open her notebook. "Well, what's on the agenda for today?"

"Dr. Roger Delaney's due in any minute." Delaney was a psychiatrist and a Catholic. The captain had strongly recommended that Ray call him in on the case, since the department had used him before. They were to answer all his questions and give him as much data as he requested on the strangulations in the hope that he could work up a profile of the killer. Ray wasn't sure he believed in psychiatry's effectiveness in searching out murderers, but he was ready to try most anything. Hell, they'd even resorted to a psychic in the Weston case. To say

SHATTERED VOWS

nothing of the fact that Renwick's request had had the flavor of an order. Ray aimed the finished plane into the waste basket. And missed. "You ever work with him before?"

"Once, years ago. We had a missing eight-year-old girl who'd been taken out her bedroom window. Delaney tried to give us a feel for the kidnapper."

"Did it work?" He picked up another piece of graph paper.

She leaned back, remembering. "I believe he narrowed it down to a young man, probably a loner type, insecure in his relationships with girls his own age, who probably wouldn't harm his victim." Her eyes turned bleak. "His description was very accurate, but his prediction was not. We found her body before we found her eighteen-year-old loner-type killer."

Before Ray could comment, the captain appeared in their doorway. "I need you on something, Meg." Hardly anyone ever saw Renwick smile. He was close to retirement, with bad feet and a bum heart. But he usually smiled at Meg, and did so now.

"Sure. What can I do for you, Captain?"

"Got a woman down the hall in room two with a six-year-old who says she's been molested. I could call in Sharon Yost with the Special Unit. But I'd really like you on this."

Meg rose, her lips a thin line. Of all the gruesome things they ran across, she hated child molesters the most.

"See if you can get the girl to open up. So far, she hasn't, not to any male detectives." Far from a chauvinist, Renwick wished he had half a dozen more like Meg in his precinct. She was not only as good as or better than any man in the field, but she could work miracles with weeping women and scared kids. "Keep in mind that the kid might have an overactive imagination, may have made the whole thing up and the mother's running scared."

"Right." Meg left the cubicle.

"Let me know," Renwick called after her, then turned back to Ray. "I assume there's nothing new on our serial killer."

"Just this." Ray handed him the forensics report.

Renwick read it quickly. "Well, that sure narrows down your suspect list to half of Detroit."

A tall man with a pencil-thin mustache appeared in the doorway alongside the captain. "Dr. Delaney," Ray said, "come in, please." Ray introduced the man to Renwick.

"I certainly hope you can help us, Doctor." Renwick shook hands, then returned to his office as Ray indicated the chair alongside his desk.

"So, what can I get you, Doctor?" Ray glanced at his empty Styrofoam cup. "Want some coffee?"

Delaney crossed his legs, studying the detective. Despite Vargas's facial hair, the psychiatrist saw a mature man with quick intelligence and an ingrained impatience that apparently he had learned to mask fairly well. "No coffee, thanks. I drink too much of the stuff."

"Yeah, me, too." Ray tossed his cup.

"Basically, I need you to brief me on what you know so far about the murders, to describe the victims, the crime scenes, anything that will help me put together a profile."

Ray reached into his file drawer and pulled out a manila folder. "It's all in here. Might be easier if you read it."

The cop didn't want him here, Delaney speculated, didn't believe in his work, and had probably been pressured to call him. Delaney could live with that. Most people had their doubts. "A psychological profile is more than facts on papers. In order to capture this man, you need to know his emotions, what drives him to kill, how he feels and thinks. Even so, all I'll be able to give you is an educated opinion." He shifted in his chair and stroked his thin mustache. "Why don't you just start talking, tell me about the case from the time you were called to the first victim, and let me hear your professional observations."

Damn, but he didn't want to do this, Ray thought. Dispassionately, he briefed the shrink on the details of the case. It took him only three-and-a-half minutes to run through the facts as he saw them.

A man who didn't waste words, Dr. Delaney thought as he caught Ray's frown. "Look, I know you're not convinced I can help. I don't want to be here any more than you want me here."

Ray had the good grace to look chagrined. He reached for a large envelope. He wouldn't apologize for his skepticism, but he would cooperate, on the off chance that the shrink could pick up on something they'd missed. He owed that much to the victims and to their families. "I can't let this evidence out of my hands, but here are the mass cards he leaves on the bodies, the wires, the broken chain pieces."

Delaney studied the contents of each plastic envelope carefully.

"We've got a sketchy physical profile. The lab has two hairs taken from under the fingernails of one victim. We think this guy's medium height, brown-haired, Caucasian, twenty-five to forty-five."

"A big, strong man, would you say?"

"Not necessarily. The severity of the wire cutting into the neck suggests strength and even height, but the victims may have been kneeling or crouching. We believe he's had the element of surprise on his side in at least three of the cases. There was no struggle there, nothing to indicate the victims tried to defend themselves in any way. The fourth was strangled, then dumped into a backyard pool, so we're not sure where he killed her or the circumstances surrounding the act. And he could be high on adrenaline."

"Or religious fervor."

Ray leaned back in his chair. "You think he's an angry Catholic with an ax to grind with the church, taking it out on the nuns?"

Delaney set aside the evidence envelope. "From what I've heard and read so far here, I think he's a very troubled man. Repeatedly asking for forgiveness indicates a tortured soul, not necessarily an angry person."

"You think it's sexual? Most serial murders are, when they're random, though he hasn't assaulted any one of the women."

"No seminal fluid found on or around the victims?"

Ray shook his head. "He merely happens upon them and zaps them."

"Actually, I doubt that. I think he chooses his victims first, then stalks them, waiting for his chance. It can't be coincidence that all four were blond and blue-eyed."

So he'd picked up on that, Ray thought. "Yeah, we've thought of that. But it's not easy to stalk a nun. With the exception of one of these victims, their world was pretty much limited to church, school, and convent. We've checked out every man, woman, and child connected to St. Matthews in any capacity, and they're all clean."

"How about the altar boys? Some of them are in their late teens. How about parishioners, volunteers? Family members of the victims?"

Ray ran a weary hand across his face. "The investigation is ongoing. The number of people you refer to is well over two thousand."

"I can appreciate what a task that must be." Dr. Delaney stood, picking up the manila folder. "Can I take these and study them?"

"Sure. I had those copies made for you."

"Thanks. I'll call when I've finished my analysis." He glanced down at the paper airplane on the floor next to the waste basket, but decided not to comment.

Ray stood. "What's your gut feeling so far?"

Delaney tapped the folder on the back of the chair. "Notice the dates? Closer together each time. I'd say he's coming unglued pretty rapidly."

Ray's frown returned. "So he'll kill again."

"That would be my guess. And soon."

Terrific. Ray watched the doctor walk away while the knot in his stomach tightened.

It was a beautiful Sunday in May, the sun shining down on the parking lot at St. Matthews. The area had been cleared of cars and cordoned off to accommodate six amusement park rides, as well as booths selling ethnic food—German, Polish, and Hungarian—a large tent offering games of chance, crafts for sale, and an ongoing bingo game.

At one of the outdoor booths, Rosie Pulaski expertly turned the kielbasa she was frying, the heat from the small burner reddening her cheeks. It was so nice to see so many folks enjoying the day, she thought, putting behind them the awful business of those poor nuns getting killed. Satisfied with the progress of the sausage, she turned to stir the sauerkraut, a bright smile on her broad face. Rosie loved the spring fundraising festivals the church put on each year.

"Rosie," Father Hilliard called out, strolling to her booth. "I headed straight here for your wonderful sandwich. Nobody makes kielbasa like you do."

"Hello, Father," she beamed. Over her shoulder, she gestured to her friend, Helen Koberski. "Fix a special for Father, will you, Helen?" She turned back to the priest. "It's good to see so many people out, yeah, Father?"

"It is indeed." The older priest's face was deeply etched with worry lines, several new ones since all the trouble had begun in his parish. He was seriously contemplating early retirement. The fear that gripped his people was wearing heavily on him, and he was losing confidence in his ability to minister to them.

Rosie's friend, Helen, was taller than Rosie and quite thin. But her smile was just as wide as she handed the priest a paper plate piled high with a mouth-watering lunch. *"Smacznego!"* she said in Polish. "Enjoy, Father."

"Thank you." He reached for his wallet.

Rosie stopped him. "Your money's no good here, Father. It's on the house."

"Are you sure?" he asked. Every year for as far back as he could remember, these two little ladies had contributed their wonderful Polish food to help raise money for the school, and had never accepted a dime from him.

"Go on with you," Helen said, waving him along as she wiped her hands on her apron, then turned to serve a paying customer.

SHATTERED VOWS

Rosie rolled her shoulders as she plopped the cooked sausage into the keep-warm cooker, then put on another fresh batch to brown. Only 2:00 P.M., yet her feet were burning and beads of sweat were trailing down between her heavy breasts. If the kids in the school didn't need so much, she'd quit volunteering.

As she reached for another loaf of bread, she saw a young man approaching the booth, and her smile quickly returned. "Wladek, you made it."

Her tenant strolled over, his brown hair neatly combed, his short-sleeved shirt freshly pressed. He smiled at her. "How's my favorite girl, Rosie?"

She forgot her sore feet and felt like a teenager again. "I'm fine. You're looking spiffy." She glanced over his shoulder. "No girlfriend again this year?"

His dark eyes laughed at her. *"You're* my only girlfriend." Leaning forward, he inhaled the tantalizing aromas. "Can I have one of your specials, with a big pickle, please?" Looking past her, he waved to Helen, who smiled at him.

"Sure, sure." Rosie shuffled about, fixing his plate herself. "You been in the tents yet? Lots of nice prizes this year." She spooned a dollop of horseradish sauce alongside the sausage she'd placed on a large slice of Russian rye.

"Yeah." He reached into his pocket. "I won something for you pitching balls at milk bottles." He held out a pale pink handkerchief with deeper pink crocheting around the edges, the whole thing wrapped in cellophane.

Rosie finished scooping a generous portion of sauerkraut on his plate and turned back to him. Her eyes widened at the lovely gift. "Why, you sweet boy." She looked up at him. "Are you sure you don't want to give that to your mama?"

A shadow passed over his face and he quickly shook his head as he held the handkerchief out to her. "My mama's gone. This is for you."

Rosie handed him the plate and took the small package, holding it reverently. Rosie didn't get many presents anymore, large or small. Her priest son sent her more rosaries than she could use, and her married son sent a check. The money helped, but the fact that he didn't take the time to pick out something special for her hurt. "It's beautiful. Thank you."

Wladek was once more his smiling self. "Sure." He held out a five dollar bill.

She waved it away. "I can't take that. You enjoy your lunch."

Pocketing the money, he thanked her. "Think I'll go get some root beer. See you later, Rosie."

Holding the hankie to her nose, she realized it smelled like his aftershave. Like her own son, the boy was. More thoughtful than her own sons, really.

"We're not going to have much to give Father if you keep giving away everything free," Helen groused.

"Oh, hush," Rosie said, bending to place her precious gift in her black purse beneath the counter. "When your daughter and her four kids come, we give them each free, too, no?"

Helen shook her head. "Yeah, I guess."

"So, okay." Happy, Rosie returned to her frying pan.

It was Monday evening and he felt bone-tired. Ray stepped out of the shower and grabbed a towel.

SHATTERED VOWS

It'd been a bear of a day, with every cuckoo in the free world stumbling into the Beaubien precinct over the last twelve hours. He'd needed to clear his head, so he'd called Mark and played a little basketball. They'd spent a couple of hours shooting hoops and Ray was pleased at the kid's progress.

At least in basketball. On the home front, it wasn't so good. Mark's mother's fiancé had broken off their engagement, which had pleased Mark, but Dr. Abigail McCarthy definitely hadn't been happy. When he'd arrived at the pretentious English tudor, she'd taken Ray aside and told him she felt he was responsible for the breakup of her relationship.

That had floored him. He'd had it on the tip of his tongue to tell her to go stick it, but Mark had been standing on the porch. Instead, he'd turned his back to the boy and very quietly told the good doctor that perhaps it was high time she took responsibility, not only for her failed relationships but for her troubled son. As her bright red mouth had turned into a hard, grim line, he'd signaled Mark to join him, climbed into his wagon, and driven off. In his rear-view mirror, he'd watched with no small amount of satisfaction as she'd stomped back into her three-story home.

Ray wrapped the towel around his waist and left the bathroom. Hamlet was waiting for him outside, and he bent to pat his large head. "Miss me today, boy?" The dog looked up with soulful brown eyes. "Yeah, I guess so."

He padded barefoot downstairs and into his kitchen, Hamlet on his heels. He wasn't hungry; he'd taken Mark to the golden arches after their workout and they'd both stuffed themselves. But all that great, greasy food had made him thirsty. He popped the tab on a Bud Light and took a long swallow. Then he walked into the living room, stretched out in his Barcalounger, and picked up the phone.

He had a night off and, if he got lucky, he might be able to persuade Toni to come over.

She wasn't at the restaurant so he tried her at home. He was about to hang up when she answered, her voice sleepy. "I'm sorry if I woke you."

On the couch in the enclosed back porch with the blinds drawn, Toni stretched lazily. "It's all right. I fell asleep reading, I guess. It's catching up with me, I think."

He gave up hope that she'd drive over. "I'm sure you can use the rest. How'd your day go?"

"Fine. Uneventful. Tiring. Anything new?"

He hated it that every time they talked, the subject of the stranglings came up. But he couldn't blame her for needing to know. He told her about Dr. Delaney and the fact that the lab had sent another report that indicated that the trace substance on the brown hairs *might* be a type of chemical fertilizer. "Do you know when your back lawn was fertilized last?"

Toni brushed back her hair, sitting up. "No. We have a gardener. I'll ask Dad. You think it might have blown into the pool under that heavy cover?"

"It could have. Or its possible the killer works as a landscaper. Of course, he could have passed a truck carrying some kind of fertilizer that blew into his hair." The possibilities were endless and inconclusive. Ray tipped back the can and drank deeply.

"I see." She stifled a yawn. "I got something in the mail today that at first startled me. But I'm glad to have it, nonetheless."

"What's that?"

"Mo's gold chain and her cross. Someone must

have found it and sent it to me. The clasp is off, but the rest is intact. Mom gave it to her ages ago and—"

"Say that again." Ray sat up in the chair, his heartbeat accelerating.

"I said that I got Mo's gold chain and cross in the mail and—"

"Did you keep the envelope?"

"What? I don't think so. Why, is it important?"

He'd never told Toni about the necklaces missing from the other victims. The sonofabitch was toying with them. "I need to pick that up, Toni. Do you think you could find the envelope?"

"Probably. I opened the mail in the kitchen. I think it's in the garbage can there." She hesitated. "What's this about?"

Already standing, he told her about the killer's M.O. and heard her gasp. "Don't be alarmed. I'm coming right over. Are your folks home?"

"No." Toni scrambled to her feet, wide awake now. She narrowed her eyes, trying to see through the blinds that covered the three walls of windows on the porch. Was he out there, the person who'd sent her Mo's necklace, the man who'd strangled her cousin? Was he watching her now?

Ray heard the fear in her voice and nearly swore out loud. "Is your security alarm set?"

"Yes. I always set it the minute I walk in."

"Good. Wait for me. Try to handle the envelope by its edges and don't touch the chain anymore. I'm on my way." He slammed down the phone and turned the air blue as he raced upstairs to dress. Hamlet loped after him, his ears raised as he sensed his master's alarm.

* * *

The same block lettering as the mass cards, printed on a common white envelope in blue ballpoint ink. Couldn't be more ordinary than that. Whatever else the creep was, he was damn cautious. Ray took hold of the envelope with two fingertips at one corner and dropped it into a plastic evidence bag, even though he was pretty certain they'd find no prints.

Standing in the glare of the kitchen light, he turned to Toni. She was wearing a blue denim shirt that hung down almost to the hemline of her white shorts, its sleeves rolled up over her slender arms. Those arms were crossed over her chest in a defensive gesture by now familiar to him.

She'd let him in moments before, and had silently led him to the kitchen table. He'd wanted to take her in his arms, to offer some small measure of comfort for the fear he saw reflected in her face. But her stiff demeanor didn't welcome the intrusion. He could see a nervous muscle twitch near one eye as she looked up at him. "I didn't even think to connect the printing to the mass cards. How could I have been so stupid?"

Giving in, he slipped an arm around her slim shoulders and felt her tremble. "Because you're not used to seeing something sinister at every turn."

"What kind of a sicko are we dealing with here, a man who collects souvenirs from the women he kills?"

"It's not as uncommon as you might think."

Toni stared at the gold chain and cross still on the table. "Mo was so happy the day Mom gave her that, the day she'd taken her vows. It ... it belonged to Mo's own mother." She turned in Ray's arms, pressing her cheek into his chest, and closed her eyes as he tightened his hold on her.

Ray was running out of words of comfort. Usually, he kept his distance from the families of victims. Usually, it wasn't up to the police to offer comfort. But this wasn't a usual case.

He could tell she wasn't crying, but through their embrace he felt her labored breathing, her chest rising and falling rhythmically. He hadn't wanted to care for her, but he knew that he did. He didn't love her, of course.

Ray Vargas didn't fall in love. Love wasn't something he gave much thought to. He'd seen what loving Marianne had done to his father. She'd used and abused his father shamefully, all in the name of love. His father had claimed to love both Ray and Pete, but his obsession with his young wife had caused him to neglect his two sons.

Then there'd been the woman he'd married, Ray thought, bitterness seeping into him all over again. Sharon had claimed to love him, and all the while she'd been sleeping with God-only-knew how many guys. Love was a word invented by Hallmark and perpetuated by FTD. It didn't belong in Ray's vocabulary.

Nevertheless, he felt for Toni, wanted to ease her grief, her pain, and now, her fear. He stepped back from her, wondering how to tell her to be even more careful without scaring the hell out of her. "Listen, I'm a little concerned that this guy mailed this to you. Apparently, he knows that you and Mo were related. First the pool, now this."

Toni sighed deeply. "It's like a message, isn't it? A warning. But why me? I'm not a nun and he seems to have singled out nuns."

So far, Ray thought. He stuck his restless hands

into his jeans pocket. "I wish I knew why." He followed her into the dim family room where only one lamp was burning. "How's your security system at the Glass Door?"

Toni curled up in the corner of the pastel floral couch. "We've never had a problem with it. We set it at night and disconnect it each morning."

But during the day, anyone could come and go. Someone pretending to be a customer, a delivery person; someone who hired on as a waiter so he could watch her. *He* knew what *she* looked like, but they couldn't recognize him. "I think I'd like to stop in tomorrow and look through your personnel files."

"All right. What are you looking for?"

He pulled a leather hassock close to her, sat down and rested his elbows on his knees. "I'm not sure. Something that doesn't fit, that jumps out at me." He gave her a physical description of the killer, based on what they knew so far. "That fits hundreds of men, thousands. But maybe there's someone new on your staff. I want to weed out the guys who resemble what I've just told you, and new employees especially. It's not much, but we have to start somewhere."

"Other than that, we just pray he doesn't decide to kill another nun or come after me before you get him, right?"

"Praying's *your* department. Mine is the slow, methodical elimination of possibles until we get to probables."

"Comforting." Threading her fingers through her hair, she turned to gaze out into the gloomy night. There was no moon and even the streetlights seemed muted. The large trees out front were in full foliage now, casting vague dancing shadows that skittered across the lawn in a light breeze. Toni shivered.

Ray reached out to take her hand. "I wish I could make all this go away, Toni."

She felt suddenly contrite. None of this was Ray's fault, yet she'd been making him feel as if it were. "You've been great. I'm sorry. I guess I'm just in a mood."

He eased alongside her, pulling her to him. "You have every right to be." He could suggest no alternatives. She was as safe in her parents' home and in her work place as she was likely to be. She couldn't hole up somewhere until it was over, and he couldn't keep her with him every hour of the day and night. His mind raced around, trying to come up with answers. "Why don't you have an answering machine here at the house?"

"Dad hates them."

"Could you talk him into one? I'd feel a lot better if you let the machine pick up everything, and report to me any unusual calls. Count the hangups, too."

"You think he'd call here?"

"I doubt it. These are just precautions. Have your father record the message, brief and businesslike. Don't let anyone on the staff bring anyone to your office unless they've cleared the person with you ahead of time. Don't drive anywhere alone. Get a car phone. Lock your doors. Don't—"

"Don't live, don't enjoy. But don't worry." She lowered her head, her hair curtaining her face. "Oh God, Ray. When is this going to end?"

Rather than try to answer, he brought her back into his arms and took her mouth. She responded instantly, her lips open, and her tongue warm. Her kiss thrilled him, as always.

But again, he wondered if she really wanted *him*, or someone, anyone, to kiss away the pain.

EIGHT

"Toni, are you awake?" John Garette asked from his daughter's bedroom doorway.

Blinking toward the shaft of light coming in from the hallway, Toni brushed back her hair and turned over. "I am now. What's wrong, Dad?"

"It's your mother. She's vomiting blood." His voice was unsteady, unsure. "Do you think we should call the doctor?"

Already out of bed, Toni grabbed her robe and pulled it on as she hurried to the bedroom her parents shared. She found Jane lying on the pale peach sheets, her face a startling white. "Mom, how long has this been going on?"

Before Jane could answer, John's voice came from behind Toni. "She tells me over a week, but never as bad as tonight."

"I'll be all right after I rest a bit," Jane said, sounding frail. "I probably broke a blood vessel."

"No," John insisted. "There was too much blood for it to be just a broken vessel."

"Was it bright red?" Toni asked, recalling a first aid class she'd taken ages ago. Bright red blood indicated something entirely different from dark, almost black blood. She saw her father nod, then walked over to the opposite night stand. Well aware that her father's characteristic strength failed him when it came to his wife, she knew she'd have to take over. She opened the drawer, found the address book her folks kept there, and flipped through its pages. Quickly, she picked up the phone.

"What are you doing?" Jane asked.

"I'm calling Dr. Jonas."

"No, Toni," Jane protested weakly. "Don't fuss."

Dialing, Toni ignored her mother and waited impatiently for their family doctor to answer his private line. The bedside clock showed just past two in the morning. She prayed the doctor was home and was relieved when he answered. She explained the situation and listened to Dr. Jonas's response. "Fine. We'll leave immediately."

Toni hung up. "Mom, I'll help you dress. Dr. Jonas will meet us at the emergency room at Bon Secour." The hospital was only ten minutes away.

"I'll help her dress, Toni," John said, coming to life now that there was a plan of action. "You go change."

"I hate to be such a bother," Jane murmured. Yet she had to admit she was concerned. The pain had deepened and the amount of bleeding had put the fear of God in her.

"You need to be looked at, Mom," Toni said, smoothing her mother's hair back from her forehead. "This isn't going to go away without treatment."

"All right, if you think so." Jane sat up, resigned to the situation.

Toni studied her father and decided he was capable of getting them both ready. "I'll put some clothes on and be right back." Already removing her robe, she hurried to her room.

SHATTERED VOWS 151

* * *

Ray stood at the one-way glass and watched Meg interact with six-year-old Kimberly Everett, the little girl who'd told her mother she'd been molested. Also seated at the table with them was the girl's mother, Molly Everett, and Dora Haynes, a child psychologist. A physical exam by a medical doctor had confirmed Kimberly's claims. More than merely molested, bad as that was, the little girl had been raped. Ray ground his teeth. The report revealed that the child had been penetrated so deeply, her uterus had a tear at the crest. Kimberly was scheduled for surgery to repair the rip, but whether or not she'd ever be able to have children was still an unknown.

"You're not afraid of me, are you, Kimberly?" Meg asked.

The solemn-eyed child with the ponytail looked at Meg, but didn't answer. Her mother patted her hand while Mrs. Haynes smiled reassuringly.

Meg and Ray were both aware that Kimberly hadn't spoken to any police officer or to the psychologist since the day her mother had first brought her in. Molly Everett seemed desperate to find out who had harmed her child, but Kimberly seemed too traumatized to speak. All she'd ever said since that day was, "I want to go home."

"It's all right if you don't want to talk, Kimberly," Meg went on. "All of us here want to help you. You told Mommy that someone hurt you. We want to find out who, so that person will never hurt you again." She smiled warmly at the child, who kept studying her but didn't return the smile. "Just nod or shake your head if you know the answers to my questions, Kimberly. Tell me, do you know who hurt you?"

The little girl glanced at her mother, then looked back at Meg and slowly nodded.

"Good, that's good. Can you tell me, was it a man? A grown-up man?"

Again the glance at Molly and the slow nod.

The child psychologist had warned Meg before the session began that the young girl might freeze up at any moment or commence to cry, as she had at her office. Or she might react with a stoicism that belied her young years, repressing the experience. Meg attempted a process of elimination, since Kimberly's exposure to grown men had been limited.

"Was it your doctor, the one Mommy takes you to when you're sick?"

The girl shook her head no.

The Everetts were well off and lived in a large home off Lakeshore Drive in Grosse Pointe Shores. Dr. James Everett was a highly respected pediatric eye surgeon and Molly had come from money. "Was it someone who works at your house, someone who cuts the grass or delivers groceries?"

Kimberly's lips were pressed tightly together as she shook her head again.

Here goes nothing, Meg thought as she focused on the child, avoiding the mother's eyes. "Was it a man who lives with you, Kimberly? Your daddy, maybe?"

At that, Kimberly Everett let out a wild wail and buried her face in her mother's throat as her mother gasped, first in outrage, then in shock. The child's sobs were deep and painful to hear as Mrs. Everett, realization of her worst fears showing on her face, whispered in a trembling voice, "Oh my God. Please, no!"

Behind the glass, Ray's hands curled into fists. "The bastard," he said aloud, though no one else was in the room. Meg had suspected the father after her first attempt to get the girl to talk. Ray wished to hell she'd been wrong.

For another minute, he watched the child weep, joined now by the mother. Then Ray left the booth, hating his job today.

"Don't you think you should have gone with them?" Ray asked Meg. His partner had just returned, seating herself at her own desk opposite his, looking weary and angry at the same time.

"I couldn't insist," she said defensively. "Molly Everett wanted to go home and confront her husband herself. She's reeling from what she learned today."

"You mean to tell me she never suspected? Doesn't the woman read? Over half of child molestation cases involve a relative. Incest is getting as common as dirt water." He crushed his Styrofoam cup and tossed it into the basket. "Judas Priest, the woman's too damn smart to have her head in the sand."

"Maybe she doesn't. Maybe she just needs time to adjust."

"Or maybe she knew all along and looked the other way." Many a mother had, Ray thought, while the father methodically worked his way through each and every female child.

Meg didn't agree. "Give her a break, Ray. We don't know. Just because she has a degree and money doesn't mean she's smart. Or worldly. She could have had a sheltered upbringing. Besides, the medical report indicates that the abuse hasn't been going on for long."

He didn't feel like giving anyone a break today. The strangling case was gnawing at his nerves; he was worried about the madman possibly stalking Toni; Mark's mother was giving the kid a hard time about the hours he was spending with Ray; and the arsonist and possible murderer had been sprung out on bail by some shyster lawyer. No, he wasn't in a charitable mood. "Not going on for long? Is that supposed to make us feel kindly toward the good doctor? He saves kids' eyesight by day and screws his six-year-old daughter by night, and we're supposed to forgive him? *Once* is one time too many, Meg."

"I know that. And I didn't ask you to forgive him. But I couldn't *make* Molly let me go with her. The child didn't actually state that it was her father who raped her. That could be implied, given her reaction to the question I asked, but you know as well as I do that I can't make an arrest based on implications alone." Suddenly uncertain, Meg rubbed at a spot over one eye where a headache was threatening. "Maybe I'm out of my element here. I'm Homicide. What do I know about counseling kids? They put me on this because I'm a woman and for no other reason."

Ray felt contrite. He shouldn't have taken his shitty mood out on Meg. "You're not only a woman but a damn fine detective. I'm sorry I shot my mouth off. It's not you, or even this case. It's just everything." He attempted a smile. "Or maybe it's my time of the month." The phone on his desk rang and Ray reached for it, glad for the interruption.

"Ray? It's Toni. Have you got a minute?"

She sounded uncharacteristically subdued, and he was immediately concerned. "Toni, what's wrong? Where are you?"

"I'm at Bon Secours. Dad and I brought Mom in around three in the morning. They've diagnosed her with bleeding ulcers."

Just what they needed. "How's she doing now?"

"We won't know for a while. I just donated some blood for her." At the phone cubicle outside Jane Garette's room, Toni sighed deeply. "The doctor says we have to eliminate worry and stress from her life. Jesus, how do we do that, especially with that maniac still on the loose? Mom had a flare-up of this same thing years ago, when Mo's mother died. But she's been fine until these stranglings began."

What could he possibly say that would ease her mind? "I wish I could tell you we've got the sonofabitch behind bars."

Toni felt the push of tears behind her burning eyelids. She was tired, worried, scared. "Can't you tell me anything? Have you got any new leads? This . . . this animal is destroying my family. Are you at least any closer to getting him?" Her voice was agitated, beyond her attempts to control it.

Ray couldn't do much about alleviating her fears. Or his own. He wished to hell he had answers for her. "No, Toni," he said quietly. "Nothing new. There were no prints on the gold chain and only smudges on the cross. Still nothing for us to go on."

She felt deflated suddenly, left with little hope and too many problems not of her making. "I knew you'd say that. I don't know why I called."

"Do you want me to meet you there?"

"What for?" She brushed back her hair, wanting nothing more right now than to go home and hide in her bed under the covers, childish as she knew that to be. "I'll be all right. Sorry I bothered you." She hung up and slowly walked back to her mother's room.

"Toni, wait . . ." But then Ray realized he was listening to a dial tone; he swore inventively. What the hell was he supposed to do, work miracles? Whip a rabbit out of a hat who'd lead them down the yellow brick road to the killer, just waiting to be caught?

"Ray," the desk sergeant said from the doorway, "someone to see you."

Ray slammed down the receiver and turned to glance into the hall waiting area. Mort Ziltzer was sitting on the edge of a wooden chair in his baggie chinos and filthy tennis shoes, a hopeful look on his scruffy face. The perfect topper to an already perfect day, Ray thought.

He felt like going out and getting drunk. Not roaring drunk, but the peaceful, slide-off-the-chair, roll-onto-the-floor-and-go-to-sleep kind. Except he was on duty. And he was a man unused to shirking his responsibilities.

"Send him home, Ray," Meg advised.

Ray got up, knowing he couldn't possibly send the poor misfit home. Walking as if he carried the weight of the world on his shoulders, he went to meet Mort.

The man stood up as Ray reached him. "I hate to bother you, Detective Vargas, but I wanted you to know how bad it is. You gotta do somethin' with her."

"Come with me, Mort." Ray led the way down the hall into an empty office, wondering how the woman who rented the apartment above Ziltzer managed to put up with his constant complaints.

"Now she's got a blender, see," Mort went on.

"It's buzzin' and whirrin' all the time." He shuffled after Ray. "A man can't think with all that racket going on. You gotta do somethin'."

The Olds needed a tuneup and a new muffler, and he still hadn't replaced the headlight, Wally thought as he drove toward a new job across town. He'd have to have the car taken care of real soon, because the cops stopped vehicles in such condition. He couldn't afford that. Nosy cops might get suspicious, ask a lot of questions he didn't want to answer.

He glanced in his rearview mirror and saw no cop cars around. He'd be okay. The Lord would watch out for him until his mission was completed. No one suspected him, a friendly guy with a ready smile who lived above the little widow lady, Rosie. Wally stopped for a light, thinking of his cheerful landlady. She called him Wladek, which was Polish, he knew. It had been her father's name, she'd told him. He knew Rosie really liked him, and he felt good about it.

His own mother hadn't liked him. She'd given him the Olds years ago, and it hadn't run all that well back then. She'd bought Clark, his older brother, a brand-new car. Wally didn't get good grades in school like Clark. Mama had yelled at him constantly as far back as he could remember. Wally, you like the girls too much. Wally, you like to stay out late. Wally, you never get your chores done. Wally, you hang around with bums. On and on she'd ranted and raved.

Mama hadn't approved of anyone he knew, not until Terry. She'd loved Terry almost as much as he had. Finally, she'd been happy with him, smiling, inviting his girl to dinner. Everything would have been all right if only ...

If only he hadn't gotten impatient, letting the evil take over. If only Angie hadn't told on him. If only Terry had forgiven him.

The light changed and Wally stepped on the gas. No use thinking about all that. It would never be all right again, not really. He had to move on, to complete his mission. The dreams were starting again, the pressure building. Soon it would be time. He'd have to be more careful, though. The cops weren't real bright, but they were persistent. He'd seen how they were constantly buzzing around St. Matthews. The Reverend Mother cluck-clucked around her nuns like a shepherd herding in the sheep.

But he was smarter, Wally knew. They wouldn't catch him until he was good and ready. Until he was finished. The thought pleased him. He'd have smiled, except his head was beginning to hurt.

He turned the Olds into the employee parking lot of Mt. Carmel Hospital on Detroit's west side, parked, and turned off the engine. He was lucky that jobs were plentiful in his line of work, and no one asked questions when he quit suddenly. He got bored easily and didn't like to stay in one place day after day. Owners of small landscaping companies liked guys who didn't ask for benefits and didn't mind being paid under the table. That saved them money. He always found a job when he needed one at schools, hospitals, churches, and even private homes. Because he was good with growing things.

For a moment, he rested his head on the steering wheel, feeling tired and headachey. There was no rest for the wicked. Mama used to tell him that. He had work to do and he mustn't give in to the weaknesses of the flesh. Praying for strength, Wally got out and walked toward the service door.

She missed him. It was that simple, and that complicated, Toni thought as she drove down the expressway on her way home from the Brass Door.

She'd spent the whole day unpacking things, setting up her new office, filling in where help was needed as the new chef arranged his kitchen. She felt hot, but pleasantly tired. The new place was coming along fine, her mother was out of the hospital and resting comfortably at home. And yet, she felt a sense of unease. She hadn't stopped to think why until she'd started the long, solitary drive home.

She missed Ray.

She'd been horrid to him three days ago when she'd called at the precinct, then proceeded to hang up on him when he hadn't provided the answers she'd wanted to hear. That had been rude and uncalled for, and decidedly unlike her. Ordinarily, she'd chalk it up to fatigue and worry. But it was one thing to excuse yourself and quite another to expect someone else to do the same. Without an apology.

Decision made, she put her right blinker on and aimed the Mercedes toward the off ramp that would lead her to Ray's house. It was late May, 7:00 P.M., not yet quite dark. She had no way of knowing if he'd be home, but she decided to chance it. If he wasn't, perhaps she'd leave him a note. It was better than letting this go on. Minutes later, on his porch, she rang the bell repeatedly. Hamlet, his front feet up on the couchback normally forbidden him, his nose plastered to the picture window, greeted her with his deep bark. Ray's wagon was parked in the side drive. Maybe he'd gone for a walk, or a run. Or . . .

Toni smiled. That was probably it. He was at the park two blocks down playing basketball with Mark. She decided to walk over.

The lights illuminated the far court where a slim boy and a tall man were shooting hoops. At the cyclone fence, she stopped to watch, far enough away that she didn't think either could easily see her.

Ray was wearing a gray sweatshirt and cutoffs, as was Mark, almost as if the boy had deliberately copied the man's attire. He was several inches short of Ray's six three, all skinny legs and thick sandy hair. Slowly, he dribbled the ball feinting left, then right, trying to keep Ray from getting control. Suddenly, he shifted to the left, leaped high in the air, and aimed a fast one. It sailed through the hoop, clean as a whistle.

Pleased, Mark jumped up again in celebration. Ray sprinted over and thumped his shoulder, offering congratulations. "Way to go," he said. The kid grinned, something he'd been doing more of lately.

Ray checked his watch. He'd better get Mark home and not give his mother more reasons to complain. "You probably have homework to do yet tonight, right?"

Mark wiped his warm face in his sleeve. "Yeah, a little. But I can do it later."

"Finals next week. I think we'd better call it a night." Seeing the disappointment the boy tried to hide, Ray rushed to reassure him. "Maybe we can get in another evening of chess in a couple of days, okay?" The boy was good, possessing a keen intelligence. He'd beaten Ray soundly in their last session.

"Sure." Mark looked up and spotted Toni leaning against the fence post. Immediately, he turned self-conscious and shy, lost control of the ball he'd been bouncing, and ran off after it.

Ray turned, saw Toni, and moved to the edge of the court. She was wearing her Reeboks with pink cotton slacks and a loose T-shirt that read DARE TO BE DIFFERENT beneath three dalmation pups with pink dots. He hadn't been expecting her, and was surprised how the sight of her warmed him. He wished it didn't. "Hi."

"Hi. I came to apologize." She thought his gray eyes looked inscrutable and a little cool, and wondered if he was angry with her. "I've been rude to just about everyone lately. I'm sorry."

He shrugged. It wasn't her rudeness that bothered him. It was his unexpected pleasure at seeing her. "Don't worry about it."

She touched his arm lightly. "But I do. I shouldn't have jumped on your case. You, of all people, who has helped me the most. I just feel so ... so frustrated."

"Join the club." He turned and motioned Mark over, then introduced them. "I have to drive Mark home. Will you wait for me with Hamlet?"

His eyes were still guarded, but no longer cool, Toni noticed. "I'd like that." She swung in step with them as they walked back to Ray's place. "You two look pretty good out there."

"Next year, Mark's going to make the team, right, buddy?"

The boy shrugged shyly, ducking his head.

Ray kept up a line of chatter in an effort to put Mark at ease, but his mind was on Toni. Had she come to him to apologize, or seeking reassurance or comfort? Or had she come to him because she honestly missed his company? And, the even bigger question, why did that matter so much to him?

On the porch, he unlocked the door as Mark got into his wagon. Hamlet rushed out to greet them, then bounded over to visit a bush before following them inside. "Make yourself at home,." Ray told her. "There's a pitcher of iced tea on the counter and beer in the fridge. I'll be back in twenty minutes."

He watched a mysterious smile form on her face as she bent down to pet his dog. Somewhat baffled, Ray left.

He was back in nineteen minutes, twelve seconds, by his watch. Letting himself in the back way after putting his wagon in the garage, he wondered why Hamlet wasn't there at the door to meet him. By the time he got to the foot of the stairs, he thought he might have stumbled on the answer.

One Reebok was on the bottom step, the other halfway up. He could see her pink slacks draped over the upper banister, where Hamlet sat at attention, his big brown eyes curious. In a playful mood, was she?

Ray took the steps two at a time and heard the shower start up as he reached the top. In the middle of the hallway lay her T-shirt, and hanging on the bathroom doorknob was her bra. Grinning now, he turned to Hamlet, who had moved to his side. "Sorry, boy, you're going to have to sit this one out." The dog cocked his head, as if hurt not to be included, then circled around and went to lie down nearby.

Ray stepped into the steamy room. Red silken underpants were on the tile floor next to his blue rug.

He could just make out a shadowy form behind the glass shower door. He set a record for stripping off his clothes, then opened the door. She was standing under the spray, her golden hair plastered to her head, a bar of soap in her hand and an invitation in her eyes. He stepped in.

He didn't waste time on preliminaries but moved under the water and pulled her into a deep, open-mouthed kiss. She dropped the soap.

They hadn't been together in far too long and he was hungry for her. Her little seduction scene had worked. He was hard and ready in seconds. His hands went exploring as eagerly as her own. He backed her up against the tile wall and gripped her bottom, then he lifted her. She wrapped her long, slender legs around his waist and he plunged inside, long and deep, his eyes closed as he filled her. Completely joined with her, he slowed, kissing her again, letting her adjust to him.

She'd taken a hell of a chance, Toni thought as ripples of desire skittered along her nerve endings. If he hadn't reacted exactly as he had, she'd have had egg on her face and a lot of explaining to do. In all her life, she'd never deliberately seduced a man, just like she'd never sought one out and all but thrown herself at him. Twice now, she'd done that with Ray.

What was there about him that drove her to this uncharacteristic behavior? she wondered even as her lips sought his.

She'd never dreamed it could be so exciting, kissing a man with a beard. The hair on his face was soft to the touch and his mouth was hard, aggressive, unrelenting. She kissed him back with a rising passion, recognizing his special taste, already so very familiar. Then she moaned low in her throat as he began the rhythm, and arched to meet his thrusts.

She wanted it to go on and on, and held off as long as she could. Finally, she crested so fiercely that she almost stopped breathing. Her head fell to his shoulder as she went limp in his arms.

Bracing against the wall, Ray closed his eyes and felt himself splinter as the aftershock waves gripped him. Water splashed and slid down their slippery bodies, yet he scarcely was aware of it. He knew only Toni, felt only Toni, thought only of Toni.

He didn't want to let go of her and she seemed perfectly willing to stay where she was. But his knees were none too steady, so he slowly released her. "You sure know how to get my attention," he said, watching her thread her fingers back through her wet hair.

"I'm a conservationist, didn't you know? I knew you needed a shower and I certainly did. Why waste water?" Sliding her arms around his neck, she drew him back for another long, thorough kiss.

He was loving it, but the water was already cooling. Stepping back, he found the soap and began running it over her body, stopping to admire how beautifully she was made. As he rinsed her off, his mouth dipped to catch the drips from the points of her breasts, and he felt a rush of renewed interest. He made quick work of sudsing himself and rinsing off before stepping out and grabbing two towels.

"Let me," Toni said, joining him on the blue rug and reaching up to towel-dry him. But before she was even half finished, he had her in his arms and was carrying her to his bed. "We're going to get your bed all wet," she warned as he lay her down.

"I don't care." He was already hot, hard, and

throbbing. His mouth locked to hers, he raised himself above her and slipped inside.

They took their time and ended together in a shattering climax. Afterward, still damp but temporarily sated, Ray shifted to his back and moved her on top of him, still joined together. "I'm really glad you decided to drop by," he whispered.

"Mmm, so am I."

"Was it really just to apologize?" He didn't know what else he wanted to hear, just knew he wanted more.

Toni propped her elbows on his chest and met his questioning gaze. "That was part of it."

"What's the rest?"

She knew exactly what it was, had known for some time, but hadn't admitted it even to herself. She'd suspected even before she'd gone to bed with him the first time. She was falling in love with him, and the news didn't thrill her.

She feigned avid interest in playing with the hair on his chest, dropping her eyes. "I missed you. There, I've said it."

He digested that a long minute. "And you're not pleased that you do, is that it?"

Sighing, Toni disengaged herself and shifted to her back. "You could say that. I really didn't want to get involved with anyone, as I told you a while back. But . . ."

When she didn't go on, he decided to prompt her. "But?"

She curled toward him, raising a hand to caress his beard. "But I find that, despite my best efforts to stay away, here I am again."

His arms encircled her, drawing her closer. "I'm glad."

Her eyes darkened, growing serious. "Are you?

Are you really?" He had been just as adamant about no involvements. Had he changed his mind? Was she in this all alone? Would he admit to his feelings, whatever they were?

"Yes." He studied her, trying to read her thoughts. "I didn't go looking for this either. But whatever's between us is damn hard to ignore, wouldn't you say?"

After what she'd just experienced in his arms, could she deny that? "Yes, it is."

"What are we going to do about it?" he asked, wondering what his own answer to that question would be.

The ringing bedside phone prevented Toni from having to reply. Reaching over, Ray grabbed it, already frowning. Late evening calls were rarely good news. "Vargas."

He listened for several seconds. "Where did you say?" Again he listened, his frown deepening. He scarcely noticed Toni easing back as he sat up. "Right. I'll meet you there." He hung up quietly.

"What is it?" Toni asked, afraid of the answer.

"That was Meg. There's been another strangling, on the west side this time, at a Catholic hospital."

"Oh my God," Toni whispered as Ray walked to his closet.

NINE

"What do you mean, this one's different?" Toni wanted to know as she shrugged into the shirt Ray handed her.

"First, the location's some distance from the strangler's usual area. Even though Sister Bernie was killed some ways from St. Matthews, she did teach there." Ray zipped up his slacks and reached into the closet for a clean shirt. "This victim's a Felician nursing nun working the night shift at Mt. Carmel Mercy Hospital, Meg tells me."

Toni buttoned the shirt as she sat cross-legged on the bed, watching him. "Apparently, he's branching out. Or he's run out of blond, blue-eyed nuns from St. Matthews."

Tucking in his shirt, Ray walked to his dresser, picked out a pair of socks, and sat down in his bentwood rocker to put them on. "The other thing is that there's a witness who believes he saw the guy."

"Oh, thank God. This could be it." Tossing back her hair, Toni wondered if she should go home or wait for him here. She wanted to get the news on the latest murder as soon as possible.

"Maybe, maybe not." Ray went back to the closet for his loafers. "Witnesses, especially in high-profile cases, can be unreliable. Everyone wants to help catch a murderer. Sometimes they'll say things they think you want to hear."

"But Meg has him there and is questioning him?"

Ray grabbed a tie, looped it under his collar, and reached for his sportcoat. "The witness is there, but Meg's meeting me at the scene. We'll undoubtedly question him together." He gathered his wallet, loose change, and keys from the dresser and turned to her as he pocketed them. "I shouldn't be more than a couple of hours." He longed for a repeat of the one night she'd spent with him. "Why don't you . . ."

"Why don't I go with you? I can get dressed quickly and I won't be in your way, I promise." She sent him what she hoped was a pleading look.

"I can't allow a civilian on the scene, Toni." Nor would he take her if he could. She was too close to this case. The killer had a line on her. Ray couldn't take a chance that the strangler might still be on the premises. Mt. Carmel was a big hospital. "Will you wait?"

She could tell there was no further argument that would move him. "Probably. If it gets late, will you call?"

"If I can." He leaned down and touched his mouth to hers, torn between being on his way and staying with her. Rotten timing, that call. He could see the tops of her breasts through the unbuttoned opening of the shirt. How could she look so damn sexy wearing his clothes?

Toni felt him trail two fingers along her cheek, then he hurried out. Hamlet bounded in as he opened the door, then reversed himself after checking her out and racing after Ray. She heard the backdoor slam shut and in moments, Hamlet was back. He greeted her bare foot with a long lick, then lay down on the floor alongside the bed.

With a sigh, Toni scooted back toward the headboard and picked up Ray's pillow, hugging it to her as she breathed in his scent. But instead of thinking of her lover, her mind was across town in a distant hospital where another savage murder had taken place.

A shudder raced through her as she closed her eyes at the thought.

The men from forensics were patiently brushing their black dust over every possible surface of the nurses' station on the fourth floor as Ray ducked under the crime-scene tape cordoning off the area.

Meg gestured to him immediately. She and Dennis lived in a two-story condo on the west side, not more than five miles from Mt. Carmel. She'd arrived an hour ago. "The hospital staff has evacuated patients in the immediate area and moved them to other rooms. This floor's already been thoroughly searched. Half a dozen uniforms are starting to check out the other floors. I don't hold out much hope that we'll find anything though."

"You never know, Meg," he told her. "The guy's got to make a mistake sometime." He walked around to the other side of the nurses' desk and bent down to pull back the sheet someone had placed over the body.

The nun wore the same abbreviated habit of skirt, blouse, and jacket, but with a nurse's cap pinned onto her blond hair. She was slender and pretty, somewhere in her late twenties. The by now familiar green wire was still twisted around her neck as she lay on her back with one leg bent under her.

Ray surmised that she'd fallen from the chair. Her sightless brown eyes were open.

"Whoa. Brown eyes?"

"Yes, I was surprised, too. Her name is Sister Irene," Meg filled Ray in, referring to her notes. "Her supervisor said she preferred the night shift because it was quieter. She was taking some day classes and sometimes managed to get in some studying during the wee hours."

"She wasn't on duty alone, was she?"

"No, but the supervisor was on break and the other nurse on duty was with a patient at the far end of the hall. This wing is orthopedics and many patients aren't ambulatory. Apparently, Sister Irene was seated at the desk doing some paperwork when the strangler approached her from behind."

Ray spotted the broken end of a chain near the wire. "Did you find a mass card?" he asked, rising and covering the body.

"I was beginning to think this might be a copycat killing, until I found it." She removed a plastic envelope from her jacket pocket and handed it to him. "I mean the location's way off, so I figured some nut case might just want attention. But the card's the same. Only, the message is different."

Ray studied the five words written in the same block lettering. HAVE YOU FORGIVEN ME YET? Something else caught his eye as he opened the envelope's sliding seal and took out the card, holding one corner with his fingertips. He stared at a round smudge over the word *me*. "Did you see this?" He pointed to the spot with his index finger.

Meg leaned in for a closer look. "Not until now. Looks like a damp spot blurring the ink."

"Like maybe a drop of something. The paper's porous, so any liquid would make an impression."

"Water maybe, or sweat?"

"Could be. Can they get a DNA reading from a drop of sweat?" Ray slid the card back into the envelope, sealed it, and gave it back to Meg.

"I don't know. I think it's only from blood, tissue, semen, or saliva, but I'll have the lab check it out."

"Good. Has Doc been called?"

"It's late and I didn't see much point. I thought he could get us all we need tomorrow from the autopsy. But it's your call. I'll phone him if you want."

Ray shook his head. "No, I agree." A phone was ringing at the nurses' station around the bend and several subdued figures in white with rubber-soled shoes were going about their work. The pager came on seeking a Dr. Fulbright. The faint sound of a siren could be heard coming nearer. There was an antiseptic smell in the somewhat stuffy air. A typical night in a metropolitan hospital.

Except for the dead nun on the floor.

"So where's our witness?" Ray asked, hoping the guy was on the level. It was about time they had a break.

"I've put him in the supervisor's office with a cup of coffee. The guy's pretty shook up." Meg led the way around the police barrier. "I've already talked with the super and the other nurse. They say they saw nothing unusual."

They passed a room where a patient moaned in his sleep. Another was sitting in a chair as if it were high noon instead of nearly midnight. Ray wondered how often the nurses checked on these people. He hated visiting hospitals almost as much as morgues.

"Our witness's name is Charley Ames," Meg told him, still reading from her small notebook. "He's a maintenance man who's worked for Mt. Carmel for fifteen years. I called in a check on him anyway."

Ray nodded as she stopped at a closed door. "Have you asked him any questions yet?"

"Not really. He was so nervous when I got here that it was all I could do to calm him down. I thought it best to give him time to compose himself. He's sixty-four and has high blood pressure. I think he told me that so we'd take it easy on him."

Ray opened the door. The man on the couch along the wall looked up quickly, his eyes wary. Charley Ames was slight, no more than five-six, balding, with a large mole on his left cheek. The hands that held a burning cigarette trembled as Ray walked in and introduced himself.

"I never seen a dead body look like that before," Charley blurted out, the shock of finding the dead nun still uppermost on his mind. "I mean, I seen lots of corpses, you know. Like when someone dies and they put a sheet over them and wheel them away on a gurney. But nothing like that poor sister." He drew deeply on his cigarette.

"Not a pretty sight, I know." Ray pulled a chair over for Meg, who continued taking notes. He leaned his hip on the supervisor's desk. "Tell us how you found the body, Charley."

He took another drag, then snuffed out the butt in a small tin ashtray on the end table next to a sign that read THANK YOU FOR NOT SMOKING. "Like I told one of the other cops, I passed Sister Irene around about ten-thirty. I was wheeling my service cart down toward the end of the hall where I usually start, you know."

Nervous, tobacco-stained hands lit up another cigarette before he went on. "She smiled at me like always. She's a real friendly lady, you know. Some people never noticed janitors. But Sister Irene always asked about my wife. She knew my Clara from when she had her hip replaced last year. Irene likes Clara." His expression clouded. "I mean, she *did*. Jeez, I can't believe she's gone. I got a daughter around her age." He rubbed a hand along his chin. "Young women ain't safe nowhere these days. I tell my wife and daughters, don't go nowhere after dark." Charley inhaled deeply.

Only this killer didn't kill only after dark, Ray thought. "So you walked past Sister Irene with your cart and she smiled at you," Ray prompted. "Then what?"

"Then I saw this guy get off the elevators down the hall from the nurses' station, but I just gave him a quick look-see, you know. Lots of people around a hospital all hours. I don't pay much attention. I mind my own business, you know."

"Can you tell us what he looked like?"

"He was wearing work clothes, sort of like mine. Dark pants and a blue shirt. He didn't turn my way so I didn't get too good a look at his face. Like I said, just a quick glance."

"Did he appear to be in a hurry?"

"Nah. He just sauntered out of the elevator, looking toward the desk."

"Did Sister Irene greet him?" Ray asked as Meg recorded the man's comments.

Charley peered through the smoke of his cigarette. "I didn't hear her if she did."

"All right, go on."

"Then Sister Florence came out of the room next to the end and asked could I go in and clean up before I did the floors. Some guy got sick and missed the pan."

"How long were you in that room?"

"Eight, ten minutes, tops. I come out and no one's around except that same guy standing by the elevators. He don't look left or right, just steps in when it comes and then he's gone. I don't think nothing about it 'cause, like I said, people come and go. If I stood around checking them all out, when would my work get done?" Charley sucked on his cigarette some more.

"Okay, then you started scrubbing the hall floor?"

"Not scrub. Just wash, you know. Sudsy water, then a sponge rinse. They scrub with the big machines and polish with wax every Saturday."

Which was more than Ray had ever wanted to know about hospital floor maintenance. "Right. You *washed* the floor. Where was the nurse who'd called you in to clean up the room?"

"She left before I finished. Took the dirty linen out of there. I didn't see her until later, when I yelled after finding Sister Irene."

"Was that when you'd worked your way down to the nurses' station from the end of the hall?"

"Yeah, that's right. I was pretty hot by then, so I thought I'd get a drink. Sister always kept some cold drinks in her desk. I walked up to her and she was kind of slumped over, you know. Like she'd fallen asleep." Charley punched the cigarette butt out almost viciously. "I ain't never seen her fall asleep on the job before, but still, I didn't think nothing was wrong, 'cause I know she works real hard, goes to school and all. But I thought I'd better wake her 'cause if old Beecher came out—that's the super—she'd have a shit fit."

"And there still wasn't anyone else out in the hallway or anywhere you could see?"

"No, no one. So I walked around and touched her shoulder, real gentle like. She scared the hell out of me when she fell over onto the floor. Holy shit!" Charley turned pale, reliving the scene, as he fumbled in his shirt pocket for another cigarette.

"What did you do then?" Meg asked.

"I yelled. I mean, I know you're not supposed to yell in a hospital, but hell, I couldn't worry about that right then. No one came right away so I picked up the phone and called security."

"Did you check Sister Irene for a pulse?"

"Nah, not me. I didn't touch her. I don't know nothing about taking pulses." Charley had a feeling neither of these two cops smoked, but he didn't much care. He lit up again.

The small room was turning blue with smoke, but Meg didn't say anything. She knew the cigarettes were holding the poor guy together. "How long before security arrived?" she asked.

"I don't know, coupla minutes. By then Beecher was there and Sister Florence, too. I don't mind telling you, I was shaking like a leaf." Sticking the cigarette in his mouth, he smoothed back his sparse hair with shaky fingers. "I don't like being around dead people. No, ma'am."

"Let's get back to this man you saw," Ray continued, bracing his hands on the desk edge and crossing one foot over the other. "I know you had only a glance, but was he tall or short? Was he thin or stocky? What was the color of his hair? Since he wasn't turned toward you, I don't suppose you saw his eyes?"

"Nah, not his eyes. He was kinda medium height, you know. Little taller than me, probably. His build was just average, you know. Not lots of muscles, not skinny either. His hair was ... was brown, I think. Yeah, it was brown. Medium brown. 'Bout like yours, Detective." He sent Ray a shaky smile.

Great. Medium height, medium build, medium brown hair. Like Doc had suggested, the guy was Mr. Average. "You say he was wearing dark pants and a blue shirt. Work clothes. Were the pants black or blue or maybe dark green?"

Charley screwed up his face thoughtfully as he drew smoke into his lungs. "Navy, I think. Yeah, probably navy blue."

"Was the shirt long-sleeved? Buttoned down the front or pullover?"

Charley tapped his denim shirt at his chest. "Like this one. Collar, buttons, long sleeves."

"Did he have the sleeves rolled up or buttoned at his wrists?"

Charley brushed a weary hand over his face. "Geez, you sure want a lot from a quick look. Maybe five seconds I saw him, you know. Not rolled up, I don't think. Down to his wrists, I'd say. I'm not real sure about that, but I think so."

"How old of a man would you say he was?"

"Lots younger than me, that's for sure. Not even thirty. More like mid-twenties. Thick hair, you know. I always wanted thick hair."

"When he walked, did he walk straight, without a limp? What about his shoes? Did they make a noise on the floor as he moved?"

"Christ, I don't know. I didn't notice no limp. I didn't hear any noise his shoes made. Most of us work around hospitals are told to wear rubber-soled shoes, you know. On account they want it quiet and they don't want no scuff marks on the floors." He held up one foot. "Like these." Black, soft-soled shoes that tied.

"You say most people who work around hospitals. Do you think this man works here at Mt. Carmel?"

"I couldn't say. I never saw him before. We got lots of guys work here. Janitor staff, laundry, kitchen help, lawn people in summer and snow removal in winter, maintenance, engineering. No way I coulda met them all."

And over fifty percent of them used some form of wire in their work. Terrific. Ray turned to Meg. "Can you think of anything else?"

"Charley," she began, "would you be willing to come to the station in the morning and describe the man you saw to our police artist? He could make a couple of sketches and maybe with your help, we could get a reasonable likeness of this guy."

"I dunno." Charley sucked the last bit out of his butt before smashing it out. "I gotta finish my work tonight. I usually sleep late."

Meg was persistent. "About two o'clock? I know you liked Sister Irene. You want to help us catch the man who did this to her, don't you?"

"Yeah, I guess." He wrinkled his brow. "Do you think this is the same guy in the papers, the one who got those nuns on the east side?"

"We can't be certain until all the evidence has been analyzed," Ray told him, pushing off from the desk. "But it certainly looks like it."

Charley got up slowly, favoring his right knee. "Okay, I'll be there tomorrow. You gotta catch that bastard. My wife's a Catholic, you know. She's going to cry when I tell her about Irene."

"Thanks for your help," Ray said. "Here's my card. If you think of anything else, please call me."

Meg returned the chair she'd been using. "And I'll meet you at the station tomorrow at two." She also handed him her card.

"Yeah, okay." He shuffled out, wishing he could end his shift right now. Damn, but he was going to be late getting home. Clara worried about him. He'd have to phone her next break.

In the office, Meg looked up at Ray. "What do you think?"

"If he has trouble providing details for the artist's rendering, let's see if we can't get Charley to agree to hypnosis. He may have seen a lot more than he's aware of."

Meg remembered a case she and Ray had worked on in January, where the eyewitness to a shooting had blocked out the memory due to fear. Under hypnosis, she'd been able to provide them with enough information to bring about an arrest. "Good idea. Ted Riordan sure helped us out a while back. Remember?"

Leaving the office, Ray closed the door. "Yeah, that's the guy I was thinking of." At the nurses' station, the medics were placing Sister Irene's body onto a gurney in preparation for the ambulance ride to the morgue. "I'll beep Doc from home and leave a message about this one. Maybe, if I press, he can get us a report by noon tomorrow."

Meg flipped her notebook shut, shoved it in her pocket, and stifled a yawn. "I guess that's all we can do tonight."

Ray checked his watch. Just past one. He hoped to find Toni fast asleep in his bed. He decided against calling her. At this hour, he could make it home in under thirty minutes. "Come on, I'll walk you to your car."

Wally lay on the hard mattress in his dim bedroom, wearing only blue shorts, his skin feeling damp and clammy. A feather pillow Rosie had given him was bunched under his head and an ice bag rested on his forehead. He listened to the loud pounding of his heart as the two candles he'd lighted on the dresser flickered.

The headache would subside soon, he knew. He'd returned to his flat, hurried upstairs, and stripped off his sweaty clothes. He always sweat like a pig after one of these. Tomorrow, he'd go to the laundromat. He hated to smell bad.

He'd like to take a shower or a bath, but he didn't dare turn on the water at this hour. Rosie would hear and maybe ask questions. He couldn't afford to arouse her suspicions. He'd have to mask the perspiration odor with his aftershave.

Carefully, moving slowly, he removed the icebag and waited. Yes, the pain was gone. Thank God. He put the bag on the floor and reached for the towel he'd brought in. Slowly, he blotted the sweat from his face and body. This upstairs flat was always stuffy and warm. Maybe he'd buy a fan. Summer was almost here and soon the humidity would make it really close up here. He had trouble sleeping anyway. Circulating air would help.

Turning, he reached to the nightstand and picked up the fine gold chain. This cross had etchings on it that he couldn't make out in the pale moonlight coming in through the sheer curtains Rosie had hung on his bedroom window. No matter. He'd examine it more thoroughly tomorrow.

Then he'd add it to the silver box on his dresser with the rest of them. He had three altogether. The first sister wasn't wearing one, or maybe he'd missed it. And he'd mailed one to Toni Garette because he'd wanted her to have something he'd touched. He'd driven by the cop's house on his way back tonight. Her car had been in his driveway again.

He was getting worried about Toni. She was spending too much time with that detective. Was he trying to talk her into doing sinful things, acts that would spoil her purity? Wally hoped not as he sighed heavily.

Five angels he'd sent to heaven, and only three souvenirs.

There'd be more.

Wally placed the chain and cross back on the nightstand and closed his eyes. Tonight he would rest. He always slept best on nights like these.

Her car was gone and the house empty, except for his sad-eyed Great Dane. Ray felt just as sad.

Carrying his jacket and unbuttoning his shirt, he walked upstairs, the dog trailing after him. It was quiet, which is the way he usually liked his home, especially after a grueling jaunt out to view a murder victim and interrogate a witness. But the quiet didn't do much for his spirits tonight.

In his bedroom, he hung up his jacket and tossed his tie on the dresser. That's when he spotted the note propped in his hairbrush. He opened the single sheet.

It's late and I have an early morning tomorrow. Please call when you get home no matter the hour. I really would like to know what you found out.

Toni.

Ray stripped down to his briefs, lay down on his bed, and dialed her number. He was surprised to realize he'd memorized it. She answered in the middle of the first ring.

"Hi. I just got back. I wish you were here. Hamlet misses you."

In her own bed with her favorite pale yellow sheets, Toni smiled. "Just Hamlet?"

"Yeah. The dog's got no pride."

"You probably have enough for the both of you."

He smiled. "All right, so I miss you, too."

It pleased her to hear him admit it. "I borrowed your shirt. I'll return it."

"Good. How about right now?"

"I don't think so. What did you find out at Mt. Carmel?"

He stretched out and told her about his night. "The witness's description is too vague to be of much help. Unless the janitor remembers more, or the police artist is able to get more from him, we may have to resort to hypnotizing the guy. Even that doesn't always work."

"But the DNA test might tell you something." She wanted to put her hopes on something, anything.

"It could. Like his blood type. But even if we had a good reading on it, without suspects to test how would we get a match? And as of this minute we don't have a single suspect."

Toni let out a frustrated breath, going over in her mind all he'd told her. "Brown eyes this time. That's a switch. And a nurse instead of a teacher. What do you make of it?"

Ray yawned tiredly. "Damned if I know. From what we can gather, he looks like everyman, which means no one appears to notice him. He fits in well a lot of places, so he must do some kind of work that allows him to come and go without suspicion. He wears work clothes most likely, but that applies to literally dozens of blue-collar professions."

"Do you think he stalked this Sister Irene, too?"

"If not, then he had to have happened on a nun all alone on the fourth floor who was young, slender, and blond when the urge to kill came over him. That's too coincidental for my book. I believe he stalks them, but I can't prove it."

"This new message is scary. 'Have you forgiven me yet?' seems to imply that he'll keep killing until he gets some sign that he's been forgiven for whatever sin he's harboring. I wonder, is he asking God for forgiveness, or some mortal?"

"Yeah, it would help to know that." Ray thought of all the young victims he'd seen over the past few weeks. "Well, *I* sure as hell am not going to forgive him."

"No, me either," Toni whispered. She was safe in her bed in her room in her home. Yet she didn't *feel* safe. "I wish you were here with me."

Ray smiled at the thought. "I'll bet your mother would love that."

"My mother has nothing against you."

"She would if she knew what I'd be doing if I were there in your room with you."

A delicious memory drifted through her mind as she recalled that shared shower. "I'll toss down a rope ladder from my bedroom window and you can climb up. No one will be the wiser."

"Don't tempt me." Ray gave in to a yawn as he glanced at the clock. "I guess we'd better say goodnight so we can catch a little sleep before the alarm goes off."

"Thanks for the update."

"I'll call you tomorrow." Ray hung up, turned off the light, and placed his hands beneath his head.

The scenes form his busy day kept whirling through his mind, mingled with the short time he'd spent with Toni. And inevitably, his thoughts drifted to the sweet-faced sister who'd had her young life snuffed out so cruelly. "I'll get him for you, Sister," he whispered into the darkness, then closed his eyes.

TEN

Meg sat at her desk waiting for Charley Ames. She was scheduled to take him up to Kevin Kiefer, the police artist. The hospital maintenance man was already fifteen minutes late and she wondered if she should call his home or give him a little more time. Ray was at the morgue, meeting with Doc about their latest strangling victim.

The *Detroit Free Press* was open on her desk, the killing of the fifth nun making the headlines. How did the media get their information so quickly? she wondered. Reporters often dropped in to various precincts, waiting for a story to break, but this latest murder had taken place practically in the middle of the night. Yet here were all the gory details in the morning edition, waiting to scare the hell out of everyone as they sipped their coffee.

She perused the article again as the phone rang. "Sergeant O'Malley," she answered.

"Meg, this is Toni. Have you got a minute?"

Meg set aside the paper. "Sure. What's up?"

"I've been reading about the strangling last night." She didn't want to reveal that she'd talked with Ray about it, that she'd been with him in his bed when he'd received the call. Their relationship was no one's business, after all. "I have an idea I want to run by you."

Why would she want to run an idea by her? Meg wondered. Unless Ray had already rejected it. Curious, she said, "Okay. Let's hear it."

"Have you thought about assigning an undercover policeman to St. Matthews, dressed as a maintenance man, perhaps, so he could monitor people who come and go? Or what about having a woman go undercover as a nun? You know, someone fitting the description of the nuns who've been targeted by the killer. What do you think?"

Meg thought that Toni read too many detective novels. "Well, we *have* used undercover officers on occasion."

Toni's voice, which had been hesitant, became enthusiastic. "I thought you might have. I didn't think Ray would go for this, so I called you. He seems to have this idea that methodical police work will eventually win out."

She was really worked up over this, Meg thought. Of course, her cousin had been one of the victims and Meg knew that the killer had sent her Mo's necklace. Toni certainly had just cause in wanting to lock the guy up. "While your idea has merit, it also presents problems. First of all, the strangler's now killed in and around St. Matthews, on the lower east side, and in a hospital corridor clear across town. How could we know where to position our man—or woman?"

Toni hadn't thought about that, but she was quick on the rebound. "All right, so there's more than one location involved. Surely your budget would allow several cops to go undercover, when so many lives are at stake."

She was persistent, Meg would give her that.

"Perhaps. But, although this man is obviously disturbed, he's quite clever. He's killed five women and left not a genuine clue as to his identify or his whereabouts. We could station half a dozen undercover officers—provided we got the approval—and they could be at several designated locations for days, weeks even. Yet our killer could be stalking someone in an entirely different part of town. We haven't the staff or budget to send an officer to every parish and hospital in the archdiocese."

"I realize that." Toni was getting annoyed. Meg was shooting holes in her idea left and right. "You don't think putting just one at St. Matthews would work?"

"I couldn't hazard a guess. As I said . . ."

"Yes, I know what you said. Could you at least mention my idea to someone in a position to authorize it, whoever that might be?"

Toni wasn't going to give up. "That would be Captain Renwick. I'll certainly tell him about our conversation." And perhaps Ray also, Meg thought.

"But you don't think your captain will go for it?"

Through the doorway, Meg spotted Charley Ames standing in the hallway, looking confused. "All I can do is try, Toni. Listen, someone I need to see just walked in. Can I get back to you on this later?"

"All right. Thanks for your time." In her office at the Glass Door, Toni hung up, feeling frustrated and annoyed. Of course she was a mere layman, not trained or even familiar with police procedures. But she knew her idea had merit. And yet, she felt as if Meg hadn't taken her seriously.

She blew at her bangs as she leaned back in her chair. The madman had to be caught, and soon. Her mother tried, but she still wasn't her old self. By watching her diet, the bleeding had stopped and the pain hit her only occasionally. But there was a pale listlessness about Jane that worried Toni.

The grand opening for the Brass Door was scheduled for the coming weekend, and Toni wasn't even sure her mother would be up to that. Jane so seldom left the house these days, and she had been so active before, spending time at the restaurant, shopping, lunching with friends. Her father had curtailed his activities, even his golf outings, over concern about his wife. Toni hated to see the changes in her parents that had taken place since Mo's death.

Sighing, she picked up the list she'd been putting together, names of people she planned to invite to the opening, and tried to concentrate on that rather than agonize over the murders any more today.

"Well, what do you think?" Meg asked Ray as she walked into their office and handed him the police artist's sketch of the strangler, based on Charley Ames's description.

Ray looked up from the report he'd been reading and studied the sketch. The man had a round face with lots of brown hair. Ordinary eyes, nose, and mouth. There wasn't a single outstanding feature about him. "Like we said, Mr. Everyman. Kevin's pretty good at reading between the lines. Even he couldn't get Charley to remember anything unusual about the guy, eh?"

Disappointed, Meg sank into her chair. "I'm afraid not. If we release this sketch to the media, they'll make mincemeat of us."

"Let's get ahold of that hypnotist. Charley still willing to go under?"

"He seems to be."

"Set it up for next week." He held out the report

he'd been reading. "But before you do, take a look at this."

Meg leaned forward and grabbed the sheet. "Oh, the lab report on the spot on the mass card. Well, I'll be damned. Perspiration, like we thought."

"Yeah, but unfortunately we can't get a DNA fix on drops of sweat. However, they found traces of cellular debris, too."

"I've read about that. Tiny particles of skin sloughing off when we sweat, not visible to the naked eye."

"Right. They're still studying that, but even if they can pinpoint a certain set of characteristics, we don't have a suspect to match up."

Meg thought of something. "Did they ever check any of the other mass cards for possible drops of sweat? Maybe the guy has some disease and perspires more than average."

"Or maybe he was a little nervous while he twisted wire around the throats of his victims and dripped all over the place. Anything's possible, I guess. I'll call the lab and see what tests they ran on the other cards."

"Too bad he didn't cut his finger. A drop of blood would have been more conclusive for DNA testing."

"I suppose, but just as useless without a suspect to test."

"Still, if we've eliminated, say a workman at St. Matthews who might have a sweating problem, we might want to interview him again. He might have an allergy problem, a skin disorder, scaley hands that are always damp or a drippy face."

Ray smiled. "You don't think we'd have noticed a guy like that?"

"Maybe, but why would we? We talked with so

many. Can you remember any one person with, say, an eye twitch or a nose that ran constantly? I can't."

"Hey, Ray," Officer Chet Hemsley called out as he stuck his head inside the doorway, "I think you better come with me. We just brought a guy in who's asking for you."

Frowning, Ray stood up. "Asking for me? Who's that?"

"Guy who lives in the Gratiot Apartments. He took a twelve-gauge shotgun, broke into his neighbor's apartment and went on a rampage. Said her appliances were making him crazy. Damn good thing she wasn't home. His name's Mort Something-or-other."

Ray stared at the handcuffed old man in his wrinkled clothes, his scraggly face hanging low. "Judas Priest."

Every investigative team resorted to the good cop–bad cop routine occasionally when questioning a suspect. Ray thought he and Meg did it really well. Yet that wasn't why she'd asked him to be present while she interviewed Dr. James Everett, whose daughter, Kimberly, had by her actions indicated that her father had molested her. Though it wasn't a homicide case, Meg had asked for Ray's help on this one since the captain had told her to follow up. She wanted another set of ears in case she missed something. And a witness in case the doctor's high-priced lawyer claimed police brutality or harassment.

Kimberly's mother had confronted James, but he'd vehemently denied the charges. Meg and Ray had guessed that he would. Molly Everett wasn't convinced of her husband's innocence and Kimberly had refused to talk about the subject, period.

It was up to them to get the truth.

He was a handsome man, Ray thought, as they entered the interrogation room. Tall, with classic features and beautifully tailored clothes. And dark eyes that were cool and confident as he carefully folded his neatly manicured hands over a manila folder in front of him.

His attorney, on the other hand, was not handsome but he was equally confident. J. Lewis McIntyre had a gray fringe of hair which made his full black mustache beneath a very large nose all the more startling. He also had no chin. He wore a pinstriped suit with a vest from which hung a heavy gold chain and pocket watch.

Meg introduced everyone, then took the last of three chairs at the small table as Ray went to stand by the window. "Thanks for coming down, Dr. Everett. We'll try not to keep you too long."

"You'll keep me only long enough to allow me to read my statement," Dr. Everett said in a silken voice as he removed a sheet of paper from his folder. He cleared his throat before beginning. "I am an outstanding member of the community, on the board of directors of three universities, a respected pediatric eye surgeon of some renown. I have not committed a crime of any sort. Either present me with charges of something you can prove or stay away from me and my family. Be prepared to face harassment charges if you do not abide by this." Replacing the paper, the doctor sent Meg a chilling look.

"I see." She removed two pieces of paper from her folder and handed them to Dr. Everett's attorney, who immediately began to read.

"What's that?" Everett asked, his voice just a shade uneasy.

"It's a statement signed by your wife that she has reason to believe that you've sexually assaulted your six-year-old daughter, Kimberly. And also the medical report by the doctor at St. John's Hospital, where I believe you're on staff, as to the damage that has been inflicted on your little girl."

The doctor's eyes narrowed. "I am as outraged by what happened to Kimberly as her mother. As to Molly's accusations, our marriage has problems and she's using this to attack me." His well-modulated voice had risen with each word.

"Are you aware that your daughter begins to weep when your name is mentioned as possibly being the man who hurt her?"

"How dare you! You had no right to lead my daughter—"

"Jim!" J. Lewis McIntyre held up a hand boasting a heavy gold pinkie ring to silence his client. "Say no more." He tossed both papers back to Meg. "These don't implicate my client in any way. We agree that Kimberly has been assaulted. By whom is yet to be determined." His small pale eyes challenged them. "Shouldn't you be looking into that rather than harassing a man of Dr. Everett's impeccable reputation?"

Meg dug out still another report and pushed it toward the attorney. "I have here a statement by a child psychologist who has interviewed Kimberly for six one-hour sessions. Based on the information she's gathered, she is ready to testify under oath that she believes that the girl's father is responsible."

McIntyre glanced at the statement, then tossed it back. "This is rubbish, one silly quack's opinion." He got to his feet. "If and when you get something concrete, call me. Until then, leave my client alone or we'll press harassment charges." He turned to the doctor. "Come on, Jim. We're through here."

His confidence restored, Jim put on a smug smile and followed McIntyre out. Neither looked back.

"Shit!" Meg gathered up her papers, disgusted.

Ray pushed off from the wall. "What did you expect, that he'd cave in and admit everything? You know you don't have any real proof."

Meg grabbed her folder and stood, her blue eyes angry. "What am I supposed to do, let him get away with this?"

Ray walked over, slipping an arm around her shoulders. "No, babe. You're supposed to sit tight until you do get some evidence. And you will."

"Just how am I going to do that?"

Ray hated to say it aloud. "He'll trip himself up sooner or later. Because, Meg, he isn't going to stop molesting her. He thinks he's gotten away with it now and he's going to continue. But Kimberly will speak up one day. Then, we'll get him."

"Meanwhile, that . . . that animal is having sex with a small, frightened little girl, and we have to just sit tight and wait."

"That's the system, babe." He opened the door. "Come on, let's call it a day. I'll buy you a beer."

She knew he was right, but that didn't make the news any easier to take. "I don't think so. I think I'll go home and make some pasta for Dennis. He's on early shift this week." She followed him out of the room. "Some other time?"

"Sure. Catch you tomorrow." Ray strolled back to their office to check for messages.

* * *

SHATTERED VOWS

Dr. Roger Delaney took the chair alongside Ray's desk on Friday morning and set down a manila folder. "My conclusions are all in there."

It had been the week from hell, Ray thought as he leaned back in his chair. There'd been the strangling of Sister Irene, with its accompanying media frenzy and public demands for the police to "do something," Mort Ziltzer's arraignment and subsequent order for psychiatric evaluation, and Dr. James Everett's cocky denials, as well as half a dozen routine matters. He'd worked twelve-hour-plus days, eaten far too much fast food, and fallen into bed exhausted each night, only to start the whole thing all over again the next morning.

And he hadn't had a chance to even call Toni.

"Why don't you save me a little time and just tell me about your conclusions?" Ray asked the clinical psychologist.

Delaney crossed his long legs. "Like I mentioned the last time we met, the man is plagued by guilt. In his own eyes, he's a sinner. He's begging for forgiveness."

"From God, you mean?"

"Not necessarily. Might be some person or persons he's wronged. Whether actually or in his troubled mind, we don't know."

Ray handed him a note with the new message left with Sister Irene, HAVE YOU FORGIVEN ME YET? "This was written on the last mass card."

Dr. Delaney read it and nodded. "Yes. He's sacrificing these young nuns to atone for hurting someone, someone he hopes will forgive him soon. My guess would be that he won't stop killing until he feels forgiven."

A muscle in Ray's jaw clenched. "I wish to hell we knew who could forgive him."

"I wish I could target someone for you."

"Have you come up with some sort of a profile on this guy?"

Delaney smoothed his thin mustache. "It's a tough one with so little to go on. The best clues we have to his motive are the mass cards. His choice of murder weapon indicates that he has easy access to that particular wire, but it's so common that literally hundreds of people in the area use it."

"Yeah, that's for sure."

"His habit of ripping off the chains holding the crosses could mean that he likes a remembrance of each killing, to relive them when he's alone. Or it could be symbolic of a gift he'd given someone once and perhaps she rejected. Collecting souvenirs of killings isn't unusual with serial killers, so it's hard to say."

Everything was iffy. Ray felt his blood pressure rise. "So you really can't give us anything definite?"

"No, but then I'd told you that from the start. These are educated guesses only." He became thoughtful, gazing ceilingward. "I'd wager he lives alone. That way, no one can question his comings and goings, his erratic hours, his odd collection of women's broken jewelry. His work may take him all over the city, east side to west. He's likely to be shy and sensitive, particularly with the opposite sex. He may hold a job and be well thought of by his coworkers and friends, who don't know anything about his secret life."

Ray had a hard time buying that. "I wonder what it was that triggered this whole series of killings."

"Maybe it isn't his first. Maybe he's killed before elsewhere. Have you looked into similar stranglings in other states?"

He'd done that after the third dead nun. "We came up empty on the same M.O."

"Have you looked into other nuns who may have lived or worked in and around the areas where these five were killed? Maybe one was a relative of his. Maybe one died and he feels responsible for her death, which would explain his need for forgiveness."

"That's a thought. So you don't think this guy's a loner?"

"Not necessarily. He may work helping others, odd as that sounds. The killings took place at a church, a school, and a hospital. The people who work around these places are all giving, volunteers, donating time."

Ray nodded. "We've concluded that he wouldn't stand out as being a visitor to either of those institutions, so he must work around the place. But doing what?"

"Good question."

"He's damn careful, you know. Not too many people can go about their days, kill five women mostly in broad daylight or in a lighted area, and leave not a clue."

"Of course. He's smart enough to be cautious. He knows he's a fallible man, one who's made mistakes, who needs forgiveness. He doesn't want to be caught until he's completed his mission."

"Which is?"

Delaney allowed a small smile. "If we knew that, we would probably be halfway home." Something else occurred to him. "This recent strangling occurred only a couple of weeks after the last one, right?"

"Two weeks, two days, actually."

"Yes. I believe I mentioned that the closer together the killings, the stronger the indication that he's becoming unraveled. He's probably showing signs of strain to his coworkers and those who live around him. He could be nervous, distracted, sweating."

Ray's head went up. "Did you say sweating?"

"Yes. Nervous people often perspire freely. Is that significant?"

Ray explained about the drop of sweat on the last mass card.

Delaney smiled, as if he'd just won a prize. "There you are. He's likely sweating a lot over these killings."

"That makes two of us."

Delaney paused a moment, as if wondering whether or not to speak his mind. "I know you're a cop, Detective, and it's your job to apprehend murderers and punish them. But I hope you understand that this man is very disturbed and he's screaming out for someone to help him, to forgive him. But there's no one."

Ray sat up straighter, his face growing stormy. "*He* needs help? Damn it, Doctor, don't turn bleeding heart on me here. How about the families of those innocent young women? How about the world that's lost teachers, nurses, counselors to some probable drifter, some misfit, some dangerously disturbed creep? You want me to feel for him? You've come to the wrong cop." Pushing his chair back, Ray rose angrily.

The doctor sighed. "I do understand how you feel."

"No, I don't think you do. When was the last time you leaned over a young nun with a wire twisted around her neck and her eyes bulging out of

SHATTERED VOWS

their sockets? Do that a couple of times and tell me how sorry you feel for the bastard then."

Delaney hesitated, then nodded and slowly rose. "You're right, of course. You're absolutely right." The detective remained silent, standing with his back to him, looking out the window. "I hope my findings are of some help." He turned, then, and left.

He'd be damned if he'd apologize for the way he felt, Ray thought, struggling to clamp down on his anger. Crying for help. Right. Swiveling about, he walked with angry strides to get another cup of coffee.

Ray got out of his wagon and ran up the three steps leading to the McCarthys' door. He'd honked his horn as usual, which was Mark's signal that Ray was there for their scheduled basketball practice. That way he'd avoided talking to Mark's barracuda of a mother. Ray had talked with the boy earlier and Mark said he'd be waiting. Maybe he hadn't heard the car horn. Ray rang the bell and stepped back, waiting.

After a minute, he rang again, till finally he heard footsteps approaching. Dr. Abigail McCarthy swung open the large front door and regarded him frostily. "Mark ready?" Ray asked.

"I'm afraid not." The voice was hard and brittle. "Mark's decided he no longer wants to see you. My engagement's on again and Donald and I are taking him to the Bahamas for a week as soon as school's out. We'll be married there. So, Detective, your services will no longer be required. Mark will have a new father very soon." The thin lips parted in a parody of a smile. "But we do thank you for your past attention."

When she began closing the door, Ray stopped her. "Could I just talk to Mark a minute?" Something smelled rotten here, he thought.

"I'm afraid not. Donald's taken him to the golf range to hit some balls. They enjoy each other's company so much."

She was lying, Ray thought. Not just to him but to herself. Mark hated golf, had told him so several times. Still, there seemed little he could do in the face of Abigail's open hostility. "All right, then," he said.

He turned and walked back to his car. He'd try to intercept Mark after classes one day, just to hear it from the horse's mouth. If Mrs. McCarthy was right, and he was getting along well with his father-to-be, Ray would be the first to be pleased. But if not ... well, Ray wasn't sure what he could do. Maybe call Mark's therapist.

He drove away, feeling sorry for the poor little rich kid.

Maybe he shouldn't have come, Ray thought, looking around at the sophisticated crowd gathered for opening night of the newest restaurant in Birmingham, the Brass Door. Like the original on the east side, the restaurant's entranceway was distinctive—this door was made of thick polished brass from floor to ceiling, and most impressive. There was a large oak bar at the back, two spacious dining rooms with white linen on the tables, and small brass planters as well as brass candlesticks with tall white tapers. Pale peach-colored draperies and carpeting softened the elegant decor.

He recognized several prominent auto executives and their wives, a couple of local politicians, and even Jane Rayburn, the restaurant critic of the *Detroit News,* among the guests. But they weren't the reason for his unease.

And it didn't have anything to do with his attire, either. He'd known just what to expect and had worn gray pleated slacks, a white shirt with thin black and gray stripes, and a black Geoffrey Beane sport coat set off by a red paisley tie. The reason was he wanted her all to himself, the lady of the hour, who was very busy. And very lovely.

Toni was elegant in white linen contrasting beautifully with her tan, her hair just touching her shoulders, her eyes bright with excitement. She worked the room, stopping to chat with this one and that, laughing with a young twosome, congratulating an older couple on an anniversary, kissing babies—in this case, young Joey Varner, son of Luke and Stephanie.

Ray sidled over.

"I warn you, Toni," Stephanie was saying, "don't jiggle him too much. He just ate a huge plate of french fries."

Fourteen-month-old Joey ignored his mother as he tried to pull off Toni's gold hoop earring. "Mine," he stated emphatically.

"The kid's got good taste," Ray said as he joined the small group.

Toni turned to him, her gaze taking in his attire, and smiled her approval.

"That he does," Luke said proudly. "I've been teaching him. Go for the gold, kid."

Toni pried loose the child's sticky little grip and handed him a pretzel she'd nabbed from a passing waiter's tray. "Try this instead, fella."

"No," Joey said, shaking his head. A persistent chubby hand stretched toward the earring again. "Pretty."

Stephanie reached to take her son back. "Come here, squirt, before you ruin Toni's dress and rip out her earlobes." Joey immediately went to work trying to pry open the rhinestone buttons on his mother's dress.

"Like father, like son," Ray observed with a laugh, then glanced around. "Where are Sam and Carly?"

"They were here earlier," Toni explained as she stepped back out of the way of a waiter carrying a loaded tray. "Carly wasn't feeling too well, so they left. The baby's due in a couple of months." Unobtrusively, she signaled a waitress that the occupants of a certain table were waiting impatiently for their check.

"I think we're going to hit the road, too," Luke said, slipping his hand around his wife's waist. "The little guy's got to get to bed and our little Annie's with the sitter."

Stephanie laughed. "That means that the big guy's sleepy. Toni, the place is fabulous. I know you'll do wonderfully well."

Toni beamed. "Thanks, I hope so." She spotted her parents talking to a couple at the bar. "Please stop and say a word to Mom and Dad before you leave. They're both such worry warts."

However, Toni knew how pleased her father was at seeing his dream come true. Earlier, his eyes glistening, he'd thanked her. It was a moment she'd always remember.

Stephanie leaned in to hug Toni, as did Luke. As his wife carried Joey toward the Garettes, Luke turned to Ray, his face expressionless as he ran a hand along his friend's lapel. "Nice threads. On duty tonight?" He glanced over at Toni, who was conferring with her maître'd two tables over. "Or is this a social call?"

Ray shoved his hands into his pants pockets. "Just came to wish the Garettes success in their new venture."

"Uh huh." Luke watched his friend, his expression curious.

Ray saw Toni toss her hair back in a familiar gesture as she laughed at something the maître'd said. She hid her nervousness well, he thought. He shifted his gaze back to Luke, who was still studying him intently. "All right, I came because I'm keeping an eye on Toni. Both personally and professionally." Taking his friend aside, he explained about the envelope she'd received from the killer. "He knows of her connection to one of the slain nuns and he knows where she lives. And maybe a whole lot more."

"Do you have her under surveillance?"

Ray shook his head. "Not enough to make it official. Renwick would never give me the okay."

"So you're taking up the slack?"

"I try, whenever I can. She's not real cooperative. She's so damn independent."

Luke nodded as he watched his wife and son with the Garettes. "You don't have to tell me about independent women." He turned serious. "You remember that Sam all but moved in with Carly when that stalker was after her? Damn good thing he did, too. If it's getting serious, you might want to give that some thought."

"I remember, all too well. But Toni lives with her parents."

Luke shrugged his broad shoulders. "Talk her

into moving in with you, or wouldn't you want that?"

Ray met his friend's steady gaze. Yeah, he'd want that, but he doubted that Toni would. "I'll think about it."

Luke grinned and patted his shoulder. "See you."

Ray scanned the room and found Toni at the far end of the bar, talking with one of her bartenders. He slipped up behind her as she finished and leaned close. "How long are you planning to be here?" he asked, already knowing the answer.

She swung around. "I'll be here for the duration tonight. This is it, Ray, the thing we've worked toward for months."

Ray nodded and check his watch. Only eight. "Does that mean two?"

"More like midnight or a little after." She touched his arm appreciatively. She was glad he'd come but he was quite a distraction, looking so incredibly wonderful. Good enough to eat. She straightened his tie a fraction.

"Okay. I'll wait." He glanced toward a small table along the side. "Maybe I'll even sample the fare."

She brightened at that. It would keep him busy. "Come on, I'll seat you myself." She led the way, then handed him a large folded cardboard menu, which had a replica of the brass door on its cover. "Here you are."

"Any chance you could join me for a bite?" he asked, sitting down.

She surveyed the crowd as she considered his offer. "Maybe a little later, when the diners thin out."

He took her hand in his, brought it to his mouth, and kissed her fingers. "I'll be right here."

His beard tickled her skin and his gesture warmed

her. She remembered how that beard felt trailing along her ribcage, across her stomach and . . . Toni cleared her throat. "I'll join you as soon as I can."

Ray watched her go, his eyes automatically scanning the room for anyone, anything that could pose a threat to her. A tall waiter in a tux with a soft-pleated shirt walked over to take his order. He decided on scampi and pasta, then sat back. The mayor of Birmingham walked in with Detroit's flamboyant major. It would seem that everyone who was anyone was here.

The waiter brought him iced tea in a crystal goblet with a thin slice of lemon. He sipped it for a while, then checked his watch again. Twenty after eight. He wished to hell Toni would hurry back.

Lord, how he hated waiting.

The Olds slowed as it passed the jammed parking lot with uniformed attendants racing about, whipping Jaguars and Caddies and BMW's into designated spaces. He'd read about the opening of the newest Garette-owned restaurant. He'd driven over hours ago to see the family arrive for the event, all dressed to the nines.

The uppity parking lot attendant had waved him past impatiently, as if he and his old car had no business being there. But Toni had arrived just then and had seen the incident, and scolded the attendant. Then she'd gazed after the Olds, which was already moving down the street, looking apologetic, as if she wished she could call him back. Of course, he couldn't allow her to see him, for she'd surely recognize him. But her gesture had warmed him all the same.

He envied the easy way she had with people. He

envied her family. All their lives they'd had everything, while he'd had nothing. No fun, no love, no laughter, no acceptance. He'd like to run inside that fine establishment and scream that no one there was without sin, just like he himself.

But he knew they wouldn't listen to him. Today, people didn't care about morality. There'd been a time when he hadn't, either. He'd let the sins of the flesh rule him. He'd changed, though—his mind, his ways, his feelings. But too late for anyone who mattered to him.

And there was nothing he could do. His family, lost to him forever over his transgressions. They couldn't forgive him, nor would they ever forget. They'd pushed him out of their lives. And the sweetest angel of all had been turned against him. By his own family, by Angie, by gossip.

Of course, he was as much to blame. He'd been a sinner, but hadn't he paid? Wasn't he still paying?

Laughter rang out as someone left the restaurant, and he looked over. No, it wasn't Toni. He'd seen the cop, all duded up, walk in awhile ago. He was probably waiting for her.

Wally drove the Olds to a side street and parked under a tree. He'd had only enough money to have the muffler fixed, not the headlight or tuneup. Next payday. He could see the door from where he sat. He would wait for Toni to come out.

It made him feel so good inside to watch her.

ELEVEN

Toni fanned her hair over the seatback of Ray's station wagon as she leaned back with a weary sigh. "You were easily the most attractive man there tonight," she told him.

"Yeah, right. I really outshine all those upwardly mobile, house-in-the-suburbs, two-car-garage, crabgrass-is-my-favorite-topic yuppie types." He turned off Maple onto Woodward Avenue heading south, deciding he didn't want to race along the expressway. It was nearly one in the morning, still warm, the June sky full of stars. A night not meant to be hurried.

Toni turned her head to study his profile. He wasn't smiling, but he didn't look angry, either. "Why do those people make you uncomfortable? I imagine you grew up in pretty much the same environment, from the little you've told me about your early years."

He sent her a quick glance. "And I walked away from all that, didn't I?"

Toni was quiet a long minute. "Maybe one day you'll tell me the real reason you did."

Ray's eyes flicked to the rearview mirror. An older model sedan with only one headlight had been behind them for some time now, keeping a consistent distance of two car lengths back. He narrowed his gaze, trying to determine if the driver was a man or a woman, but the windshield was tinted. Probably nothing.

"Are you ignoring me?" Toni asked, puzzled by his silence.

He brought his attention back to her and smiled. "I'd probably be more attentive if you'd slide over closer."

"The seat belt won't let me."

"There's a third set for the middle passenger." Digging around, he found one end and held it up.

Toni inched over, making the switch. She placed her hand on his right thigh and felt his reaction as his muscles flexed at her touch. "Is this better?"

Keeping his left hand on the wheel, Ray reached with his right to thread his fingers through hers, feeling his gut tighten at her nearness. "Much." Her scent wrapped around him as he drove and he suddenly wished that he'd taken the faster route.

Her folks hadn't been all that thrilled when Toni had announced that she wasn't going home with them. Her mother's face had looked surprised, then concerned. John Garette had frowned his disapproval, but Toni had ignored both reactions, taken Ray's hand, and told them not to wait up for her. At her age, she shouldn't have to explain herself to her parents, yet he knew she didn't like worrying them. How much safer could she be than with a cop? he asked himself. Unless it was danger of another sort that troubled them.

"Your parents don't approve of me," he said simply.

"Of course they do. They don't approve of my going out at one in the morning and perhaps not coming home until morning, like I've done before with you."

"They think you lead a celibate life?"

With her free hand, Toni brushed back her hair. "My mother married the first man who'd ever kissed her. The *only* man. Does that tell you anything about how she thinks? She doesn't *want* to think that I might not be celibate, because then she might have to face issues foreign to her."

"Hard to believe, in this day and age. Doesn't she go to movies, read books, watch the soaps?"

Toni pretended shock. "My mother, watch soaps? You've got to be kidding. She watched Oprah once and said she thought it was disgusting the way people aired their dirty linen in front of millions of viewers." She fell silent for a moment. "It's not that she's a prude. Or that she's not aware these things go on. It's just that she prefers to think that her only daughter is immune to these baser urges."

He smiled at her phrasing. "And are you?"

Toni shifted her hand, settled it over his zipper, and closed her fingers around him. Her jerked in reaction and she laughed. "Oh, yeah, I'm immune, all right. And I see that you are, too."

Ray squirmed. "You'd better let go until we get home or I'm liable to drive up a tree." Still laughing, she lifted her hand and stroked his thigh gently, which wasn't much of an improvement. Ray glanced into the rearview again. The one-eyed car was still behind them.

It was time, he decided, to do a little testing. Nonchalantly, he swerved into the left lane and speeded up, passing several cars rather quickly. His eyes shifting from front to rear, he moved back to the right lane, eased up on the gas for a mile or so, then repeated his actions. The dark car was some distance behind them and not changing lanes.

"What are you doing?" Toni asked.

"The car behind us had a broken light and it's been bugging me the way it shone into my mirror." Which was only half the story, but he didn't want to alarm her.

Keeping watch as he slowed again, he saw that after several blocks the car in question turned off to the right. It had probably been his imagination on overdrive. Forgetting the incident, he laced his fingers with Toni's and drew her closer to his side, liking the way she felt next to him altogether too much.

"I'm glad you waited for me," she said, her voice low and suggestive.

"Me, too." Ray stepped on the gas pedal, giving in to his desire to get home quickly.

"He hates to be left outside," Toni said as Ray pulled her into his arms in the kitchen. An exuberant Hamlet had met them at the door, and Ray had let him out into the fenced yard. The excited dog had quickly visited a couple of bushes, then dashed back to jump up against the screen door, wanting to get back in.

"Tough," Ray said, nibbling on her delicious neck.

"He's no trouble when he's in here with us," she persisted, listening to the dog's low whine. "Have a heart. He's been alone all day."

"He's a pest," Ray said, shifting his attention to her small ears. "Did you come over to visit me or my dog?"

Toni leaned back her head, as if considering her

answer thoughtfully. When he realized what she was doing, he nipped her earlobe. She yelped. "Hey! No fair."

"No fair preferring my dog over me." Ray shrugged out of his jacket and tossed it onto a chairback as he walked her backward into the living room.

Her hands moved to undo his tie. "This is beautiful. Where'd you get it?" She fingered the silken material.

Ray gave out an exasperated sigh. "Now she wants to discuss clothes. Listen, lady . . ."

Her mouth pressed suddenly to his, stopping his complaints. She rose on tiptoe, thrusting her hands into his hair. As he deepened the kiss, Toni stepped out of her heels and rubbed against him.

It had been a long, tiring day, a backbreaking week. But she didn't want sleep, didn't need rest nearly as much as she needed this. This mind-altering diversion that chased away her fatigue, provided her with a shattering release followed by a welcome lethargy that was better than any drug, she was certain. Wanting him, needing him, she gave herself up to the kiss.

His hands were on the back zipper of her dress, sliding it slowly downward, when the doorbell shrilling interrupted them. Startled, they jumped apart.

"Who could that be at this hour?" Toni murmured.

He could ignore his barking or whining dog, but the cop in him could never disregard his ringing phone or buzzing doorbell. "This better be good," he muttered as he ran a hand through his disheveled hair and walked to the front door, checking the .38 he'd tucked into the small of his back at his waist.

He bent to look through the peephole he'd had installed awhile back as he flipped on the porch light.

What he saw had him swearing under his breath just before he swung open the door.

The man on the stoop was tall, slim, and moviestar handsome with blond hair, Paul Newman blue eyes, and huge dimples. His grin was cocky as he leaned against the doorframe. "Hi, big brother. Long time no see."

With a resigned sigh, Ray stepped back. "Pete." He turned and saw that Toni had slipped on her shoes and zipped up her dress. She looked at him, a question in her eyes. "Toni, this is my younger brother, Peter Vargas."

All smiles, Pete walked in. "And you are?" he asked Toni.

"Toni Garette," she answered, moving to sit alongside Ray, where he'd settled on the couch wearing a look of impatience.

"Nice to meet you." Pete studied them, noticing Ray's tie hanging open and Toni's slightly swollen mouth. "Hope I didn't interrupt anything." His grin widened.

Ray frowned. "What brings you to town?"

Pete dropped into the chair by the fireplace and boyishly shoved back a lock of curly hair. "Hey, we're family, right? Only family we got left. Thought I'd see how you're doing. It's been how long, two or three years, right?"

"Two years, three months," Ray replied.

Feeling the tension in Ray although she wasn't touching him, Toni decided to see if she could ease the situation. "Where do you live, Peter?"

He shrugged, his hands moving restlessly on the chair arms. "Here and there. Most recently in Atlantic City." The carefree smile came easily, though it was a little worn around the edges. "Now there's a town for you, man. Action like you wouldn't believe. The beautiful people at play." He glanced around the room. "Nice little place you've got here, Ray."

"How's Melanie?" Ray asked, his voice guarded.

Pete leaned forward, his elbows on his knees, his hands gripping one another. "We've split. She's . . . she's pregnant. I told her I don't want kids." He looked up at Toni and gave her his heart-stopping smile. "Do I look like father material to you?"

No, he certainly didn't, Toni thought. Thinking she'd best stay out of this, she kept quiet.

Ray ground his teeth so hard he was surprised they didn't crack one by one. "Where is Melanie living?"

"In Cleveland. A real nowhere town." He shook his handsome head. "Man, I hate that place."

"You got a job?" Ray persisted, wondering why he periodically went through this charade.

Pete cleared his throat. "Actually, I'm between jobs right now. But I've got some irons in the fire. An offer should be coming in any day now." His expression turned solicitous. "I just need a little something to tide me over until one of them pops."

"What about Melanie and your baby?" Ray wanted to know.

"She'll be all right. She's planning to move back with her folks after she gets out of the hospital."

"The hospital? Is the baby here already?"

Pete waved the question away. "No, not for another five or six months. She's got morning sickness so bad she's dehydrated, so they put her in until she straightens out. She's been throwing up for three, four months. Man, I couldn't stand it no more, you know? She can't cook, can't stand the smell of food, she looks like hell. Who needs it?"

Who, indeed? Toni thought. How could such a fiercely responsible man like Ray have such a totally irresponsible brother? She wanted to grab Pete and shake that charming smile off his face. She could only imagine what Ray wanted to do with him.

Rising, Ray walked to the desk in the corner of the living room and found his checkbook in the top drawer. Quickly, he wrote a check and walked back to stand in front of Pete, holding it out to him.

"I hated to ask again, but I'm a little down on my luck." Pete shot a glance toward Toni, looking a shade embarrassed, then back to Ray. "This is just a loan. I'll pay you back." He stood up.

A loan. Where had he heard that before? Ray wondered.

"Hey, bro, you made this out to Melanie and me. I just told you, we've split."

"I heard you." Ray shoved his hands into his pants pockets, the urge to hit his own brother creeping up on him. "You can't cash it without her signature. I want you to go to her and give her half. You can do what you want with your half, but don't come to me for more. I mean it this time, Pete."

"Yeah, yeah. But Ray, like I said, I hate Cleveland. My car's not the best and I'm not sure it'll make the trip."

"Then get on a bus. You split that with her—and mind you, I'll find out if you don't—or you give it back right now." His eyes were hard.

Pete's handsome face turned bitter, almost ugly. "You've never liked me. You've always been jealous that Dad loved me more than you."

With a weary sigh, Ray walked to the front door

SHATTERED VOWS 213

and opened it. "You better leave before I change my mind and rip up the check."

Anger reddening his cheeks, Pete turned to Toni. "You'd better think twice before getting mixed up with this sonofabitch." With that, he hurried past his brother and down the steps. The night swallowed him up as the door closed behind him, the sound of the lock clicking overly loud in the silence.

Slowly, Ray walked back to the couch, sat down, and leaned his head back. He closed his eyes, wondering as always after a bout with Pete, where he'd gone wrong.

Toni wasn't quite sure what to say or do. "Would you like me to get you a drink?" she asked cautiously.

"No."

She was quiet a few moments. "Maybe I'd better go . . ."

He reached for her hand and held on tightly. Finally, he opened his eyes and looked at her. "I don't need a drink. I need you."

In his eyes, she saw how hard those words were for him to say, to admit to her. She'd needed him twice, and he'd been there for her. She could do no less. "I'm here."

Getting to his feet, still holding her hand, Ray led her up to his bedroom.

Pillow talk. It wasn't something she'd participated in much. She'd heard it often led to true confessions and emotional probings, something she'd thought it best to avoid. But tonight was an exception.

How to go about it was the question, Toni thought.

In the afterglow of good sex, Ray lay naked on

his bed with Toni nestled against him. He felt so comfortable with her, so right. Not during his brief marriage or any of his temporary alliances had he ever felt this way about anyone. Perhaps he ought to take that next step, to give her a glimpse of his not so rosy past to see if she'd still want to hang around afterward. After the scene with Pete, he could hardly ignore things. He'd appreciated that she hadn't asked any questions, not until he was ready to talk, though he was certain she had many. Mellowed by their lovemaking, he thought that now he could tell her, now he could open up a little.

Placing his hand on her hair as her cheek rested on his chest, he began talking, thinking it easier if she wasn't looking right at him. "My father's name was Joseph Vargas," he began, almost in a monotone, as if reciting an old, familiar story. "He came from a hard-working family of Hungarian immigrants who owned a grocery store and saved every dime so he could have the best education. He graduated from Harvard with a business degree and it didn't take him long to start making money. He married his neighborhood sweetheart, Isabel, my mother. They tell me she was not only beautiful outside but inside, too. She died when I was four and I hate it that I don't remember her very well."

Surprised that he'd embarked on such a story without her prompting, Toni shifted slightly so she could see his face. He kept his eyes on the window across the room, where moonlight filtered in through the slatted blinds.

"Dad threw himself into his work. Soon he was known throughout Massachusetts for his strong opinions, which appeared regularly in his three newspapers, and for the small television station he bought and expanded. There'd even been talk of his running for public office. When he was thirty-five, he hired a nineteen-year-old named Marianne, whom he fell for like the proverbial ton of bricks. He married her after knowing her only three months. When I was seven, they had Pete."

Unaware he was doing it, he stroked Toni's back and smoothed her hair, his thoughts on the past.

"To say that Marianne was a clever golddigger isn't giving her enough credit. My father was so crazy about her he didn't notice she was frittering away most of his money. She favored her son over me, naturally, and pretty soon, so did Dad. I wasn't a very happy kid."

She heard the hint of bitterness and lingering pain in his voice. She was an only child, until Mo had come to live with them, but her experience couldn't have been more different from Ray's.

"Dad did keep his promise and sent me to Harvard," Ray continued, "on the educational trust fund he'd set up when I'd been born. Just as I completed my first year, Marianne left him, but by then, Dad was down to one newspaper, having lost most everything else. She cleaned out the bank accounts, even somehow managed to cash in Pete's educational trust account. But unfortunately, she didn't take her son with her, which was too bad, since Dad was in no condition to raise a teenage boy."

"He was pretty shaken up when Marianne left?"

"To say the least. He was grief-stricken, as if she'd died. He started drinking, let himself go, and lost interest in his few remaining businesses. He was so nuts about her that he simply couldn't handle life without her. In short, he gave up."

Toni raised herself up on her elbows. "What happened?"

"I graduated from Harvard in May. He died in June."

"I'm so sorry, Ray."

He returned the pressure of her hand in his. "I'd seen that one coming. What I hadn't given much thought to was my fifteen-year-old half-brother."

"You don't mean that there was no one else left to care for Pete?"

His smile didn't hold much humor. "That's exactly what I mean. He was already a problem, having been spoiled by his mother and overindulged by Dad after she left, mostly because by then it had become a habit to give Pete everything he asked for."

"What did you do, a new graduate, only twenty-two?"

"I went to work for a friend of Dad's who'd bought one of the papers. Dad had lost the house, so I got an apartment near the high school so Pete could walk there." Ray shifted slightly, remembering. "He got kicked out for skipping classes. I got him into another one and he was expelled for cheating. One damn thing after another. When he turned sixteen, I managed to get him a used car and he took it out joy-riding, got drunk, and crashed it. Walked away without a scratch, but the car was totaled. Then, when he was seventeen, he got a girl pregnant and I didn't know what the hell to do."

"Lord, what a mess. What *did* you do?"

"The girl's father was furious, but he didn't want his daughter marrying Pete, which was very astute of him. He talked her into an abortion and I made Pete get a job and pay for it. He was so damn mad at me that he skipped town."

"So you paid for the abortion, I'll bet."

He let out a shaky breath. "You'd win. I didn't try to find him. By that time, he was eighteen and frankly, I was sick of cleaning up his messes. I wasn't real happy working at the paper. That hadn't been the plan. I had a friend who'd gone into law enforcement and worked his way up to lieutenant on the Boston force. I talked with him and decided to enroll in the police academy. The month I graduated, I went home one night and found two guys waiting for me. It seemed that Pete had gotten into gambling real heavy and owed them a bundle. They wanted to know where he was. I hadn't a clue. They didn't believe me. They beat the hell out of me and left me in the hallway of my apartment building."

"Oh, God." Toni's heart went out to him. He'd been through so much and yet he was still so sympathetic to the pain of others. "Is that when you got on a bus headed for Detroit?"

"Yeah. I needed to get away from Pete and all his problems. He was keeping me broke and messing up my life. I wanted to start over somewhere clean."

"So you joined the police force here."

"Yeah. And met this nice girl who thought it would be real exciting to marry a cop. Only she soon learned that it wasn't."

The puzzle pieces were finally slipping into place. "After you left her, is that when you decided that going it alone was a lot less hurtful than trusting someone again?"

For the first time since he'd begun his purging dissertation, he met her eyes. "You're pretty smart, you know? Like you once told me, a dose of people using and abusing you can make you swear off the opposite sex."

"I also said I hadn't given up on men, I'd just become more cautious. Do you think I'm using you?"

He drew her up closer, feeling her breasts slide up his chest, not in the least surprised that he was growing hard with just that little touch. "Hell, no. I'm using you. As a sounding board, as a beautiful diversion, as an outlet for my lustful needs." He gave her his slow smile. "But there is a difference this time, Toni."

She hadn't liked being called a diversion, beautiful or otherwise. "What's that?" she asked, feeling wary.

"The difference is that I've come to need you despite my best efforts to fight it." He hadn't meant to say that much, hadn't known until just this minute that he needed to say it.

"Oh, Ray," she whispered softly, knowing how hard the admission was for him.

"After all I've just told you, you must realize that I come with a lot of excess baggage, some that I've been unable to shake loose. Pete keeps finding me and I keep shelling out good money after bad. I know that I'm an enabler, as the analysts like to word it. A co-dependent, keeping him from standing on his own two feet and taking responsibility for his life and the lives of people like Melanie and his baby."

Toni agreed, yet understood. "What else could you have done, walk away from your only living relative?"

"That would probably have been the smart thing to do."

"When we care about people, we don't always act wisely. Love makes us do crazy things, at times."

He drew in a deep, shaky breath. "The L word. How do you feel about it?"

She saw the tension on his face and wondered how he couldn't have known long before this. "I've been afraid of it for years, not trusting where it might lead me." Moving up, she framed his bearded face with her hands. "With you, I'm not afraid, though maybe I should be. I'd told myself I didn't want to let myself love someone because I didn't want to be hurt again. I don't believe you'll hurt me. I trust you." *And I love you,* she finished in her thoughts. But something made her hold off telling him just yet.

When she lowered her mouth to his, he felt the sting of emotion behind his eyes as his arms crushed her to him.

On the phone in her office at the precinct, Meg heard someone approaching, whistling off tune. Swiveling about, she looked up to see Ray walk in. *Whistling?* He never whistled. She returned her attention to Father Hilliard on the other end of the line as Ray sat down at his desk.

"What did you say the woman's name was, Father?" Meg asked.

"Dolores Falconi," the priest answered. "She and her husband, Mario, were members of St. Matthews for a long time, then moved up to St. Clair about three years ago. They bought a house on the water because they both love to fish."

"I see," Meg said uncertainly. "And why is it she called you?"

"She read about the stranglings here at her former parish, of course, and she got to thinking. The Falconis had a daughter who was killed about two years ago. At first, they'd thought she'd fallen out of their small boat and drowned one afternoon. But when the body was found, they discovered something grisly."

"And that was?" she prompted.

"Angie had a wire wrapped around her neck."

He had Meg's full attention now. "Did the St. Clair police investigate?"

"Dolores said they came out, asked a lot of questions, but nothing was ever resolved. Mrs. Falconi thought I ought to call you. Maybe there's no connection, but . . ."

"I'm certainly glad you did, Father. Can you give me the Falconis' phone number, please? We'd like to talk with them."

"Sure, sure." He shuffled papers a moment, then came up with the right one and read Meg the number. "Do you think the same person who killed Angie Falconi might be involved in our stranglings?"

"I really couldn't say until we've talked with her parents and the St. Clair police. Thank you so much for calling, Father Hilliard."

"Anytime. Please let me know if you learn anything."

Reassuring him that she would, Meg hung up and looked at her partner. "You're certainly in a good mood," she commented, wondering when Ray had taken up whistling.

"Why not? It's a beautiful day out there. We don't get a hell of a lot of great days in Michigan." Ray removed his jacket and hung it on the back of his chair.

Meg indicated the page she'd been taking notes on. "This might cheer you even more." Quickly, she explained Father Hilliard's call.

"Sounds promising. Let's phone Dolores Falconi and see if she's free to talk with us. If so, we can drive up and stop at the St. Clair Police Station and take a look at their file on the daughter."

Maybe, at last, they had a lead, Ray thought.

Meg picked up the phone.

* * *

The small tourist community bordered Lake St. Clair. Vacationers and summer dwellers and year-rounders alike enjoyed boating, fishing, swimming, and watching the big freighters head up toward Lake Huron. It was a sleepy little town, and its inhabitants had chosen to live there for just that reason.

Driving along the main road that paralleled the water, Ray took in the large homes, situated on high ground, with terraced lawns and privacy hedges. Most were owned by the summer people. As the road wound northward, smaller houses, many clapboard add-ons, dotted the shoreline. Small bait shops and boat repair places were tucked in here and there, and the squeals and laughter of children on summer vacation, most bicycling on the winding sidewalks, filled the air. The breeze blowing in through Ray's open window smelled of newly mown grass.

"Summertime and the living is easy," Meg commented as they passed a youngster sauntering along eating an ice cream cone that dripped onto his chin and shirt.

Ray caught sight of the street name he'd been seeking and hung a quick right. The road wound downward, hugging the grassy banks of the lake. Dappled sunshine filtering through leafy trees overhead warmed the breeze and sent shadows dancing across the hood of his wagon. Number 17 was the last house on the right of the dead-end street.

Parking out front, Ray got out and looked around. The small house was painted gray and could have used another coat. A white Chevy sat in the graveled drive and a carport housed a small boat up on a hoist. A short, dark-haired woman came out the side door, wiping her hands on a terrycloth towel.

Meg walked to greet her. "Mrs. Falconi?"

"Yes. Please, come inside." She swatted at a buzzing fly. "I made a pitcher of tea."

They introduced themselves and accepted a frosty glass of iced tea with a chunk of lemon, then sat down on a floral couch under a picture window that overlooked the calm lake. The decor spoke of the owners' Italian heritage with fringed lamp shades and crocheted doilies on the arms of the overstuffed furniture. And it was all so spotlessly clean that Ray wondered if the lady of the house was obsessive/compulsive.

Dolores Falconi perched on the edge of a maple rocker across from them and held out a framed photo of her daughter. "This was my Angie." She swallowed back the tears that came every time she thought of their loss. "Beautiful, no?"

"She was lovely," Meg assured her, handing back the picture and taking out her notepad. "Can you tell us what happened?"

Dolores dabbed at her eyes with the towel. "I wish I knew. Angie was a good girl. Only that one time she got in trouble, back when she was just a teenager. After that, she learned her lesson. She had a good job at the St. Clair Bank, bought a little car. She dated a little, but not much. No one special. She was kinda quiet, you know."

Ray set his tea down on the glass-topped end table. "What kind of trouble was Angie in when she was a teenager, Mrs. Falconi?"

Dolores glanced furtively out the window. "My husband's out there fishing in one of our boats. He don't know the whole story. Angie, she wasn't wild, you know. Just young. She got pregnant, but she didn't tell anyone. Only something went wrong and she lost the baby. I didn't find out till the doctor called me from the hospital after she collapsed at work one day. He told me she miscarried." She twisted the towel in her trembling hands. "We never told her father. Mario couldn't handle knowing his daughter wasn't a virgin, you know."

Like a lot of fathers. "And the baby's father?" Ray asked.

The woman's face grew angry. "Angie wouldn't tell me his name. With my bare hands, I would kill him. My Angie was a good girl, sweet, innocent."

"Can you give us names of men she was dating around that time?"

"Men? Not men, just boys."

"How old was she when this happened?"

"Eighteen. Right after graduation. Thank God we kept it quiet. We told everyone she had a bad infection." Her deep brown eyes were sad. "Either one of you got kids?" When they shook their heads, Dolores nodded. "They give you a lot of pleasure, but a lot of pain, too."

"Could you give us a list of some of the boys then, her classmates, maybe neighbors?" Meg asked.

"Sure, I remember a couple of them. But who cares now, so much later, who the father was? The baby's gone, Angie's gone."

"It might be important," Ray answered. "How old was Angie when she died?"

"Twenty-three, just two years ago. We moved here the year before. Terrible, it was terrible."

"I understand you thought it was a boating accident at first," Meg said.

"That's what the cops thought, but me? I never thought so. Angie, she could swim like a fish." She sniffled into her towel. "They pulled her out of the water and there it was, this wire around her neck." Tears flowed freely now. "Oh, God, I never want to see such a sight again. No mother should ever see such a thing."

"Mrs. Falconi, do you remember anything particular about the wire?" Meg asked.

"Like what? It was just a wire. A long wire."

"Was it silver or copper in color?" Ray asked.

"No. I remember like it was yesterday. It was green."

TWELVE

The first thing anyone meeting Ted Riordan noticed was that at thirty-five he hadn't a hair on his head. As the hypnotist sat down in the chair alongside his desk, Ray tried to refrain from running a hand through his own hair. He'd never understood why men shaved their heads. "Thanks for coming over, Mr. Riordan."

The smile was quick, genuine. "No problem. Glad to be of help, if I can." Riordan spent most of his energy trying to help people stop smoking or overeating. Working with the police was far more challenging and prestigious, even if no money was involved. The mention of his occasional affiliation in his ads lent authenticity to his credentials.

"You spent some time hypnotizing Charley Ames yesterday?" The maintenance man from Mt. Carmel Hospital had been scheduled for a 10:00 A.M. session.

"Right. I had him under over an hour." He patted the envelope he'd placed on Ray's desk. "I recorded our session and brought you the tape so you can listen to the whole thing when you have time, if you like."

"I appreciate that. For now, can you tell me, did he remember more about the man he'd seen at Mt. Carmel the night Sister Irene was strangled?"

"Yes, some. Charley's an ideal subject. He went under easily and talked freely, although he often veered off and rambled quite a bit. He kept returning to one thing regarding the suspect, that the man had really thick brown hair." Ted smiled. "Those of us lacking in that department seem to zero in on others more abundantly blessed."

"Right. What else?"

"Apparently the man never looked at Charley straight away so he doesn't have a recollection of eye color. The face, he recalled after some probing, gave the impression of roundness, almost like baby fat."

Ray frowned. "Was the man that young?"

"Charley guessed him to be in his mid-twenties."

That came as a surprise, probably because most serial killers were at least in their thirties or older. "I see. Anything else."

"The clothes he was wearing. Dark green pants and shirt."

"Dark green. Work clothes, I imagine."

"Yes. The sort you can buy at Sear's or such places. A lot of jobs call for the type, Charley went on. He has some himself. They also come in black, navy, gray."

"Did he recall hearing the man say anything?"

"No, not a word. Not even after he started walking away did he hear the faint sound of someone talking behind him. People under hypnosis often recall conversations on the periphery that they've overheard, but aren't aware of consciously. But not this time."

Maybe there hadn't been a conversation between the man and Sister Irene. Maybe she hadn't looked up when he'd stepped from the elevator, still engrossed in her paperwork. Maybe after Charley had gone into the patient's room to clean up, the man had managed to circle behind the nun and kill her before she even knew he was there. There'd been no sign of a scuffle, no indication of a struggle. She'd died quietly, slumping forward, her head resting on the desk until later when Charley'd touched her and she'd slipped to the floor.

"Is there anything else he said during the hour he was under that might help us?"

Ted ran his hand over his bald pate and shook his head. "Not really. It took me a while to lead him around to discussing the murder. He's understandably frightened at having found the body. He's got the feeling that maybe this killer works at the hospital and he's fighting a case of nerves, seeing someone lurking in every shadow. I wouldn't be surprised if the man quit his job, he's that upset."

"That'd be a shame."

"Yeah, well, most people get nervous even thinking about murders." Ted stood, ready to leave. "The average person doesn't run across a dead body in the average workday. Of course, you see it all the time, so you're used to it."

Ray rose as well. "You never get used to it, Mr. Riordan."

The hypnotist looked unconvinced as he turned away, then swung back suddenly. "One thing I forgot to mention—Charley recalled smelling something, a strong scent. And he was very definite about what it was."

"And what was it?"

"Old Spice aftershave. It's the same brand Charley uses."

It was unseasonably hot by Tuesday afternoon. Ray wished he could remove his jacket, but he was wearing his piece. Unlocking his car door, he turned on the engine and opened the windows. He'd let some of the heat out before turning on the air conditioning.

He sat behind the wheel for a minute, thinking he'd spent a long and fruitless morning interviewing maintenance men and groundskeepers at Mt. Carmel Hospital. He'd struck out on this possibility. Not one fit the description Charley'd given them under hypnosis. However, there appeared to be a good reason for that.

Like many hospitals, Mt. Carmel farmed out their groundskeeping tasks. An assortment of nurseries kept up the flower beds and planted new trees and shrubs to replace damaged ones. Lawn maintenance service contractors came weekly to cut grass, trim shrubs, prune trees. But not necessarily would the same men go to the same place every week.

The company currently servicing the lawn was Westland Maintenance. They employed twenty-four men who worked a variety of shifts and were sent to over thirty locations throughout the west side and suburbs. And that was just the larger jobs, the hospitals, libraries, schools, and malls. They also had about a hundred private clients whose home lawns were attended to by members of the Westland crew, another dozen or so men.

Only about three dozen men to check out, Ray thought with a sigh. And, as if that weren't bad enough, Westland was new on the job at Mt.

Carmel. Before that, they'd used United Lawn Maintenance Company, which employed sixteen men. Terrific.

He closed his car door and shifted into drive. No point in putting it off. He'd grab a quick burger and head over to Westland first. Leg work. How he hated it.

The call came in at eight on Wednesday morning, the caller a young boy whose voice was in the process of deepening. The desk transferred it to Ray's desk phone. Having just gotten his first cup of coffee of the day, he picked it up. "Vargas here."

"Hi, Ray. I . . . I didn't know if I should call you at work." The voice was low and hesitant.

Ray swallowed a hot mouthful. "Mark, is that you?"

"Yeah. I . . . I just wanted to say goodbye."

"Goodbye? Where are you going?" He thought he knew. The Bahamas with his witchy mother and the man who'd soon be his stepfather.

"A vacation, I guess. Mom says I'll like it, but I don't want to go. Being with them every minute sucks. I mean, they act so goofy, holding hands, kissing in public. They embarrass me. I don't know why they want me along. They hardly even know I'm there."

The stepfather who was bonding with her son, or so Abigail had told him. "I went to pick you up the other night. Your mother said you were out on the driving range with Donald."

"Yeah. She made me go with old stupid." The boy's voice was filled with disgust. "I told him I hate standing there hitting those dumb balls for hours, but he kept saying I'd get to like it. The day hell freezes over, you know."

Ray sat down and leaned back, wishing he knew what to say. "Maybe he's trying, Mark. Since your mother's determined to marry him, you're probably going to have to learn to like him. Think you can manage that?"

"No. He's stupid, acting like a teenager around Mom. And she giggles at everything he says, even when it's something really dumb like the airhead jokes he's always telling."

"What kind of work does he do, Mark?"

"He's a stockbroker. He wants to take me to work with him one day and show me the ropes. Hell, I don't want a jerk like him showing me *anything*. He calls me *son*, never uses my name. He makes me want to throw up. I tried to teach him to play chess and he couldn't catch on, so he told me it wasn't a game for a *real* man. Shit!"

Ray understood the boy's frustration, but he doubted that things would improve for Mark in the immediate future. Abigail was more interested in her own pleasure than her son's happiness. "Have you tried telling your mother any of this?"

"Geez, man, did you ever try talking to my mother?"

Ray was silent.

"She doesn't care how I feel. She's happy and I should be, too, according to her. I'm such a lucky kid, she told me. I have everything any *normal* boy could want. Why can't I be happy?" There was a brief pause. "Ray, you think maybe I'm not normal?"

"Mark, I think you're a hundred percent normal. Just like me. Of course, there are those who don't think I am, either." He got a chuckle from the boy, but not a heartfelt one. "I wish I could tell you something that would solve your situation. All I can say is, you're nearly sixteen. You'll soon be old enough to make some decisions about your life apart from your mother's influence. Like we talked about that day when we were playing chess, the choices we make, in that game and in life, can make or break us."

He was quiet a long moment. "She doesn't want me to see you anymore. Did she tell you that?"

Ray struggled with a rush of anger. "Yeah, she did. Look, maybe when you come back from this trip, you and I together can try to talk with her again and see if she'll change her mind about that." He'd have to bite the bullet and make nice with Abigail. Ray hoped he could manage that. "Okay?"

"Yeah, I guess." He sounded more dejected than when they'd begun talking.

"What about John? What does he have to say?" John Cramer was Mark's therapist.

"He tells me I should give Donald a chance, maybe I'll like him if I do. Only I never will. The guy's a nerd, Ray, with his vests, his wingtips, and his *Wall Street Journal* always tucked under his arm."

"Why don't you try thinking of this as temporary, Mark? Two years, that's all. You can stand anything if you know one day it'll be over."

"Two years is forever, Ray."

The hopelessness he heard in the boy's voice got to him. "When do you get back from this trip?"

"We're leaving Sunday and we'll be gone a week."

"All right. I promise I'll find a way to get your mother to let us go on being friends after you get back." Maybe marriage would mellow Abigail. Ray really liked the kid. Being around him was no hardship. "I'll involve John, if I have to. I'll *make* your mother listen. What do you think?"

"If only you could, that would help."

"I'll be in touch a couple of days after you return, okay?"

"Okay. 'Bye, Ray."

Ray sat listening to the dial tone after the boy hung up, wondering how he was going to keep his promise, how he was going to get past the barracuda in order to help Mark McCarthy.

Rain pelted against the windows of the twelfth floor of the Pontchatrain Hotel, a sudden summer squall that had the sky darkening in midday and the river that separated downtown Detroit from Windsor, Ontario, rolling and pitching from the restless wind. Inside, in a kingsize bed, the two people totally engrossed in one another hardly noticed the escalating storm outside.

Ray hadn't known he could feel so much pleasure as he'd impatiently undressed Toni, stripping layers from her with trembling hands. The neat little business suit, one of many she owned, fell piece by piece onto the thick blue carpeting, followed by silken swatches he'd almost ripped from her. His eyes had grown hungry while he'd quickly shed his own clothes as she'd watched him from her kneeling position on the pale blue sheets.

Need for her pounded through him as he knelt with her, lacing his fingers through hers. Her skin was fragrant, delicate, the texture like fine satin. He sent his mouth on a journey of discovery as her breath trembled from her. Hands still locked, he followed her down and watched her eyes widen as he filled her completely. She arched to take him deeper.

Now he could feel her own need vibrate through her, drawing him in, as slick, damp skin slid over warm, moist skin. He held off the moment, watching her climb, until she became greedy and finally desperate. Her fingers curled around his as she changed from passive to frenzied. She moaned her demands and begged for release as he held her in check, increasing their pleasure by delaying the inevitable.

Outside, the rain battered against the glass, vying for attention, and still neither heard nor noticed. Hands locked, hearts pounding in sync, he thrust deeply, then withdrew until she raised to urge him back, then thrust again. His eyes on hers, he emptied his mind of everything but this woman who filled his thoughts more thoroughly than anyone he'd known.

There in the room he'd rented and coaxed her to come to because he couldn't wait for night to fall, he took her with a raging hunger he was very much afraid would never let him be. As he swallowed her cry of completion, he wondered how he'd ever again manage to be without her.

"This wasn't supposed to happen," Toni said, her voice husky as she lay with her legs still tangled with his.

"What wasn't? Taking a few hours off in the middle of the day?" His arm moved her fractionally closer, wondering why he could never quite get close enough to this woman. "We deserve it."

Shifting her hair back, Toni angled so she could look at him. "I mean falling for you." She still hadn't said those three little words, waiting to be sure he felt the same. "I hadn't intended to."

"That makes two of us."

"I'd thought I'd enjoy myself with someone I truly liked and admired. Good sex between two good friends. Then, when it was over, I'd hoped to walk away with no bitter feelings, no self-recriminations."

He was interested in how she'd analyzed the situation. "And?"

"And I realized awhile back that I'd been kidding myself. It wasn't going to be that easy. The thought of walking away from you devastates me."

He smiled, tugging her ever nearer. "Good, because I don't want you to walk away."

"I'm not sure I know how to deal with feelings this strong, because I've never had them before. I'm not sure I'm prepared to deal with any of this."

He shifted her so they were only a breath apart. "You don't have to deal with anything alone. I'm right here with you." The words, so foreign to his thinking just a few weeks ago, sounded right, sounded true. "We'll work this out together."

She smiled at him then. "Together. What a nice word." She closed the gap between them by touching her mouth to his. His arm around her tightened as he deepened the kiss. She felt him stir against her and wondered if she dare take the time for another go around. She had scheduled a meeting with a new catering crew she'd hired for three this afternoon.

Then his tongue took possession of hers and she forgot the time, the caterers, and everything else.

Ray heard the shower turn on in the bathroom and settled back to wait his turn. He couldn't remember

SHATTERED VOWS   235

the last time he'd been so crazy to have a woman that he'd thrown caution to the winds and all but kidnapped her in the middle of the day. Even now, if he let his mind drift just a bit, he'd find himself wanting her again.

But he had to get back to work and so did she. His beeper on the dresser across the room reminded him that he was on call even when it was silent.

Snapping on the bedside radio, he lay back, his crossed hands under his head. He stretched lazily, feeling good. Feeling better than good. He toyed with the idea of joining Toni in the shower, then decided he'd better not. If he made her too late for her appointment, she'd hesitate the next time.

Eyes closed, he listened to a collection of show tunes with half his attention until the newscaster interrupted with a late-breaking story about a gunman who'd gone berserk in a west side police station, killing several people and wounding more. There was little else he could say at this time, but urged his listeners to stay tuned for full details on their regularly scheduled newscast on the hour.

Sitting up, Ray reached for the phone and called Beaubien. The sergeant on duty had the details they were keeping from the public until next of kin could be notified.

Among the dead was Sergeant Dennis O'Malley, Meg's husband.

It was too nice a day to be buried. Ray would have preferred a dark, threatening sky or even a downpour. A man as fine as Dennis O'Malley had been shouldn't be stuck in the ground on a bright day wreathed in sunshine.

He stood next to Toni, along with Luke and

Stephanie and Sam and Carly, the six of them off to the left of the flag-draped casket under a funeral tent on a slight rise at White Chapel Cemetery. Dennis had been born into a big, boisterous Irish Catholic family. It seemed to Ray that he could spot at least two dozen relatives of all ages who resembled the O'Malleys. Then there was the Ryan clan, Meg's people, many redheads like she. A well-liked couple, many of their friends were present, too.

A very social guy, Dennis would have liked the turnout, Ray decided.

"There have to be three hundred people here," Carly whispered to her husband. She shifted from one foot to the other, her advanced pregnancy causing some discomfort. Six more weeks to go. She couldn't wait.

"At least," Sam agreed. He hated seeing Meg look so small, so pale and forlorn. She'd adored Dennis. He wondered how she'd manage to go on. Gripping his wife's hand, he felt sympathy for Meg's loss.

"It's all so senseless," Stephanie added. "The man was gunned down while sitting at a desk."

Luke was always the philosophical one. "Maybe when it's your time to go, it doesn't matter where you are."

"I'm not sure I agree with that," Toni chimed in, thinking of Mo and the other sisters who'd been killed so viciously while minding their own business, just like Dennis. "There are too many loose canons wandering our streets."

Ray's jaw tightened, feeling as if everyone blamed the police for that sorry state. Did Toni blame him in particular for not having captured the strangler thus far? "If only loose canons walked around with signs on their foreheads that they were about to commit a heinous crime, we could pick them up more easily."

Silently, Toni squeezed his hand, wishing he wouldn't take every remark personally, wishing he didn't feel responsible for every crime in the city, for every wrong in the world. She kept her voice low, for his ears only. "I know it isn't easy, standing by and watching terrible things happen repeatedly, unable to get a handle on who's doing them."

He turned to her, his eyes bleak. "Do you?"

"Yes."

He stared at her a long moment, then turned to see Captain Renwick making his way toward Meg as the brief graveside ceremony ended. "Let's go say a few words to Meg." Even though he knew there were no words that would give her comfort on the day she buried the only man she'd ever loved, he had to try.

Ray stood at the back of the courtroom as Mort Zitzler's court-appointed attorney stated the old man's case. Psychiatric evaluation showed that Zitzler had a history of disturbances and disorders dating back to a troubled childhood, abandoned by his parents, growing up on the streets. He was undereducated, had worked sporadically all his sixty-seven years, and was living on a small social security check that barely paid his rent, much less for other necessities.

Mort had confessed that he often bought cat food on sale and doled it out to himself for dinner, claiming he loved fish. He was not senile, had never been a drinker or drug user, but showed signs of mental deterioration and had a very low I.Q.

Shoving his hands in his pocket, Ray thought that

Mort Zitzler was an example of the leftovers of society. No one wanted them, no one knew what to do with them.

The judge ordered them remanded to a minimum-security facility and ordered more testing and psychiatric counseling. Ray knew that after he'd served his time, Mort would be released back into society. They simply didn't have the space to keep them for long nor treat them until cured. If a cure was even possible.

Mort would fall between the cracks and be free to commit another crime, perhaps more devastating than shooting up someone's apartment. The next time, it might be the someone.

As Mort was led out of the courtroom in handcuffs, he glanced back and spotted Ray. "Detective Vargas," he called in his shaky voice. "Can't you help me? They're gonna lock me up. No one listens. No one cares."

His stomach muscles clenching, Ray followed him out. He would talk to the man, try to reassure him. It was the least he could do. "I'm here, Mort," he told the old man.

"Move along, buddy," the burly escorting officer said to Mort, ignoring Ray and poking his charge in the back, all but shoving him down the corridor.

"Hey," Ray said, tapping the officer's shoulder, "you don't need to talk to him like that. There's no call to be so rough."

The cop spoke over his shoulder. "Stay out of it, mister. He's a criminal and a loonie besides."

"He's a human being."

Disgusted, the cop swung around to face Ray. "He shot a—"

"He shot a microwave oven. Let's keep things in perspective, officer." Ray's voice was steely.

The cop spotted Ray's I.D. dangling from the breast pocket of his sportcoat. "Right, Detective Vargas. Sorry."

"I'll take him down." Ray took hold of Mort's thin arm. "Come on, Mort. I'll see that you get settled in."

She stood on the porch ringing the doorbell, feeling a little foolish. It was late and Toni didn't know why she'd come. She'd spent the day racing between the two restaurants, someone always needing her attention, her input, her decision. By ten, she'd had it, and had set out for home. But halfway there, she'd felt an overpowering urge to visit Ray.

She pressed the bell again, then stepped to the window and peeked into his living room. Ray's car was in the drive and several lights were on inside. Hamlet was up on the couch, barking a welcome. And still Ray hadn't come to open the door.

It was too late for him to be down at the park with Mark, and besides, Mark was probably still in the Bahamas with his honeymooning mother and her new husband, or so Ray had told her. He might have gone for a run, but she doubted he would this late. Where was he?

She heard a car coming down the street and looked over her shoulder as a dark sedan with tinted windows moved slowly past. The night breeze picked up her hair and tossed it about. Toni shivered and decided to try the door, though she didn't think Ray ever left it unlocked.

It turned easily.

Hamlet bounded over to greet her with a deep-throated woof, then licked the hand she held out.

"Ray?" she called out. But all she heard was the dog panting.

Surely he hadn't been the victim of a robbery, for nothing looked disturbed. The whole neighborhood knew Ray was a police officer. His jacket was hanging over the newel post of the upstairs railing, his loafers beneath the coffee table, as if shoved off while he'd been sitting on the couch. *The Detroit News* was scattered over the floor as if thrown by an angry hand.

Murmuring reassurances to Hamlet, Toni tossed her purse onto a chair and wandered toward the back of the house. In the kitchen, she saw further signs that Ray had been here, and quite recently. A steak, charbroiled to shoe leather stage, sat on a plate alongside barbecue tongs and a hot pad. Then she saw something that offered up the best clue so far.

The top to a bottle of Chivas and an empty glass.

"Where's Ray?" she asked Hamlet, returning to the living room. "Where is he, boy?" She watched the dog scamper up the stairs. Slowly, she followed.

He was sitting on the edge of his bed, barefoot, his shirt hanging open and his hair mussed. On the nightstand stood the half empty bottle of scotch. Toni wondered if it had been full when he'd started.

Ray stood up, weaving only slightly, then thought better of it and sat back down. "I said I was coming. Guess you didn't hear me."

She walked over to him, more surprised than anything. "When did you decide to get a little drunk?"

He gave her a silly grin. "I'm not just a little drunk, honey. I'm shit-faced."

"All right. When did you decide to get shit-faced, and why?"

"I dunno when. This afternoon." He felt quite

proud that he wasn't slurring his words. Not too damn many guys could drink half a bottle and not slur. He blinked, trying to get Toni's face in better focus. "I called you awhile ago. They said you were at the other place."

She frowned. "I didn't get the message."

"That's 'cause I didn't leave one." He reached for the bottle, lifted it to his mouth, took a long swallow, then made a face. Grimacing, he held it out to her. "Here, have a drink. It's good stuff."

"I can tell you're really enjoying it." She took it from him and placed it back on the nightstand. Sitting down alongside him, she noticed that his face had taken on a sadness. "Is something wrong?"

With exaggerated slowness, he turned to face her. "Is something wrong? The question should be, is something right? Judas Priest, Toni. Nothing in the whole friggin' world is right anymore."

She put her hand on his back, caressing it soothingly. "Tell me what happened."

He gave a grunt. "What didn't happen. Meg's husband is sitting behind a desk when some slimeball decides to go on a shooting spree and kills him. A madman is loose somewhere in the city and he's strangled five innocent nuns. Five. Count 'em."

The job was getting to him, and why shouldn't it? He faced the dregs of humanity day in and day out. How many cheery days did a cop ever really put in? Damn few, she'd wager. She took a deep breath and touched her cheek to his shoulder. "I know. There are so many wrongs you'd like to right. Too many."

"I can't get a handle on him, Toni." His voice had gotten wavery, so he cleared his throat. "Who is the bastard and why is he killing the sisters? I *need* to find him, to solve this, to end it all."

"You will."

"Yeah, sure." He reached across her for the bottle, took another swig, then set it down hard. "I solve so many. Like poor old Mort Zitzler. He says his neighbor's appliances are talking to him and interfering with his thoughts, and when no one buys that story, he shoots the place up, still trying for attention. Well, he's got a ton of it now. Locked up in prison, psychologists pokin' into his brain. Know what they're gonna find?" He didn't bother to wait for her answer. "That he's all alone and hurting and no one cares about the poor old bastard."

She wondered if she could get through to him. "You can't solve everyone's problems, Ray. You can't be there for all these people who are so needy."

His eyes burned into hers. *"I'm* needy, Toni. Tonight, I'm real needy."

She slipped her arms around him, still uncertain if everything had piled up on him or if something new had happened. "I'm right here. Will I do?"

"Yeah, you'll do." He placed trembling hands on her cheeks and kissed her more gently than she'd have ever imagined. She tasted regret mingled with scotch.

When she drew back and looked at him, Toni saw that tears were trailing from his eyes and disappearing into his soft beard. "What is it, Ray? What else happened?"

He lowered his hands from her face and reached for her fingers, his grip strong, almost painful. His face twisted as he struggled not to cry. "So many die, Toni. So many good people. I can't stop it, no matter how hard I try. Maybe I should give up."

"No." She tightened her hold on him. "You

mustn't give up. You're a cop, a damn fine one. You make a difference in people's lives."

"Oh, yeah?" His mouth was a thin line as the tears continued to fall. "What kind of a difference did I make in Mark McCarthy's life?"

Here it comes, she thought, her intuition telling her this was what had sent him so uncharacteristically to the bottle. "What about Mark?"

Ray swallowed hard and forced the words out. "His barracuda of a mother and his new stepfather brought him home from their trip to the Bahamas two days ago. He called my office, but I was at Dennis's funeral and didn't get the message until late that night. I called awhile ago and Donald answered. Abigail was too upset to come to the phone, he said."

He seemed unable to go on, his face a study in anguish. Toni waited until he got himself under control.

"Mark took his mother's handgun and shot himself in the head last night."

"Oh God, no!" Toni pulled his head to her chest and held him tightly, her own eyes filling with tears.

"He was going to turn sixteen next month," Ray said, his face pressed to her, his hands kneading her back. "He never had a chance, Toni."

She didn't know what to say to that. Long ago, she'd read that if someone was determined to die, they'd find a way. Only she hadn't thought it of anyone so young.

Eyes as bleak as a winter sky looked into hers. "I need you, Toni. I never wanted to need anyone, but I do need you."

"It's all right," she whispered. "I need you, too." Opening her arms, she pulled him closer, rocking him in the age-old rhythm of comfort as he wept for Mark and all of the world's unfortunates.

The dusty Olds sedan crept by the detective's house for the fourth time. Slowing to a stop across the street, Wally rolled down the tinted window and peered at the two-story colonial curiously. Something didn't seem right.

He'd followed the Garette woman from her Birmingham restaurant and passed on by when she'd pulled into the drive behind Vargas's station wagon. Making a slow U-turn, he'd seen her on the porch for some time, then watched her enter, though he hadn't noticed the cop anywhere in sight. Did she now have a key?

He felt a surge of disappointment at the thought. If Vargas gave her a key, that probably meant that they'd become a couple. Jealousy shivered through him. He'd been part of a couple once and his lonely heart longed for that still. From the start, when he'd started watching Toni, he'd known deep inside that she wasn't as good and pure as his angel. But he'd gotten so much pleasure from looking at her, from thinking about her, from imagining her with him the way Terry had once been.

But wait. If Toni had a key, she wouldn't have had to stand on the porch, waiting to be let inside.

The lights were on all over the place, upstairs and down. What was going on? Through the thin curtains on the front windows, he'd seen Toni walking from room to room, then she'd disappeared. Had she gone upstairs? Wooden blinds were on the upper two windows and, although they were slanted, he couldn't see inside. Had she phoned him ahead, planned to meet him here and then rushed up to his bed?

Wally's body heated as his mind pictured them. He didn't want to think of beautiful, blond Toni Garette with those long legs and that perfect skin giving herself to that bearded cop. Only bad girls did that outside of marriage. His mother had told him that repeatedly, and so had Father Hilliard in the confessional when he'd admitted that he had these powerful urges that wouldn't let him be. They'd both told him to think pure thoughts to drive away the bad ones.

He'd tried, he'd honestly tired.

Maybe Toni wasn't in the cop's bed. Maybe he was only a friend to her and she'd heard he was sick. Toni had such a good heart, she'd probably come to take care of him.

Yes, that was probably it. Wally felt better picturing that scenario. He'd seen her go toward the kitchen, probably to get his medicine and maybe a bowl of soup. She'd carried that upstairs and was feeding the detective, he decided. She'd make sure he was comfortable, then she'd leave.

Wally picked up the picture he'd taken of Toni with the new zoom lense he'd bought for his camera months ago. He'd taken pictures of all the others, too, before he'd sent them to be with the Father. They were in his dresser drawer. This one showed Toni hurrying out the side door of her restaurant and rushing to her car. She hadn't been aware he'd been parked on a side street, aiming his camera through a partially open window.

For one split second, she'd glanced his way and he'd snapped her. She wasn't smiling and she looked preoccupied, but her eyes were bright blue and her hair was so shiny and pretty. He wished he could touch it, like he'd once touched Terry's. With a shaky hand, he put the picture back on his dash.

He rubbed his forehead where a dull headache made itself known. They were starting again. Not so bad yet, but definitely there. He was fighting them, praying they would ease up. He didn't want to start looking for another angel. He wanted peace.

Nothing had changed at the cop's house. Lights still on and no one in sight. Wally debated about staying until Toni came out so he could follow her home and make sure she was safe. But he still hadn't gotten his headlight fixed and she might spot him behind her now that there was hardly any traffic. Besides, he had to get up early tomorrow.

He had a job to do on the west side and he hated to be late.

THIRTEEN

"You're sure you're up to this, Meg?" Captain Renwick asked, his usually stern face a study in compassion.

"Yes, absolutely." She'd lost weight in the two weeks since Dennis's death, and she knew she was pale and a little shaky. But when the captain had called, she'd been more than ready to return. Work meant there would be less time to grieve, to weep, to rail against the fates.

In the other chair facing Renwick's desk, Ray studied her with concern in his eyes. She was a hell of a trouper, but at what cost? "You don't have to do this, Meg. The psychologist said that it's possible I could win Kimberly's trust."

Meg shook her head. "No offense, Ray, but the child needs a female. It's been proven that she's been raped by a grown man, most probably by her father, whom she once trusted. In the mind of a six-year-old, I'm sure she equates all men with pain right now. It'll take years of analysis and counseling to make her trust another adult male." She could have wept for that much alone. but there was so much more that had happened to the poor child.

Her mother had been killed in the kitchen of her

luxurious Grosse Pointe home at three in the afternoon two days before, while Kimberly had been upstairs in her room. According to Dr. Everett, he'd come home early and found his wife with multiple stab wounds, bleeding profusely and near death. He'd told police that just before she'd died in his arms, Molly had whispered that a long-haired, hippie-type man had forced his way in, demanded money, and grabbed a kitchen knife when she'd told him she didn't keep cash in the house.

From the beginning, the police had been suspicious of the doctor's story. There were eleven stab wounds in Molly Everett's body, indicating a rage killing rather than a robber turned killer. If an intruder had killed her, he'd had to have been covered in blood since the kitchen floor, counters and even some walls were sprayed with it. A neighbor woman and her three children had been in their backyard pool, which faced the Everetts' kitchen door, and she'd seen nor heard no one enter or leave, not even the doctor himself. And Dr. Everett's receptionist said he'd left the office shortly after noon, which left nearly three hours unaccounted for.

"Has the doctor been formally charged?" Meg asked.

"Not yet. We're cooperating with the Grosse Pointe police on this one, but they agreed that since you'd met with Kimberly several times, it would be best if you talked to her again."

"Is she staying there in that house alone with her father?" The very thought had Meg curling her fists.

The captain shook his head. "She's with her maternal grandparents. They live several blocks from the Everett house. They're understandably upset about their daughter's death, and don't believe Everett's story for a minute. They've never liked him and so they're willing to allow you to talk to Kimberly provided Dora Haynes, the child psychologist, is present."

Meg turned to Ray. "I haven't read the reports, but you have. You think he killed his wife?"

Ray leaned forward. "I'm sure he did. I was behind the glass when the boys on the hill interrogated the doctor. Naturally, his smarmy lawyer was present. The way Everett described the man his wife struggled with reminded me of reruns of *The Fugitive,* absolutely insisting he's innocent. As far as I'm concerned, the guy's lying, sure as hell."

"He killed her because she wasn't letting up on accusing him of molesting Kimberly?" Meg conjectured.

"I think so. Let me run this possible scenario by you. Let's say our good doctor came home unexpectedly. His wife's at the store so, not wanting to miss a golden opportunity, he gets cozy with his daughter again. Suddenly, he hears Molly return, so he sneaks downstairs, trying to leave before she sees him. But she catches him. Remember, the groceries were still on the counter unpacked. She guesses what he's been up to. Earlier, she'd made it clear to him that she wasn't allowing him to be alone with Kimberly ever again, and had even discussed filing for divorce. She's finally had it and threatens to call the police. He gets scared, realizes the threat she poses to his career and decides to shut her up."

"It sounds logical," Meg said thoughtfully.

Captain Renwick glanced at the file. "I read somewhere here that the wife's family is the one with the money. Lots of it. Of course, as a pediatric eye surgeon, Everett makes quite a bit, but it was her family who funded his plush office. I imagine he was afraid that if they believed Molly's accusations, they'd throw their considerable clout behind her and discredit him."

"And that'd be the end of his lucrative practice," Ray added. "After all, he works with children. We're also checking into his patient list to see if there have been any previous complaints against him. But this is tricky. If we act before we have an airtight case against him, that smart-ass lawyer of his will slap a defamation-of-character lawsuit on us."

Meg checked her watch. She'd been right to come back to work. Here, the time flew by. At home, she'd wandered from room to room like a sleepwalker, the minutes like hours. "What time did you say we're to meet with Kimberly?"

"In half an hour," Ray answered.

"Will you come with me? I'll feel better if you're there on the other side of the glass." She hated to ask, but knew she wasn't back to her old self yet. Would she ever be?

Ray stood. "Of course. Come on. I'll drive."

"Good luck," Captain Renwick said.

Rosie Pulaski bent over her small flower garden in her fenced-in backyard. The geraniums were doing so well this year. She snapped off a couple of dead blossoms so the new ones could take their place. And the pansies were in full bloom, yellow and purple. She'd tied her two rose bushes to small poles to keep them upright. Ah, how her Joe had loved to see roses on the table. Roses for my Rosie, he'd say.

Straightening, she smiled at the memory, then gave in to a frown as a sharp pain ran up her back.

She'd been at it an hour now. Too long for a woman her age. She'd pay the price tonight, probably needing a heating pad to ease the aches. But who didn't have a few?

She'd just finish to the end of the row of marigolds, pulling out the stubborn weeds from the ground softened by a brief early morning rain, and then she'd quit. Bending again, she heard the sound of a car chugging down the alley. She recognized Wladek's Olds as it turned into her garage. She'd told him he could park it there since she didn't own a car.

It was barely ten in the morning and she wondered why he was back so soon. She'd heard him leave around seven and knew that most days, he was gone for hours, sometimes late into the evening. A couple of times, she'd even fallen asleep after the news, and he hadn't returned home yet. Just last week, she'd asked him what kind of work he did that he worked such odd hours, but he hadn't answered her, changing the subject instead. She hadn't minded, really. As long as he paid his rent, where he worked was none of her business.

She heard the car door slam hard and, with one hand pressing into her sore back, she turned toward the sidewalk leading from the garage. It wasn't like Wladek to be so noisy. He came through the door quickly and made for the back stairs, not even glancing her way as he rubbed at his forehead.

"Wladek, good morning," she called after him.

He stopped and turned to her, looking puzzled. She saw that he was sweating heavily, the armpits of his gray shirt stained and his face damp. He appeared confused. Rosie took a step toward him. "Are you all right?"

"Awful headache." He swung back and gripped the railing. "Gotta lay down."

"I've got aspirin in the house," she offered. Moving closer, she could smell that cologne he always wore. Maybe that strong stuff was giving him his headache. Rosie had read in the paper that lots of people were allergic to certain smells and that they could cause headaches and even upset stomachs. But she decided not to mention the article to him just now. "You want me to get some for you?"

"No, I'll be all right." He shifted a trembling hand to the back of his head where the pain was traveling upward. Mostly it centered above his eyes, almost blinding him. He wasn't sure how he'd managed to drive home, the ache was so bad. His eyes hurt from the sunshine and he was sweating again.

He started up the steps slowly, each movement costing him. It was happening again, just like all the times before. Maybe if he took a couple of Tylenol and laid down in a dark room with a cold cloth, the misery would leave him. Please, God, he prayed as he climbed.

"Maybe I should come up with you, fix you a nice cup of tea?" Rosie suggested from the bottom of the steps. He really did look terrible, and the poor boy had no one. How could someone so young and such a nice boy have no family, no friends to visit?

"No! Just leave me alone." His voice was harsher than he'd intended, but he had to make her see. He didn't want her or anyone else in his private place.

Rosie took a step backward, a little hurt by his sharp tone. But she had a forgiving heart and knew that when people didn't feel good, they often said things they didn't mean. She'd nursed her mother for years before the old woman's death and had been the object of her sharp tongue more than once.

SHATTERED VOWS 253

"All right," she called up to him as he fumbled with his key. "I'll be home all day if you want anything."

Just what he needed, his landlady watching and listening, Wally thought. Why didn't she go to one of her card clubs or church meetings and let him be? He got the door unlocked on the third try and almost lunged inside. He shoved the chain in place and stripped as he walked to the bathroom. He let the water run until it was cold, tossed down three Tylenol, and then wet a washcloth.

The bedroom blinds were down, like he always had them. He opened the window, hoping for a breeze. He still hadn't gotten that fan he'd been wanting. Wearing only his briefs, he lay down, put the cloth on his forehead, and closed his eyes.

Please, Lord, make it go away, he prayed.

In the backyard, Rosie stood looking up at the closed door. This was the second time she'd seen her tenant act oddly. About a month ago, he'd come home late one evening. She'd been sitting in her rocker on the back porch, visiting with Helen. He'd hurried past them, hardly answering their greeting, mumbling to himself all the way up the stairs. He'd been sweating then, too, and it hadn't even been hot. That night, she'd heard him pacing for what seemed like hours.

Rosie returned to finish her weeding. The boy needed to see a doctor. She wasn't one to run to doctors herself. But there were times when a person had to give in. He didn't look good and twice now, he'd mentioned having a bad headache. Then there was the sweating. Maybe that's why he didn't have a girl. He was embarrassed by those terrible sweats.

Later tonight or tomorrow, she'd wait to catch him when he was feeling better and suggest he go see her doctor. Dr. Tomaszeski was a nice man and didn't charge an arm and a leg. He'd fix Wladek up just fine.

Humming to herself, Rosie yanked at the offending weeds.

The Grosse Pointe police station was on Kercheval, on the Hill, as the area was known. It was an old building, not very large, made of red brick with fairly small rooms. Meg, Kimberly Everett, and Dora Haynes sat around a maple wood table. Standing behind the one-way glass, Ray stood with his hands in his pockets alongside Police Chief Harold Munser.

Dora had explained that Kimberly was still reticent, but that she did speak when she wanted to. She hadn't cried when she'd been told her mother had died. She'd withdrawn instead to a place her grandparents and Dora wondered if she'd ever willingly leave, a place in her mind where no one could hurt her again.

Ray watched the child twist the red braided hair of her Raggedy Ann doll and avoid the eyes of both adults.

"Kimberly, do you remember me?" Meg began gently.

Taking her time, she looked at Meg, then slowly nodded.

"Good. Are you enjoying staying with your grandparents?"

"I love Nana and Grandpa," she said. "They're going to take me to Disneyland soon."

Meg felt encouraged that the child had answered. "That should be fun. I was there last summer." With Dennis and two of his nieces. They'd had such a good time. But she couldn't afford to think of that just now.

"Did you see Mickey?" the small voice asked.

"Uh-huh. And Minnie and Goofy."

Kimberly lowered her eyes to the doll again, her expression heartbreakingly sad. "I wish my Mommy could go with us."

Dora's hand patted the little girl's arm comfortingly.

"I know what you mean," Meg went on. "It's so hard losing someone you love." Meg swallowed, hoping she was saying the right things. "I just lost someone I love, too."

Kimberly's eyes were solemn. "Do you miss her?"

"Him, and yes, I do. Very much."

"Did someone kill him with a big knife?"

How terrible to have a six-year-old know about such things, Meg thought. "Yes, someone did. With a gun, not a knife."

"Did you tell the secret? Is that why they did it?"

Meg became even more alert. "I didn't have a secret. Do you have a secret, Kimberly?"

The child twisted the doll's braid back and forth. "Good girls don't tell secrets."

"Who told you that?"

Kimberly glanced toward the door, then at Dora. Finally, she whispered, "Daddy."

"Do you and Daddy have a secret?"

She nodded. "I didn't tell. Honest, I didn't."

"I believe you, Kimberly," Meg told her. "What did Daddy tell you would happen if you told the secret?"

The girl's expression became agitated. "That Mommy would die." Suddenly, without warning, a sob escaped from her. "I didn't tell the secret, but still, Mommy died. I was a good girl. Why did Mommy have to die?" She hurled herself into Dora's open arms, her cries deep and anguished.

Barely able to remain composed, Meg let her weep the worst of it out. She handed Dora a tissue and watched the woman dry the small face and brush back her blond bangs. She waited until Kimberly was reduced to small hiccups. "This secret that Daddy told you not to tell, Kimberly. Can you tell me what it is?"

The little girl shook her head. "If I tell the secret, bad things will happen." She was trembling, frightened now.

The psychiatrist turned her attention to Meg. "Sergeant O'Malley, I think we should end this session. Kimberly's worn out."

"Just a couple more questions." Meg glanced over at the tape recorder on the table, then back at Dora. "You want to see this monster behind bars as badly as I do, don't you?"

Reluctantly, Dora Haynes nodded.

"Kim," Meg said, leaning forward, "does the secret involve the bad things Daddy was doing to you?"

The little girl's eyes grew wider as she looked from Dora to Meg, but no more tears came as she regarded them silently.

"Did Daddy ever take your panties off and ... and do things that hurt you?" Holding her breath, she waited. She'd stretched the boundaries here and knew that if Kimberly's grandparents had been present, or an attorney, they probably wouldn't have allowed her to continue. "It's all right to tell us, honey. No one is going to hurt you again, I promise."

Kim hugged her doll to her chest and finally, she nodded.

Meg wanted the words on tape. "What did you say? I didn't hear you."

"Yes," the child whispered. "Daddy hurt me, but I didn't tell." Her little face fell apart. "Why did Mommy have to die?"

On the other side of the glass, Ray let out a breath he'd been holding far too long.

"Hanging's too good for the guy," the chief muttered.

Christ the King Catholic Church on the west side of Detroit was in a lovely old neighborhood that had seen better times but was struggling to remain decent despite a recent rapid turnover in area residents. The new influx of young families was welcome and many felt that the community would band together, fix up their homes, and keep out the riff raff.

Spearheading such a drive was Father Jim Morris, the fifty-something pastor who was deeply involved with his parishioners. He'd arranged counseling for troubled youths, meetings for single parents, and meals-on-wheels for shut-ins. He'd also enlisted the six remaining nuns at the parochial grade school connected to the church to help, as well as the dozen or so lay teachers.

And he'd agreed to hold evening confession one Thursday a month for his members who couldn't make it in on Saturday afternoons. He sat in his confessional on a warm Thursday night, mopped his damp forehead, and checked his watch. A quarter to eight. Fifteen minutes more and he'd lock up. Quite a few people had come from six to seven, but only a couple of stragglers after that, including the young sister who'd just finished. Stifling a yawn, Father Jim sat back.

Sister Mary Jon left the confessional and silently moved to the last pew to say her prayers of penance. An older couple near the front, kneeling and praying, were the only other people in the church. Mary Jon lowered the kneeler and folded her hands as she bowed her head.

A third grade teacher, Sister Mary Jon was twenty-eight, slender and blond with huge blue eyes. Her parents hadn't wanted her to become a nun, but ever since early childhood, Mary Jon had felt she had the calling. She loved teaching and loved the little ones. She'd been at Christ the King for two years and felt very much at home in the small convent, the other sisters like family to her now.

Some minutes later, when the belfry clock struck eight, Father Jim turned off his light and exited through the confessional door, closing it quietly. He saw a couple walking hand in hand down the center aisle headed for the rear doors. Only Sister Mary Jon was still praying. He decided to go to the sacristy and remove his vestments. He'd lock up back there and by then, sister would undoubtedly be finished.

He walked past her at a brisk pace, thinking what a shame it was that churches these days had to be locked up at night to keep vandals out. It shouldn't be like that. Churches should always remain open as a sanctuary for the troubled, the oppressed, the lonely. When he'd been a boy, things had been different.

He must be getting old, Father Jim decided as he began to unvest.

SHATTERED VOWS

He was nearly finished when he heard an odd sound. Pausing, he cocked his head, listening. There was only silence. Perhaps he'd only imagined the small grunt, the quiet thud. He put his eye to the peephole the former pastor had had installed so he could check the number in his congregation attending each mass. Father Jim saw no one. Even Sister Mary Jon was gone.

Quickly, he locked up and adjusted the lights so that only the vigil lamps were on. Then he walked along the side aisle toward the main doors, intent on locking them as well before heading for the parish house, where the housekeeper would serve his evening meal. Father disliked hearing confession on a full stomach so he always made it a point to eat afterward.

As he was about to round the bend of the last pew, he saw a figure clothed in black slumped on the floor, resting on the kneeler where Sister Mary Jon had been minutes before. He reached over to touch her shoulder, hoping she hadn't fainted. "Sister, are you all right?"

Father Jim got no response, so he tugged on her shoulder, turning her over. It was then that he saw the wire around her neck, the blue eyes gaping open, her blond hair spilling out of her head piece.

"Oh my God," he whispered, then hurried to the phone.

"Sonofabitch," Ray said as Dr. Lester Freemont bent over Sister Mary Jon's body. "I knew something like this would happen." It had been nearly five weeks since the last strangling, that of Sister Irene at Mt. Carmel Hospital. "I had this feeling that he was going to strike again."

"Ease up, Detective," Doc said as he removed one of his rubber gloves. "You couldn't possibly have known where or when." With the fingertips of his other gloved hand, he held the familiar mass card he'd found on the floor alongside the nun's body, as if casually tossed there by the killer. "This might be of some help."

Ray leaned closer. The message had changed again. TERRY, PLEASE FORGIVE ME. "Finally, we've got a name. Now if we only knew who Terry was."

Doc slipped the card into a clear plastic evidence envelope, then put the envelope in his pocket. "I'll send it to the lab just in case." He stared at the usual green wire. "He's damn clever. There's not enough surface on a wire to pick up a print and there's been nothing on the cards except that one drop of sweat. He probably wears gloves."

Ray had bent close to the body and now straightened. "Lean down and tell me if you smell anything on her."

The doctor did as Ray asked and came up sniffing. "Smells like strong cologne of some sort. I've smelled it before, but I can't think of the brand name."

"How about Old Spice aftershave?"

Freemont grinned. "Yeah, that's the stuff."

Toni sat at a side table with Ray and sipped her wine. Over the rim of her glass, she watched him finish his pasta. The man should have been Italian, the way he loved noodle dishes of any kind, she thought. She was glad to see he was eating at all considering his expression when he'd popped in on her. Of course, she'd known his gloomy mood had been the result of the sixth strangling victim found last night, and she could hardly blame him for being a little down.

Ray made an effort to keep his mood upbeat. "That was just about the best fettucine alfredo I've ever had," he told her as he sat back with a contented sigh.

"I'll tell Alphonse you said so."

He raised a questioning brow. "Alphonse? Doesn't sound Italian to me."

"He isn't. He's German, but his menu reads like a tour of Europe." She set down her glass. "Tell me about your day and I'll tell you about mine."

"I have a feeling I'd choose yours. I spent the day chasing down old boyfriends of a woman named Angie Falconi, who was strangled a couple of years ago. Someone dumped her body in Lake St. Clair."

"I remember you telling me about that awhile back. Did you get anywhere?"

He shrugged. "Not really. None of the guys whose names were given me by Angie's mother are viable suspects. However, her closest girlfriend said that Angie had been dating some guy on the sly because her mother disapproved of him. Trouble is, the friend never knew his name or much of anything else about him." Ray suspected the man in question had been the father of the baby Angie had miscarried. But again, he didn't have enough to go on. "I'm considering a return trip to her parents' home. Maybe they know more than they think they do."

Toni frowned. "How do you mean?"

Ray finished his wine before answering. "Sometimes we know people, but we're so used to them coming around that we don't think anything of it. A family friend, a neighbor's kid, a guy who often gave her a ride home. Maybe I can jog the mother's memory." Or the father's. He'd like to talk with Mr. Falconi, the one who supposedly didn't know his daughter had been pregnant. Maybe he knew more than his wife suspected.

"What about this name on the latest mass card? Any clue as to who 'Terry' might be?"

"Not so far. I've gone through the parish list of names from St. Matthews and I've come up with four Terrys. Two were males, a boy of six and an Irishman, family man type. There was a middle-aged woman with six kids who'd only recently moved to Detroit, and the other one died recently. Another dead end." He was getting used to them. "We badly need a break here."

Toni leaned forward. "What about that suggestion I made a while back, that a female police officer dresses as a nun and lures the killer out? Ray, it's not a bad idea and I can't imagine why both you and Meg dismiss it so easily."

They'd had this conversation before. He didn't like the idea then and he didn't now. "I've explained this, Toni. It's very risky and we really don't train our female officers to act as decoys. Meg would probably do it, because she's gutsy enough, if the captain asked her. But you know she's an emotional wreck right now." He'd told Toni about the way Meg had handled the little girl earlier in the week. "She fell apart after we left Kimberly that afternoon. Cried all the way back to Beaubien. She's too fragile right now. I wouldn't let her do it."

Toni folded her napkin and placed it on the table. "You're never going to catch this guy otherwise. He's too smart, too slippery."

His face took on a hard look, one he seldom showed Toni. "Will you leave police work to the police?"

The last thing she wanted to do was fight about this, or anything, with Ray. She reached over and touched his hand. "I'm sorry. But I just hate what this case is doing to you."

"We'll get him, Toni. And I'm fine." He knew he didn't sound particularly fine, but it was the best he could do.

The maître'd came over just then, needing a word with Toni. She excused herself and left him alone. He poured himself another half glass of wine from the carafe and forced himself to relax.

Ray knew he'd been pushing too hard lately, which was why her suggestion had caused him to react. He'd been letting too much get to him which was why he'd come to see Toni tonight. She was a leveler, keeping him on safe ground. She always made sure he had a good dinner and a relaxing glass of wine, no junk food. And she said she'd be ready to leave soon and would follow him home. Holding her in his arms was like holding the world at bay. He was better able to face things with her in his life. He knew she hadn't wanted to rile him, but only to help.

It had taken him a lot of soul searching and four long months to realize that he needed her in his life. He knew she cared deeply about him, but he wondered how she'd fare as a cop's wife. He could tell how listening to him talk about some of his cases filled her eyes with a concern she tried to keep him from seeing. Could she handle the stress of his job? She was already almost as worried about the strangler as he. Hell, he wasn't handling stress all that well himself these days.

He'd never gotten quite so shit-faced as that night she'd found him barely able to sit upright in his bedroom. At least not since his teens. But Toni had stayed with him, held him as he'd cried like a baby. She'd remained there all night, while he'd slept it off. The next morning, he'd been embarrassed and apologetic, but she wouldn't listen to a word of it. Sometimes, we all need to let it out, she'd said, absolving his actions while understanding his motives.

She was a rare one.

Toni walked back to the table, finished with work for the day, her shoulder bag on her arm. "Ready to go?"

"You bet." Ray tossed some bills on a table, even though she never allowed the waiters to give him a check, rose and took her arm. "Your place or mine?"

"Yours is more private, I think." Mom was getting used to her frequent disappearances, but her father still frowned when she came home in the morning to shower, change, and go to work. Still, she never wavered, looking them both in the eye, daring one or the other to question her. Toni knew that they were aware that if they did, she'd probably move out.

Her parents didn't want that, but she was beginning to feel the strain of being an adult still living under their roof. Soon she'd have to make some changes, but she didn't quite know what kind just yet.

In the parking lot of the Glass Door, Ray leaned down to kiss her as she climbed behind the wheel of her red Mercedes, its convertible top down. "See you at my house," he said, closing her door.

"Race you there, Detective," she called after him as he walked to his station wagon. When he waved her suggestion aside, she laughed and roared out of the lot.

She felt good, happy and in love. She hadn't felt

SHATTERED VOWS 265

so good in a very long time. Even the recent strangling couldn't put a damper on her mood tonight. It was overdue, she thought, turning south on Jefferson and easing into traffic.

She was far too happy and preoccupied to notice a scruffy dark Olds with a recently repaired headlight following two car lengths behind her convertible.

Wally felt good, too. Ever since his visit to Christ the King, the headaches had stopped again, the sweats were gone, and he was at peace. Another angel had joined her sisters in heaven.

He wanted to follow Toni Garette home to make sure she was all right, then he'd go to his flat and sleep deeply. But as he zigzagged in and out of fairly heavy traffic, he saw that the cop's station wagon was also following Toni's convertible. Was that cop going to her house?

He'd forgiven Toni for staying to take care of the detective because he'd probably been sick last week. But why was she hanging around him still? Was she afraid that she might become a victim like her cousin had been? Didn't she know, couldn't she tell, that he had no interest in harming her? He just liked to watch her, to fantasize about her. She was so beautiful with that silky hair and those long legs, so like Terry.

Suddenly, her Mercedes turned onto the expressway. He barely had time to switch lanes and follow. But this wasn't the way to her house. Was she going to that cop's house? Sure, there he was, right behind her. Gripping the wheel angrily, Wally followed at a safe distance.

Not wanting to believe the worst, he took a shortcut and parked down the street from the cop's brick colonial, turning off his headlights and scrunching down in the seat. In minutes, they drove up, Vargas parking in the drive and Toni pulling in behind. Wally watched the cop walk to her car and help her out. Then he pulled her into a close embrace and kissed her right there on his front lawn with other cars passing by and a neighbor two doors down sitting on his porch steps.

Had they no shame? His mother had told him that such things were done only in private and only by married people. The devil was at work in you if you did bad things in public and outside of marriage. Wally'd known that from as far back as he could remember. God would punish the ones who didn't listen. Hadn't he had to punish Angie because she'd been a sinner? And hadn't he been punished by losing Terry forever?

Watching the kiss go on and on, Wally grew agitated. Then, arms around each other, laughing, they went into the cop's house. Wally saw that no one bothered to turn on the downstairs lights. Only one lamp came on, the one in the upstairs bedroom. He ground his teeth as he felt his hands grow damp.

He'd thought Toni was different, that she was pure like the others. But she wasn't untainted like all his sweet sisters. She was like Angie.

She would have to be punished.

FOURTEEN

Ray studied the medical examiner's report on Sister Mary Jon with a frown of annoyance. Not a damn thing different from all the others, he thought. The killer had apparently yanked off the woman's necklace, according to Doc's findings on her bruised neck, but no broken remnants were found this time.

Next, Ray picked up the newest mass card left by the strangler and studied its message. Who was "Terry" and where was she? he wondered. Meg was at Christ the King, going over the parish records with Father Jim, trying to find the person named Terry in that community. They'd checked with every parish for miles around and been unable to locate the one that used that particular mass card.

Feeling they could use all the help they could get, they'd released the information on the mass cards to the newspapers the previous day. Both morning and evening editions had run pictures alongside the article asking for help from anyone who might have information to share with the police investigators. So far, there had been no calls.

Ray tossed aside the card, took a sip of lukewarm coffee, and sat back in his desk chair. All over the precinct, he could hear the hum of activity, the usual ringing of phones, the scuffling of feet arriving or leaving the building, the voices both loud and low. A usual day at Beaubien. He blocked it all out and concentrated, going over every scrap of information they had so far on the strangler.

They'd gone through the records of St. Matthews, checked out all the nuns at the convent and their families, as well as Father Hilliard and his assistant. Ray had personally revisited the Falconis the previous day and had talked with them both. Mario didn't speak very good English, had said very little and abruptly had gotten up and gone fishing. His escape, Ray decided.

Dolores could remember no more than what she'd already told him, no matter how differently he worded his questions. Angie apparently had always been very secretive about her dates since the age of thirteen, and she'd been caught lying to her mother more often than not. He'd left the small town of St. Clair no wiser than he'd arrived.

Department personnel had checked out the green wire and they'd found it everywhere. Florist shops, groceries that sold flowers, greenhouses, nurseries, construction sites, lawn maintenance companies. But no one could come up with an employee, past or present, who resembled the generic sketch the police artist had made based on Charlie Ames's description.

Again, they'd gone door-to-door in the old neighborhood where Sister Bernie's parents lived, trying to ascertain if anyone had seen a stranger the evening of the nun's strangling. No one claimed that they did, nor had they heard anything.

Old Spice was their only other lead, and enough men used the inexpensive aftershave to make that clue useless.

One stinking dead end after another.

Someone had to know something. But who? The phone on his desk rang sharply, interrupting his musings. He grabbed it, wishing for a miracle. "Vargas."

"It's Father Hilliard, Detective."

Probably calling to see why they didn't have the killer locked up, Ray thought with a sense of discouragement. "Yes, Father."

"I just received a call from a parishioner that I thought you ought to know about. Emily Watson's sister-in-law Hannah does volunteer work at the Franciscan Monastery on Grand Boulevard. You know the place I mean?"

"Not really, but I've heard of it." He did know they hadn't visited there in their search. "What about it, Father?"

"Well, Emily said that Hannah Watson thinks she knows something about those mass cards found at the scene of each strangling. Would you be interested in talking with her?

Is the pope Catholic? Ray thought. "I certainly would. Give me the address, please, Father."

Hannah Watson was an attractive black woman with soft brown eyes and rimless glasses. She shook hands briefly with Ray and led him into a small office off the monastery's anteroom. "I didn't know if I should bother you with this, Detective," she said after checking his I.D. "But Emily said I ought to call."

"We appreciate any help you can give us, Ms. Watson."

The woman seated herself behind her desk. "Emily's a member of St. Matthews and she's been concerned about the tragic deaths of the sisters. Of course, we all are."

"Right. Father Hilliard mentioned that you might have some information about the mass cards?"

"Yes. When I saw the sample in yesterday's paper, I knew I had to call." She opened her center desk drawer and handed him a small white card. "This is the mass card we use here at the monastery. It appears to be the same as the one pictured in the newspaper."

Ray took the card and checked it out. There it was, the pen-and-ink sketch of the risen Christ in one corner and a lighted candle in the other. "Yes, this is the same."

"Emily said that the killer left one with each one of the sisters." Hannah pursed her lips in disapproval. "Are you Catholic, Detective?"

"No, I'm not."

"Well, when a parishioner purchases a mass card, the name of the person for whom the mass is to be said is typically recorded in our book so the brothers have a record of it. We fill out the mass card for the purchaser. Some people send it to the family of the deceased or keep it themselves."

"I understand."

"Several months ago, a man came in here and bought twelve of these."

Ray narrowed his gaze. "Twelve?" Six down and six to go? Good God, he hoped not.

"Yes, and he took all twelve with him. He didn't give us any names for our register book. Instead, he said he'd send us a note with the person's name on it each time he wanted a mass said. That alone was odd, but then just yesterday, after seeing the newspaper article, I mentioned the man's odd purchase to

SHATTERED VOWS

Brother Ralph and he told me something even more disturbing."

"What was that?"

Again, she opened the drawer and removed a packet of notes. "We've checked the dates on these notes that were sent in. There'd been one received after the death of each sister, with her name printed on it and a mass requested for her." She handed him the notes.

Ray studied the block printing he'd come to recognize. He could see that the papers had been handled so there'd be no use checking for finger prints.

"Up until yesterday, Brother Ralph saw nothing unusual in someone wishing to dedicate a mass to each fallen sister. But after our conversation about the twelve mass cards, we both revised our thinking." Hannah folded her hands nervously. "I hope I did the right thing by calling you."

"You definitely did. Do you have the name of the man who bought the twelve cards?"

"No, I don't. It's not required that they give us their names. He paid in cash, that I remember."

Ray sucked in a disappointing breath.

"Of course," Hannah went on, "I have seen him around here often."

He looked up hopefully. "Can you describe him?"

"I can try." She tipped her head as if picturing the man. "He's white, young, no more than mid-twenties. Sort of medium height with brown hair. Nothing too outstanding about him, except he's always been very pleasant. He has a nice smile."

The description Charley Ames had given them, Ray thought. "And each time that he comes in, does he purchase more mass cards?"

"He's not stopped in to the office before or since, just that once."

"Then how is it that you've seen him often? Does he attend mass at the monastery?"

"I don't know that he does. He does work around the monastery. The flower beds, lawn cutting, trimming the bushes. That sort of thing."

Bingo! Ray kept his expression unchanged. "Do you know who hired him?"

"Undoubtedly Brother Ralph."

"Is he in? I'd like to talk with him."

"I'll go see." Hannah rose and exited down a long hallway in her silent shoes.

Ray fidgeted as he waited. The purchase of multiple mass cards didn't really pinpoint a killer. But it certainly did bear checking out. He heard footsteps and turned to the doorway.

Brother Ralph was tall and thin, his body wrapped in the dark brown robe and rope belt of the Franciscan Brotherhood. His smile was warm as he shook hands with Ray. "Hannah here tells me you're interested in Wally."

"Would that be your groundskeeper?"

"He is that, on and off. It's a volunteer position, but Wally's been helping us out for a couple of years now."

"And his last name is?"

Brother Ralph frowned, thinking. "Lambert, I believe. Yes, Wally Lambert. That's it."

"Do you have an address for him?"

The man shook his head. "No. He's not a member here, although I have seen him at mass occasionally. Many folks attend our masses, including transients. We don't keep all their names on file because they come and go. Sometimes we don't see them for months, then up they pop."

"How regularly does Wally work on your grounds?"

"For a while there, he'd been dropping by to help out once a month or so. But I haven't seen him for a while."

"Did you maybe get his phone number? This could be very important, Brother Ralph." Ray was feeling his frustration mount again.

"I tried once, so I could call him when we needed trimming or pruning done, and so on. He told me he didn't have a phone, but that he'd check in. That's usually what he did, gave me a call and asked if I needed any work done, then he'd come by if I said yes. He must be employed as a landscaper; he's very good with plants and shrubs. As far as I know, he helps us out because he's Catholic and knows we don't have much in the way of funds."

"Would you recall what kind of car he drove, or did he even have a car?"

Brother Ralph rubbed his chin. "Yes, an older car. Buick or Oldsmobile, I'd guess. Dark color, blue or black. He was always having trouble with it, one thing or another. I remember once I told him he'd better get a new muffler because his vehicle was making quite a bit of noise."

Ray jotted down a few quick notes. "Would you describe this man to me, please, Brother?" He listened and heard basically the same description Hannah had given him. "Did you notice *anything* unusual about him? Was he nervous; did he perspire more than average?"

Brother shook his head, but Hannah spoke up immediately. "I *do* remember that. When he was in the office, his face was damp and his hands were sweating. And it was winter, early March I believe."

Right before the first strangling, Ray thought. "Anything else?"

"He's pretty average, I guess you'd say," Brother

Ralph said. "I'd find it hard to believe that such a nice young man had anything to do with the death of five sisters."

"Six," Ray corrected.

Ralph fingered the heavy rosary that hung from his rope belt. "Even worse. We'll offer up prayers for him tonight."

Ray pocketed his notebook and rose. "Perhaps you could include a few prayers that we capture him."

"Yes, of course. We've been doing that all along."

"Thank you for your help, both of you." He held out a card to each. "If you remember anything else, or if Wally Lambert shows up here, please call me right away. And don't let on that you've talked with me."

"Certainly." The man looked a bit taken aback to find himself even peripherally involved in a conspiracy.

"There is one other thing," Hannah said, causing Ray to turn back to her. "I don't know what brand he uses, but the man reeks of cologne. He must bathe in the stuff. I had to air out the office after he left."

Driving toward St. Matthews, Ray tried not to get too excited about this first real possibility. At least he had a name, someone to start searching for to see if he fit the profile of the killer put together by Dr. Delaney and their one eyewitness. If he could locate this Wally Lambert and put him in a lineup for Charley Ames to view, would he pick him out? Even if he did, that alone wouldn't prove that Wally strangled Sister Irene. But it would place him at Mt. Carmel Hospital on the night of her death.

Ray angled around a slow-moving bus, his thoughts on his next stop. He didn't want to blow this. Many a case had fallen apart because care wasn't taken in collecting evidence and in following procedure. If he could tie this man to St. Matthews and some of the west side locations such as Mt. Carmel and Christ the King, then they'd have a strong reason to pick him up for questioning, even if Charley's identification fell through.

Ten minutes later, he turned into St. Matthews parking lot and walked over to the convent. As he rang the bell, he glanced down at the flower beds bordering the small cement stoop. Roses were in bloom, pale pink to bright red, half a dozen of them. They were obviously older bushes because they were thick-stemmed and filled with blossoms. Due to the heaviness, each one was fastened to a staking pole, held in place by thin green wire.

Leaning down to have a better look, Ray touched one end of a wire and decided it was the same sort he'd held in his hand after each strangling. Swearing under his breath that he'd missed the obvious, he straightened as the reverend mother opened the door. Recognition brought a frown to her round face, but she politely invited him in.

In the sitting room, he wasted no time. "Reverend Mother, do you employ a groundskeeper here at St. Matthews, someone who works on the flower beds and shrubbery?"

"Indeed we do. A lovely young man has been our landscaper for some time. His name is Wally Lambert."

Ray felt an adrenaline rush. "Could you give me his address, please?"

"Let me check." With a slight rustle of her skirts, she left the parlor and went into the adjoining office where a typist was busy at her machine. She returned in moments with a Rolodex card file. "The rectory office has a more complete listing of our parishioners, but I might have Wally's card in here." She shuffled through the L's a moment, then looked puzzled. "Well, odd as it may seem, he's apparently not a member of St. Matthews."

"There must be some record of him," Ray said. "How does he get paid? How do you know when he's coming to work?"

"Yes, of course there's a record. Let me check with Father." She moved to the phone at the side table and dialed quickly.

Ray leaned forward, his elbows on his knees, as she spoke quietly into the phone, her back to him. Impatiently, he waited.

The woman hung up and turned back to Detective Vargas. "Well, that explains it. Wally is one of our volunteer workers. We don't pay him. He does the landscaping as his gift to the parish. According to Father Hilliard's assistant, Wally doesn't have a phone, but he calls in periodically to see if he's needed. Then he just shows up." She smiled at Ray. "We have other volunteers with similar work arrangements. For instance, the ladies of the altar society, who clean the church and launder the linens, and the florist, who supplies the flowers for the altar."

"Are you saying that no one here has Wally Lambert's address or phone number?" Ray said, sounding somewhat incredulous.

Mother Magdalen's smile faded in response to what she considered a bit of a reprimand. "Yes, that's exactly what I'm saying. I'm also telling you

SHATTERED VOWS

that that's not a terribly unusual situation at any number of churches. You can't always hold volunteers to definite hours. They donate their free time and that often varies. Can you tell me what this is about?"

Ignoring her question, Ray forced himself to regroup. "Can you recall the last time you saw Wally here?"

The woman looked thoughtful. "Not really. I recall seeing him at the funeral masses for the sisters, and ..." Suddenly, her eyes grew wide. "Oh, dear. You're not under the impression that Wally Lambert is somehow involved in those terrible stranglings, are you? Why, I've had many conversations with him and he's the sweetest young man."

Right. Every killer had someone who thought he was sweet. "Let me ask you to describe Wally, if you would," he countered evasively. He listened with growing excitement as Mother Magdalen gave a description that matched the others. But what good would that be if he couldn't locate the man?

Ray decided to use another tack. "Reverend Mother, do you recall anyone named Terry who might visit here or be a parish volunteer?"

The woman shook her head. "I don't know of a Terry. But then, I've been here less than two years." Rising, she went to the office doorway. "Carmella, would you know of someone named Terry who might have volunteered here?"

Carmella turned from her typewriter. "Not a volunteer, but I remember a nun who used to be here in the convent. Her name is Sister Theresa Roberts, but everyone called her Terry."

Ray got to his feet and walked closer to the

dark-haired secretary. "You say she used to live here?"

"Yes, that's right. She was assigned here right after taking her vows. She taught school right across the street. That was before you came, Mother."

Ray was growing impatient. "You say she left. Do you know where she is now, Carmella?"

The secretary wrinkled her brow. "No, I don't remember ever hearing where she went. One day she was here, the next gone."

More frustration. Ray turned to the reverend mother. "Could you call in the other sisters, please? I need to ask the ones who lived here back then if they remember Sister Theresa and if they might know where she is."

Mother checked her watch. "If you'll have a seat in our parlor, I'll tell our sisters that you'd like a few minutes of their time. School will be dismissed in twenty minutes. They'll be free after that."

It was the best she was going to offer, he knew. "Thank you," Ray told her, then sat down to wait.

The sisters assembled at three-thirty. They were a bit more animated than at his last meeting with them, Ray decided. Of course, that had been right after Sister Ronnie's body had been found, and they'd all been stunned.

As soon as Mother Magdalen explained the purpose of his presence, Ray began questioning them, first about Wally Lambert.

"He's always so polite," Sister Agnes, an older nun with shrewd blue eyes volunteered.

SHATTERED VOWS

"I give him a wide berth," said Sister Clement, the nun Ray had tagged as being quite feisty during their last session. "Not because of anything he does, but because he always smells so bad."

"Describe what you mean, please?" Ray asked.

"He splashes some cheap cologne on and usually smells worse than the fertilizer he uses," she answered.

Then Ray asked about Sister Theresa Roberts.

"Terry's a lovely person," Sister Lillian answered quickly. "I hated to see her leave us."

"Do you know why she left?" Ray asked.

"No," Sister Lillian admitted. "It was sort of hush-hush." She shot a look at Mother Magdalen in apology.

"What does Sister Theresa look like?" he asked.

"She's so pretty," Lillian answered, smiling. "She has blond hair and huge blue eyes."

Could she be the woman the strangler was thinking of when he killed, Ray wondered, the "Terry" he kept asking for forgiveness from?

"I know why Terry left here," Sister Agnes said confidently. "She asked for a transfer because a man she'd known before she took her vows wouldn't let her be. He kept coming around, following her, phoning her constantly."

"Oh, yes, I remember that now," Lillian said, nodding.

"Do you know the man's name?" Ray asked. "Did any of you see him?" Was he the killer who had stalked Sister Theresa first, before he snapped and stalked the nuns he killed?

"Not me," Agnes answered. "Not any of us. Mother Frances was in charge back then, and she fielded all the calls. She died last year, but I'm certain she never let him inside the convent." Agnes shook her head sadly. "It was a bad time for poor Terry. He frightened her, I can tell you."

"Sister Agnes," Ray began, addressing the one he thought knew the most about the matter, "do you know where Terry went from here?"

"None of us knows. Terry appealed to the archdiocese for the transfer and asked that her whereabouts be kept secret."

"Did the man continue to call after she had left?"

"Oh, yes," Sister Agnes said. "But after a while, after being rebuffed repeatedly, he finally stopped."

"Was he from around here, do you know?" Perhaps he could trace the man through his family.

He heard a chorus of "I don't knows" and saw all of them shake their heads. There was only one thing left to do. He thanked them all, then asked to see Mother Magdalen alone.

When she'd closed the door to her office behind the whispering nuns, Ray came right to the point. "Reverend Mother, this is a police matter. There is some indication that the man we're seeking in the strangulations might be the same man who was involved with Sister Theresa."

"And you think that's Wally Lambert?"

"It's a possibility. I need you to call the archdiocese and explain the gravity of the situation. I must know Sister Theresa's whereabouts." He would go in person if he needed to, but Ray was hoping this might save time.

The Reverend Mother didn't have to be persuaded. She was as anxious to find the murderer as anyone. She went immediately to the phone.

Ray paced the small office until Mother Magdalen hung up the phone and turned to him. "Sister Theresa Roberts is living in Nazareth, Michigan, at our mother house."

"Could you give me that number and may I use your phone?"

She wrote down the number and Ray quickly dialed. A Sister Grace answered. He asked for Sister Theresa, only to be told that the nun was on a trip and was due back late Friday afternoon. He wouldn't be able to reach her until then, since Sister Theresa was on a camping trip and left no phone number where she could be reached. It was only Wednesday. He reminded himself to be patient. Ray thanked her and hung up.

"I can't thank you enough for your help, Reverend Mother." Ray walked with her to the door.

"We're only too glad to assist you. Are you planning to visit Sister Theresa?"

"Yes, ma'am. I plan to be there on Friday when she returns."

The Tigers were losing a doubleheader. Ray wasn't really a big baseball fan, but he enjoyed stretching out with a can of beer and watching a game on television now and then. Tonight, he was too distracted to pay much attention.

Half-heartedly, he reached into the bowl of popcorn that Toni had made, grabbed a scant handful, and nibbled on it as his mind wandered back over the day's events.

He'd gone back to the precinct after his visit to St. Matthews and checked the name Wally or Walter Lambert by every possible method. No fingerprint records on file under either name, no phone listing, no income tax records on file with either IRS or the state. He had discovered a social security number, but they didn't have his address. The driver's license was valid, but the address he'd listed turned out to be a building that had been torn down two years ago. No auto or hospital insurance on record anywhere. Ray had even faxed the F.B.I. and come up empty-handed.

The man was practically a non-entity.

Ray did learn a little at Christ the King. Father Jim verified that they'd had a man known only as Wally who'd worked on their grounds on and off for about two months. Strictly as a volunteer. No, they had no known address for the man.

He'd called the two landscaping companies that had handled the grounds for Mt. Carmel Hospital, but neither had heard of Wally Lambert. However, the one owner did say that they often took on extra part-time help during peak seasons and didn't keep very good records since those men weren't entitled to benefits and were often paid in cash.

Terrific.

His only hope lay in Sister Theresa "Terry" Roberts. Friday, he'd drive to Nazareth and . . .

"Wow! What a play!" Toni all but upset the popcorn bowl as she cheered on her team. Turning to Ray, she noticed that he'd been lost in thought. "Hello? Are you off somewhere?"

Chagrined, he gave her a sheepish smile. "Yeah, sorry. What's the score?"

"Seven to five, our favor." She studied his face, noting the worry lines that she'd sworn weren't there when she'd first started seeing him. It was the strangler who'd put them there, she was certain. "Something troubling you about the case?"

He didn't want to tell her about the new developments. First, she'd want to go with him to Nazareth, he knew, and he couldn't permit that, so they'd probably quarrel over it. Second, if things didn't pan out, he didn't want to disappoint her. "Oh, you know. Same old, same old."

She lifted his arm and slipped under it, nuzzling his bearded cheek. She was relieved when he tightened his hold on her. Lately, it seemed that the only way she could capture his attention was to initiate some kind of love play. Her parents were at the restaurant, and they were alone in her home for a change. She hesitated to spoil the mood, but she badly wanted him to solve the murder case.

"Have you given any more thought to the suggestion I made?"

Ray frowned, searching his memory. "What suggestion was that?"

"The one about planting a couple of undercover officers at St. Matthews and a few other places to keep watch, see who comes and goes. Trained people know what to look for. They might—"

"I told you to forget that, Toni. It isn't feasible. The man's killed people from east side to west. We'd have to use a dozen or more. We don't have that kind of manpower."

"Did Meg even ask your captain?" Probably not, she thought.

"You may have noticed Meg's had a lot on her plate lately." Ray straightened, sitting up. He was feeling irritable and anxious, and knew he shouldn't be taking it out on Toni. But, as he'd told her before, he wanted her to stay out of police business.

"I realize she has. But maybe if *you* approached Captain Renwick, he'd—"

"I certainly will not. The idea's ludicrous. You

watch too much TV." He picked up his can of beer and drained the last of it.

"Fine." She crossed her arms and stared unseeingly at the screen.

He'd done exactly what he'd told himself he wouldn't do and that was to get her royally pissed off. "Listen, I know you mean well, but trying to solve major crimes isn't for amateurs. You might try trusting me a little. It's my job, my responsibility. I'm the one who goes to bed at night and sees the faces of those young women when I try to sleep, and I'm the one who has to answer to their families. I'll find the sonofabitch. But these things don't happen overnight."

She was fuming, but she was *not* going to let him see that. He was doing it again, taking responsibility for the entire case, for all the nuns vulnerable to the strangler, for their families. For the whole frigging mess. "You don't have to fight the world alone. There are people who can help."

"Not in this, you can't. I have to do this myself. I want you to stay out of it. Period."

Very slowly, she turned to him. "I don't take orders very well. Do you want to rephrase that?"

"No. You're not trained, you're not a police officer. You don't know all the ramifications."

Toni felt like popping him, but instead she balled her hands into fists. "I'm not suggesting someone grab an Uzi and stand guard at St. Matthews. But I don't see why you treat my suggestions as if I were a slightly slow five-year-old who wanted to play cops-and-robbers. You aren't the only one in this world with a working brain, you know."

With difficulty, he hung on to his temper, forcing himself to speak calmly. "I respect your intelligence. But in this area, you have no experience, no expertise. I don't presume to tell you how to run your restaurants. I don't expect you to tell me how to run this investigation." Pointedly, he checked his watch. He'd better leave before this whole thing blew up and they both said more than they intended. "It's late. I think I'll shove off." He stood and picked up his jacket.

He saw that she was tight-lipped and staring straight ahead, not speaking, not rising. Damn, but he didn't need this right now. "Listen, Toni. I'm sorry if I offended you. I know you have a stake in this because of Mo. But when you take the time to think about it, you'll probably realize I'm right."

She swiveled to face him, her eyes blazing. "You're so goddamn used to running the world and everyone in it, absolutely certain you know what is right for every breathing soul. Every criminal, all your friends, even your brother."

His gray eyes turned smoky. "You don't know what the hell you're talking about."

"It must be a heavy burden, being in charge of the universe like that, responsible for us all. I'm surprised you're not stoop-shouldered under the weight of all you've taken on, without checking first if any of us *want* to be taken care of, I might add."

"That's not the way it is. Toni—"

"It's *exactly* the way it is." She waved a hand in dismissal and turned from him, afraid if she didn't that he'd see the tears in her eyes. "Just go. Go look after your world and everyone you've decided needs your guidance. I've gotten along so far without your help. I think I can muddle through the rest of the way without it, thank you very much."

Grinding his teeth, he slung his jacket over his shoulder and glared at her. He couldn't think of anything he could say that would change the situation between them. Wordlessly, he turned and left the house.

It wasn't until she heard the door slam behind him that Toni gave in to her angry tears.

FIFTEEN

On Thursday, just before noon, Ray leaned back in his desk chair at the precinct, cradling the phone at his ear. "Thank you for calling me back so promptly, Dr. Delaney."

"No problem, Detective Vargas. What can I do for you?"

"I wanted to run something by you, Doctor. Hypothetically and, of course, confidentially." Since the early days of the investigation, Ray had reluctantly revised his opinion of the doctor's worth, conceding that he might actually offer a measure of help.

"I understand. Go ahead."

"This has to do with the strangler, the one you worked up a profile on recently. We have a possibility here on his motivation and I wanted to see if you think what we learned is consistent with what you know of serial killers in general and this one in particular."

"I'm listening."

Ray checked his notes, then related to Delaney what he suspected, that a man had been stalking a certain nun a couple of years ago so persistently that she'd had to relocate and left no forwarding address for fear he'd follow her. After relating everything he'd learned to the psychiatrist, he paused. "Of course, I don't know yet if this groundskeeper—the man we've discovered has worked at all the various locations where the stranglings took place—is the same man who harassed Sister Terry. But it would tie in with the messages he's left on the mass cards." Quickly, he brought the doctor up to date on what he'd learned at the Franciscan monastery as well.

Delaney cleared his throat. "Stalking is very much consistent with some serial killers, as we've discussed before. Others kill randomly. As to motivation, it could very well be that our man became fixated on a particular nun in the past—viewing her as the personification of the unattainable female, for example—and then stalked her. When she moved out of his life, he turned to others as representatives of her, killing them and asking her forgiveness."

"But how would you explain the two-year hiatus between the time Sister Terry left the area and when the stranglings began?"

"In my studies of serial killers, this is not unusual. Perhaps they meet someone who keeps them on the straight and narrow for a time. Life seems to be going along well and the need to kill is pushed into the background. But that state usually doesn't last. Then again, in this case, we have no proof that your man ever killed before this time. Perhaps after the object of his obsession left, it took him two years to build to a strong enough level of frustration to actually kill. Then again, he could have killed others elsewhere that we know nothing of yet. Or maybe he'd been searching for her and finally realized he'd never find her, and so his madness manifested itself in uncontrollable killing rages."

"You think he's out of control?" Ray asked, afraid of the answer.

In his office, Delaney stroked his thin mustache. "It would seem he's moving in that direction. The murders are becoming more frequent. I'd say he's becoming seriously unraveled, perhaps he even senses that the police are getting close."

Ray went on to tell the doctor about Angie Falconi. "My partner's in St. Clair right now talking to Angie's parents, questioning them about Wally Lambert."

"It's obvious that Angie Falconi's death is connected to the nuns'. And Angie's folks were once members of St. Matthews. That can't be dismissed as coincidence."

"I agree. If Sister Terry also knew Angie Falconi, then I'd say we're close to resolving this thing." Ray sighed. "Of course, we still haven't a clue as to this guy's whereabouts." Ray had considered putting out an all-points bulletin for the man, but they still had so little to go on. A vague physical description and a name. He hesitated involving the media, for fear their man would go into hiding or move away.

"He can't hide from the police forever," Delaney said. "But don't underestimate the guy's intelligence. In my studies, I've come to find that serial killers have almost a sixth sense about how not to get caught."

"Oh, I know he's damn clever," Ray said.

"Look at Ted Bundy. He left a trail of blood everywhere, but none seemed to fall on him. Time and again, he left the crime scene without a single eyewitness. These guys are not only shrewd but lucky."

"Let's hope this guy's luck is running out. Doctor, thanks for confirming my suspicions."

"Any time. And I wish you luck in catching him."

"Thanks. we'll need it." Ray hung up as Meg walked in.

Feeling exhausted as she had for weeks now, Meg sat down at her desk and ran a hand through her windblown hair. She needed a haircut, she thought. And a manicure and a vacation, one where she'd be sightseeing from morning to night and have no time to sit around and think. Maybe after they put away the strangler.

"What'd you find out from the Falconis?" Ray asked.

"I got the father to open up finally."

"How'd you manage that?"

"Dolores wasn't home and I found Mario down by the lake, getting ready to go out on his boat. His English isn't very good, but I was able to make out what he said just fine. Even though his wife and daughter had tried to keep him in the dark, he'd known that Angie had been seeing someone. Dolores didn't know who, so Mario decided to find out."

"Worried fathers make good sleuths," Ray commented as he drained his lukewarm coffee.

"You got that right. He followed Angie one night in a car he'd borrowed from a friend so she wouldn't recognize him. He watched them park at a motel and go inside, and it nearly broke his heart."

"Don't tell me he stormed inside?"

"No, though he wanted to, poor man. Trouble was, his daughter was in her twenties and he didn't want her to leave home, so he couldn't risk that big a blowup. But he did talk with her the next day. She apparently had a good job at a bank, and Mario didn't want her mixed up with a common laborer.

Even though Mario worked in a factory until his retirement, he wanted more for his only child."

"What kind of a laborer was this guy Angie dated?" Ray asked hopefully.

She smiled wearily. "A landscaper named Wally. Mario didn't know the last name. She'd dated him awhile back, when they'd lived in the old neighborhood around St. Matthews, and now Wally had looked Angie up in St. Clair. The father told her she could do better. Angie said she knew that now, that they'd quarreled and she wasn't going to see him again. Two weeks later, they found her body in the lake."

"And that happened two years ago?"

"Almost two years to the day the first strangling victim was found, yes."

"I think we've got our man. On paper. Getting him physically is going to be much more difficult."

"Let's hope Sister Terry can shed some light on his whereabouts." Meg opened her appointment book disinterestedly, then closed it. Lord, but she was tired. Bone-tired. She felt as if she could sleep a week. Yet she scarcely was able to get in more than a couple of hours at a stretch before her eyes would pop open, she'd notice the empty place next to her in bed, and reality would slam into her. Then the grief would take over.

Ray was checking his own schedule. "I'm sure she hasn't kept in touch with him if she moved away to avoid him. But I'm hoping she knows his family and the Falconis. Maybe we can track the guy that way." He made a note, then placed his book in his inside pocket. "You want to come with me to question her in Nazareth tomorrow?"

"I suppose." She really should, Meg thought. She knew Ray was uncomfortable in the presence of nuns and could use her Catholic assistance, as he called it. But she'd give anything to just go home and forget about all she should be doing.

Ray studied her across the two desks. "I think you need to get out of here. I can handle this alone. Meg, take a little time off. You came back too soon. I'll clear it with the captain."

For just a moment, Meg closed her eyes. Then she shook her head and looked at her partner with a shaky smile. "You forget that I'm Catholic. I'd be so steeped in guilt at leaving you to do all the work that I wouldn't be able to rest anyway."

"That's silly. I can certainly question one small nun without help. I want you to gather up your stuff and go home. I don't want to see you around here for at least a week."

"Won't you miss me even a tiny bit?" she teased. Then she winked at him. "Of course not. You've got Toni."

Ray didn't answer as he suddenly found the file in front of him enormously interesting.

Studying him closely, perhaps even more attuned because of her recent loss, Meg began to get the picture. "You've quarreled."

Gritting his teeth, he wished she'd have left five minutes ago. "It wasn't exactly a quarrel. Toni made a suggestion on how I should solve one of our cases—a rather stupid suggestion, I might add. I told her I'd promise not to tell her how to run her restaurants if she'd get off my back about my work."

Meg let out an uneven sigh. "I imagine she took that well."

He shrugged. "Laymen have no business sticking their noses in police affairs."

"She cares about you. Maybe she was just trying to help."

He slapped closed the file he'd been pretending to read. "I don't need her help. I don't need *her.*"

She'd been down this path with Ray before, Meg thought. Only this time, it was different. Because Toni was different from anyone else he'd ever dated since she'd known him. Toni was the genuine article and she loved him, warts and all.

Gathering up her courage, Meg crossed her arms on her desk and stared across at him. "Do you love her?"

He felt the muscle in his jaw clench, then open, then clench again. "I care about her, not that it's any of your business. But I stand by what I said. I don't want her hurt and I don't want her messing in police business."

"Papa knows best?"

He glared at her. "What's that supposed to mean?"

Meg steepled her fingers as she searched for the right words. "Ray, the only person whose actions you're responsible for is you. You care about Toni, but it doesn't give you the right to tell her what to do and what not to do."

"Do you want me to stand by and let her get hurt? That creep sent her Mo's necklace and dumped a body in her pool. He knows who she is and where she is."

"I'm aware of that and so is Toni. She's not stupid or careless. She's undoubtedly taking precautions. You can't take responsibility for everyone. It didn't work with Pete and it won't work with Toni. If you love her, trust her."

His scowl deepened. "What makes you think I love her?"

She smiled. "Because I've seen you with her. You can deny your feelings till the cows come home. Your actions give you away." When she saw his expression, she zeroed in. "Love isn't really a four-letter word, Ray."

"It is to me. Love never got me anywhere." Not with his father, his stepmother, his half-brother, or his ex-wife. "Love does nothing but make people act irrationally."

Slowly, she shook her head. "You're wrong, partner. Love is the only reason for being here. Without it, we're empty shells, lonely and lost."

Ray softened his voice. "Meg, you're grieving right now, so you remember only the good times. Or maybe, for you and Dennis, there *were* only good times. But trust me, it's a rarity when two people remain in wedded bliss. It's simply not for me."

"I suppose not, if you make up your mind that it isn't. And yes, there were some down periods in our marriage. But if you love someone, you forget the petty problems between you. They'll work themselves out." She remembered how annoyed she used to get because of Dennis's habit of leaving wet towels on the bathroom floor. Now, she'd pick them up daily, hourly, if only he were back with her.

Swallowing a sob, she met Ray's thoughtful gaze. "I'm not one to dish out advice freely, especially unasked-for advice. You know that. But if I could, I'd tell everyone to take every minute you have with the one you love, and milk it dry, use it for all you're worth. Enjoy that love and cherish it. We never know when the one we love will be snatched from us."

A bit embarrassed by her sentimental tone, Meg cleared her throat and stood. "Forgive me for meddling." She walked around their desks and wound her arms around Ray's neck. "You're a terrific guy, you big lug. Go to her." Straightening, she grabbed her handbag. "You're sure it's okay if I take off?"

"Absolutely." Ray stood, too.

"It's Thursday. I won't take a week, but I will stay away till Monday. All right?"

"It's a deal."

She stepped up to him again, grateful when his arms came around her and tightened for a long moment. Stepping back, she blinked to avoid the tears that were always so close to the surface these days. "Thanks, Ray."

He leaned down to press a kiss to her forehead. "Rest well."

After she left, Ray sat back down. For several minutes, he thought over what Meg had said. And he thought about Toni.

He was sorry he'd jumped all over her case the previous night. It was just that she was so goddamn stubborn sometimes. All right, so was he. She'd made a few good points, he'd thought on the drive home, and Meg had made a few as well. He was a responsibility nut and maybe even a control freak when it came to his job. But he'd stand on his original opinion that Toni should stay out of police business.

But he hadn't needed to be so hard-nosed about it.

He dialed the Glass Door and waited. She came on the line as usual, crisp and businesslike. He swallowed nervously. "Hi."

Toni tossed down the pen she'd been writing with and leaned back in her desk chair. "Hi, yourself."

"Are you still speaking to me?" He toyed with a pencil.

"Apparently so."

Ray took a deep breath. "Sometimes I have a big mouth." When she remained silent, he went on. "I was out of line last night."

"You'll get no argument from me on that."

Meg's words echoed through his head. "I care about you, Toni. A lot."

She let out a shaky breath. "I care about you, too, Ray. But I won't be bullied, not by you, not by anyone. With or without you, I'm my own person."

"I'm learning that." He noticed that she didn't laugh. "Give me a little time and I'll get it right."

She supposed that that was as close to an apology as she was likely to get from him. "All right."

"Can you meet me somewhere for lunch?"

She had a lot of work to do, she thought. And besides, maybe a little time apart would be good for them. "I'm up to my ears over here right now. Rain check?"

"Sure. I've got a couple of important appointments tomorrow. I'll call you afterward."

"That'll be fine." She waited while the silence lingered.

"I guess that's it then."

"I guess so."

"Toni?"

"Yes?"

"I'm glad you're not angry with me anymore."

Why did he have to sound so much like a little boy? she wondered.

Rosie Pulaski clicked off her television set. It was midafternoon and her soaps were over. That *General Hospital,* she thought, reaching for her crocheting. Hard to believe that there were people in the world who acted that way, everyone sleeping with everyone else. Shaking her head, she couldn't see the sense of it.

Her sister who'd been dead for five years used to say, why borrow trouble? At least with your man, you know what you've got. Rosie chuckled at the memory. Not that she'd ever considered any other man than her Joe. There was a widower named Eddie at the senior center connected with St. Matthews who always flirted with her. But she never took him seriously. She would leave the running around to the folks on television.

Rosie arranged the soft yarn in her lap and reached for her hook. She made blankets for newborn babies, then donated them to the church to distribute to the poor. And lap robes and slippers for the elderly that Father Hilliard took periodically to nursing homes. She hated sitting idle and she was pleased that her handiwork benefited others.

She paused as she heard the pacing resume upstairs. Wladek was at it again, she thought with a worried frown, gazing up at her ceiling. He'd been walking back and forth all night. Now, there it was again.

The boy was troubled, but she hadn't a clue as to why. The previous day, she'd taken up a dish of stuffed peppers to him, knocking at his back door. It had taken him quite a while to respond, though she'd known he was in there. When he finally came to the door, he'd looked awful, his hair mussed, his clothes wrinkled and his face sweaty. He'd peered out at her almost as if he didn't recognize her.

Then he'd refused to open the screen and take the food. That was the first time he'd ever done that, for she knew him to be a good eater. He'd said he wasn't hungry. She'd asked if he was all right and he'd nodded. Then she'd asked why he was home in the middle of the day and he'd gotten agitated. He'd raised his voice, telling her he'd quit his job, but she wasn't to worry about the rent because he'd get another one soon. Then he'd slammed the door shut.

Rosie didn't know what to do. The mild-mannered tenant she'd been so pleased with for two years had changed, seemingly overnight. If only she knew where his family was, she'd call someone. But she didn't have one friend's name or even the name of the place where he worked.

Sighing, she shifted in her chair. What was a body to do? Nothing, Helen had advised her when she'd confided in her friend. Wladek was a grownup and she had no business interfering. Which Rosie knew was true. But she'd been thinking of him like a son, and his rejection hurt her.

Still, she couldn't help someone who refused her help. Trying to put the whole thing out of her mind, she clicked the TV back on, hoping Oprah's guests would distract her.

Toni sat on the bed, struggling with tears that wanted badly to fall. The large box that she'd taken out of the closet was open. Tucked inside were the nun's duds, as Mo had called them, that Toni had picked up from St. Matthews convent a couple of weeks after her funeral. At the time, wanting no fresh reminders, she'd placed the box in the closet of the bedroom Mo had had as a young girl growing up in the Garette house.

Today, Toni had decided to take them down.

She fingered the soft cotton blouses, the black skirts and slacks, the jacket. In the bottom were two pairs of sensible shoes Mo had hated and seldom worn, except when Reverend Mother had reminded her that she was a little out of step. Sisters were allowed to dress in street clothes these days in many orders and quite a few did. But you had to choose, either full habit, abbreviated habit, or street clothes. The church frowned on mixing and matching.

Slowly, she picked up the short veil Mo had also often as not removed as soon as she'd stepped foot inside. Sisters weren't supposed to be vain either, but Mo had always been a little proud of her beautiful hair. Toni remembered going over to St. Matthews to pick up Mo one afternoon and finding her playing basketball with the grade school girls in the gym, her headpiece on the sidelines, her hair flying and tennis shoes on her feet. Feeling a sob catch in her throat, Toni closed her eyes.

Would she ever get over missing her fun-loving cousin? Would her mother ever truly be the same as she'd been when Mo had been a part of their lives? Would her father be the carefree man he'd once been, the one who used to leave the house whistling each day?

Mo had died so violently, so uselessly, at the hands of a madman. Maybe if he were caught, if he were put away some place where he could never harm anyone again, they could all rest easier. But so far, he was still on the loose, wandering around in the free world, while Mo rested in a silent grave.

It wasn't fair.

Dabbing at her eyes, Toni turned back to the few remaining things they had left of Mo. The police seemed indifferent to her suggestions about trying to flush out the killer. Meg was sympathetic but noncommittal, too wrapped up in her own grief to be of much assistance. As much as she cared for Ray, so far he'd been unable to get a bead on the strangler. And any day now, there'd be another senseless murder, another poor, innocent sister dead because of some maniac.

It had to end.

Toni slipped off her shoes and began to undress. She glanced out the window and saw that it was not quite seven and still light out. She'd left work early, knowing her parents would probably stay later. She had something she needed to do, something she'd spent several days planning. She'd wanted to do it with Ray's blessing and the police backing her up. Apparently, that wasn't to be.

She stepped into Mo's skirt and fastened it. They were nearly the same size so everything should fit. She picked up the blouse, then hesitated for a moment and discarded it. Hurrying to her room, she rummaged around in her drawers until she found a white cotton turtleneck. Returning to Mo's room, she put it on.

Next she picked up the circular piece of hard plastic she'd fashioned from some discarded pieces on her father's workbench in the garage. Arranging it in place under the high collar of the turtleneck, she decided it would do as a deterrent. At least, if someone snuck up on her and managed to slip a wire around her neck, the hard material would prevent serious damage. And maybe stop him in his tracks long enough for her to respond and do him some bodily harm in return.

If the police would do nothing, she would do something. Maybe it wouldn't work, as she'd been told repeatedly. But doing something was better than sitting around stewing over it all, feeling helpless. So the previous night after Ray had left in anger, she'd finalized her plan.

Shrugging into Mo's jacket, Toni slipped her feet into the plain black flats, then reached for the headpiece. Angling this way and that at her mirror image, she finally got it in place and anchored it with several bobby pins. Standing back and regarding herself objectively, she decided she was every bit the nun—at least on the outside. She had one more thing to get before she was ready to leave.

In her nightstand drawer was the .38 pistol her father had purchased for her years before, with a valid permit, for protection when she worked nights at the restaurant. John Garette had taken her to the shooting range and taught her how to use the weapon. But despite all the preparation, Toni had always felt odd carrying it in her purse. Her mother, for whom John had gotten an exact duplicate, felt the same and never took hers along either.

At last, she had a use for the weapon. The jacket had deep pockets. Toni checked the gun to make sure it was loaded and that the safety was on. She placed it in her right pocket and stuffed in several Kleenexes to disguise its shape. Again, she checked herself in her cheval glass. Yes, she definitely looked the part.

The bedside clock indicated five to seven. Confessions would begin at seven, she knew. She wasn't a member of St. Matthews, but knew from her conversations with Mo that only the candles that burned in the wall sconces and an altar lamp were left on during evening services in order to save on the electricity bill. In subdued lighting, she was sure no one would recognize her.

It seemed logical to try the place where the stranglings had first begun and the parish where most of the victims were members. Toni didn't think of herself as particularly brave, which was why she'd taken certain precautions. Nor did she consider herself foolish, which was why she'd taken her loaded gun. It was simply that someone had to do something, and she saw no other volunteers at the ready.

After locking up and setting the alarm, Toni hurried to her car and drove to St. Matthews.

It was oddly cool in the cavernous church, almost as if the building were air-conditioned, though Toni knew it wasn't. The stone walls always gave a feeling of dampness, yet it wasn't as stifling as the lingering summer heat and humidity outside.

As she made her quiet way down the center aisle, she saw that several people were lined up at the one confessional in use and others were kneeling at scattered pews, likely saying their penance. Still, there were no more than a dozen people in attendance, including the priest and herself.

She chose a pew halfway down the center aisle, and immediately knelt down, crossed herself, and began her prayers. She certainly needed God with her tonight for, despite her determination to lure the strangler out into the open, she had a curled fist in her stomach and nerves dancing along her spine.

An hour passed all too slowly. Toni found herself jumpy, looking over her shoulder frequently, starting at the slightest sound. Perspiration dampened her brow despite the cool interior. From under lowered brows, she watched a slow but steady trickle of parish members go into the confessional, then leave minutes later. Some walked out of the church afterward, others stayed to pray.

By eight o'clock, only two women and a man were left, along with a weary Toni. The two women left moments later. The man stayed in the last row. Surreptitiously glancing his way, Toni's hand

SHATTERED VOWS 303

slipped into her pocket, her fingers closing around the .38.

Fifteen minutes passed and two couples entered with three children in tow. They walked to the vigil lights. Next, two teenage girls came in, crossed themselves, and knelt in the front pew. Toni wished they'd all leave so the killer would surface.

Yawning expansively, Father Hilliard came out of the confessional and looked around. He noticed that there were several people in the church including a nun. Father didn't recognize her as one of St. Matthews' sisters. She was probably visiting a family nearby. She'd be safe with so many others around. He doubted if anyone else would be coming to confession tonight. There was a night game on television he didn't want to miss. He decided to leave for now and walk back later to lock up. He made his way to the rear doors.

Twenty minutes later, everyone had left except the man wearing dark work clothes who seemed to be waiting, as she was. Toni braced herself. Surely it wouldn't be this easy, ferreting him out the first time she tried it. Nervously, she checked her neck piece and found the heavy plastic still in place. If he approached her, she'd grab the gun and face him down. Hopefully, she wouldn't have to shoot him. But if it came to that, she'd think of Mo and pull the trigger.

A new thought struck her. How could she keep the gun trained on him while going for help? She hadn't figured on the whole church emptying out, and the priest leaving so soon. Usually confessions went on till around nine at most parishes. If the killer didn't show tonight, next time she'd bring her cellular phone. Then, she'd be able to summon help while holding her gun on him.

It all sounded so good in the planning stages. But so far, the star performer had failed to show up.

Just then, the man in the rear stood up, his feet on the stone aisle making a shuffling sound. Suddenly alert, Toni released the safety on the gun and held it in a strong grip inside her pocket. In her other hand, she held a rosary her mother had given her years ago. If necessary, she'd throw it at him as a diversionary tactic.

She heard him slowly walking toward her. Her muscles were so tense she felt they might literally split. Moisture gathered beneath the hard collar and dripped down to her breasts and along her back. She didn't dare risk a glance at him now. He was almost abreast of her when the back door creaked open.

"Dad, I'm back here," called a teenage male voice. "Sorry I'm late picking you up."

As Toni swiveled about, the man in the dark work clothes turned. "Where you been, Robby? I was just gonna go try to find a phone to call you."

"I got out of work a little late," the boy told his father as the older man joined him.

"Okay. Let's go. Mom hates it when we're late for supper."

As the two men left, Toni let out a shuddering breath that could probably have been heard in the sacristy, she thought. Then she laughed out loud at herself, breaking the tension. "Not tonight," she whispered and got to her feet, her knees still a little wobbly.

Her eyes still watchful, she hurriedly left and made her way to her car parked in the lot. Before

SHATTERED VOWS 305

she removed her hand from her pocket, she glanced around and saw no one. Two cars were parked down by the rectory, but they were empty. Steadier now, she unlocked her door and got behind the wheel. Motor running and doors again locked, she sighed.

As much as she'd hated the last two hours, she'd managed to get through them. If only the killer had shown up. But he hadn't. Next time, she'd bring her phone and be even more prepared.

That thought in mind, she flipped on the headlights and pulled out of the lot. Because she was still trembling, she turned on the radio, needing a sense of normalcy. The strains of Kenny G came rolling out, soothing her. She headed east, then veered north toward Grosse Pointe and home.

The man hunched down in the dark Olds straightened, but didn't hurry to rush after the little red Mercedes. He knew where it was probably going. When he saw that Toni Garette had pulled out into traffic, he followed at a safe two-car distance.

Wally scratched his head in confusion. Why was Toni wearing a nun's habit? She certainly couldn't have joined the convent that quickly. He didn't pretend to be a good Catholic, but he knew that sisters had to go to school almost as long as priests. Was she wearing her dead cousin's things as sort of a memorial? That didn't make sense either.

What was she up to?

He trailed along behind, following a path to her home. So she wasn't going to visit the cop tonight. Did he even know she was hanging around St. Matthews dressed up as a nun? What purpose would she have in mind?

As he slowly turned onto Lakeshore Drive, it came to him. She'd dressed up as a nun because she wanted to die. She wanted him to come to her, like he'd gone to the others, and send her to a better place. While the police were trying to catch him, Toni was trying to join her cousin and the others.

His head began to ache as he considered it. Could that really be her plan? Or had that bearded cop set her up as a decoy to lure him.

Peering in his rearview mirror, Wally scanned the other cars on the road. Detective Vargas was the one in charge of the case and he drove a Ford station wagon. There was none in sight. No cop cars either. Of course, he could be in a totally different car to throw him off.

As they cruised north along the winding street, the Olds several lengths behind the Mercedes, he kept watch. Traffic was fairly heavy on this Thursday evening. He could spot no one car that stayed with them all the way. No, he was probably just getting paranoid.

Still, his head was hurting really bad by the time Toni turned in onto her street. Wally decided not to follow her there, but keep on going. At Vernier, he made a left and headed for the expressway home. He'd have to get there before the headache made his vision blur. That had happened to him several times, and had scared the hell out of him.

He knew that Rosie had noticed his actions lately. But that couldn't be helped. He'd been so agitated a couple of times there that he'd had to pace, had to walk off the nervous energy or he felt as if he'd explode. He hadn't dared go to any of his jobs lately. He'd seen the cops going around questioning everyone. He couldn't risk being caught before his mission was complete.

Wally rubbed his forehead as he turned onto the expressway. Another fifteen or twenty minutes and he'd be in his flat with the new fan he'd purchased keeping him cool. Already, his hands were slippery with sweat.

Feeling himself near the breaking point, Wally looked out the windshield, his gaze drifting heavenward. *Please, when will it all end?*

SIXTEEN

Nazareth was a small town nestled in the Irish Hills of Michigan, so small that it seldom appeared on any map. You had to know where you were going to find it, or stop to ask along the way. Ray had been told that the road leading to the small town veered off from the old two-lane thoroughfare that had been the only good route to Ohio before the interstate highway had been built in the late fifties.

The mother house of the Sisters of St. Joseph was in a valley, one of many in the green rolling hills that dotted the area. Approaching from the country road, Ray saw that the main convent was an old three-story building made of reclaimed brick. The archdiocese representative had told him that the nuns who lived there did community work mostly. He wasn't sure what that included. The retreat also housed retired nuns, troubled nuns, and some novitiates.

It was four on a sunny Friday afternoon as he pulled into the blacktop parking lot and walked to the large wooden front door. He rang the bell and heard the chimes echoing inside. The round-faced sister who greeted him reminded him of someone right out of *The Sound of Music,* with her full habit and warm smile. She was Sister Bertrice, the one he'd spoken with on the phone.

Apologizing for the necessity, she asked to check his I.D. even though she'd been expecting him. Satisfied, she smiled at him. "Isn't it a beautiful day out there," she said as she reluctantly closed the door behind him. It was cooler inside, but far less sunny. "Too nice a day to be indoors." She led him toward a book-lined study and indicated a corduroy couch to the far left. "Please have a seat, Detective Vargas. May I get you something cool to drink?"

"No, thank you. Is Sister Theresa back from her trip yet?"

"No, but we expect her shortly." She glanced at her watch. "I'm going to ask you to excuse me, but if you'll wait here, Sister will join you as soon as possible."

They'd told him late afternoon, but he'd been prepared to wait, albeit impatiently. Ray had a feeling the young nun held the key to this important investigation. "Certainly, Sister." He walked toward the couch as she slid closed the double doors, leaving him alone.

He had nothing to do but look around, which was an ingrained habit anyway. The two arched windows behind the large oak desk at the opposite end had heavy black wrought-iron grillwork outside, as a safety precaution rather than merely decorative, he guessed. Even here, away from urban crime, Ray thought, they had to be careful. Of course, a house full of women would be easy prey for a couple of skilled B & E men.

The desktop held only a small shaded lamp and a leather-covered bible on its shiny surface. Hands in his pockets, Ray perused the bookshelves and was impressed with the eclectic collection. He wondered if each sister had brought some of her favorites or if most of the books had been donated. Restlessly, he wandered over the uneven flooring, listening to the squeak and creak of wood polished to a sheen. He caught the scent of lemon oil mingled with the faint musty smell of old books.

Finally, he settled on the couch and picked up a newspaper from the coffee table. The minutes dragged by as he tried to concentrate.

It was more than an hour before he heard a slight knock at the doors before they slid open. Ray stood expectantly, then stared in shocked surprise.

Sister Theresa Roberts could have passed for Toni's sister.

She was slender, with pale skin untouched by makeup, high cheekbones, a patrician nose, and large blue eyes. Her thick blond hair fell to her shoulders. She held her headpiece in her hand as she smiled an apology. "I'm so sorry to have kept you waiting, Detective Vargas." She held out her hand.

He shook it as he tried to shake off his astonishment. "I appreciate your seeing me. You must be tired from your trip."

"Oh, no, it was fun. Sister Naomi and I took six of the eighth grade girls from St. John the Divine parish camping for three days and nights." Her laugh was musical. "Fourteen-year-olds sure have a lot of energy."

"I'll bet." He waited until she seated herself in a brown plaid chair across from the couch before he, too, sat down. "Did Sister Bertrice tell you why I'm here?"

"Only briefly." A flash of pain crossed her fine features. "She mentioned something about Walt

Lambert. I'd almost gotten myself to the point of believing I'd heard the last of him."

Ray decided to move slowly, to ease her into the story. "How long since you've been back to St. Matthews?"

"A little over two years. What is it, Detective? Is Walt in trouble?"

"I'm not sure yet. Can you describe him for me?"

"It's been some time. He may have changed. He's about five-nine or ten, built solid but not muscular or heavy. He's got very nice hair, brown and quite thick. His eyes are gray and he tans easily."

"That's his physical description. Can you describe his personality?"

She was wearing black slacks and now crossed her slim legs, her hands in her lap betraying a hint of nerves. "He's a paradox, Detective. He can be so sweet, so very charming. Then, for hardly any reason, he can turn moody and emotional, argumentative and pretty obnoxious."

"Would you consider him violent?"

She looked taken aback. By his questions, she knew that the officer had never met Walt. Yet this had to be serious or he'd never have mentioned violence. She'd prayed so hard for Walt all the years she'd known him, yet he'd turned from the right path apparently. "I'd have to say that, if he doesn't get his way, or if something gets in the way of what he wants, yes, he could be violent. I certainly was afraid of him. With the full knowledge of the archdiocese, I took out an order of protection against him back when I lived at St. Matthews. You may already know that. He wasn't to come within ten feet of me, the convent, the church, or my parents' home."

"Did Walt comply with the order of protection?"

"No, not even for a day. He tried to bully his way into the convent. He'd come into the school and stand outside my classroom. He'd send me letters and call me continually." She brushed back a fall of her hair and sighed. "It was terrible. I hate thinking about that time."

"I'm sure. Did you notify the police when he was in violation?"

She shook her head. "I know I should have, but it would have meant jail time for Walt. I didn't want him to have a record, just to leave me alone."

Ray leaned forward, his elbows on his knees. "I'm sorry to trouble you this way, Sister. But this is important. Very important. And you may be the only person who knows Walter Lambert well enough to provide us with information."

"But I haven't seen him in so long. What about his family?"

"Were they members of St. Matthews?"

"Yes. They lived on the next block from my folks' house on Georgia Street. It was a nice neighborhood when we were growing up, but it's changed so much now."

"I've checked St. Matthews' parish records. There are no Lamberts listed. And no Roberts either, I might add."

"My parents moved to Florida several years ago. I don't know what happened to Walt's people."

"Did you know them?"

The woman nodded, frowning. "Mr. Lambert worked at Chrysler, drank quite a bit, and was rarely home. Mrs. Lambert was a big woman with a loud voice, very critical of Walt, though she seemed to like me. Walt has an older brother who got straight A's, a football star and all-around great guy. She adored him. Walt never quite measured up to Clark and he was always getting in trouble. Minor stuff, but Mrs. Lambert was always on him about something. I used to feel sorry for him."

"Would you mind my asking what sort of relationship you had with Walt?"

Sister Theresa drew in a deep, steadying breath. "I suppose I thought it was love at the time. You see, I was eighteen and I'd been dating Walt for a couple of months right around high school graduation. I'd always felt drawn to the church and had talked of studying for the sisterhood since I was about ten. But Mom kept saying I'd have to be absolutely sure. So I tried to keep an open mind, getting involved in school, dating, and so on."

She was taking the long route. Ray tried to move her on. "Did you go steady with Walt?"

"No. He asked me to, but I thought that was too much of a commitment for the way I felt. I took a job at a bank after graduation, still undecided about what I wanted to do. Walt kept coming around and then one day, he said he loved me and asked me to marry him. I was fond of Walt, but I just didn't know if marriage was for me. I went to our pastor and discussed my confusion. He told me it might be best, since I was so undecided, that I go away for a few weeks and think things over. My mother's sister lives in Orlando so I went to spend the summer there."

"How did Walt take that?"

"Not well. But I asked him not to contact me, that I had a lot of thinking to do. And I promised him an answer when I returned. But at the end of summer, I still wasn't sure. He became more and more insistent about marriage. My parents were highly annoyed at his many calls and the way he'd just show up, often late in the evening."

"Would you say that he was obsessed with you?"

Sister Theresa set aside the headpiece she'd been fiddling with and looked at Ray. "At the time, I didn't see it that way. I was extremely naive, Detective. But after all I went through with Walt, I'd have to say that he was."

And maybe still is. "Did he call you Theresa?"

"No, everyone calls me Terry."

"So then, during your time in Florida, you decided to reject Walt's proposal in favor of the convent?"

Terry dropped her gaze and chewed on her lower lip for a moment. She could feel her cheeks reddening, and threaded her fingers together agitatedly. "An incident occurred that helped make up my mind for me. You see, from the first time we began dating, Walt was always trying to ... to get physical. Over and over, I told him that I didn't condone premarital sex, but he ... he ..."

"He had trouble accepting your decision?"

"Yes. I was adamant that he accept that. But I found out that Walt had turned to someone else while I'd been gone." Clearing her throat, Terry forced herself to continue. The reverend mother had urged her to be cooperative in every way with the police.

"Practically the day I came back, I learned that a friend of mine was in the hospital, so I went to see her. She'd been in a boating accident, but that wasn't all of it. She'd been dating Walt the summer I was away and they'd gone to a motel together. When my friend learned she was pregnant, Walt became angry. But later he invited her to go waterskiing with him. He was driving the boat when she'd fallen—hard. Later, she had a miscarriage and wound up in the hospital. She told me that she was certain Walt had tried to hurt her."

Ray sat listening as the puzzle pieces fell into place. "What is your friend's name, Sister?"

"Angie Falconi."

"Did you know that Angie's dead?"

"Yes. My mother wrote me some time ago that Angie had died in still another boating accident. I'd thought it ironic at the time, especially since she was an excellent swimmer."

Again, Ray decided to postpone telling her the truth about Angie's death until he heard the rest of her tale. "What did you say to Walt after you visited Angie in the hospital?"

Nervously, she uncrossed her legs. "We had an awful quarrel. I accused him of having killed his own child. He cried, begged my forgiveness, pleaded with me to give him another chance to marry him. But I simply couldn't. We all have a point beyond which we cannot forgive, Detective, even us Catholics. For me, he'd passed over the line. Not only did his baby die, but he could have killed Angie. So I told him I never wanted to see him again. But at least, he'd helped make up my mind for me. The next day, I told my parents that I intended to enter the convent. And I've never regretted my decision."

Ray leaned back, appearing casual yet inside he was humming with excitement, the way he often was when everything was clicking. "Did he leave you alone after that?"

"For a while. As a novitiate, our days are very long and quite busy. The convent wasn't receptive to his many attempts to see me. He did stop for a time. But after I took my final vows and was assigned to St. Matthews, the harassing began again, worse than ever."

"What did you do?"

"I tried talking with him, always with someone else present. I told him I thought he was sick and desperately needed counseling. He didn't agree. He kept it up until the other sisters were getting frightened. I got the restraining order. He ignored it. Finally, I had no choice but to ask for a transfer and some sort of promise that my whereabouts be kept unknown." She let out a shuddering sigh. "For two years, I've been blessedly free of him and happy." Her eyes were serious as they met his. "Are you going to tell me what he's done?"

From the little time he'd spent with Sister Terry, Ray knew she was strong enough to handle the news. Yet he hated to be the one to tell her. "We have reason to believe he's responsible for the murder of several nuns in various Detroit locations, mostly at St. Matthews."

"Oh dear God." Terry's hands flew to her face and her eyes glistened with tears. "It never entered my mind, even though I've been following the story in the papers." She swallowed around a sob that tried to escape. "If only I had made the connection, perhaps I could have prevented some of those poor nuns from getting killed."

"Don't blame yourself, Sister," Ray said quickly. "There's no way you could have known. And even if you did make the connection, it's unlikely you would have been able to stop him. He's covered his tracks extremely well."

But she was scarcely listening to him. "How many sisters have died?" she asked, her voice tremulous.

"Six."

SHATTERED VOWS

"Oh Lord." She crossed herself and bent forward, agonizing.

He decided he'd best reveal all. "We also think Walter Lambert is responsible for Angie Falconi's death."

The nun brought her head up. "Angie, too? But why? Why is he doing these dreadful things?"

Ray removed the mass cards from his pocket and handed them to her. "He's asking for forgiveness. At first, we thought he might be imploring God to forgive him. But it seems his pleas are directed at *you*."

Her face reflected her sorrow as she studied each card, lingering on the last one. Finally, she looked up. "Despite what you said, this is my fault. I specifically told Walt I could never forgive him for killing his child. It . . . it must have sent him over the edge."

Ray reached for her hand, hesitantly at first, then more confidently as her fingers curled around his and she closed her eyes. He saw tears roll down her cheeks and wanted badly to offer her a measure of comfort. "The man is obsessed, Sister, and although you're the object of that obsession, you didn't cause it. Stalkers are disturbed individuals. Most of the ones we read about unfortunately do commit murder. But stalking laws are on the books now, making it possible for us to get them off the streets *before* they do serious harm. But back when Walt was hounding you, there were no such laws in effect yet."

"If only there had been."

"There's no way you could have known or stopped him. He apparently strangled Angie right after you left St. Matthews two years ago."

She let go of his hand, found a tissue in her

pocket, and wiped her face. "What set him off on this more recent killing spree?"

Ray sat back. "I wish I knew."

"Have you got him in custody? What does he say?"

"We haven't apprehended him yet. That's one reason I'm here. Do you remember anyone he was close to, someone he might be living with? We've checked all our sources. He's probably driving, yet there's no car registered to him, nor a license plate. His driver's license is valid, but the address on it is a building that's been torn down. No fingerprints on file, no juvenile record. We're groping in the dark."

"There've been no witnesses?" she asked.

"We have one witness who cooperated with our police artist in putting together a sketch that we could run in the papers. Our problem is, he has no distinguishing features; apparently he looks generic, sort of everyman."

She grew thoughtful. "Yes, I guess he does. There is one thing, though. He perspires terribly when he's nervous or upset. His mother was always on him about something. And he gets headaches, really bad ones."

"Did he visit a doctor for those conditions, do you know?"

She shook her head. "I wouldn't know. It's been seven years since I was dating him."

"Can you give me the names of his parents and a friend or two?"

"His parents are Alma and Henry Lambert, but I have no idea where they are if they're not at the old address. I believe his brother Clark's in the service, but I don't know which branch. As to his friends, he didn't have many back then that I'm aware of. Walt's not one for large gatherings. He's not exactly a loner, but he prefers small groups. Or he did when I knew him."

"How old is he and what line of work was he in?"

She hesitated, thinking. "He'd be twenty-six now. When I knew him, he worked for Carson's Nursery on Eight Mile Road. He had big dreams about going to college, and about possibly owning his own business. But I doubt he ever achieved either. He's a dreamer, not a hard worker. And when things go wrong, he tends to blame those around him rather than take responsibility himself."

"You saw all that in him, yet you still considered marrying him?" Ray asked, puzzled.

The woman pocketed her tissue. "I was only eighteen, Detective Vargas. I saw what I wanted to see—his handsome smile, his sense of humor, the way he would bring me flowers. A cluster of violets. He charmed me. Until I stepped back and took an objective look at him." She shivered involuntarily. "But never did I dream he'd turn out to be a killer."

Ray checked the small notebook he'd been jotting things in. He asked for the address of the Lambert house and she gave it to him. Then he tried a long shot. "Do you recall if Walt often wore a lot of aftershave?"

She nodded. "Yes, I remember that. Because of the sweating, I think. I told him once that I was allergic to the one he used, so he stopped wearing it around me."

"What brand was it?"

"Old Spice."

She walked with him to the heavy front door. "If there's anything else you think of, please call me."

He handed her his card. "And thank you so much for all your help."

"I don't need thanking. Just find him, please. Walt needs help before he hurts someone else."

"I'll do my best." Ray walked through the open door, but before he'd stepped off the porch, she called him back.

"You mentioned that he was probably driving a car, but you don't know what kind. He used to drive his mother's Olds. He once said it was the only thing she'd ever given him. It would be close to fifteen years old by now, if it's still running. Dark blue, as I remember."

"Thanks again, Sister." Suddenly anxious, Ray hurried to his car and immediately put in a call to the Department of Motor Vehicles asking them to check on an Olds registered to an Alma Lambert.

Maybe they were finally going to get lucky, he thought as he started back to Detroit.

They weren't hearing confessions at St. Matthews on Friday evening. However, the Rosary Altar Society ladies were just finishing their meeting in the downstairs hall as Toni arrived. She watched them file through the church, several staying to say prayers, as she stopped halfway down the aisle. She felt more secure tonight with her gun in her jacket pocket and her cellular phone in the black purse she laid down on the wooden pew.

Getting out her rosary, she knelt and assumed a prayerful posture while her alert eyes took in every corner of the church. Only women were present— seven, to be exact—and herself. She knew that the church would be kept open until around nine, when

Father Hilliard would come to lock the doors. It was barely seven.

She dreaded the next two hours.

Two of the women left, whispering loudly as they walked to the rear. Toni continued facing the front. She wished the others would leave, for the strangler wouldn't make his move unless he found a nun alone. She reached up to loosen the bobby pin holding her headpiece in place and saw that her hand was trembling. Small wonder, being that she was lying in wait for a killer.

Her father was at the Glass Door that night, since his gin rummy card-playing cronies were meeting there for a dinner *sans* wives. Her mother was at a Tupperware party; Toni prayed that Jane wouldn't return home before her and spot her wearing Mo's habit. She hadn't heard from Ray. When they'd talked the previous day, he'd told her he had several appointments, but nothing more specific.

She'd walked over after parking under a street lamp near the convent tonight, thinking that if the killer saw her Mercedes in the church lot, he'd be deterred. Nuns usually didn't drive red convertibles. She wanted him to think she was a new nun who was staying at St. Matthews convent. She wanted him to see her as a victim.

She wanted to get this over with.

Wally paced the upstairs flat, his emotions in turmoil, his thoughts in a frenzy. He ran damp, trembling fingers through his hair and pressed a fist against his forehead. The headache wasn't going away.

He'd been at home since returning the previous night, but he'd barely slept. Even with the fan on, it was hot, and his head hurt badly. He'd changed clothes three times, and still he was wringing wet. He couldn't stand another minute of it.

He would have to go to her.

He didn't want to put Toni Garette out of her misery, even though she'd seemed to be asking to die last night. He enjoyed watching her, imagining her with him, daydreaming of her. She reminded him so much of Terry ... But he had no choice. He had to make the headache go away, and there were no other pretty ones left. It was probably for the best, anyway. Toni had changed. She was with the cop now, and probably no longer pure.

But he would send her to heaven, where God in his infinite mercy would cleanse her if she repented for her sins.

Hurriedly, he went into the bathroom. No time for a bath. He quickly stripped, then splashed on cologne before dressing in clean clothes. Back in his bedroom, he opened the top dresser drawer and took out mass card number seven. The last thing he did was clip off a piece of green wire from the spool and put it in his pocket.

The headache was blinding. He put on sunglasses even though it was evening. They didn't help much. He had to hurry, had to get to her, had to send her to her heavenly father. Then, he'd be at peace.

Chanting to himself, Wally clumped down his back stairs. Rosie was taking out the garbage as he passed on his way to the garage. Ordinarily, he'd stop and chat with her, but tonight he couldn't spare the time. He heard her call out his name, but he ignored her and climbed behind the wheel. Mumbling to himself, he managed to get the key in the ignition. His hands were already wet again with sweat. He swore aloud as the engine turned over. He shoved it into reverse and the car jerked out into the alley. He sped away, a prayer on his lips.

Hands on her ample hips, Rosie watched her tenant drive off. For some time, she'd thought something was bothering Wladek. Now, she was sure. What it was, she didn't know. But she meant to find out.

Turning back into her yard, she fastened the gate and glanced upstairs as she walked toward her house. Of all things, Wladek had left his back door open.

A blessing in disguise, she thought, grabbing the painted railing and making her slow way up the stairs. She hadn't been inside the flat, since she'd rented it to him two years ago. If it was dirty, she'd clean it for him as a surprise. Maybe that would put him in a good mood so she could talk him into seeing her doctor.

Opening the back screen, Rosie prayed she wouldn't find too bad a mess.

It was eight by the time Ray got back to the city. As he debated with himself whether to go home or stop in at the precinct, his car phone rang. "Vargas, here."

A rookie named Scott was calling about his DMV inquiry. "I found a 1980 Olds Delta 88 registered to an Alma Lambert, Detective. Want the address?"

Ray listened as the kid read out the address of the old Lambert residence. Really current information here, he thought. "What's the plate number?"

"C as in Charley, N as in Nellie, D as in Denver, nine, eight, two."

Driving with one hand, Ray copied down the information on the pad resting on the seat.

"Anything else I can do for you?" Scott asked.

"Yeah. I want an all-points bulletin out on that car. Should be a dark blue."

"Suspect's name?"

"Walter Lambert. Wanted for questioning in several murders."

"Considered armed and dangerous?"

Ray thought that over. Was a thin green wire a weapon? It was if someone had used it to kill six women. Correction, seven, if Angie were included. Was the Walt that Sister Terry had described dangerous? Damn right, he was. "Yeah, armed and dangerous."

"You got it."

Ray clicked off. Maybe he was jumping the gun, maybe not. Dr. Delaney had said the killer was falling apart, ready to crack. On the one hand, if Walt got wind of the manhunt and decided to go underground in a city the size of Detroit, they might never catch him. On the other hand, it was doubtful that he had the connections to help him hide out for long.

And just possibly, they might prevent another killing if they took him in tonight.

There was no reason to go in to the station right now. He'd have to soon enough when the boys in blue picked up Walt. He hadn't had dinner yet, so maybe the best thing would be to go home, have something to eat, and sit down to wait.

Jane Garette maneuvered the key into the lock. Her front door swung open at last and she hurried inside. Quickly, she punched in the alarm system code, then relaxed. Setting down her purse, she flipped on several lights.

Walking into the kitchen, she called out her daughter's name. No answer. Toni's car hadn't been in the drive, but then, she often put the Mercedes into the garage if she planned on staying home for the evening. She turned off the kitchen light and tried to remember if Toni had mentioned that she had plans that night. She didn't think so. Perhaps someone had called or something had come up.

Or maybe she was with Ray Vargas.

Jane decided to go upstairs and change into a robe, pulling pins from her hair as she climbed the stairs. Toni didn't talk about Ray, but as her mother, Jane could see that her feelings for the tall detective had grown steadily. Marriage to an officer was not what she'd wanted for her daughter. But who got to choose these things for their children?

If Toni loved him and was loved in return, that was all that mattered. The man was certainly attractive, in a rough-and-tumble way, that beard giving him a dangerous look. Jane supposed that was a plus in his line of work. She'd lost count of the number of nights Toni had apparently warmed his bed, so it had to be serious between them. Her daughter had never been one to get involved that way unless her heart was in it.

On her way to the room she shared with her husband, John, Jane glanced into Toni's bedroom. She'd passed by before she had registered the open box spread out on her daughter's bed. She walked back for a closer look. Her worst fears were realized. Heart thudding, she pulled out Toni's nightstand drawer.

"Dear God," Jane whispered as she reached for the phone.

* * *

Ray had just veered off the expressway onto the exit nearest his house when his car phone rang again. It was the desk sergeant at Beaubien.

"Had someone on the line real anxious to talk with you, Ray."

"Who was it?"

"Lady named Jane Garette, calling from her house. Says her daughter's missing and she fears she's in trouble."

An adrenaline rush had Ray swerving around a city bus while with the other hand, he slammed his red flashing light atop the car, then turned on his siren. "Tell her I'm on my way."

SEVENTEEN

Wally was not having a good evening. Nothing was going right. Friday night traffic on Warren Avenue was heavy, tempers short, cars changing lanes seemingly on a whim. The Olds was acting up, making an odd thunking sound. He no sooner had one thing fixed on the darn thing than something else went wrong. He should really junk it and get another car. Except he didn't have the money.

Worst of all, sweat was running down his face, rolling into his eyes, clouding his vision.

He reached for the handkerchief on the seat and mopped his forehead, then took off his sunglasses and wiped around his eyes. The thin cotton material was so damp it hardly did the job. Nervously, he wiped his hands on his pant legs, then ran the handkerchief around the steering wheel. Just in time, he grabbed the wheel and steadied the Olds before it swerved into the fast lane.

And his head was splitting.

If only there was a pill he could take that would help with the headaches and the sweats. But nothing helped except . . . except what he had to do to make the pain go away.

St. Matthews was about a mile ahead. He could

see the high steeple jutting into the evening sky. Not much farther now.

She'd be there again, he had a feeling. Toni wanted to die and he'd help her. By sending her to a better place, he'd be at peace again. It always worked like that.

A flashing light behind him caught his attention. Wally peered into his rearview mirror. Realization slammed into him as he recognized the vehicle, and his pulse began to pound.

A police car was signaling him to pull to the curb.

Ray made it to the Garettes' home on Lakeshore Lane in record time. Pulling into the circular drive, he jumped from the car almost before he'd shoved it into park.

Jane had been watching for him and opened the door. "I'm so glad you were available," she said, ushering him inside.

"What is it? What's happened to Toni?"

"Maybe nothing. Maybe I'm overreacting." Feeling uncertain, Jane shoved a pin up into the hair she'd hastily redone.

He was breathing hard from the breakneck drive over and from the fear that had clutched his heart ever since he'd heard the words *Toni's in trouble*. "Let me decide that. Tell me."

"Come upstairs and I'll show you instead." She started up, anxiety causing her to move faster than usual. "I came home a short time ago and was walking past Toni's room when I noticed something odd. Ordinarily, she's not a risk taker, but I fear that her grief over Mo's terrible death and her desire to have her killer put away may have pushed Toni over the edge."

Ray followed her anxiously.

At Toni's doorway, Jane paused, indicating the clothes on the bed. "You see."

Moving past her, Ray saw an outfit of Toni's that he recognized, thrown rather carelessly aside as if she'd removed her clothes hastily. But the thing that made his blood run cold was the open box on the bed. It held a pair of clunky black shoes, two black skirts, and two white blouses. He wanted to reject the thought that popped into his head. "Are these your niece's things?"

"Yes," Jane said, entering the room. "Awhile back, Toni picked them up from St. Matthews convent. We decided to store them in the closet of Mo's old room."

"Then you wouldn't know if any pieces are missing?"

"I went through the things when we first brought them home. Mo's jacket isn't here, nor her slacks. Her headpiece is gone, as well as a pair of shoes." Her eyes bright with fear, Jane looked up at him. "Toni mentioned to me once that she felt the police should dress a female officer in nun's clothing and plant her as a decoy to draw out the killer. I told her to stay out of police business. How I wish now that I'd been more insistent."

Ray drew in a shaky breath. He and her mother had both warned Toni, and she hadn't listened. Toni marched to her own drummer, which was what Meg had been trying to tell him. He had to respect that, he knew.

But look where it had gotten her.

He hadn't listened to any of her suggestions either, and apparently that had made her even more determined to find a way. He should have guessed what she might do. He struggled with the guilty knowledge that he'd pushed her to this action. "What time did Toni leave the restaurant?"

"I don't know. I was out with friends. I left the restaurant about four. I could call and—"

"No, never mind." What difference did that make? Ray thought. She had a head start on them, but maybe it wasn't too late to intercept her. He thrust a hand through his hair, trying to think as Toni would. "Probably she'd go to St. Matthews . . ."

"Yes, that's what I thought, too. Most of the sisters who died were from that parish." She shook her head worriedly. "I can't imagine Toni doing something so foolish, though she's always had a mind of her own."

Ray's mind was racing. Two of the slain sisters had been killed inside a church as they knelt in prayer. That would be the logical place to start, and Toni was fairly logical. "I'll find her." He turned to go, then swung back. "Are you familiar with a man named Walter Lambert?"

"Wally? Yes, of course. He's our yard man. John hired him this spring. He's doing a great job." Suddenly, Jane grew suspicious. "Why?"

Damn. Why hadn't he thought to ask yesterday when he'd learned the man's name? Ray chided himself. That's most probably how the maniac had learned that Toni and Mo were related. And why he'd chosen to dump Mo's body into the Garettes' pool. Had he also been stalking Toni? "It's not important now," Ray said, and nearly ran from the room.

"Wait!" Jane called to him.

At the top of the stairs, he turned back impatiently.

"John bought Toni a gun some time ago. A .38. She knows how to use it. It's missing from her drawer."

Oh God, Ray thought. Civilians with guns, even when they'd had a few shooting lessons, made Ray nervous. He ground his teeth as he started for the stairs. "Thanks. I'll let you know."

Maybe they'd be lucky, Ray thought as he took the stairs two at a time, and some cop this very minute had spotted Walter Lambert's car from the APB that was out. Or maybe the bastard had sensed the police were closing in and was holed up somewhere. He'd sent Toni her cousin's necklace, but hadn't tried to contact her since, that he knew. Toni hadn't mentioned seeing anyone suspicious following her, and she was always alert, especially since Mo's death.

Slipping behind the wheel of his station wagon, Ray shoved the key into the ignition. Meg's words came back to him as the engine roared to life. *Love is the only reason we're here, Ray. Without it, were empty shells.*

He hadn't thought he'd ever fall deeply, hopelessly in love. But now, as fear gripped his heart, he realized he'd loved Toni all along. He was a man who'd found it difficult to believe, but he sent a prayer heavenward now. *Please, let me be in time.*

Then, on tires that screamed seemingly in protest, he roared out of the drive and headed for St. Matthews.

Rosie Pulaski's mouth dropped open as she stared into her boarder's bedroom. Two candles had been left burning on the dresser and another on the nightstand. What had Wally been thinking of, leaving without snuffing out the flames?

Bending down, Rosie blew out the low one on the nightstand first. It was short and squat. If the hot wax dripped over, it could easily catch the bedclothes on fire. She'd never dreamed the boy would be so careless.

Moving to the tall dresser, she stood on tiptoes, but still couldn't reach high enough to blow out the long tapers. She stretched her hand for the brass holder and snuffed out the first one. But before she reached for the second, she noticed a picture. Picking up the frame, she studied the colored snapshot in the candlelight.

A man and woman stood holding hands under a tree. The man was a young Wally, smiling the way he so seldom did anymore. The woman was no more than a young girl really, with shoulder-length blond hair and eyes so blue they jumped out at you even in this small photo.

So he had had a girl once. What had happened to her that Wally didn't see her anymore? Rosie wondered. He'd never mentioned her name. Certainly, he'd never brought her here, although she'd told him that if he wanted to ask a friend over, she'd cook them a fine meal. He'd never once taken her up on her offer.

Rosie set the picture back on the dresser and noticed that a cluster of violets were placed in a small glass bowl alongside where the photo stood. The same kind of violets he often gave her. Maybe the girl in the snapshot was dead, which would explain why he brought her flowers. Perhaps she was buried far away and he couldn't go to the cemetery, and this was the next best thing.

SHATTERED VOWS

She hadn't thought of poor Wally as grieving, but maybe that was why he was acting so peculiar lately.

When she'd entered, she'd found that most of the flat was fairly clean. His clothes hamper was stuffed with dirty clothes in the bathroom. She'd opened the window to air out the room. Men so seldom thought of things like that.

There was no dust to speak of and he was neat to a fault. The kitchen looked as if it had hardly been used; his refrigerator was almost empty.

She wasn't ordinarily a snoop, Rosie thought to herself. And even this time, the very first time she'd come into his private place, she only did it to make sure everything was all right. And thank God she had, given the candles. Lately, Wally hadn't been getting home until late. He'd probably forget that he'd left the candles burning. She wouldn't have to tell him she'd been in.

She was about to blow out the last candle when she noticed a silver box on the dresser. Curiosity got the best of her and she picked it up. It was heavy and probably had been expensive, though it was quite old. Carefully, she removed the lid.

Inside were several strands of broken gold chain and five gold crosses. Slowly, she examined each one. They were all a little different. How very odd that he would keep such things. Putting the box back, she decided it was none of her business.

The top dresser drawer was slightly ajar. Rosie knew she shouldn't look any further. But she couldn't help herself. She had an uneasy feeling that something was amiss here. Nothing she could put a name to, just a feeling. Acting on that feeling, she pulled open the drawer.

At first glance, the contents looked harmless

enough. A small stack of white undershirts alongside a pile of white undershorts. But there was more. To the far left was a spool of some sort. Rosie picked it up, looking it over. Thin green wire wound around a cardboard spool. It was the sort she'd used herself to tie up her rosebushes.

Then it hit her. Green wire. The stranglings of those innocent nuns had been done with green wire just like this. She'd attended all four funerals at St. Matthews. She hadn't personally known any of the sisters, but as a Catholic, she'd felt she had to go to pray for them.

She'd had a police officer come to her home and ask questions after the first strangling, just as he'd gone to the homes of all parishioners of St. Matthews. She'd served him coffee and they'd chatted about the injustice of the murders, about how long she'd been a member, and so on. He'd told her about the green wire used in the strangling, and she'd also read about it in the paper. She remembered that she hadn't been of much help, but he'd been nice all the same.

As she held the wire spool in one hand, she reached in to the right side of the drawer with the other. Her heart leaped into her throat as she realized what she held. Mass cards. Five of them, all blank. She'd seen these before. In the newspaper when the police had asked for help from anyone who might know what parish gave out these specific cards.

Replacing the wire spool, she checked the cards again more closely. Yes, she was certain these were the ones in the article. Her hand flew to her mouth as she stifled a cry.

Dear God.

What could all this mean? Surely not what she

was thinking, what she was fearing. Surely her sweet-faced tenant, Wladek, wasn't involved somehow in those awful killings.

Rosie noticed a small stack of photographs and picked them up. She gasped out loud as she recognized the nuns who'd been killed, one leaving the school, another getting into a car, a third walking to the convent door.

That did it. She couldn't stay quiet over her discovery. She couldn't wait for him to return to confront him about the articles. She had to do something and quickly. Her conscience would never let her be if she didn't.

Father Hilliard would know what to do. Rosie had asked for his advice many times in the past.

Picking up the wire spool and clutching the mass cards and pictures, she left Wladek's flat and hurried downstairs. He had no phone, but she did. She'd call her friend, Helen, and ask her to drive over to St. Matthews to show her discoveries to Father.

As she made her unsteady way down the steep steps, Rosie began to pray.

He was breathing hard and sweating furiously. Wally didn't know exactly how he'd managed to get away from the cop car, but another quick look in his rearview mirror assured him that he'd shaken the black-and-white.

Luck had been with him when a group of senior citizens had trailed across the street after alighting from a touring bus. He'd stepped on the gas and made it through the intersection just before the light changed and the crosswalk filled with elderly people walking slowly. The cop had been stuck while he'd zigzagged through traffic, made several turns, and come out on the street leading to St. Matthews.

Maybe he had a taillight out, Wally thought as he mopped his brow again. This damn car almost got him in trouble. It couldn't have been the muffler, for he'd gotten that fixed, and the headlight, too. Yeah, probably something in the rear, like maybe his tailpipe was dragging. Tomorrow, he'd take the Olds in and get it fixed up, but good.

After his headache was gone. After a good night's sleep. After he sent the pretty one to join the others.

Wally reached St. Matthews Church parking lot and saw not a single car there. Gazing around, he spotted the red Mercedes in front of the convent. Pulling into a space, he smiled.

Did she think to fool someone by parking there? Surely not him. He knew her, knew her car, knew why she'd come.

Turning off the engine, he wiped his hands one last time. He felt a sudden calm flood his being. It was always like that just before it happened. Stepping out, he fingered the wire in his pants pocket. Knowing it was there reassured him. Slowly, surveying the area, he walked up the stone steps.

Soon it would all be over.

Toni was extremely discouraged. She'd been at St. Matthews since seven and it was past eight-thirty. Her knees ached from the constant kneeling and her nerves were stretched taut. Her hands on the weapon in her jacket pocket was cramped from grasping it.

And still he hadn't come.

The ladies had finished their prayers some time ago and left. One young couple had walked in about an hour ago, strolled to the vigil lights, lighted a candle, and knelt down to pray. Then they'd also left.

She'd been alone ever since.

Toni rolled her shoulders to relieve her tense muscles. Maybe both Meg and Ray had been right, after all. Hanging around one church apparently wasn't the answer. The killer could be almost anywhere. This seemed to be an exercise in futility. All she'd managed to get so far were sore muscles and a large dose of frustration.

Maybe the killer was no longer killing. Maybe the police had learned something about him that had them ready to close in, and he'd sensed the danger and was hiding out somewhere. Ray had told her he had several important appointments that day, but he hadn't told her with whom or where, or even on what case he was currently working.

Toni sighed and leaned back, her buttocks resting against the edge of the pew seat. As an undercover agent, she was a bust. She hated to admit defeat, hated to have to tell Ray that her plan hadn't worked.

Stifling a yawn, she checked her watch again. Enough already. Time to give it up and rethink the whole thing. Somewhat stiffly, she rose.

And nearly gasped out loud as she saw a man standing in the center aisle not more than a dozen feet from her.

In the passenger seat as her friend Helen drove along the quiet residential street, Rosie twisted a hankie in her nervous hands. Glancing down at her lap, she saw that it was the pink one that Wladek had given her the day of the fair. Her eyes misted.

"Can't you go any faster, Helen?" Rosie's voice shook as her unspoken fears nearly choked her. Never in her life had she prayed so sincerely that she was wrong about the things she was thinking. *That sweet boy can't be a murderer.* She wouldn't believe it, not unless she heard it from his own lips.

"Do you want me to get a speeding ticket?" Helen asked peevishly. She was annoyed with her friend, who hadn't told her what this mad dash to St. Matthews was about, except to say that she had to see Father Hilliard immediately.

"This may be a matter of life and death, Helen," Rosie stated, realizing that she sounded dramatic. But better to be safe than sorry. Once you knew something, or suspected something, you simply had to talk with someone about it. To keep it to yourself might do more harm than good.

Helen rounded the corner and St. Matthews came into view. She headed for the rectory. "Father Hilliard's probably in his living quarters at this hour."

"Wait," Rosie said, gazing out her open window. "There's Wladek's car by the church entrance. Park over there."

Helen frowned. "I thought you wanted to talk with Father Hilliard. What's Wladek got to do with this?"

"I'll tell you later. I want to talk to Wladek face to face." Impatiently, she waited for Helen to maneuver her Chevy next to the Olds.

"Wally," Toni said, breathing a sigh of relief. "You frightened me for a moment there. I didn't hear anyone come in." Recognizing their yard man, she re-

SHATTERED VOWS 339

laxed her hold on the gun in her pocket. "Are you a member of St. Matthews?"

"No. I do some work for them. The flowers and shrubs, you know." He hadn't been sure she'd recognize him. She usually just rushed past him when he was working on the Garette property, on her way somewhere, breezily waving to him as she drove off. Except the day they'd found her cousin's body in the pool. He'd liked to have hung around for that, but he'd decided it might be too dangerous.

Stepping closer, he casually wiped his hands on his pants as he looked her over in the dim light of the wall sconces. "Why are you dressed like a nun?"

Toni leaned against the back of the pew in front of her. "It's a long story. I don't have time to go into it right now."

He moved to block the row where she stood. "Are you thinking of becoming a sister?" he asked.

She didn't know Wally very well, hadn't ever been so close to him before. Fleetingly, she thought that he looked odd. His eyes were dark and intense, and he was sweating profusely. Why? she wondered, since it was quite cool in the church. A sickeningly sweet odor emanated from him. "No, not at all. I don't think the sisterhood is for me." She started toward the aisle, but stopped when he didn't step out of the way.

"That's good, because I don't think you'd qualify. You're not pure like the others, are you, Toni?"

"Pure? I don't know what you mean. What others?" Toni said, frowning.

Wally felt confused. His head was pounding and she wanted to fence with him. "You know very well what others. The sisters were pure and untouched, but you aren't, are you? You've given yourself to that bearded cop, haven't you? You've lain with him, let him do things to you. You're not married to him, but you've sinned with him, haven't you?"

Alarm bells went off in Toni's brain as she tensed. The others. The pure sisters. The killer was a man of average height with thick brown hair, Ray had told her. They'd found a drop of sweat on one of the mass cards. The sweet smell was that cheap cologne. Everything added up. How could she not have spotted it earlier? And here, he'd been right there, working in their yard all along. In her pocket, her fingers tightened on the gun.

He was mad. She knew that now, and knew that reasoning with him was a waste of time. But perhaps she could distract him somehow. "Detective Vargas is on his way, Wally. He's supposed to meet me here. He knows about what you've done. It's all over."

He seemed flustered, his eyes darting to the doors and back again. "You're lying. No one knows you're here." Quickly, he withdrew the piece of wire from his pocket and stretched it between his two hands. "You want to die. That's why you've dressed up like a nun, because you want to join the others. You're not worthy of wearing those holy clothes. But I'll send you to your heavenly father anyway." He took a step closer into the pew.

"Don't come any nearer." Toni removed her hand, holding the gun. "I know how to use this. Stop right there."

"You don't understand," he said as he took another step. "I have to send you to heaven. You know you want me to help you." He smiled then as a feeling of righteousness came over him.

* * *

SHATTERED VOWS 341

Huffing in her haste, Rosie heaved open the heavy door of St. Matthews. No one was in the vestibule.

Helen, right behind her, grabbed her friend's sleeve. "What are we doing here, Rosie?"

"Shhh! Be quiet." Rosie walked through the arch and stepped into the center aisle.

Wladek was standing in one of the middle pews and he had a piece of wire between his hands. It was true, all of it, she thought. A nun was standing near him, holding something in her hand. Dear God, she had to stop him from hurting still another sister.

"Wally!" Rosie yelled. "Don't do it."

He swung toward the voice, recognizing his landlady in a split second, then turned back to Toni.

Taking advantage of his momentary distraction, Toni got off a shot aimed at his legs.

But he was too fast for her, deflecting her shooting arm with a hard chop of his hand to her forearm. The bullet hit the stone floor, spraying shards in every direction. The gun dropped to the floor, landing next to his feet. He grabbed Toni, yanking her body back against his solid chest. "I tried to help you, but you wouldn't listen."

At the sound of the shot, Helen ducked behind the last pew, crouching down, her thin lips murmuring a prayer.

Unmindful of her own safety, Rosie rushed down the aisle. "No, Wladek, please. You have to stop. Jesus, Mary, and Joseph, don't let another sister die."

"Rosie, go home," he ordered. "This is none of your business." Sweat dripped down his face, nearly blinding him as he tightened his hold on Toni. Why had his landlady come here tonight? Didn't she know he had to do this, that it was his God-given mission? "She's not even a nun. Go home!"

But Rosie didn't stop, talking all the while she hurried to him. "Of course she's a sister. Please, Wladek, come with me. We'll talk with Father Hilliard. Everything will be all right. You'll see."

Sweating profusely, Wally bent to pick up the gun Toni had dropped, while his other arm kept his hostage in a stranglehold. He didn't want to hurt Rosie. *Please God. Make her go home.*

At the end of the pew, Rosie paused, taking in the sister's fearful eyes. She reached an imploring hand out toward Wladek. "Don't hurt her, please."

Slowly, Wally raised the gun and aimed it at Rosie.

Ray hadn't engaged his siren, though he'd had his light flashing. If Walter Lambert was anywhere near St. Matthews, he didn't want to frighten him into action in case Toni was actually there. Careening around the corner, he drove like a madman until finally, the church was just ahead.

As he neared, he saw Toni's Mercedes parked near the convent. But it was the dark blue Olds sitting in the church lot next to a rundown Chevy that had him swearing as he jerked to a halt in front of the front doors. He took a few precious seconds to call for backup from all area patrol cars. As he hurried up the stairs, he drew his weapon, but kept it down and slightly to the back.

Holding his breath, Ray shoved open the church door, which creaked loudly. He cursed under his breath as, stealthily, he crept across the foyer.

Inside, Wally heard the back door open and snapped his head in that direction.

Sensing his attention diverted if only for an instant, Toni decided that if she didn't act now, she might not get another chance. Raising her foot, she stomped down hard on Wally's instep, the solid heel of Mo's shoe making itself felt, she was certain. She heard a gratifying crunch right before he gave out with a yell and loosened his hold on her. Seizing the opportunity, Toni pulled away from him and ran in the opposite direction toward the far wall.

As she rounded the bend, she heard a man shout from the rear of the church.

"Walter Lambert!" Ray called out from alongside the back pew, where a thin woman cowered on the floor. Already in his shooting stance, he levered his weapon on the trembling man. "Police! Drop your gun."

Rosie cast a frightened look at Ray as she shook her head. "Don't shoot him, please. He's sick."

His headache nearly blinded Wally, while a new pain shot through his foot and up his leg. Sweat pouring into his burning eyes, he stood undecided, confusion wracking him. Toni was the cause of it all. If she'd just stayed home and not tried to trick him, none of this would be happening.

Fear clogging his throat, he swiveled and shot in her direction. He was gratified to hear her body hit the floor with a muffled thud as he swiftly swung the weapon back in the direction of the bearded cop. "You're next," he muttered.

Ray took a step nearer, but he couldn't shoot because the older woman was too close to Walter. And he couldn't take the time to check on Toni even as fear for her safety overwhelmed him. "Give it up, Walter," he said, trying not to think of how badly Toni had been hit.

"Wladek, no more," Rosie cried out, and rushed with her hands extended, intending to hit his arm so the shot would go wild. But she was too heavy to be fast enough.

Tears running down his face, Wally squeezed the trigger. The bullet tore through Rosie's shoulder, sending her back over the pew where she dropped awkwardly to the floor.

There was no one left to shoot but himself, Ray thought as he walked up the aisle. His training echoing in his mind, he would do all he could to take the man in uninjured. In the distance, he heard sirens approaching as his backup arrived. "Drop the gun, Walter. You're finished."

Poor Rosie, Wally thought. He hadn't meant to harm her. She was the only person who'd ever been truly kind to him. "I'm sorry," he whispered to her. Gazing heavenward, he released one last prayer. "Please forgive me." Then he put the gun into his mouth and pulled the trigger.

Ray averted his gaze as blood splattered everywhere.

After a moment, he went to the fallen woman and checked for a pulse. Her heartbeat was weak but steady. He prayed Toni had fared as well as he turned and rushed to the back.

He found her on her side, lying next to a large stone pillar. Bending, he turned her over and heard her groan. He thanked a God he wasn't sure he believed in as he pulled her to him. Her eyes fluttered open, looking disoriented. She struggled to sit up and he eased her back down. "It's all right," he told her. "It's all over."

"What happened to Wally?" she managed weakly.

"He killed himself," Ray said, feeling no pity for the man who'd taken so many lives. "He saved the state a lot of money."

She closed her eyes, shuddering.

Ray had been standing too far back to see where she'd been hit. He eased back, his hands checking her. "Where does it hurt?"

"My head," she said, gingerly touching a raised bump. "I got to the floor before he hit me. My head hit the pillar and I must have passed out."

"Thank God you're all right." Since the moment he'd gotten the call telling him that she might be in trouble, he'd been scared to death. Not only fearing for her life, but afraid for himself, of what it would be like if he lost her.

Two armed police officers chose that moment to rush into the church. "Over here," Ray called as he helped Toni to her feet. As he settled her in the back pew, he told one of the uniforms to radio for two ambulances, then led the other cop up to where the thin lady was holding the chubby one's hand.

Father Hilliard stood alongside the ambulance gurney while the attendants strapped down Rosie Pulaski. "You're going to be just fine, Rosie," he told her. "I understand you were very brave tonight."

"Oh, Father," she managed through her tears, "I still can't believe that that sweet boy was . . . a murderer." She squeezed Helen's fingers with her good hand. "My friend and I are both in shock."

"Would you like to ride to the hospital with your friend?" the ambulance attendant asked Helen.

Helen looked doubtful. "My car is there, in the lot."

"Don't worry, Helen," Father told her. "I'll see that it's safe." He held out his hands for the keys. "You go with Rosie."

"Bless you, Father," Rosie said.

"I'll be by the hospital to visit you tomorrow,"

the priest said as the attendant released the wheels and pushed the gurney into the ambulance, then helped Helen inside.

Standing off to the side, Ray slipped his arm around Toni as they watched the other ambulance drive off with Walter Lambert's remains in a black body bag. He knew he'd have to be the one to tell Sister Terry, and he didn't look forward to it. Although she'd be relieved that he'd never kill again nor bother her any longer, he knew she'd feel guilty about his death and the others' always.

"I can't believe it's finally over," Toni said as they walked toward Ray's car after saying goodnight to the priest.

Ray sucked in a deep breath of fresh air. "Thank God it is."

Stopping at the station wagon, she looked up at him. "Are you on speaking terms with God again?"

He slipped his arms around her, their bodies touching as he leaned back at the waist to look into her eyes, very blue under the streetlights. "Yeah, we had a chat tonight. He listened while I pleaded with Him to let you live. I guess He heard me."

"Thank you for that."

His expression grew serious. "What made you think you could take on a guy who'd killed six women and left not a clue? You could have been killed."

"But I wasn't, and it worked."

"It was far too great a risk."

She cocked her head. "You mean like the ones you take every day?"

"Yeah, like those." He tightened his hold on her. "Could you handle the stress of that, day in and day out, going through with me what I just went through in there with you?"

She sighed. "I wasn't sure before, but I am now. And I think I'll leave the police work to you from now on."

Her words made him smile. Then he grew serious again. "I learned something myself tonight. Actually, I heard it the other day, but I didn't believe it until tonight, until I thought you might be lost to me. Love is all that's really important, Toni. Without it, we're empty shells."

"I think I always knew that," she whispered.

Ray lowered his head to kiss her long and hard. "I love you," he said into her neck as he gathered her close.

"I love you, too."

Stepping back, he noticed the fatigue on her face and knew her mother would be worrying. "I'm taking you home. I'll get one of the officers to drive your car."

"You cops sure are pushy," Toni said, then reached up to kiss him again.

NOW THERE'S NO NEED TO WAIT UNTIL DARK!
DAY OR NIGHT, ZEBRA'S VAMPIRE NOVELS
HAVE QUITE A BITE!

THE VAMPIRE JOURNALS (4133, $4.50)
by Traci Briery
Maria Theresa Allogiamento is a vampire ahead of her time. As she travels from 18th-century Italy to present-day Los Angeles, Theresa sets the record straight. From how she chose immortality to her transformation into a seductive temptress, Theresa shares all of her dark secrets and quenches her insatiable thirst for all the world has to offer!

NIGHT BLOOD (4063, $4.50)
by Eric Flanders
Each day when the sun goes down, Val Romero feeds upon the living. This NIGHT BLOOD is the ultimate aphrodisiac. Driving from state to state in his '69 Cadillac, he leaves a trail of bloodless corpses behind. Some call him a serial killer, but those in the know call him Vampire. Now, three tormented souls driven by revenge and dark desires are tracking Val down—and only Val's death will satisfy their own raging thirst for blood!

THE UNDEAD (4068, $5.50)
by Roxanne Longstreet
Most people avoid the cold and sterile halls of the morgue. But for Adam Radburn working as a morgue attendant is a perfect job. He is a vampire. Though Adam has killed for blood, there is another who kills for pleasure and he wants to destroy Adam. And in the world of the undead, the winner is not the one who lives the longest, it's the one who lives forever!

PRECIOUS BLOOD (4293, $4.50)
by Pat Graversen
Adragon Hart, leader of the Society of Vampires, loves his daughter dearly. So does Quinn, a vampire renegade who has lured Beth to the savage streets of New York and into his obscene world of unquenchable desire. Every minute Quinn's hunger is growing. Every hour Adragon's rage is mounting. And both will do anything to satisfy their horrific appetites!

THE SUMMONING (4221, $4.50)
by Bentley Little
The first body was found completely purged of all blood. The authorities thought it was the work of a serial killer. But Sue Wing's grandmother knew the truth. She'd seen the deadly creature decades ago in China. Now it had come to the dusty Arizona town of Rio Verde . . . and it would not leave until it had drunk its fill.

Available wherever paperbacks are sold, or order direct from the Publisher. Send cover price plus 50¢ per copy for mailing and handling to Penguin USA, P.O. Box 999, c/o Dept. 17109, Bergenfield, NJ 07621. Residents of New York and Tennessee must include sales tax. DO NOT SEND CASH.

WHO DUNNIT? JUST TRY AND FIGURE IT OUT!

THE MYSTERIES OF MARY ROBERTS RINEHART

THE AFTER HOUSE	(2821-0, $3.50/$4.50)
THE ALBUM	(2334-0, $3.50/$4.50)
ALIBI FOR ISRAEL AND OTHER STORIES	(2764-8, $3.50/$4.50)
THE BAT	(2627-7, $3.50/$4.50)
THE CASE OF JENNIE BRICE	(2193-3, $2.95/$3.95)
THE CIRCULAR STAIRCASE	(3528-4, $3.95/$4.95)
THE CONFESSION AND SIGHT UNSEEN	(2707-9, $3.50/$4.50)
THE DOOR	(1895-5, $3.50/$4.50)
EPISODE OF THE WANDERING KNIFE	(2874-1, $3.50/$4.50)
THE FRIGHTENED WIFE	(3494-6, $3.95/$4.95)
THE GREAT MISTAKE	(2122-4, $3.50/$4.50)
THE HAUNTED LADY	(3680-9, $3.95/$4.95)
A LIGHT IN THE WINDOW	(1952-1, $3.50/$4.50)
LOST ECSTASY	(1791-X, $3.50/$4.50)
THE MAN IN LOWER TEN	(3104-1, $3.50/$4.50)
MISS PINKERTON	(1847-9, $3.50/$4.50)
THE RED LAMP	(2017-1, $3.50/$4.95)
THE STATE V. ELINOR NORTON	(2412-6, $3.50/$4.50)
THE SWIMMING POOL	(3679-5, $3.95/$4.95)
THE WALL	(2560-2, $3.50/$4.50)
THE YELLOW ROOM	(3493-8, $3.95/$4.95)

Available wherever paperbacks are sold, or order direct from the Publisher. Send cover price plus 50¢ per copy for mailing and handling to Penguin USA, P.O. Box 999, c/o Dept. 17109, Bergenfield, NJ 07621. Residents of New York and Tennessee must include sales tax. DO NOT SEND CASH.

"MIND-BOGGLING... THE SUSPENSE IS UNBEARABLE...
DORIS MILES DISNEY WILL KEEP YOU
ON THE EDGE OF YOUR SEAT..."

THE MYSTERIES OF DORIS MILES DISNEY

THE DAY MISS BESSIE LEWIS DISAPPEARED	(2080-5, $2.95/$4.50)
THE HOSPITALITY OF THE HOUSE	(2738-9, $3.50/$4.50)
THE LAST STRAW	(2286-7, $2.95/$3.95)
THE MAGIC GRANDFATHER	(2584-X, $2.95/$3.95)
MRS. MEEKER'S MONEY	(2212-3, $2.95/$3.95)
NO NEXT OF KIN	(2969-1, $3.50/$4.50)
ONLY COUPLES NEED APPLY	(2438-X, $2.95/$3.95)
SHADOW OF A MAN	(3077-0, $3.50/$4.50)
THAT WHICH IS CROOKED	(2848-2, $3.50/$4.50)
THREE'S A CROWD	(2079-1, $2.95/$3.95)
WHO RIDES A TIGER	(2799-0, $3.50/$4.50)

Available wherever paperbacks are sold, or order direct from the Publisher. Send cover price plus 50¢ per copy for mailing and handling to Penguin USA, P.O. Box 999, c/o Dept. 17109, Bergenfield, NJ 07621. Residents of New York and Tennessee must include sales tax. DO NOT SEND CASH.

HAUTALA'S HORROR AND SUPERNATURAL SUSPENSE

GHOST LIGHT (4320, $4.99)
Alex Harris is searching for his kidnapped children, but only the ghost of their dead mother can save them from his murderous rage.

DARK SILENCE (3923, $5.99)
Dianne Fraser is trying desperately to keep her family—and her own sanity—from being pulled apart by the malevolent forces that haunt the abandoned mill on their property.

COLD WHISPER (3464, $5.95)
Tully can make Sarah's every wish come true, but Sarah lives in teror because Tully doesn't understand that some wishes aren't meant to come true.

LITTLE BROTHERS (4020, $4.50)
The "little brothers" have returned, and this time there will be no escape for the boy who saw them kill his mother.

NIGHT STONE (3681, $4.99)
Their new house was a place of darkness, shadows, long-buried secrets, and a force of unspeakable evil.

MOONBOG (3356, $4.95)
Someone—or something—is killing the children in the little town of Holland, Maine.

MOONDEATH (1844, $3.95)
When the full moon rises in Cooper Falls, a beast driven by bloodlust and savage evil stalks the night.

Available wherever paperbacks are sold, or order direct from the Publisher. Send cover price plus 50¢ per copy for mailing and handling to Penguin USA, P.O. Box 999, c/o Dept. 17109, Bergenfield, NJ 07621. Residents of New York and Tennessee must include sales tax. DO NOT SEND CASH.

Prepare Yourself for

PATRICIA WALLACE

LULLABYE (2917, $3.95/$4.95)
Eight-year-old Bronwyn knew she wasn't like other girls. She didn't have a mother. At least, not a real one. Her mother had been in a coma at the hospital for as long as Bronwyn could remember. She couldn't feel any pain, her father said. But when Bronwyn sat with her mother, she knew her mother was angry—angry at the nurses and doctors, and her own helplessness. Soon, she would show them all the true meaning of suffering . . .

MONDAY'S CHILD (2760, $3.95/$4.95)
Jill Baker was such a pretty little girl, with long, honey-blond hair and haunting gray-green eyes. Just one look at her angelic features could dispel all the nasty rumors that had been spreading around town. There were all those terrible accidents that had begun to plague the community, too. But the fact that each accident occurred after little Jill had been angered had to be coincidence . . .

SEE NO EVIL (2429, $3.95/$4.95)
For young Caryn Dearborn, the cornea operation enabled her to see more than light and shadow for the first time. For Todd Reynolds, it was his chance to run and play like other little boys. For these two children, the sudden death of another child had been the miracle they had been waiting for. But with their eyesight came another kind of vision—of evil, horror, destruction. They could see into other people's minds, their worst fears and deepest terrors. And they could see the gruesome deaths that awaited the unwary . . .

THRILL (3142, $4.50/$5.50)
It was an amusement park like no other in the world. A tri-level marvel of modern technology enhanced by the special effects wizardry of holograms, lasers, and advanced robotics. Nothing could go wrong—until it did. As the crowds swarmed through the gates on Opening Day, they were unprepared for the disaster about to strike. Rich and poor, young and old would be taken for the ride of their lives, trapped in a game of epic proportions where only the winners survived . . .

Available wherever paperbacks are sold, or order direct from the Publisher. Send cover price plus 50¢ per copy for mailing and handling to Penguin USA, P.O. Box 999, c/o Dept. 17109, Bergenfield, NJ 07621. Residents of New York and Tennessee must include sales tax. DO NOT SEND CASH.